"Filled with both menace and heart, *Phoenix Island* stands out in all the right ways."

—Melissa Marr, *New York Times*
bestselling author of *Carnival of Souls*

"Fast-paced, exciting. . . . This action-packed novel combines adventure with extreme violence."

—*Kirkus Reviews*

"The pacing and smooth prose will have suspense fans waiting for the next book."

—*Publishers Weekly*

"Gritty, grim, sometimes unrelenting, but always with an underlying theme of hope."

—*Blogcritics*

"A crazy fun ride to read. . . . Packs quite the wallop."

—*The Hub*, YALSA

"A tribute to the indomitable human spirit that challenges the mob and chooses values over expediency."

—F. Paul Wilson, *New York Times*
bestselling creator of Repairman Jack

"*Phoenix Island* is one of those rare books that stay with you. I couldn't stop thinking about it long after I had read it. I loved the characters, the action, and the world."

—Tripp Vinson, executive producer of *Intelligence*

"Fantastic . . . Superbly suspenseful, unpredictable and frightening. Welcome to the world of *Phoenix Island*. It will blow you away."

—Mark Sullivan, *New York Times*
bestselling author of *Rogue*

"Di[x] . . . of color and vi-
olen . . . another page."

—*The Daily Quirk*

PHOENIX ISLAND

JOHN DIXON

G
Gallery Books

New York   London   Toronto   Sydney   New Delhi

G

Gallery Books
A Division of Simon & Schuster, Inc.
1230 Avenue of the Americas
New York, NY 10020

First Gallery Books trade paperback edition October 2014

GALLERY BOOKS and colophon are registered trademarks of Simon & Schuster, Inc.

For information about special discounts for bulk purchases, please contact Simon & Schuster Special Sales at 1-866-506-1949 or business@simonandschuster.com.

The Simon & Schuster Speakers Bureau can bring authors to your live event. For more information or to book an event contact the Simon & Schuster Speakers Bureau at 1-866-248-3049 or visit our website at www.simonspeakers.com.

Interior design by Davina Mock-Maniscalco

Manufactured in the United States of America

10   9   8   7   6   5   4   3   2   1

Library of Congress Cataloging-in-Publication Data

Dixon, John
  Phoenix Island / John Dixon
      pages cm
    1. Mercenary troops—Fiction. 2. Boxing—Fiction. 3. Orphans—Fiction. 4. Science fiction. I. Title.
  PZ7.D6445Ph 2014
  [Fic]—dc232013033616

ISBN 978-1-4767-3863-5
ISBN 978-1-4767-3865-9 (pbk)
ISBN 978-1-4767-3870-3 (ebook)

THIS IS FOR MY WIFE AND BEST FRIEND, CHRISTINA,
WITH ALL MY LOVE.

Never give in—never, never, never. . . .
—Winston Churchill

Battle not with monsters, lest ye become a monster. . . .
—Friedrich Nietzsche

1

WEARING A STIFF BLUE JUMPSUIT AND HANDCUFFS, Carl sat with no expression on his face and waited to see what they were going to do to him this time.

They were going to come down hard on him. The judge might even dismiss the case straight to adult court, and then Carl would be looking at jail time, as in *real* jail, no more juvie, no more boys. Men. Thieves and rapists and murderers. Shanks and gangs. Everything. He'd be lucky to survive a month.

The Dale County Juvenile Court didn't look like a courtroom. It was just a narrow room with two folding tables set end to end. No judge's dais, no jury box, no spectators' gallery. Just the tables and a dozen or so uncomfortable metal chairs flanking them. Carl smelled new carpet and coffee. Fluorescent lights buzzed in the drop ceiling overhead. A furled American flag leaned in one corner, pinned to the wall by a podium pushed up against it to make room.

He avoided eye contact with his foster parents, who sat at the other end of the table, next to Ms. Snyder, the probation officer, and stared instead at his bruised and swollen hands—the scars on his knuckles reading like a twisted road map of the great lengths he'd traveled to arrive here.

Out in the hall, somebody laughed in passing. Carl heard keys jingle. A cop, probably.

The cop in this room looked bored. His leather gun belt creaked as he shifted his weight, watching the judge shuffle through a tall stack of papers.

Carl's mouth was dry and sour with the waiting. Directly across the table, the judge picked up a white Styrofoam cup. Then he put it down and set some papers to one side of the others. Then he looked up. He had watery eyes and deep lines in his face. His hair was a gray mess, and he needed a shave. Despite his robe, he looked more like a burned-out math teacher than a judge. Looking again at the white cup, he finally spoke.

"Could somebody please get me another cup of coffee? Velma? Would you mind?"

A tall woman said okay and stood up and left the room.

"You are an orphan," the judge said, turning his attention to Carl.

"Yes, sir."

"It says here your father was a police officer?"

"Yes, sir."

"And what does that make you?"

"Sir?"

"The sheriff?"

Chief Watkins snorted. "*I'm* the damned sheriff."

"Language, Chief. I'd hate to have to find you in contempt of court."

Carl read the men's voices: just a pair of good old boys, having a little fun while they sat one more case together.

Chief Watkins nodded. "Sorry, Your Honor."

"That's all right." Then, looking up at Carl, he said, "You're kind of a hard-ass, aren't you, son?"

Chief Watkins cleared his throat.

"It's all right, Chief. It's my court. I'll be in contempt if I see fit. Answer the question, son. You fashion yourself a hard-ass?"

Carl shrugged. "I don't mean to be."

"You don't mean to be."

"No, sir."

"And you know what that sounds like to me?"

"No, sir."

"That sounds like every kid who comes in here." He looked at the paper. "It says here you're a boxer?"

Carl nodded. "I was."

"Chief Watkins used to box a little, didn't you, Chief?"

"A few smokers back in the navy. Nothing official."

The judge said, "Our friend here had more than a few fights. How many was it altogether, son?"

"Eighty-seven," Carl said.

"And out of those eighty-seven matches, how many did you win?"

"Eighty-five."

The judge raised his shaggy brows. "That is a good record. Were you a champion?"

"Yes, sir."

"What sort of champion?"

"Seventy-five, ninety, and one fourteen."

The judge tilted his head, then grinned a little. "No, son, I'm not talking weight classes. I meant what level of champion. City? State? National?"

Carl nodded.

"All three?"

"Yes, sir. Junior Golden Gloves, PAL, and AAU."

Officer Watkins's gun belt creaked as he leaned back. "That's pretty good."

Carl relaxed a little. Talking boxing did that, made him feel like more than just a throwaway kid awaiting sentencing. Still, he could tell this judge viewed himself as a shoot-from-the-hip kind of guy. A judge like this, he might throw you in a dungeon for life or let you go scot-free, either way, just to see the look on your face.

The judge said, "When I asked if you were a boxer, you said 'was' rather than 'is.' Is that correct?"

"Yes, sir. Was."

"Was, then. Have you retired?"

"It's just, I keep moving so much. I haven't been able to fight—box—for a while."

"Indeed."

Velma returned and handed the judge his coffee. "Thank you, dear," he said. "Mr. and Mrs. Rhoades, are you sure you wouldn't like some coffee? All right, then. Do you all have anything you'd like to say?"

Carl's new foster parents looked nervous. He wondered if they had ever been in a courtroom before. Probably not. He felt bad, dragging them in. Mr. Rhoades had almost certainly missed work, and Carl could see Mrs. Rhoades had been crying. She told the judge they hadn't known Carl long, but he'd been a good boy, very respectful, and Mr. Rhoades nodded. Listening to them, Carl felt a renewed pang of loss. Things could have been good here. Really good.

The judge thanked them, riffled through his papers, and said, "Carl, why did you hurt those boys?"

Carl cleared his throat before saying, "They wouldn't stop."

"Could you elaborate, please? I'm trying to decide your fate right now, and I'd like to think I gave you a chance to share your side of the story. I don't know how it is back in Philadelphia, but it's not every day I deal with a kid who's beaten up half the football team. Wouldn't you agree, Chief Watkins?"

"Yes, Your Honor. I'd say this is downright idiosyncratic."

"Idiosyncratic, yes. So, Carl, do you mind telling me a little more about whatever it was that led up to this unfortunate incident?"

"I was just sitting there, eating my lunch, and then I heard them laughing, and I looked over, and I saw this one kid—I think his name is Brad—picking on this little kid. Eli something."

"Yes," the judge said. "Eli Barringer and Brad Templeton. Brad's home from the hospital now, in case you were wondering. His jaw's wired shut. He'll be sipping breakfast, lunch, and dinner through a straw for the next six months, according to his father. Did you know them?"

"Sir?"

This judge asked questions like a slick boxer used a jab. You never saw them coming, and just when you thought you'd found your rhythm, he knocked you off-balance again.

"This boy, Eli, for instance. Was he a friend of yours?"

"No, sir."

"You just decided to defend him, then. And did you know Brad Templeton?"

"No, sir."

"What I'm trying to comprehend is why you would do something like this. No grudge to settle; no attachment to the victim. Why don't you tell me a little more about how it all happened? Maybe even why."

"I don't know." Carl remembered Eli's thick glasses, his hunched body, and worst of all, his smile—his braces full of white bread and peanut butter. "I just . . . I don't like bullies. I mean, I can't stand them. They were making fun of this kid, and he was sitting there, laughing, because he didn't know what was going on, and everybody kept laughing at him, so I got up and walked over and told them to stop."

"By *them* you are referring to Brad Templeton?"

"Yes, sir."

"An interesting choice of words, *them*. This is not the first time something like this has happened."

Carl shook his head.

"I've read your records, son. It took me a good portion of yesterday evening. I must say, to employ Chief Watkins's terminology, that I found your history rather idiosyncratic."

They looked at each other for a second, and the judge said, "Carl, you've been in eighteen different placements in the last four years, and that's not counting short stays like the place where you got that jumpsuit you're wearing. Eighteen. A dozen and a half foster homes, group homes, and juvenile detention facilities in Pennsylvania, New Jersey, Ohio, and"—he glanced down at the papers—"Idaho. How was Idaho?"

"Cold, sir."

"Cold, yes. I'd imagine. You've accumulated one of the longest rap sheets I've ever seen for a juvenile, and you've only just turned sixteen. And yet something stands out to me. They're all, every last one of them, the same charge—assault—each stemming from the same sort of situation that brought you before me. Someone gave someone else a hard time, and you took it upon yourself to teach him a lesson. Good God, son, I lost track of how many people you have assaulted. And it's not just other children. Oh no. You've punched foster parents and teachers and mall security and even a police officer. A police officer? Son, don't you have a brain?"

Carl looked down. "He had some skateboarder up against the

monkey bars, and he kept yelling at the kid and slamming him into the bars, so—"

"Stop," the judge said. "There is no *so* when you don't like something a police officer is doing. You had no role in that situation. You're lucky he didn't shoot you. I would have shot you. Chief, wouldn't you have shot him?"

"Hands like that? Yeah, I'd have shot him."

Carl wished these two would drop the cutesy act and get down to business. The longer he sat here, the more it felt like disaster brewing.

The judge said, "I don't know whose decision it was to move you all the way down here to North Carolina and drop you into Jessup High, but I intend to find out, and I further intend to have his hide nailed to my shed by sundown." He glanced at Velma, and she nodded and made a note on a clipboard. "You are a rare person, Carl Freeman. Other than fighting, your record is absolutely spotless. No theft, no drugs, no underage drinking. If it weren't for the fighting, you'd look like a candidate for the glee club."

Carl had heard all of this before. "I don't look for trouble. . . . If they would just stop."

The judge tented his fingers and narrowed his eyes. "Very interesting, Carl. Very interesting, indeed. You said it again. *They*. Do you feel these people—Brad, the policeman in Ohio—are all in on this together? Part of some club or something?"

"I'm not crazy."

The judge tapped the stack of papers before him. "Your record implies otherwise, I'm afraid. Either you are insane or, at the very least, *downright* idiosyncratic. It's like you have a superhero complex or something. Mild-mannered schoolboy by day, raging lunatic by night."

Heat rose through Carl's chest and into his face, and his knuckles began to ache again. Why didn't anybody understand? "If I don't stop them, nobody will. Not the kids, not the teachers, nobody. Everybody just sits back and watches. The kids pretend they think it's funny, because they're too scared to say anything, and the teachers pretend they don't see it because they're too lazy to do anything. What am I supposed to do?"

"Lower your voice," Chief Watkins said. He was still leaned back with his big forearms crossed over his chest, but his eyes bore hard into Carl's.

The judge patted the air. "That's okay, Chief. I'm glad the boy's letting his hair down." Then, to Carl, he said, "Now, these boys you attacked, Brad Templeton and the others, they're well-known in the community. Put on car washes, sell candy bars door-to-door, you might know the type. Their mothers and fathers, I see them at the Elks Club on Friday evenings. In the fall, we show up a bit later on Friday nights. See, football is quite popular here in our little corner of the world. Disturbingly so, in fact. It approaches religion at times. You can see the sort of trouble you've caused me?"

Carl nodded, thinking, *Here it comes. The jabbing's over; here comes the KO punch.*

The judge continued. "Jessup's football season is over before it even got going. The boys with broken noses will be okay, but the ones with busted ribs and wired jaws are out for the season. There are on that team other kids, good kids counting on football scholarships. Who will even scout a team with the record Jessup's going to have this year? No one, that's who. So these boys, instead of going on to college, they'll just mow lawns and load cases of beer into people's trunks for the rest of their lives." The judge stared directly into Carl's eyes, and for the first time, Carl saw anger there. "These are the real victims of your crime. They might not even know it, but I know it, and you know it, and their parents know it. The town is screaming for your blood, son. They'd like to string you up on the fifty-yard line and then feed what's left to the pigs."

"I'm sorry about those other kids." Carl lowered his head. He *was* sorry. They had never crossed his mind. Worse still, he wasn't sure he could have stopped himself even if they had.

"I believe you are—sorry about them, I mean—but what interests me is, are you sorry about the other boys, too, the ones you hurt?"

Carl remembered the deep green mountainside beyond the cafeteria windows, rags of fog lifting away like departing ghosts. A strange world far from home, everything darkness and void. Remembered the boys, their cruelty, their laughter when he'd told them to stop. Remembered the fight, all of them coming at him, and then . . . kids on the floor, bleeding, Carl turning himself in.

He raised his eyes and shook his head.

The judge's mouth went thin. "I didn't think so. While I commend your honesty, I must publicly acknowledge that a criminal who shows no remorse for his crimes is, of course, a criminal likely to perpetrate those same crimes in the future. With those hands of yours, I could charge you with assault with a deadly weapon. Eight counts. Forget the juvenile detention center. Chief Watkins would drive you straight to the state penitentiary, where you could serve out a sentence of, oh, a decade or two, right alongside full-grown men. Does that sound good to you?"

"No, sir."

"Or I could hand you over to Windy Pines. They'd put you in a padded cell and drug you up so heavily you wouldn't be able to tie your own shoes. Do you like the sound of that?"

"No, sir."

"The trouble is, I have to live with whatever decision I make here today, and despite your singular idiosyncrasy, I believe you have the potential to become a good man someday. Your father was killed in the line of duty?"

"He died as a result of wounds sustained in the line of duty." If it sounded like a line Carl had said before, it was. Many times.

The judge sighed. "Carl, it is my belief that you are at the present time, regardless of your potential, incapable of controlling your temper should the aforementioned situation arise again."

Carl nodded.

"Judges in the past have taken every approach, from absolute leniency to draconian severity. Nothing has worked. And yet, you have within you this potential. Even your criminal acts have a certain nobility about them, as if you ascribe to a higher code than the rest of humanity. But make no mistake; they are crimes. In light of these factors—the nature and number of your crimes, your seeming inability to control your temper, and the positive potential I see in every other aspect of your character and behavior—I hereby sentence you to Phoenix Island, a military-style boot camp, the term of confinement to begin immediately and to end at the date of your eighteenth birthday, at which point in time you will either return to North Carolina to serve out the remainder of your sentence, a term of six months to three years, at the state penitentiary, or you will earn placement through Phoenix Island, at which time this court will declare your debt paid in full and will furthermore expunge your juvenile record."

Carl swallowed with difficulty. Jail or freedom. Nothing in between.

"There is no parole from Phoenix Island. It is a terminal facility, meaning you will remain there until you are legally an adult. Fail to learn from this opportunity, and I predict you will spend the rest of your life in and out of prison. If, however, you make the most out of this situation, and you learn to give others a second chance, just as I have given you here today, you will be able to lead a good life as a productive member of our society. You get control of that temper of yours, and I think you'd make one hell of a cop."

"Thank you, sir."

The judge looked Carl dead in the eyes. "There will come a day, son, when you will need to determine exactly who it is you intend to be."

"Yes, sir."

The judge finished his coffee, set the empty cup on Carl's file, and turned to the others. "Questions?"

Ms. Snyder asked for the location and visiting hours.

Yeah, right, Carl thought. If there were two things you learned as an orphan, they were endings and beginnings. Mr. and Mrs. Rhoades were no more likely to visit than were Carl's dead parents.

The judge closed the matter. "I'm afraid that's confidential, Ms. Snyder, and irrelevant, as well. Phoenix Island allows no contact with the outside world."

2

THE PLANE SHUDDERED, angling downward, and Carl thrilled at the sight: an island covered in thick jungle, except at the center, where three peaks of raw stone rose sharply through the forest canopy. As the plane descended, he spotted a few clusters of buildings and thin roads running between them, but what really held his attention was the long sweep of sandy beach, nearly white against the deep, sparkling blue of the ocean.

Phoenix Island at last. A new start. His chance at a future.

He looked forward to getting off the plane and stretching his legs. He hoped the staff would let them swim later. He'd never been in the ocean, and he imagined what it would feel like, diving into the waves after the long, hot trip. Would it burn his eyes, opening them in the salt water?

The plane dropped, shuddering, toward a landing strip near the beach, touched down, and taxied to a stop next to a wide, paved area very black in the midday sun, the air over it wavy with heat. Nearby, beside a clump of sagging palm trees, a cluster of low block buildings squatted in the sand, looking as sturdy and businesslike as doorstops.

Out of the nearest building emerged men dressed like soldiers. They pushed a set of metal stairs toward the plane.

"Janice," the small kid with a big nose said, "cancel my afternoon appointments. I'll be at the sauna." The loudmouth hadn't stopped cracking lame jokes during the whole flight. Some of the others cussed at him, their faces as hard and scarred as Carl's knuckles.

One of passengers reached across the aisle and cuffed the small kid, and when his head jerked forward, mean laughter filled the back of the plane.

Carl tensed, the dull throb starting as his hands tightened into fists.

Rubbing the back of his head, the kid turned to Carl. "Some turbulence on this flight, huh? I'm never flying this airline again."

Carl didn't smile, didn't scowl, just turned away, telling himself, *Mind your own business. It's not your fight.* This was the end of the road, everything on the line. He couldn't throw away his future to protect someone who insisted on cracking suicidally bad jokes.

Something clunked against the fuselage. A moment later, the hatch opened, and a tall, muscular man wearing a Smokey the Bear hat swaggered aboard and glared at them.

All fifty-some passengers fell silent.

The man snapped one thick arm to the side and pointed down the stairs. "Off the plane, brig rats! Move! Move! Move!"

Carl jumped up, clutching his duffel bag to his chest, and squeezed into the flood of kids, which spilled out of the plane, down the metal stairs, and into a tropical wall of wet heat.

"What is your problem, brig rats? You will conduct yourselves in an orderly manner and in good speed, and you will line up in four ranks, at attention—and if I hear *anybody* talking, I'm going to smoke him until there's nothing left to blow away in the wind! Now move!"

Down on the tarmac, soldiers yelled and scowled and pointed, all of them jacked up like professional football players, muscles upon muscles, veins popping along their necks and biceps and foreheads. They dressed identically: camouflage pants tucked into shiny black combat boots and black tank tops so tight Carl could see six-packs through the fabric. A few wore wide-brimmed drill sergeant hats. They stomped and shouted until the kids formed four long rows on the pavement.

Stay cool, Carl thought. *Stay in the middle. Stay out of sight.*

Overhead, the sun burned even hotter than it had during the long bus trip through Texas and the mainland of Mexico before they'd boarded the plane. The air smelled of ocean salt and marshy decay.

To his right stood the small kid with the big nose. Despite the chaos, he grinned at Carl and leaned in, talking out of the side of his mouth. "Some welcome wagon, huh?"

Carl nodded but didn't smile. Smiling at a time like this would be about as acceptable as singing karaoke in math class.

Soldiers yelled, telling them to straighten the lines and move apart. "Drop your bags. Lift your arms straight out to the side like this."

A huge soldier in front of them demonstrated, lifting his arms until he looked like the world's most muscular diver about to do a triple pike in combat boots.

"Square it away, brig rats! Dress-right-dress!"

Everyone shifted, the soldiers telling them to hurry. A red-haired kid in front of Carl was crying.

One of the soldiers yelled, "Unzip your bags and dump the contents on the ground!"

Carl turned his bag upside down, dumping clothes, his shaving kit, and two pictures of his family. His only other possession hit the pavement with a loud clank and lay shining on the black pavement like a miniature sun. He had won the gold medal when he was eleven years old for being the best 90-pound boxer in the country. All of the dozens and dozens of trophies were gone, of course, but at least he'd managed to hold on to this medal over the years.

He stared at it for a second, gathering strength. He could do this. These soldiers, they just wanted to rattle his cage. They were like a fighter who came out swinging at the first bell, trying to take your head off, trying to throw you off your game. You just couldn't let them get to you.

Then a hand closed over Carl's medal and lifted it from the ground.

Looking up, he saw that this soldier was shorter than the others and even more muscular, a thumb of a man in a drill sergeant's hat. He scowled at Carl.

Carl looked back with a blank expression. He wasn't going to try to stare the guy down, but he wasn't going to punk out, either.

"Don't you eyeball me, boy. Eyes straight ahead." The guy held up the medal, snorted, and tucked it into his pocket.

"What are you doing with my medal?" Carl asked.

The soldier glared at him, kept glaring, then gave him a tilted grin, no humor in it at all. "Don't worry about it, sunshine. Put your hands on your head and spread your feet."

Carl followed the command, but anger lit inside him, and his knuckles started to ache. Where did this guy get off, taking his things?

The stout man picked up Carl's empty bag, shook it, and let it drop. "Got anything else I should know about? Drugs? Weapons? Money, phone? Anything?"

"No."

"That's 'No, Drill Sergeant.'"

"No, Drill Sergeant," Carl said, the words bitter in his mouth.

The drill sergeant patted Carl down, head to toe, then crouched to root through his things, shaking out the clothes as if on the hunt for something before tossing them to one side. Carl focused on the skull-and-crossbones tattoo emblazoned on the muscular bronze arm. The soldier used his left arm, Carl noted—a southpaw. A tattooed banner overtop the skull read *Death Before Dishonor.*

Yeah, right, Carl thought, wanting his championship gold back. Now.

"Keep these." The sergeant handed Carl the photographs: one of his mother in a red Phillies cap, the upper deck of good old Veterans Stadium visible behind her; the other of the whole family, Dad in his police uniform, Mom smiling at the camera, Carl, maybe five or six, holding their hands tight.

The drill sergeant went through the shaving kit and dropped it at Carl's feet. "Put all this back in the bag. Let's go. Hurry up."

Carl didn't budge.

The drill sergeant, who'd begun drifting down the line toward somebody else, snapped around to stare at Carl. "I told you to move."

"What about my medal . . . Drill Sergeant?"

The man snarled, eyes flashing. He rushed to Carl, shoved into him with his big chest, and leaned in so close the brim of his hat bumped Carl's nose.

Carl stared straight ahead, smelling sweat and feeling heat coming off the big muscles.

"You sassing me, kid?"

"He didn't mean anything by it, Drill Sergeant," the small kid next to Carl said.

"You took my medal," Carl said. He knew this was a mistake, but he couldn't help it; that award was the sole symbol of the only success he'd ever known.

"Your what?" The guy bumped Carl with his hat again.

Carl stared straight ahead. "My medal."

The sergeant roared with laughter.

For a second, Carl felt relief—it was all a joke—but then he noted the emptiness in the laughter and knew he'd crossed some stupid line and was about to pay.

"Drill sergeants!" the sergeant yelled. "I think I found an individual!"

In all directions, voices clamored.

"An individual?"

"Where?"

"An individual? Not on Phoenix Island!"

Then they were on him, yelling in his face, in his ears, at the back of his head.

"An individual!"

"He looks like an individual!"

"Showboat!"

"Hollywood!"

Carl gritted his teeth and stared straight ahead.

They pushed him out of the ranks to a patch of bare pavement.

"Front!" Skull-and-Crossbones yelled.

Hands pushed Carl to the hot ground. It was like pressing both his palms onto a pancake griddle. He didn't show it.

"When he says 'front,'" someone yelled, "you get into push-up position and start pushing, Hollywood."

It felt like his hands were melting into the asphalt, but Carl forced the pain out of his mind and fell into his rhythm. Up-down-up-down-up . . .

To his left, someone laughed.

Drill sergeants leapt.

"What's so funny, kid?"

"You think we're funny?"

"Get over there and join him, Stretch!"

"It wasn't me, Drill Sergeant." They pushed a tall, skinny kid onto the pavement. Carl had noticed him on the plane, the guy all smiles as he flashed signs back and forth with the other gangbangers.

"What is your name, brig rat?"

"Davis, Drill Sergeant."

"Davis, you have approximately two seconds to shut your mouth and start pushing, or you are going to rapidly develop the most debilitating migraine you have *ever* encountered. Front!"

They pushed Davis onto the ground directly in front of Carl. He yelped and rocked back. "The asphalt burned my hands!"

Carl stuck to his rhythm—up-down-up-down—and watched an arm force Davis to the pavement again. Finally, as Davis began to do push-ups, his eyes burned into Carl's, one of them dripping tattooed tears. The ink told Carl that Davis had murdered two people, one for each teardrop; the eyes told him that in Davis's gangbanger view of the world, all of this—the shouting, the push-ups, maybe even the burning macadam—was somehow Carl's fault.

"Two individuals," a voice bellowed. "What do we do about that?"

"How about . . . ? Back!"

Hands lifted Carl out of his push-up position and spilled him onto his back. A face leaned in, screaming. "When he says 'back,' you do sit-ups!"

Carl started, ignoring the burn of the pavement, which was so hot he thought his jumpsuit might burst into flames. Sit-ups, though? A boxer could rack out sit-ups all day long. Carl did a thousand a day, just out of habit.

"Go!"

They yanked Carl to his feet. Someone yelled, "When he says 'go,' you jog in place!" The voice was so close, so loud, it seemed like the guy was inside Carl's ear . . . with a bullhorn.

Carl pumped his legs up and down. Again, running was a breeze. You didn't need special equipment or a team or a gym membership to run, so it was one of the things Carl had been able to do in almost every place he'd been sent.

"I didn't do anything, man," Davis said, barely lifting his feet.

One of the sergeants reached up and cuffed Davis in the back of the head. "Lock it up, goldbrick! You just added another minute."

"How long we got to do this?" Davis asked.

Another cuff. "Two minutes longer than you did before you asked that question."

One of the drill sergeants pointed at Davis's long legs, laughing. "Man, I had legs like that, I'd sue 'em for lack of support!"

"Front!"

Carl dropped and started pushing.

And so it went, on and on: front-back-go . . . front-back-go . . . front-back-go . . . the pavement hot as fire, the sun boiling overhead, the sergeants laughing and yelling and telling them if there was one thing they couldn't stand, it was an individual. Every time they faced each other, Davis drilled his eyes through Carl's.

So stupid, Carl thought. All of it—the drill sergeants, his own mistake, the punishment, Davis's anger, everything. So, so stupid.

Front . . . back . . . go . . .

Carl pumped his knees up and down. He was exhausted from the long trip. He'd barely slept for days, and fatigue, combined with hunger and the heat, stirred his mind like a kettle of bubbling soup, out of which, like steam, rose images: Brad Templeton, Eli screaming, the judge, the sign reading YOU ARE NOW LEAVING THE UNITED STATES OF AMERICA, the assorted roadkill along the endless highway they'd driven prior to boarding the strange plane in the Mexican desert . . .

"Front!"

Carl sprawled into a push-up and started pumping away. His arms shook with effort. *So be it,* Carl thought. *They're not going to break me.* He gritted his teeth and kept pushing.

Davis's head hung low between his shoulders, and he was stuck, mid-push-up, his arms quivering. All at once, he dropped onto his stomach.

Shouting filled the air.

"Nobody told you to stop!"

"Motivation!"

"Keep pushing, individual!"

"Let's go, funny man! I don't hear you laughing now!"

Davis lay on his stomach. "I can't do no more."

"Get pushing now! That's an order!"

"I can't, Drill Sergeant," Davis said.

"Get up," Carl said. "You can do it."

"Shut up," someone told him, and pain exploded in Carl's ribs. He grunted but kept pushing.

One of them had kicked him—it surprised him. Shouting and push-ups were one thing . . . kicking, though? That was against the law.

Or at least it had been in the United States.

This was Phoenix Island.

Davis struggled through one more push-up before collapsing again.

Drill sergeants surrounded him, yelling. "Are you disobeying a direct order?" one of them said above the others.

"I can't do another—"

A combat boot thudded into Davis's ribs. He cried out and rolled into a ball. Carl saw the kicker's thick forearm, the skull and crossbones there, the words *Death Before Dishonor* suspended over Davis like a bad joke inked into bronze flesh.

Carl stopped pushing. "Leave him alone."

A hand grabbed him by the hair and lifted, then slammed him back down into the pavement. The air rushed out of his lungs, and pain spread through him.

"Back!" Someone told him. "You get sassy again, we'll take it out on your buddy."

Carl swallowed the pain and started doing sit-ups. *Buddy? Davis wants to turn me into his third teardrop.*

"You're not in Fort Living Room anymore, kid!" one of the sergeants yelled at Davis. "This is the real deal!"

"I gave you an order!" Skull-and-Crossbones said. "You have exactly three seconds to start pushing, or I'm citing you for insubordination!"

Davis lay curled on the ground.

"One!"

Get up, Carl thought.

"Two!"

C'mon, man.

"Three!"

Skull-and-Crossbones kicked him again. Davis cried out and tried to crawl away, but they hauled him to his feet, shouting that he'd disobeyed direct orders. Davis was loose in their grip, like a fighter standing up after getting knocked out for the full ten-count.

"If he's not going to follow orders," a woman's voice, cold and smooth and oddly lyrical, said, "take him to the sweatbox."

"Yes, First Sergeant!" the drill sergeants yelled as one. One tossed Davis over his shoulder and jogged off through the heat blur.

The shouting stopped. Hands yanked Carl to his feet. "Show the first sergeant respect! Attention!"

Carl had seen enough war movies to know what that meant. He stood straight with his arms at his sides and then executed what he thought of as a salute.

A compact woman with very dark skin regarded him coolly. Raised lines of scar tissue, stacked as neatly as ranked soldiers, laddered her cheeks. Speaking with an African lilt, she said, "Do not salute me, young man. I work for a living. Rejoin the ranks."

"Yes, First Sergeant," Carl said, and, lowering his hand, jogged back toward the kids. As he neared the group, he saw a jeep pull away from a low block building, two long legs dangling out of the back. Davis was off to the sweatbox, then, whatever that was. Carl hoped never to find out.

As he reentered the ranks, someone tripped him, and he nearly fell. "Way to go, Hollywood." Others hissed curses. Without even looking, Carl knew it was Davis's friends.

Great. This was going just great.

Then Carl saw the pretty girl in the back rank, staring at him, her gray eyes wide. He'd noticed her on the bus in Texas, then again boarding the plane, but they'd separated the boys and the girls, and only now did he really get to look at her. She looked frightened and stunned and exhausted, yet still beautiful, with sad-looking eyes the color of wet gravel and long hair as dark as his mother's had been, though a patch of pure white marked her bangs. White hair. And her, what? Sixteen?

Then he was back in his spot beside the small kid, facing away from her. Had he seen concern on her face? He wished he'd smiled. Then the absurdity of that hit him, and he could have laughed at himself. Smile at her? This wasn't exactly a make-out party. Still, she was very pretty. Those eyes, that hair.

His bag was gone. Everyone's bag was gone. The lines they stood in were straighter now. *Guess they had time to tidy things up while I was dying over there.* There was a gap where the red-haired kid had been. Carl glanced to the side and saw a lump under the trees. Must've fainted.

"Attention!" a drill sergeant yelled.

Everyone snapped to attention.

First Sergeant Oteka stood before them. "Welcome to Phoenix Island, boys and girls. I am First Sergeant Oteka. Allow me to explain the reality of your situation, children." She walked slowly back and forth before them. When she turned, Carl saw the pistol on her belt. "Your parents are dead."

Her words echoed in Carl's mind. *Your parents are dead.* Was she talking to him?

"You are all orphans," Oteka said.

All of us? Carl thought.

"You bit the hand that fed you, and society cast you away. You are yesterday's trash. And from this moment forward, until your eighteenth birthday, you belong to me and also to the Old Man, whom you are not yet ready to meet. I will not subject his eyes to such unwashed rabble."

She stared at them for several seconds, surveying their faces. Gunfire rattled in the distance.

"You will have no contact with the outside world," Oteka said. "No phone calls. No texts. No email. No letters. No news. No music, television, or internet." She raked her hard gaze over their ranks. "The world will move on without you. No one there knows where you are, and no one cares. Phoenix Island is your only home." She gestured toward the drill sergeants. "We are your only family."

She spoke to the soldiers, who formed a line and stood, legs apart, chins out, hands behind their backs.

"Drill Sergeant Parker," Oteka said. "Please demonstrate my sincerity."

Skull-and-Crossbones offered the formation a big smile, then walked past the line of sergeants, dumping the contents of a green bag. Cell phones, MP3 players, and games clattered to the pavement.

A quiet murmur ran through the ranks.

"Isolation!" Oteka said, and her men started stomping the devices into the ground. Screens shattered; phones snapped; iPods twisted and split. Around Carl, kids gasped and groaned, hissed and whispered, scowled and wept.

For Carl, who'd never owned electronics, this destruction wasn't of personal concern, but it was another in a sequence of danger signs. What concerned him most of all was the opening of First Sergeant Oteka's speech: *You are all orphans.* Why had they taken only orphans? He thought of the kick he had received, the rough handling of Davis. He glanced around. Here they were, on Phoenix Island, somewhere outside of the United States and its laws.

We're as dead to the world as our parents, Carl thought. *These people can do anything to us.*

3

CARL CLIMBED INTO THE LONG, OPEN FLATBED of one of the cattle trucks and found himself once again next to the small kid. Oh well, maybe it was time to make a friend—even one who told horrible jokes.

The kid smiled. "You survived."

"For now," Carl said. He felt like he'd gone fifteen rounds against a heavyweight.

"They took my PSP." The kid cursed and curled his small hands into talons. "Do you have any idea how hard I worked to get that thing?"

Carl shrugged. "Pretty hard, I guess."

"Only six hours every Saturday for about a million years." He shook his head. "I wore a chicken suit and stood at this busy intersection, waving a Chicken Hut sign."

"Ouch," Carl said, chuckling a little.

"Ouch isn't the half of it. This kid Dan Carville—he worked at the pet shop next to Chicken Hut—told everybody at school, and—"

"No prom for you."

"Yeah, that pretty much sums it up. No prom for me." The kid grinned. "I got so bored standing there in that chicken suit, I used to curse at everybody driving by. They couldn't hear me. I'd yell the worst thing I could think of, and some dumb woman would beep and wave like it was roses. It was pretty funny." He chuckled, but then his smile faded. "Now my PSP is in a thousand pieces."

Carl nodded his head. "Better your video game than your ribs."

"Sorry. It's pretty lame, complaining about my stuff when you were getting kicked like that. You okay?"

"Yeah. I've been in some pretty rough places, and sometimes staff would yell, push you up against the wall, stuff like that. But this? I didn't know they could hit us."

The kid spread his palms. "I figure we're somewhere in the Pacific, off the western coast of Mexico. You know why they build places like this outside the US, right? So they can do whatever they want without worrying about us suing them later. Whatever. Not much we can do about it now. My name's Neil, by the way. Neil Ross."

"Carl Freeman." They shook. Ross's hand was small and sweaty, but Carl didn't care. At last, he had something like a friend. Here on Phoenix Island, that mattered, even if Ross looked like a bull's-eye for the type of trouble that followed Carl everywhere he went. Bullies would eat Ross alive, and then Carl would . . .

No, he told himself. *You have to control yourself this time.* On the journey here, he'd begun to really like the idea of having a future. For years, he'd assumed all the trouble he'd gotten into would throw a pair of cuffs on any dream he might cook up. Now things were different. Staying out of trouble, earning a clean record, becoming a cop—that would really be something.

Not that he'd done a very good job of staying out of trouble so far. But still, Phoenix Island, tough as the introduction was, was his way out.

The line of trucks started moving.

"Here we go," Ross said. "Next stop, Hogwarts."

Carl grinned. He had no idea what Ross was talking about, but he could tell it was a joke.

They drove into the jungle. It was amazing—true wilderness—no pavement, no buildings, only trees and plants and gloom. A rich, damp smell filled the air, different from the mossy smell of the woods back in Pennsylvania. Underneath the jungle air dwelled a faint ripeness, something like decay. Overhead, the canopy grew so dense it blocked the sun that earlier had fried them like bacon. The light was dim, the vegetation thick. Here and there, roads branched off left or right, but the truck kept going, bouncing over frequent rough patches. Once, Carl saw something low and stubby, like a barrel with legs, running through the trees. A pit bull, maybe, or a pig. Nothing he wanted to run into, either way.

Ross said he was from Massachusetts, from some town Carl had never heard of. "Well," Ross said, "if you ever visit, drop by the pet store and punch Dan Carville in the nose for me."

Eventually they entered a bright clearing, where, off to the right, about a football field in the distance, something exploded. A plume of dirt and smoke rose into the air. Kids screamed in surprise and appreciation. Drill sergeants shouted, and the trucks drove once more into the darkness of the jungle.

The air grew thicker, redolent of swampy decay. The trucks skidded to a stop beside a high fence topped with razor wire. Off to the left, in a dim clearing dappled by strips of sunlight falling through breaks in the trees, stood whitewashed buildings with wooden porches and thatched roofs. A brown sign with yellow letters faced the road.

"Medical center," Ross read aloud, but Carl said nothing. Something about the place made his stomach roll and clench.

Two kids carried the redhead who'd fainted off one of the trucks, his arms slung over their shoulders. A gate opened, and soldiers in green shirts loaded the kid onto a stretcher. He looked dead, Carl thought.

"Whoa," Ross said. "Look."

Between the nearest building and the fence, a figure shambled into view. His mouth hung open. One bruised eye was swollen shut; the other stared blankly at the trucks. He raised a hand slowly and held it out as if reaching for something invisible.

Carl shook his head. "Poor kid looks like a zombie."

"Yeah," Ross said, "and there's Dr. Frankenstein."

A bearded man in a white coat emerged from the nearest doorway and crossed the porch. At the rail, he stepped into a strip of sunlight that caught the lenses of his spectacles, making them look like circles of flame. He shouted at the strange kid, his words angry, fast, and foreign, quick bursts of machine-gun Spanish.

The zombie kid howled and shuffled off into the deeper shadows between the trees.

The man fired another burst of Spanish, Carl picking up one word in the middle, "*ahora.*" He'd heard the word a thousand times back in the gym, trainers leaning against the ropes and urging their fighters, "*¡Ahora! ¡Ahora!*" . . . "Now! Now!" And then the man was hurrying off the porch, after the shambling kid, a snarl parting his beard as he descended the stairs.

But then, noticing the trucks and orphans for the first time, he jerked to a stop. His snarl faded, and his arms, which had been waving angrily, lowered to his sides. His beard parted again, this time with a smile, and he gave the slightest nod to the soldiers carrying the stretcher. Next, turning once more in the direction the zombie kid had fled, he raised one arm, fluttered his fingers, and called softly into the shadows, looking like a man politely requesting the service of a busy waiter.

What was going on here?

"Check it out," Ross said, pointing to the building. "There are bars in the windows. Boston Pediatric, it ain't."

The others climbed back onto their truck. "Let's roll," a drill sergeant said, and everyone started moving again. Carl saw the bearded man with eyes of fire disappear into the shadows, and before long the medical center was far behind them.

The road dipped, and after a slow descent, the truck rumbled onto a rough log bridge that crossed a wide, swampy area. Kids pointed at snakes hanging from trees.

"You get a bite from one of those snakes," a nearby soldier with a Southern twang said, "and you're one dead orphan."

On the other side of the swamp, they reentered the jungle, and the woods grew even darker. Through the murky gloom, Carl thought he saw heavy fog or perhaps smoke hanging in the trees. He pointed it out to Ross, who leaned forward and squinted.

"Holy crap," he said. "That's not fog. They're spiderwebs."

Carl shuddered. "Jeez, webs that size, what do they eat—cows?"

"Orphans," Ross said, but neither of them laughed.

The trucks topped a rise and drove through a tall gate flanked by soldiers holding what looked like automatic weapons. Carl took note of more buildings; a wide, paved lot with a tall flagpole at its center; and a high fence encircling the entire compound.

"The phoenix," Ross said, pointing to the banner fluttering atop the pole.

The flag was black and showed something like an eagle with its wings spread, red flames all around it.

"What's with the fire?" Carl said.

"Mythology," Ross said. "When a phoenix dies, it bursts into flames. Then it's reborn from its own ashes. It's used as a symbol of rebirth and—"

Their truck jerked to a sudden stop.

"Off the trucks!" a drill sergeant yelled. "On the double, orphans! Girls to the left, boys to the right. I see anybody slacking, he's going to the sweatbox. You, shut your mouth! I see anybody talk, he's going in the sweatbox. Form it up outside. Work it, orphans!"

The sweatbox. This whole place feels like a sweatbox, Carl thought, and hoped Davis would be all right.

They hurried off the trucks, and drill sergeants yelled at them and formed them up and yelled at them some more, telling them the way things would be. They would speak only when spoken to, and that sort of thing. Nothing Carl hadn't expected.

Catching a quick glimpse of the white-haired girl standing at attention with the other girls, he saw that they had female drill sergeants yelling at them. Carl forced his eyes back to his own instructor, who pointed toward the gate. "It would behoove you, orphans, to memorize that warning right now."

Carl spotted the sign just as the drill sergeant read it aloud. "Runners die!"

Someone up in a tower made a high-pitched squealing sound. Carl saw a silhouette against the sun, the black line of a rifle barrel jutting from its shadowy form.

"I note this for your safety, orphans," the drill sergeant addressing them said, and pointed toward the fence. "That jungle will eat you alive. Bad things live out there. Bad, bad things. This fence right here? It's not to keep you in. It's to keep them out. You go AWOL here, it's a death sentence."

"Hooah!" the soldier atop the tower hollered, and ripped the air with machine-gun fire.

Carl tensed but didn't break ranks. Some guys overreacted. One of the gang guys ducked down onto the pavement, eyes wide with fear.

The drill sergeant continued. "Even if, by some miracle, you made it out of the jungle alive, the ocean around Phoenix Island is nothing but teeth and blood. Hammerhead sharks. Do you read me, orphans?"

"Yes, Drill Sergeant," a chorus of voices replied.

"You better read me. And I mean Lima Charlie. Loud and clear. That water boils with monsters."

"Cool," some kid said.

"Lock it up, Chatty Cathy!"

Runners die, Carl thought. No escape, no parole: a terminal facility.

All right. He'd just dig in and tough it out. Only two years till his eighteenth birthday. Not even. Closer to one and a half.

He could do it.

CARL STOOD ON THE SCALE, wearing only boxer shorts.

"Freeman, Carl. Five feet, nine inches tall. One hundred and fifty-two pounds. Body type, meso-ecto," Drill Sergeant Rivera, who seemed way nicer than the others, told the soldier with the clipboard. "Step off the scale, Freeman, and stick your arms out."

Carl stretched his arms, pointing the fingertips.

"Seventy-four inches," Rivera said, reading the tape. "What are you, kid, a bowler or a bellhop?"

Carl grinned. He'd always had a long reach.

"Target weight?" the soldier with the clipboard asked.

Rivera studied Carl. "No fat. Wide shoulders. Monkey arms. Put him down for one seventy-five."

Carl could have laughed. One seventy-five? No way . . . and no thanks. At welterweight, he wrecked people, and nobody could rattle his chin. One seventy-five, though? That was a whole different game. Trading with light heavies was like punching a brick wall and then getting kicked by a mule.

"Get dressed and head outside, Freeman."

"Yes, Drill Sergeant."

Carl dressed quickly and hurried outside, where he joined a silent formation facing the loading dock of a large shed. They waited in the hot sun. That had been the pattern of the day: hurry up and wait, hurry up and wait.

"Quiet in the ranks!" Drill sergeants grabbed a kid and smoked him, front-back-go, for talking in formation.

Carl started thinking how stupid all this army-style discipline was, when he noticed Davis, who looked like the walking dead after only an hour in the sweatbox, and the gang guys nudging one another at the front of the formation. One bent and pulled something small and slender from the weeds at the base of the loading bay. It flashed in the sunlight, then disappeared into the kid's pocket as the others in Davis's crew grinned and nodded.

Great, Carl thought. He didn't know what the shiny thing was—a sliver of plastic or metal, probably—but he knew what they would do with it.

The metal shed door clacked and rolled open, and Skull-and-Cross-bones—*Parker*, Carl reminded himself—emerged, already yelling. "Front rank, let's go. Up the steps. Second rank, fill it in. I said hurry, orphans!"

The first rank filed into the shed and came back out carrying sheets and towels.

"Next rank, keep it tight!"

In the shed, Carl avoided eye contact with Parker. He would work on getting his medal back later. For now, he wanted to stay out of trouble. He couldn't take another front-back-go session—his muscles still felt weak and shaky—and he definitely did not want to go to the sweatbox.

A soldier handed Carl a stack of towels and sheets, and Carl started to file away.

"Hold up, Hollywood," Parker said.

Carl stopped, staring straight ahead. *What now?*

"Hey, Rivera," Parker said, taking linens from Carl's stack. "Bet you a week's pay Hollywood's a bed wetter."

Carl just stood there, doing his best to ignore the ache building in his knuckles.

"Just remember when you're wetting your bunk tonight, Hollywood," Parker said, holding up a pillowcase, then a sheet. "This one's for tears, and this one's for wee-wee." He shoved them both in Carl's face and said, "Now get off my dock before I throw you off."

Carl didn't take the bait. He rejoined the ranks and stood there, holding his stack and staring at the dirty handprints on his pillowcase until the drill sergeants started yelling, "Move, orphans, move!"

Carl sprinted. Drill sergeants shouted from all sides, chewing out any kids who dropped their linens. They hustled everyone across a quad and into a two-story block building. "Up those stairs, orphans!"

The stairwell was hot and stuffy and sour with sweat. Drill sergeants shouted from above and below, and footsteps rang loudly as kids pounded upstairs, most of them badly out of breath. Up ahead, someone fell, and Carl barely stopped himself from barreling into the guy in front of him—the kid's back so wide it practically filled the stairwell—and then someone crashed into Carl from behind and he did slam into the broad back.

Here we go, he thought.

The big guy, who had long dreadlocks and a goatee, half turned and gave Carl a look that said nothing. No scowl, no smile, nothing.

"Sorry," Carl said.

Without a word, the kid turned back around, and then they were moving again.

They passed shouting sergeants and ran down a long hall to where yet another shouting sergeant pointed through a doorway. "Into the bay! Two to a bunk! Move!"

Carl followed the others into a long room filled with bunk beds and freestanding lockers, four bunks to the right, four to the left. Behind him, sergeants yelled for other kids to keep moving down the hall to the next bay.

A soldier pointed to Carl and the huge guy, then to the bunk nearest the door. "You and you, there."

Parker's voice cursed in the distance.

Carl waited, sweating into his bedding and towels. The bay was old and smelled like a pine-tree car freshener. Most of them fighting to catch their breath, the other kids stood in pairs and exchanged glances but said nothing. Across the aisle, Ross squinted, gasping for air. The big guy with dreads wasn't breathing hard at all and exchanged glances with no one. He just stood there, staring straight ahead, steady as a statue.

Good idea, Carl thought.

Drill Sergeant Rivera came into the bay and started walking the center aisle. "Welcome to your new home, orphans. Top bunk locker to the left, bottom bunk to the right. Hooah?"

A soldier in the doorway said, "When someone says 'hooah,' you hooah back! Hooah?"

"Hooah," Carl and most of the kids responded.

Rivera paced up and down the aisle as the other soldier demanded louder hooahs until they were all screaming at the top of their lungs.

Down the hall, another bay hooah-ed.

They're all using the same script, Carl thought, and wasn't surprised when a third group started hooah-ing.

Rivera paced, telling them how it was. This was their bay. They were going to keep it clean, hooah?

"Hooah!"

He told them they would make their beds and learn to use their combination locks and always, always, always secure all items. Tonight they would march back to the supply sheds, receive more gear, clean the barracks, and shower their filthy bodies. At some point there would be inoculations, chow, and something he called "drill and ceremony," followed by an inspection. Once the barracks were clean—"and I mean shiny as your best girl's choppers"—they might get some sleep. Hooah?

"Hooah!"

Rivera stopped in front of Carl's bunk, regarding the big kid. "What's your name, son?"

"Walker Campbell, Drill Sergeant," the kid said in a deep voice.

"Take off your shirt, Campbell."

Campbell hesitated for a second, then peeled off his shirt, revealing a physique worthy of an NFL fullback.

"What in the name of General George Patton have they been feeding you, son? Tanks?"

"Mostly fruits and vegetables, Drill Sergeant."

"What's this?" Rivera asked, pointing to his shoulder.

"A tattoo, Drill Sergeant."

"Of?"

"My brother, Deonte, Drill Sergeant."

"Deceased?"

"Yes, Drill Sergeant."

"I'm sorry to hear that, Campbell. And tell me, where are your gang tats?"

Campbell looked puzzled. "Drill Sergeant?"

"Your gang tattoos."

"I'm not in a gang, Drill Sergeant."

"Never been in one?"

"No, Drill Sergeant."

"Excellent, Campbell. You're the platoon guide."

"Yes, Drill Sergeant."

"Do you have any idea what I'm talking about, Campbell?"

"No, Drill Sergeant."

"Outstanding, Campbell. I like your attitude. The rest of you orphans, Campbell here is your head honcho. You have a problem, you talk to him, not me, hooah?"

"Hooah!"

"Spectacular," Rivera said, and looked at Carl. "Freeman."

"Yes, Drill Sergeant."

"What's the square root of two hundred and seventy-three?"

The what . . . ?

"Chop, chop, Freeman," Rivera said.

"I don't know, Drill Sergeant."

"Neither do I, Freeman," Rivera said, "but I do know how to make a bed properly. Orphans, eyes on me. I'm going to show you how a soldier makes his bed, hooah?"

"Hooah!"

Carl grinned, watching the demonstration. Rivera, at least, was cool.

LATER, AFTER TWO FAILED INSPECTIONS and hours of cleaning, they got chow—a brown hash that looked like beans but smelled like old meat—

and then marched back to the barracks, where they showered and finally hit their racks. It was late. Carl was so exhausted, he was actually thankful that Campbell had claimed the top bunk. Saved him having to climb up.

"Good night, orphans!" Rivera shouted from the hall.

"Good night, Drill Sergeant!"

"Lights out!" Rivera said, and everything went dark.

The night air, hot and humid as a sauna, throbbed with a tropical chorus. Insects or frogs, or maybe both, pleading rhythmically in the darkness. Carl's mattress was hard and lumpy, and he could feel springs pressing into his back, but he didn't care. He was so tired he could sleep on the tile floor if he had to.

Maybe there really was something to the whole boot camp thing, he thought as he drifted toward sleep. Every second of their day, someone had told them where to go and what to do. *If every day is like this,* he thought, *we'll be too busy and too tired for trouble.*

It was a nice thought, the kind you could almost believe, lying in bed after a long, hard day.

But then he heard a soft sound in the darkness, a faint, repetitive grinding barely audible beneath the pulsing tropical chorus. It was a sound he had heard before, in other places he'd been put, and he sat up, instantly awake, listening, and knew that somewhere in the darkness, one of the gangbangers was scraping that sliver of found material against a bed frame, honing an edge, making a deadly shank.

4

"**P**ICK IT UP, FAT BODIES!" a drill sergeant yelled toward the back of the pack.

They'd been on Phoenix Island for a few days, and despite all the yelling and very little rest, Carl was feeling all right. He liked the way the wind rushed over his freshly shaven head, and it felt great to run, even on two hours' sleep. He was at the front of group, matching strides with Walker Campbell. The massive kid had arrived on Phoenix Island with dreadlocks, a goatee, and the build of a fullback. All he had left was the build.

They ran side by side in silence, following the trail marked here and there in yellow paint on roadside trees. They came to a fork in the road and hung a left. Carl broke the silence. "How are you doing?"

Campbell flashed him a look. "Me? I'm fine. I could run like this all day."

"Yeah, me, too. What I meant, how are you doing, you know, your hair and everything?"

Campbell smoothed a hand over his head, frowning.

His *grape*, Carl thought, the drill sergeants' word for *head* coming into his mind now.

"Okay, I guess."

"Yeah?"

"Look," Campbell said. "I don't need a buddy. I'm not looking for friends."

"Fine, by me," Carl said. He remembered the "barbershop"—half a dozen folding chairs set up on the loading dock where they'd been issued boots and bedding—and remembered the clear sense of that moment as a turning point, of the sergeants raising the stakes by actually shaving their heads, like they were really in the army or something. He remembered the buzz and whine of the razor, guys coming off the chair looking stunned, Campbell on deck, trying to talk his way out of it, calling the dreadlocks part of his religion. The barber—who was just another soldier—had laughed and said, "Religion? God's on vacation until you leave Phoenix Island."

After a few more moments of running together, Campbell shook his head a little sadly. "I knew my hair was history as soon as the judge said 'boot camp.'" He ran a hand over his head again. "Man. I don't feel like me."

Carl heard footsteps, and Drill Sergeant Parker, his skull-and-crossbones tattoo prominent as ever, pulled up alongside them. From the moment Carl had stepped off the bus, Parker hadn't stopped giving him a hard time.

"Hollywood," he said, using that nickname again. "Fall back. You're on straggler patrol. Anybody slacking back there, motivate him."

"Yes, Drill Sergeant." Carl turned and jogged back down the road, annoyed by what felt like a demotion. Now he'd have to drop all the way back and shuffle with the fat kids, the smokers, the lazy ones, and the asthmatics.

The farther back he went, the worse people looked. A soldier whose name Carl didn't know—he wasn't a drill sergeant, but one of the guys who helped during PT—demanded to know what he was doing running the wrong way. When Carl told him, the soldier laughed: "Carry on, Tail-end Charlie."

The gaps between the runners widened. Carl nodded at Ross, who looked like he was going to die. He saw a kid puking in the weeds alongside the road and reassured him he'd be all right. Near the back, he passed Davis and his buddies and was met with glares.

Davis shouted something, but Carl kept running. He was going to stay out of trouble.

Farther back, red-faced stragglers fought to breathe. One drooled.

Carl tried to be encouraging. He fell in step beside each, patted them on the back, and told them they'd be okay. A few cried. All wore looks of shock and desperation.

In the very back stumbled the redhead who people had begun calling Medicaid, since he'd gone to the medical center the first day. He looked like he might faint again.

"You're all right," Carl said and patted his back. The shirt was wet, and Carl's hand peeled away.

Medicaid shook his head, wheezing. His face was bright red and wet with tears.

"Concentrate on your breathing," Carl said. Dumb advice, considering the kid sounded about a dozen wheezes from the grave, but what else could he say?

All at once, Medicaid quit. Carl continued on a couple of steps, then looped back and jogged in place, waiting. Medicaid bent, hands on knees, struggling for breath.

"Stand up straight," Carl told him. "You can breathe better that way."

The kid stayed bent over.

"Really, it'll make you feel better. Just stand up, and your lungs will expand."

Medicaid gave him the finger.

"Nice," Carl said. After about thirty seconds, he said, "Come on. We're going to get into trouble if we don't step it up."

"I don't care."

That makes one of us, Carl thought. He'd known this place was going to be tough—military-style boot camps were famous throughout the juvenile system for their "scared straight" strategies and "tough love" tactics—but these drill sergeants genuinely did not play around. They knocked the wind out of kids, stomped on fingers—kicked Davis in the ribs—and never hesitated to deprive "individuals" of food, sleep, or both. One night, Carl had gone without dinner simply because Parker didn't like "the look on his face." He really didn't want this kid bringing down a rain of fire upon them both.

"I can't do this." Medicaid lifted the bottom of his shirt to his face and blew his nose into the fabric. The sound was long and wet, like tires driving through slush.

Carl could have puked. "Come on," he said. "Let's at least walk before somebody comes back and finds us standing here. You don't want to end up in the sweatbox, do you?"

They started walking, Carl very much aware of the mess on Medicaid's shirt.

"Heads up," a woman called from behind, and Carl heard footsteps approaching. "Wide load ahead!"

The ensuing laughter made his face burn with embarrassment.

First Sergeant Oteka passed, saying with her African lilt, "Pick it up, children." The girl running beside her glanced at Carl, then sped up the road. She was thin, running easily, her head shaved like all the others. Recognition, frustration, and embarrassment rushed through Carl as he registered her eyes.

Her gray eyes.

He felt the need to run after her, introduce himself, and explain he was playing cheerleader . . . but that would mean trouble, and he needed to avoid trouble.

Girls jogged past. Some whistled and teased. Others laughed. Others just looked disgusted. A girl with a large birthmark on her face ran past alone, staring straight ahead. *Lost in the middle,* Carl thought. *Almost invisible. Not a bad idea.*

Out-of-shape girls trickled past, red-faced and gasping, but still running.

Carl nodded to Medicaid and smiled, trying to keep his voice light and friendly. "Hey, man, we're letting the girls pass us. Want to step it up to a jog?"

Medicaid cried harder and shook his head.

Carl spat. An overweight girl in a knee brace limped past.

They started up a hill. Medicaid wheezed harder. Someone appeared atop the rise, running in their direction.

The gray-eyed girl.

Carl smiled.

She smiled back, and suddenly, Carl was very happy.

"Hey," she said, and she slowed down and turned and walked with him.

"Are you lost?" Carl asked, and instantly hated himself for making such a stupid joke.

"Oteka sent me back. Straggler patrol."

Carl chuckled. "Me, too."

"Aren't you the kid who got in trouble the first day? What did you do?"

Carl rolled his eyes. "I was being 'an individual.'"

"Well, I'm glad you survived." She smiled wider, light coming into her gray eyes, and Carl saw she was even prettier than he had thought— shaved head and all, a little patch of white stubble at the front. "I love running. This is the first time I've felt right since leaving Washington."

"DC?"

She shook her head. "The state. What a nightmare, coming here. The whole thing, you know? But now—do you think they'll let us run a lot?"

Carl shrugged. "I hope so."

"You guys aren't supposed to be talking," Medicaid said.

"Don't worry about it," Carl said, wishing he could make the kid disappear. "Concentrate on your breathing, buddy."

"He's right, though," the girl said. "I have to keep going. A couple girls are farther back."

"Yeah, *Hollywood*," Medicaid said, all sassy. "You don't want them to put her in the sweatbox, do you?"

"Hollywood?" The girl said. "That's a weird name."

"It's not my name," Carl said.

Medicaid said, "That's what everybody calls him because he thinks he's so special."

"Um, okay," the girl said, frowning a little and cocking an eyebrow. "I better go." She started running in the opposite direction.

"My name is Carl!" he called after her.

"Octavia," she called over her shoulder, and disappeared around a bend in the road.

5

"**Z**ERO-ZERO-EIGHT! ZERO-ZERO-NINE! ZERO-ONE-ZERO!"** they shouted in unison. The platoon stood at attention, lined up single file, faces forward, their left shoulders against the corridor wall. Three drill sergeants faced them, Parker in front.

Four o'clock in the morning and the walls were already sweating with humidity. The green PT shirt in front of Carl was already dark with perspiration. Above its collar, sweat-beaded blond stubble.

"Book Man!" Parker yelled.

"Yes, Drill Sergeant," Carl called. Since, thanks to Medicaid, Carl had come in last on the previous day's run, Parker had appointed him book man. That meant he had to do secretary stuff: take notes, record the day's schedule, set up the duty roster. It was a drag, and it cut into free time he didn't have.

"Get up here, Hollywood!"

Carl jogged to the front of the line. "Yes, Drill Sergeant?"

"What's your problem, Hollywood? Can't you read? Or are you just trying to screw everybody out of chow?"

"I don't know what you mean, Drill Sergeant."

"*I don't know what you mean, Drill Sergeant,*" Parker mimicked. He pointed to the whiteboard. "You didn't block out any time for your platoon to eat breakfast, Hollywood."

"Blue falcon," one of the other drill sergeants commented.

"You can say that again," Parker said.

"Drill Sergeant," Carl said. "I copied the schedule just like—"

"Oh no," Parker said. "You're not going to pin this on me, Hollywood! You just cost every orphan in this hall thirty push-ups. Front-leaning rest position!"

Groans. Movement. Outraged, Carl dropped down into push-up position.

"Get set! Hold the show. . . . Hollywood! Stand up. I didn't tell *you* to push. You're going to watch your buddies push. And then, since you decided to leave breakfast off the schedule, we'll all just go without today. How does that sound, orphans? Can I get a hooah?"

"Hooah," they mumbled.

"What are you, Girl Scouts? Get motivated! Sound off like you mean it!"

"Hooah!" Their roar filled the narrow hallway.

Parker said, "Count them off, Hollywood. This is your show."

"Yes, Drill Sergeant."

The platoon glared up at him with anger burning in their eyes.

"Get set," Carl said. "Down-up."

"Zero-zero-one!" they roared, hating him.

DAYS PASSED. Brutal days ending in fewer than four hours of sleep.

"Look on the bright side," Ross said. "As book man, you don't have to pull duty."

"Don't remind me," Carl said. "That just makes everyone hate me more." It was stupid but true. Guys resented Carl for assigning guard duty, as if it were his choice. Even the duty itself was stupid. They were society's rejects, sleeping in barracks, within a patrolled fence, on an island in the middle of nowhere. It was like locking your trash in a vault and hiring armed security guards to watch it. Absurd. More military crap, all because somebody somewhere believed if you got kids to play soldier for a while, they'd become law-abiding citizens.

The drill sergeants pushed and pushed. Mostly, it was pointless and boring, marching around and cleaning and running and forming it up and then marching some more. The drill sergeants forced them to learn rules and codes and poems and songs, and then, as soon as they'd learned something, the drill sergeants would change it on them. The barracks smelled like sweat and Pine-Sol, and everything was damp to the touch.

The staff issued them boots and uniforms, and there was a constant emphasis on maintaining and securing gear. Every couple of days, the platoon failed another inspection. More punishment. They had to square it away, the drill sergeants reminded them again and again, before the Old Man arrived.

Some of the kids were real screwups. One night, drill sergeants pulled the whole platoon out of bed and smoked them for an hour, shouting as kids duckwalked up and down the hall, hands atop their heads, loaded rucksacks on their backs, the whole thing like a bad dream. Once it got whispered across the platoon how Medicaid had caused it, falling asleep on guard duty, kids glared at him and hissed curses. Whenever Medicaid, who was too weak to duckwalk with a pack, crawled around the bend in the hall and out of sight of the drill sergeants, people would slam into him, punch him, tip him over. Carl watched with aching knuckles as the helpless kid suffered. His brain knew he had to stay out of it, had to think about his future; but the rest of him wanted to rush in there and stop the bullies—and because he didn't do that, he boiled with self-loathing. *Coward,* he told himself. *Punk.* By the end of the hour, Medicaid was bawling like a toddler, and the drill sergeants' laughter filled the barracks. They knew, and they didn't care.

As the days passed, Parker continued to ride Carl. Carl kept his mouth shut and bore up.

Other than Ross, the rest of the platoon wanted nothing to do with Carl. Campbell, who'd been named platoon leader, was all right—not friendly, but not unfriendly, either—and Carl found he could work with him.

One night, Davis and his crew came into his bay and started trash-talking, and Carl thought he was going to end up fighting all six of them. He was so sick of Phoenix Island and Parker and everybody's crap that he found himself standing there grinning as Davis laid down his rap, and even felt disappointed when it all came to nothing.

Later, Campbell surprised him by initiating conversation. "Watch those guys."

Carl nodded. "I will. Thanks."

"They're checking you now, seeing how you take it. They'll come for you when nobody's around. They're cowards, all of them. But they're dangerous cowards. I hate gangs."

"You hate them enough," Carl said, "give me a hand."

Campbell raised a brow. "And spend the rest of my time here waiting for the shank? Little guy like you, a white dude, they'll just throw you a beating. If I cross them, with my size, me being black? They'll figure they have to kill me. And they would, too. Because they can't see anything else. They can't even spell *diploma*. They're just waiting around." He shook his head. "'Get rich or die trying,' all that street mythology."

It wasn't help, but it was the longest conversation they'd had . . . a step in the right direction. Campbell was the coolest guy in the platoon. Smart, composed, tough, independent, utterly squared away. Carl thanked him again for the advice and went about his business.

Small fights broke out. Pushing and yelling, mostly. A few guys got sent to the sweatboxes and came back an hour or two later, looking wasted, like they had heatstroke or something. It rained twice a day, every day, once midmorning or early in the afternoon, and again in the night. The world felt like an overfull sponge.

He didn't see Octavia for days. Every time girls filed past, he'd look for her. He'd just started to worry that something had happened when he saw her leaving the chow hall one day. He tried to get her attention, but she didn't see him, and, lying in bed that night, he tortured himself, wondering why she hadn't been looking for him like he'd been looking for her. *Because she's not interested in you, Hollywood,* he told himself, and in the darkness of the bay, someone farted loudly.

One night after chow, Drill Sergeant Rivera called them into the back bay and let them sit on the floor. After days of dress-right-dress and square-it-away, even that small freedom felt like a godsend.

Rivera paced before them. "You must subordinate your individuality and embrace your group membership. You must work together, orphans, and you must stay motivated. Back in the world, you got yourselves into trouble, acting as individuals. Here on Phoenix Island, you're going to unlearn that. You are going to learn to work as part of a team. What is it, Ross?"

"Uh, yes, Drill Sergeant, will the team be receiving any cheerleaders? Some of the girls we rode in with looked pretty hot—"

"Lock it up, wise guy," Rivera said, but he smiled. "Give me twenty for thinking like an individual."

Some of the guys laughed. Ross started pushing.

Carl noticed the muscular redneck, Decker, whispering to one of his buddies and looking at Ross like he'd like to kill him. Decker had been giving Ross a hard time lately, but nothing too serious, and so far Ross had been able to joke his way out of it. Carl wondered how long the jokes would work.

Rivera said, "You do push-ups like those, Ross, maybe *you* ought to be the cheerleader." Everybody laughed. Rivera was *definitely* way cooler than the other drill sergeants. "Now, orphans, you're going to have some hard days here, hooah?"

"Hooah!" the platoon responded. The only guy who didn't join in was Medicaid. He sat in the back, staring at the floor and mumbling to himself. The kid had more issues than *Sports Illustrated*.

"Well, you tough those days out, and you will be amazed at the changes in you. You'll go from being boys to being men. You'll go from being individuals to being team players. Hooah?"

"Hooah!"

Rivera nodded. "Now you sound like soldiers. All right, orphans, commence personal time. Lights out at twenty-two hundred. Campbell, you need anything, I'll be down at CQ."

Personal time, Carl thought. *We're actually getting personal time tonight.* It was always on the schedule but never quite materialized. He glanced at the clock. It wasn't even 2100 yet.

"Book Man," Rivera said, "come with me. We have to run over a couple of things."

Carl followed him out of the bay. The guys started horsing around back there, making too much noise, fired up by their first bit of freedom in many days.

"How you doing on the duty roster, Freeman?"

"Not bad, Drill Sergeant. The guys don't like it, but it's working."

"Outstanding, Freeman." Reaching the end of the hall, Rivera unlocked the door on which the whiteboard hung and swung it open to reveal a dim closet. "Your office. You got your desk there, paper, pencils. File cabinet. We need you to file stuff, we'll unlock it. You even get a chair." He handed Carl a key. "That opens the closet. Do not lose it. You read me, Freeman?"

"Lima Charlie, Drill Sergeant."

"That's the way a soldier talks. I'm off to CQ for the next hour or so. You need anything, tell Campbell, and he can come tell me. After that, Drill Sergeant Parker relieves me, and I'd recommend you just hold any subsequent questions till tomorrow. Hooah?"

"Hooah."

Rivera handed him the next day's schedule and left, pausing just outside the door to smoke a couple of kids running down the hall.

Carl copied the schedule on the whiteboard, shut himself inside the closet, and went to work setting up guard duty. He planned to square this away, hit the showers, give his boots another polish, reroll his socks, and maybe even socialize a bit before lights out.

He got to work. People showed up, trying to get out of duty, but he shut them down. He went by alphabetical order, since if he followed that it was impossible to say he was playing favorites, but, as usual, some people got pissed anyway. So be it. Let them go to Campbell.

Decker and his toadies came by, all smiles, offering Carl protection from Davis's gang in exchange for Carl "forgetting" to put them on the roster. When Carl said thanks but no thanks, Decker stared at him for a few long seconds. The guy had these weird pale blue eyes that shone, cold and thoughtful, and didn't match the otherwise brutal face, which looked like it had been carved from scarred stone. Decker looked interested, amused, and angry, all at the same time . . . but mostly interested. Then he and his thugs left.

A while later, Ross showed up and got Carl laughing with an imitation of Rivera, tilting his head back and squinting a little. "Ross, give me twenty for thinking like an individual."

Carl laughed. It was perfect. "You're awesome at impersonations."

Ross shrugged. "When you're my size, good ones are a survival skill. Comedy as self-defense. How much work do you have left?"

"I'm almost finished."

"Awesome. Hurry up. We're playing Ninja in the back bay."

Ninja was, without a doubt, the stupidest game in the entire universe. Suddenly, Carl wanted to play very much.

"All right. I'll be down."

Ross left.

Five minutes later, Carl locked the closet and headed toward the back bay. Voices floated into the hall. "One, two, three . . . Ninja!"

Grinning, Carl detoured into his bay, worked his lock, secured his new key, started to close the locker, and paused, staring at the pictures hanging inside.

There was his mother, smiling at the Phillies game.

His eyes moved to the other picture. Mom again, Carl as a little kid, Dad.

He missed them terribly.

He looked at his mom's smiling face and had to swallow hard to get rid of the lump in his throat. How could somebody so full of life die so young?

Cancer. That was how. Bad luck on a cosmic scale.

Dad looked bulletproof in his uniform. *Not hardly,* Carl thought. *Not hardly.*

The man who'd shot him was a schizophrenic with the ridiculous name of Wilson W. Wilson. Wilson and his wife had fought and separated, and he'd moved out on the street. For a while, he tried to get together again, but she refused. Then one summer night, Wilson W. Wilson forced his way into the apartment with a .38 Special handgun.

Neighbors heard shouting and called the police. Carl's dad, who'd been just down the block when the call came through, was first to arrive. Wilson shot him four times as soon as he came through the door, reloaded his empty chambers, and proceeded to kill all three of his children and two neighbor boys, who'd only been in the apartment to play video games. Wilson explained to his wife that he wanted her to experience the loneliness she had forced upon him. Then he stuck the barrel in his own mouth and pulled the trigger, and that was that.

Somehow, Carl's dad survived, but Carl knew he was never going to be the same. Even at eight, Carl understood that. He loved his dad. Almost worshipped him. Before the shooting, he was a loud, good-natured man, well-known and well-loved around Devil's Pocket. He'd grown up in the Pocket, a comically wild Irish boy who'd made good in the end and upon whom they could always count on for help, whether that meant dealing with a kite stuck in a tree, or the sound of broken glass at midnight, or a murderous schizophrenic who'd decided to turn a broken marriage into a community bloodbath.

After the shooting, Carl's dad couldn't even help himself. Weather permitting, he spent his days on the front porch. His blank eyes stared from his swollen face. Scar tissue bunched the flesh where the second bullet had passed through his head, lifting one corner of his mouth in a humorless perma-smile.

Carl took care of him. He wanted to. Every moment he wasn't in school, he sat with his father. He never resented this time, and he never bought into his mother's concern that he was taking on too much, that he needed to step back a little, just be a boy. He helped care for his father in nearly every way, from feeding him to administering medication to helping him bathe. It wasn't gross or funny or weird. It just was.

It broke his mother's heart, but she couldn't afford a nurse, not on the paltry disability check they got and what little she made waitressing at the diner. So Carl did much of the work, and when he wasn't working, he sat with his father in case he needed anything.

The day the laughter started, Carl was on his way home from school with his friend Tommy, just coming onto their block. He heard laughter up ahead—mean laughter—and saw this big fifth-grader, Liam Reilly, and a couple of other kids, standing on the sidewalk, cracking up. Then he heard Liam say, "Check out the Spook."

At first, Carl thought the older boy was using some stupid racial slur, which were about as common in the Pocket as songbirds were in the suburbs. But then he saw Liam laughing and making a face and looking up at Carl's house. Up at the porch. Up at Carl's dad.

The Spook.

Liam made his face look all goofy, even doing a poor imitation of the perma-smile before bursting into laughter.

The Spook. Carl's dad.

It took Carl, who had never witnessed cruelty like this, half a block to really understand. He was vaguely aware of Tommy pulling on his arm, saying those guys were dumb, they didn't mean anything by it . . . and then Carl was at the end of the block, and Liam's friends were punching and kicking him and calling him crazy, and Liam—despite being older and bigger than Carl—was on the ground, covered in blood and moaning, half-conscious. The older boys knocked Carl down several times, but he pulled himself off the sidewalk every time and waded back in swinging, until Tommy's dad broke up the fight. The older kids were all too willing to get Liam onto his feet and peel out of there; even in his rage, Carl could see the look of fear in their eyes.

"What is it?" Tommy's dad asked, but Carl was too angry to do anything but struggle and yell after the fleeing boys.

When Tommy told the story, his dad, whose hands were rough from tree work and weather, hugged Carl hard, saying with his lingering brogue, "Oh, Jaysus, Carl boy, Jaysus. It'll be all right. I'll just have a talk with their fathers, and they won't ever say nothing like that again. You mark my words, Carl boy."

He'd been right about that. The boys never had. But the damage was done.

Carl's innocence was lost.

The fight with Liam had filled him with fury. Before Liam, Carl couldn't have imagined such cruelty; after Liam, he couldn't forget it. If someone could joke that way right in front of the house, how many people were calling Carl's dad the Spook behind closed doors? His old assumptions—that his dad was universally hailed as a hero and that most people were good, law-abiding citizens—came crumbling down, and into the vacuum of their absence raced burning rage.

Carl grew quiet. He spent all his free time on the porch, his father's tireless, silent defender. His grades dropped. It was hard to practice long division when he had the need to look up every time someone passed the front porch, had to watch and listen for the slightest clue that someone thought his dad was a joke. When people stopped by—something that happened less and less frequently as the months passed—Carl grunted in response to questions, refused to smile, and made most people so uncomfortable that they soon left.

For his mother's sake, anytime someone came by and laughed, or looked up and stared, Carl squeezed his fists and waited. Once they crossed into the next block, he tore off the porch after them, out of her sight. No matter how old they were, how big they were, or how many of them there were, he attacked without warning, without mercy, and without the slightest hesitation. Sometimes he won, and sometimes he lost, but he always fought his hardest, and nobody could keep him down. By the time he was ten years old, he had a reputation as a fearless, heavy-handed nut.

Then he got in real trouble.

His first court date was a rainy Tuesday. His mother pulled him out of school. She wore her church clothes and cried the whole ride over. She'd missed a lunch shift at the diner, but that wasn't why she was crying. She cried over the shooting and Carl's life as a caregiver and his trouble with fighting. Thinking back now, remembering how her hands had shaken as she unscrewed the cap of the aspirin bottle she carried at all times by this point, Carl realized she'd been crying about something else, too. The headaches had already started. Had she known, even then, that she had only months to live?

The previous night, waking from a nightmare, Carl had risen and gone to the kitchen, where he sweated and shook and sipped water, listening to the clock tick and staring at the closed door to the living room they'd converted into a space for his father. He went to the door and cracked it open so a little slice of illumination fell over the face of his father, who slept with his eyes slightly open, his mouth wide, that one corner still upturned. He looked pale, old. Carl saw the short gray hair, which always flaked with dandruff no matter what kind of shampoo they used on it, and the disfiguring lump from the bullet that had damaged his brain.

His mother slept sitting up in a chair beside the bed, still dressed in her work uniform. Her head hung forward like she was praying, and one hand rested on the shoulder of Carl's dad. Standing there, Carl felt something like shame, as if he'd intruded on a personal moment, and suddenly real to him was the idea of his parents *before* him: their childhoods and teen romance, their courtship and marriage, the dreams and plans they had shared. What did they do to deserve any of this? And what would Carl's mother do if the judge sent Carl away?

But the judge did not send him away. Not that first time. He talked about Carl's father and made Carl answer questions and gave him a lecture and finally sentenced him to twenty-five hours of community service and six months of professional counseling. The judge also ordered Carl to take boxing lessons, saying the sport would provide an outlet for his aggression.

Which was how he met Arthur Marcellus James, who had trained trotter horses and fighting dogs prior to establishing himself as a world-class boxing trainer. A stick-thin old man with dark skin, hooded eyes, and a thin mustache, Arthur wasn't much on warmth—he barely spoke to Carl, except to point out he was dropping his hands or raising his chin or telegraphing punches—but the man knew *everything* about boxing.

Carl missed him. He missed boxing. But most of all, he missed his parents.

Now he stood in this strange place—these *barracks*, a million miles from home—and stared up at the beaming faces of his parents. Gone, all gone. His eyes burned. His hands were cold and damp with sweat. He took a deep breath, held it for a second, and let it shudder out.

He shook out his arms and shut his locker. He couldn't take another minute swimming in old pain. Next, he'd start remembering his mother's sickness, her fight with cancer, everything. . . .

To the back bay, then. Time to lose himself in a mindless round of Ninja. All enthusiasm had left him, but he had to try. He secured his lock, took another deep breath, and that's when they slammed him up against the locker and then threw him onto his bed.

It happened so quickly, Carl had no chance to react. A dozen hands pinned him facedown to the bed. They pushed his face into the pillow, then turned it to the side so he could see Davis leaned back against the locker, staring at him, arms folded across his chest.

Davis nodded, and Carl felt something slide into his ear canal. As the point of it pressed into the softness of his inner ear, Carl felt a chill, knowing.

A pencil.

One tap, and he'd be deaf. One shove, he'd be dead.

6

DAVIS'S EYES LOOKED ALMOST BORED. "No running away this time, Hollywood."

Carl glared at him. He kept his head very still. The pencil filled his ear, its point pressing against something soft and sensitive but not doing any real damage yet. "What do you want?"

"A couple of fine ladies and a bag of weed."

One of the guys holding him laughed. Then a few of the others did, too.

Carl waited.

Davis said, "We're sick of guard duty. So, for starters, you're going to make it so we don't have to do that anymore."

"Can't. Drill sergeant said everybody has to have guard duty."

"You don't have it."

"I can't. I'm the book man."

"Well, you better work it out. I don't care how. I just know we're not covering any more guard duties. You say anything to the drill sergeants, you're dead. You understand?"

Carl understood, all right. This was their first move. If he gave in, it would be one thing after another. "Forget it."

Davis scowled. "Maybe you got a hearing problem. Ty, clean out his ear wax for him."

The wood moved in Carl's ear, sending waves of panic and rage through him. "Let me up."

Davis laughed.

"Yo!" A deep voice thundered. "What are you doing?"

Davis stood up straight. The pencil slid out of Carl's ear. Hands came away from his temple and jaw, and he turned his head to see Campbell.

"Just having a little fun with Hollywood," one of the gang guys said.

Campbell didn't even look at the kid who'd spoken. He kept staring at Davis. "You ruin free time, the platoon will tear you to pieces."

Carl could feel the grips on him loosening. He wanted to jump up and start swinging, but Campbell's cool made him hold back.

Davis grinned wider. "Easy, big man. We're almost done here. Tell you what. You head down the hall, we'll be out of here in two minutes. You won't have guard duty no more, you feel me?"

"I'm not going anywhere until you let him up. This is my platoon. I didn't ask for it, but they gave it to me. I got one month left in this place, and I'm not going to let you mess it up for me. You walk away, this never happened. You push, and I will break all your ribs. I promise."

Davis laughed. "I see how it is . . . Brother. Boss man, huh?"

Campbell looked at the others. "Let him up. Now."

A couple of the hands came away from Carl's legs. The other guys looked at Davis. He nodded. They let go of Carl.

Carl jumped to his feet.

Campbell's eyes flashed a warning.

"This ain't over," Davis said, walking past Campbell. The others followed.

Campbell watched them go. Then he turned toward Carl, shaking his head. "Man, I hate gangbangers."

"Thanks," Carl said.

Campbell shook his head again. "I knew this was going to happen. Now we got to watch each other's back all the time. Can you fight?"

Carl nodded. He hadn't told anyone about boxing. In his experience, if it got out you were a boxer, somebody always wanted to try you.

"Look," Campbell said, "I'm serious. Can you fight? For real?"

"I can fight."

* * *

DAYS PASSED.

Carl and Campbell stayed close. The Davis thing didn't go away, but it quieted down.

In the meantime, life got better. Davis still glared, Parker still barked, and training still drove them into the ground, but it was good, having Campbell and Ross to talk to.

Then there was Octavia. More and more frequently, the girls trained with the boys, and Carl saw a lot of her. Whenever they could, they ran together and ate together. Whenever they were away from the drill sergeants, they made each other laugh. The more Carl got to know her, the more he liked her. She wasn't just pretty. She was tough and smart. Funny, too. Like this one time, when they were sitting around between activities, she rolled up a piece of paper, stuck it in her ear, and just sat there, all nonchalant, saying, "What?" when he grinned at her, and then, when he said something, she went, "I'm sorry. I can't hear you. I've got some paper stuck in my ear." She was cool. And the more time they spent together, the clearer it was that she liked him, too.

They talked about their lives—not just the tragedies and triumphs, but the little, stupid things that made up so much of a person's story. She told him about the time her father had set a Havahart trap, hoping to catch the squirrels who'd been decimating his apple trees, and how he'd shouted, "Mother-of-pearl!" when he'd gone outside the next morning and found a big possum crammed into the little wire cage. "I'll never forget it as long as I live," she said, laughing so hard that tears ran from her eyes. "It's the only time I've ever heard someone shout 'Mother-of-pearl!'" Carl told her how one of his old teachers back in the Pocket would give everybody worksheets and then spend the whole period sniffing the spines of old books stacked on his desk. Then she talked about her cat, Tinker Bell, who would wait for her at the bus stop each day after school and walk her home. He talked about how some nights his dad would peel a raw potato and slice it up, and they'd stand there in the kitchen and eat it, salting each slice and laughing at the loud crunching. And she told him about her grandmother, who had lived in the Bolivian Andes, and who had visited each summer, and how the old woman would dump potatoes in the backyard and then take off her shoes and socks. "That's how she peeled them," she said. "She walked all over them with her bare feet."

They laughed a lot.

One day, the drill sergeants told them to bring pencils and marched them to the "classroom"—a bunch of folding chairs under a simple pavilion—where the cadre distributed clipboards and paper, and First Sergeant Oteka said, "Today, you will learn rudimentary first aid. Pencils out, orphans. I expect extensive notes. There will be quizzes."

Octavia patted her pockets, checked the floor around her seat, and moaned quietly.

"You okay?" Carl whispered.

She looked at him with panic in her eyes. "I can't find my pencil. Oteka's going to kill me."

Carl handed her his and raised his hand.

"Mr. Freeman," Oteka said. "Please save your questions until I have covered material about which you might ask them."

Chuckles rippled through the seats.

"First Sergeant, I can't find my pencil."

Oteka said nothing to Carl but turned her head so that he could see the rows of scars on that side of her face. "Drill Sergeant Parker, one of your orphans is unprepared for today's instruction. Please correct this."

"Yes, First Sergeant." Parker came off the column, face red, eyes flaring. He yanked Carl from his chair and dragged him to the back of the pavilion, where he pushed him up against a post and grabbed him by the front of the shirt. "Jacking with me again, huh?" He struggled to keep his voice low enough not to disrupt the class, and this forced restraint only seemed to make him angrier. He shoved Carl to the ground. "Front."

Carl started pushing.

Parker crouched down and smiled, his eyes still smoldering with rage. The guy was probably on steroids, Carl figured, all those muscles and temper tantrums.

"Just a few days, Hollywood," Parker said, "and I'm going to fix your wagon once and for all."

Carl pushed, wondering what Parker meant by *fix your wagon*. A threat, sure, but a threat of what, exactly? Not that he would show it, but the *once and for all* part bothered him even more. Was Parker trying to get Carl kicked off the island? Trying to get him sent back to North Carolina, to prison?

Parker smoked him, front-back-go, for several minutes, then said, "Here's a pencil." And Parker drove a pencil into Carl's thigh, burying the point.

Carl jerked a little with the shock and pain of it, but he remained at attention and didn't make a sound until he said, "Yes, Drill Sergeant."

Parker yanked the pencil out of Carl's leg and held it in front of his face. The sharpened part was all red. "Don't forget your pencil, now."

When Carl returned to his seat, he hid the wound with his clipboard. Octavia gave him a small, sad smile and squeezed his arm. Later, as they were lining up for chow, she gave him his pencil back . . . and with it, a note. She kept her hand on his for a second longer than necessary. "Thanks, Carl. You shouldn't have done it, but thanks. You really saved me back there."

"No problem," he said. "Um, am I supposed to read this now or later?"

"It doesn't matter," she said. Then she glanced at a pair of sergeants near the steaming serving dishes. "Actually, wait a bit."

Later, hidden away in the bathroom, he opened the note and smiled.

Dear Carl,

*Thanks so, so, so much (times a million) for what you did!
It was sweet. If we weren't here, I would take you out for ice
cream or to the movies or something to thank you. But I guess
if we weren't here, I wouldn't have needed your pencil, right?
Oh well. I'd still ask you out.*

Octavia
xoxoxo

Carl hadn't felt such a rush of happiness since he won his first national championship, all those years ago.

* * *

THAT NIGHT, Carl, Campbell, and Ross sat just inside the darkened bay, polishing their boots by the light from the hallway. It was after lights-out, so the three main bays were dark, and two guys were already on guard duty. Most of the platoon was boot polishing down at the back bay, which also stayed lit. The only other guy in this bay was Medicaid, who sat a couple of bunks in, muttering to himself. Extra boots sat beside his bed. Someone—maybe Davis and his crew, maybe Decker and his thugs—had undoubtedly forced the polish work on him, but Carl just pushed it out of his mind. It drove him nuts, but he couldn't get involved.

"I am sick of this place," Ross said. "I'm so sore my hair hurts."

"Little exercise will do you good," Campbell said. "Pack some muscle on those scrawny arms of yours."

Feigning shock, Ross said, "Scrawny? You call this scrawny?" He peeled back one sleeve and flexed. "Boom!"

Campbell chuckled. "Man, your arms look like spaghetti noodles."

"Forget muscle," Carl said. "This exercise is making us better people, remember?"

"It's so stupid," Ross said, and shook his fists overhead. "Military-style reform. They actually think that forcing us to shave our heads, polish boots, and exercise twenty-five hours a day is going to turn us into model citizens. It's crazy. The other day, I got stuck behind Decker and his toadies in chow line. The tall one, he starts talking about killing his neighbors' cats—a bunch of them—how he did it, everything. It was horrible. But these guys, they bust up laughing, like it's the funniest thing they've ever heard. Can you imagine? I'm sorry, but there's only one way to reform a kitten killer: firing squad."

"Don't give Parker any ideas," Carl said, rubbing absently at the pencil wound in his thigh. Ross was right—all this gung ho boot camp nonsense was stupid—but there were worse punishments than playing soldier.

"All I know," Campbell said, "is my eighteenth birthday arrives exactly twenty-one days from tomorrow. I'll be on the next boat out of here."

"Can't blame you," Carl said. He couldn't imagine someone actually opting to stay after their eighteenth birthday, but he supposed some did. Some like Parker.

Ross's boot brush fell to the tiles with a clatter. "You're leaving us? That's horrible. That means they'll assign a new platoon guide, and everything will change, and then—"

"Look," Campbell said, "I feel for you, but I got the whole world waiting on me. Girls, parties, music . . . you remember music?"

"I'll pay you to stay," Ross said.

Campbell laughed. "How much?"

Ross pulled out the empty pockets of his pants and grinned. "All I've got."

"Just what I thought."

"Carl will chip in, too. Right?"

Carl nodded, smiling. "All I got." He didn't like it any better than Ross did, but there was no point in going to pieces. Things would get rough when Campbell left, but Carl was happy for him.

"I already got my GED," Campbell said. "Second I walk out of here, the judge wipes my record clean. Go to community college, get this whole incarceration thing way behind me."

Ross just shook his head, looking like he'd received a death sentence.

"Hey, look on the bright side," Campbell said. "From what they've said, we're almost finished with Red Phase."

"Red Phase, Blue Phase, what's the difference?" Ross said. "We're still here, aren't we?"

Carl nodded. "Sounds like silver stars and gold stars back in elementary school. One more way to control us."

"Correction, orphan," Ross said. "One more way to motivate us."

Carl laughed.

"I don't know," Campbell said. "According to Rivera, Blue Phase is way better. More free time, better training. They even teach us survival skills."

Ross groaned. "Survival skills? More army stuff?"

Campbell shrugged. "I guess."

"Well, I hope they leave out combat training," Ross said. "Don't get me wrong. I love a good game just as much as the next guy, but I'm not entirely comfortable with the notion of some of these guys getting weapons. Davis's gang? Or Decker? That guy's a psychopath."

"Psychopath," Medicaid mimicked from the gloom. He giggled and clapped, then went back to muttering.

Campbell's face went serious. Quietly, he said, "Keep an eye on that kid. If anybody's going to snap, it's going to be somebody like carrottop over there," and nodded toward Medicaid.

Ross made a face. "Yeah, every time I see him, I think Rambo."

"Joke if you want," Campbell said, "but I'm serious. Even a strong person has his breaking point. Kid like that, he's weak. He can only take so much. They keep pushing, something has to give."

"On that note," Carl said, packing away his polish and rags, "I have to write up tomorrow's schedule."

"Put me down for sofa duty," Ross said. "Then I'll inspect the female barracks for the rest of the day."

Carl laughed. "Right." He secured his things and headed down the hall, where he locked himself in the book man closet. He put the whiteboard and marker on the desk, just in case Parker came knocking, then pulled Octavia's note from his sock. Where could he hide it? The drill sergeants were always inspecting their bunks and lockers, and they could shake anybody down, anytime, so his only shot was here, in the book room. One quick look around the room told him it wasn't much of a shot.

Just flush it down the toilet, Carl told himself. If someone found the note, he'd get in trouble, and so would Octavia. It was stupid, but they would. And they'd be kept apart, too.

He looked at the note and warmed at the sight of his name in Octavia's handwriting. No way was he going to destroy it. He couldn't let the drill sergeants take everything from him.

Where to hide it, then? Not in the desk. The drill sergeants probably checked that. The file cabinet was locked. Under it? No. They might move it to wax the floor. He looked around the rest of the room and was just about to call it quits and flush the note when he looked up and saw the silver ductwork close to the ceiling. If there was space between the duct and the ceiling . . .

He slid his chair under it, climbed on top, and stood on his tiptoes. Between the duct and the ceiling was a small gap—the perfect spot to hide something.

In fact, someone already had.

Atop the duct, blanketed in dust, sat a tube of papers held by a rubber band. He set the note on top of the duct and grabbed the papers. He started rolling the rubber band. Brittle with age, it snapped. He unrolled the pages—there were several—and saw small, neat handwriting cramming the lines. The top of the first page read *Book Man in Hell*. Below this, he read *Dear Diary. Weird*, Carl thought.

The doorknob rattled. "Hollywood!" a voice yelled outside.

Carl's heart leapt in his chest. Parker. Carl heard keys.

He jammed the scroll down his sweatpants, jumped off the chair, and said, "Yes, Drill Sergeant?" just as the door swung open.

"What are you doing in here, Hollywood, taking a nap?"

"No, Drill Sergeant."

"Drop and give me forty for making me wait. Then come to my office and pick up a stack of crap to file." As soon as Carl dropped down, Parker crossed the room and stepped on his fingers with heavy combat boots.

Carl kept pushing. "Zero-one-seven. Zero-one-eight."

He heard Parker unlock the file cabinet. "You'll file this stuff in the appropriate folders. I want it done tonight. You finish, push this tab. Eyeballs, Hollywood!"

Carl stopped pushing and turned his head.

"You're dumber than a bucket of mud," Parker said. He pointed to a knob near the top of the cabinet. "Think you can remember to lock this when you're done?"

"Yes, Drill Sergeant."

"You'd better, or I'm smoking the whole platoon in your honor— what are you doing taking a break? I didn't tell you to stop pushing. Start again."

"Yes, Drill Sergeant," Carl said, gritting his teeth. "Zero-zero-one.

Zero-zero-two." Forty more. Big deal. With all the new muscle he was packing, he could rack out two hundred.

"Oh, and Hollywood, just because I'm being a nice guy, don't think I forgot you trying to make me look bad in front of First Sergeant Oteka."

Carl kept pushing. There was no point denying it. Parker already knew it wasn't true.

Parker said, "You'll pay. And I'm not talking push-ups and front-back-go. You got . . . oh . . . about a week, I'd say. Then we'll be even." He strutted off.

Was Parker going to ship him back to the States? Carl hated Phoenix Island, but he had to stay. If they sent him back, he'd go straight to prison, and a boy in a prison would have to fight every day. He'd spend the rest of his life in solitary confinement, nursing broken knuckles and losing his mind.

Carl finished his forty and followed Parker to the drill sergeants' office, feeling the scroll start to slip down his leg. What if Parker spotted it?

He managed to get to the other office, where hanging on the door he noticed the platoon photograph. Even at a glance, he recognized faces: Campbell, Octavia, Davis. In the middle of the girls, black ink obscured one face. *That's the girl who broke her leg*, Carl thought, remembering the word the drill sergeants had used: *recycled*. The poor girl would have to start all over again with the next batch of orphans.

Parker opened the door. Carl heard the light hum of air-conditioning and felt the cool air. The hairs along his forearms rose to attention in the chill. "There," Parker said, and pointed toward a stack of papers.

"Yes, Drill Sergeant." Photographs of former platoons covered the wall behind Parker's desk. Nearly every face was blacked out. Did that mean they'd all been recycled? Carl couldn't afford to fail. His whole life was riding on making it.

Carl felt the scroll slip the rest of the way to the bottom of his pant leg. It wouldn't fall out, not with his pants tucked into his boots, but he hoped Parker didn't notice the bulge in his ankle.

"What are you looking for, Hollywood? This?" Parker reached into his shirt and withdrew Carl's medal. He'd been wearing it around his neck. Smiling, he twisted the medal so it winked in the light. "You know what this is?"

"It's my medal, Drill Sergeant."

"Wrong," Parker said. "It's a symbol. It stands for everything I hate about showboats like you. It's all shiny and flashy, and you hold it up, and everybody oohs and aahs over it . . . but what's it worth, really? Huh? What's it worth in the real world?"

"Can I have it back, Drill Sergeant?"

"I'll tell you what it's worth, Hollywood. Two cents, that's what. Just like you. Oh, you think you're special, but you're nothing. Two cents." He dropped the medal back into his shirt. "Get out of my office."

"Yes, Drill Sergeant." Carl picked up the papers and left, trembling with rage and wanting nothing more than to go back in there, show Parker just how special his fists were, and rip the medal off his stupid neck. He carried the stack of papers back to the book room, dropped them on the desk, and closed and locked the door. He climbed onto the chair, pulled the scroll from his pant leg, and stashed it back on top of the duct, his hands still shaking with anger.

He saw Octavia's note sitting in the dust. Why couldn't they just leave this place?

He hopped off the chair and threw several fast combinations, picturing Parker's face cutting and breaking under his punches. Why did the guy have to push? The pencil to the leg, the Hollywood crap, the threats and insults, the medal . . . Carl ripped another combination, liking the feel of his new muscle mass. He'd expected it to slow his punches, but it hadn't. They felt strong. They made Carl feel a bit better.

The papers he was supposed to file turned out to be medical. Height and weight, eyesight and hearing. Times and dates for their many inoculations. He opened the top drawer and started distributing paperwork into the folders, which were arranged in alphabetical order. Most were pretty thick. The first file read ALVAREZ, JUANITA. Stapled inside was a picture of the girl with the birthmark on her face.

His file was fat. No surprise there, considering how many times he'd gotten into trouble.

Stapled to the inside cover was a picture of him back in middle

school. Sixth grade, he thought. A plain black T-shirt, a poor kid's hair-
cut—the bangs chopped straight across his forehead—and a little bruise
under one eye.

Underneath the photo, someone had written *National Boxing Champion.*

He flipped through the pages, creating a choppy slideshow of school
records, disciplinary write-ups, and court reports. So much paperwork,
from so many places: counselor logs, psych evals, and feedback from
teachers, foster parents, and group homes. One from the facility at Lake
Nockamixon, where he'd spent a few months during seventh grade, said,
"Carl is well behaved. Carl is respectful to staff and other residents. Carl
says he would like to be a police officer when he grows up."

Carl says he would like to be a police officer when he grows up.
Man . . . that had been written a long time ago, back when he still told
people stuff like that. He chuckled . . . then, out of nowhere, felt
strangely sad.

He flipped ahead.

The newspaper clippings about his dad surprised him but not as
much as the articles detailing Carl's boxing victories. He grinned at an
old picture of himself, sweaty and smiling, a big trophy in his wrapped
hands, standing next to good old Arthur James. Must have been nation-
als, he thought, because Arthur was actually smiling . . . a little.

It was cool flipping through these, but strange, too. Boxing articles
didn't seem to fit this kind of folder. Whatever.

He skimmed on. More charges, more court orders, more placements,
his life beginning to take on an almost scripted pattern.

He shook his head. So much time gone.

Then he came to a page labeled SUMMARY SHEET, which looked like
just that: a stack of bullet points listed dates, charges, and institutional
placements. Very bare-bones, no real details. Someone had highlighted
all the charges in green, and neat but blocky handwriting in the margin—the same writing, he realized after a second, that had noted his national championship under that first picture—read, "A single charge,
repeated ad infinitum."

At the bottom of the page, the same handwriting—this time in red ink, not black—said, "Relocate to Idaho facility, then route as necessary to penultimate placement in North Carolina." Beside this, a date, which he read . . . then reread.

The note, which to Carl sounded less like a summary and more like an instruction, dated back to December.

Weird.

He hadn't gone to Idaho until February, hadn't even gotten into the trouble that landed him there until January, but whoever wrote this was talking about Idaho and North Carolina way back before Christmas.

That made no sense.

Unless . . .

Odd misgivings warbled through him.

Something weird was going on. Really weird. *Bad* weird.

The date suggested that whoever wrote this was either psychic or had been planning his placements months in advance. . . .

Or, he thought, *somebody just wrote the wrong date. Duh* . . . Over the years, how many people—cops, court clerks, guidance counselors—had messed up his paperwork? A bunch. One time, cops dropped him at juvie, and the intake officer looked at him funny and said, "Carla? You don't look like a Carla to me."

Carl grinned, feeling stupid—a simple clerical error had him imagining psychics and conspiracy theories—and shut the folder. He'd have another look later. It would be fun to reread the boxing articles, but he didn't have time now. The last thing he needed was Parker coming back, yelling at him for taking too long.

But maybe he did have time for one more indulgence. . . .

Finding "Gregoric, Octavia Grace," he opened the folder and smiled at the photo inside. She looked just as he'd remembered her from the first day: sad, scared, and stunned . . . yet utterly beautiful. And there was her hair, thick and dark, with that white patch in the front. Flipping through the folder, he saw school records with pictures going back to kindergarten, where she looked cute and happy. In early photos, she smiled wide, and in some of them, she was missing teeth and looking over-the-top happy, dimples and all, but in the sixth-grade photo, she didn't even smile. This was the year she'd gotten the white spot in her bangs. Maybe that was why she didn't look happy. Or maybe something bad had happened then. He'd heard of people's hair going white like that, from fright or whatever, but he didn't know if it could really happen.

This was crazy. If Parker came in, he'd feed Carl to the sharks. Besides, it was kind of weird, looking through her stuff like a stalker or something. Ready to move on, Carl froze when his eye caught a newspaper clipping in her file, its front-page headline announcing GIRL FOUND GUILTY IN ARSON DEATH OF STEPFATHER.

7

OCTAVIA DREAMED she was deep in a misty forest, everything green and gauzy. She stood on a mossy creek bank, holding the tiny hand of her little sister, both of them very happy.

But of course she had no sister.

"Wake up, Gregoric," somebody said in the darkness.

I'm still here, Octavia thought, *still here on Phoenix Island*, and the strange comfort of the sister she'd never had flitted away like ashes on the wind.

Tamika poked her shoulder. "Your turn for guard duty."

"Okay." She sat up and swung herself out of the bunk. Guard duty. Right. She was exhausted. "This is so stupid."

"Tell me about it," Tamika said, handing her the flashlight. "Wait—on second thought, don't tell me. I gotta hit the rack before my eyes fall out the back of my head."

"Right," Octavia said, and that's when she heard the shouting.

More than one voice. Two or three—wait, no . . . four—at least four different people shouting out in the hall. Most of them sounded like drill sergeants, but one was a girl. A weird twang to her accent, kind of Southern, but not the Georgia-peach thing.

Then she recognized the voice: Rice, the mean, fat girl from West Virginia.

"I don't care!" Rice shouted. It sounded like she was far away, probably in the bathroom at the end of the hall, judging by the hollow echo.

"They been going at it the last five minutes," Tamika said. "It's fixing to get ugly."

Octavia nodded.

Now drill sergeants were ordering Rice to *stand down, stand down, stand down!*

"Speaking of ugly," Tamika said, drifting toward her bunk, "this cat needs her beauty rest. All two hours of it."

"Good night," Octavia said, and went into the hall.

She was so sick of this place, so sick of playing soldier and doing stupid stuff like getting up in the middle of the night for something so obviously pointless. *If they wanted to punish us, why not just come out and say it? Why pretend we joined the army?* Most of all, though, she was sick of the shouting. Did they really think yelling would help anyone?

Spend five minutes with Rice, watch her grin as her eyes moved over the group, studying everybody, scanning for weaknesses, and you would know, even before you heard her outrageous lies, that she had spent her whole life in institutions and was going to spend the rest of her days in lockdown. She was a loudmouthed know-it-all who steamrolled people with her big voice and false confidence, the type who enveloped timid girls on day one, making fast friends. Then, days or weeks later, she would turn her back on them—boom, out of the blue, no rhyme, no crime—just to have the ugly fun of watching them suffer betrayal and struggle to comprehend how their own trusted friend could be so cruel. Once most girls got locked up, they tried to stay out of trouble, looked for a way out. Girls like Rice, though, didn't even think about the outside. They had turned inward, had become truly institutionalized. They didn't get scared; they got *interested.* They didn't look for a way out; they looked for ways to manipulate the system, ways to push buttons. Octavia had seen girls like Rice everywhere they'd sent her. There was no reforming them—and certainly not by shouting.

"Yeah," Rice hollered, "try it and see what happens!"

Octavia could see a pair of drill sergeants in the doorway of the bathroom at the end of the hall. Diaz and . . . she couldn't tell. Maybe Smith. No, too big to be Smith. Weichert, maybe.

Whoever it was, Octavia did not want to walk down there. But if she didn't, they would turn on her next, smoke her for independent thinking. Who was she to decide she didn't really need to do guard duty just because the people she'd have to report any problems to were already in the hall?

That's the number one crime around here, she thought, *thinking like an individual.*

So she walked in that direction.

"I told you," Rice's voice said. "No!" She held the *no* for a long time, drawing it out like an enraged toddler.

A two-hundred-pound tattooed toddler, Octavia thought.

The drill sergeants in the doorway—and yes, it was Weichert—shouted into the bathroom, "You are disobeying a direct order!"

Rice told them where they could stick their direct order.

It was a creative suggestion and might even have been funny, in a warped kind of way, at a different time. But right now? Not smart.

Then another voice spoke inside the bathroom. Spoke, not yelled. A soft voice.

Oteka.

"This is your final warning," the first sergeant's voice said.

Drill Sergeant Diaz glared at Octavia, seeing her for the first time, and pointed in the opposite direction. She didn't say anything—didn't need to—and Octavia happily complied, turning and heading back in the opposite direction.

She'd gone only a few steps when Rice yelled, "Stay away from me!"

Then something snapped—a horrible cracking sound—and Rice screamed. No toddler's outburst this time. Her shrieks knifed the air—*Ah! Ah! Ah!*

Oteka stepped from the bathroom, telling the sergeants, "Get her to the Chop Shop."

Octavia realized she was just standing there, frozen by the shrieks, standing there and staring back up the hall at Oteka, who—oh no . . . was looking at Octavia now, and beckoning to her.

Filled with dread, Octavia said, "Yes, First Sergeant?"

Oteka's face was just as relaxed and impassive as ever. "There has been an incident," she said, "and it is your duty to record its nature. Do you understand?"

"Yes, First Sergeant," Octavia said.

"Good," Oteka said, a faint smile lifting the facial scars that always reminded Octavia of cat's whiskers. "This is what you will write. Rice created a disturbance, disobeyed direct orders, and assaulted me. I defended myself, then sent Rice to the medical center. Are we clear?"

"Yes, First Sergeant," Octavia said. They were clear, all right. Oteka had told her what to write, and that was what she would write, but Rice hadn't sounded like she was attacking anyone. She had sounded scared.

Girls crowded in the bay doors, their faces sleepy and frightened.

"Back to your bunks, orphans," Oteka said.

They disappeared.

Octavia wished she could, too.

The drill sergeants emerged from the bathroom, carrying Rice, whose shrieks filled the hall like a smoke alarm. One of her knees had gone wonky, the leg jutting, heel up, at an angle that made no sense whatsoever.

Octavia felt her gorge rise.

"You will find the incident report forms at the CQ desk," Oteka said.

"Yes, First Sergeant," Octavia said, and hurried away. She didn't want to see Rice's leg again, didn't want to see her face, and definitely didn't want to hear her side of the story, because this time, no matter how outrageous Rice's claims seemed, they might not be lies.

Sometimes, she thought, *it's better to not even know the truth.*

THE NEXT MORNING, when the lights popped on, Octavia sat up in bed, feeling wobbly and strange, and stared across the bay at the empty space atop Rice's bunk.

Tamika asked her about it while they were lacing their boots, but before Octavia could respond, someone in the hall yelled "Red line!" and everyone flooded into the corridor, counting "Zero-zero-one! Zero-zero-two!" until they stood single file and thundered, "Zero-one-zero!"

The day had begun.

That was all right by Octavia. She didn't feel like telling the whole platoon about Rice.

She wanted Carl's take on it. He was smart, and he'd seen a lot. Most people only half listened, then cut you off, telling you what to think or do before you'd even finished talking. Not Carl. He would listen—really listen—and wouldn't interrupt, and then he'd think things over and maybe say something and maybe not. If he did, he would mean it. He wasn't the type of guy who said something just to say it.

In many ways, he seemed older. He was serious and thoughtful and something else—*wounded*, she thought, wounded but not weakened. Haunted, maybe, like he'd seen things so horrible that he could never stop seeing them—and yet he had kept these things to himself and hadn't let them make him mean or whiny.

Kind of like her.

Maybe that's why she liked him. One reason, anyway.

He was *really* good-looking, even with his head shaved, and once you got to know him, he could be funny.

She grinned, seeing him now down in the quad, talking with Ross.

She snuck up behind him, grabbed his biceps, and gave them a squeeze. "You got a permit for those guns?"

She had expected him to jump a little, then laugh.

He jumped, all right, but he didn't laugh. Not even close. He pulled away, looking . . . what? Angry? Distrustful? She was so surprised, she couldn't even guess.

"Hey," he said, his voice strange—hesitant and fake—but not nearly as hesitant and fake as his smile.

"Hey," she said. "Are you all right?"

"I'm fine."

"Um, okay," she said.

Carl just looked at her. It was *really* awkward. Her face felt hot.

"Seriously, Carl," she said. "What's going on?"

"Nothing," Carl said, and now even his fake smile disappeared.

"Did you get in trouble or something?"

He shook his head.

"You seem weird." She tilted her head a little, looked him in the eyes, and gave him half a smile, hoping he'd respond with a clue, a *not now* glance or something, but no—he only stared, like she was just some random person, nothing between them. "If you want me to leave—"

Ross stepped between them, giving her a cheesy smile. "Excuse my friend, please. He has a difficult time communicating with beautiful women. I, on the other hand, am very comfortable in the company of the fairer sex and would happily—"

"Get lost," she said, and pushed him away playfully. Inside, however, she wasn't feeling playful. She felt puzzled—hurt, really. She hadn't expected Carl to act like this, close her out.

"She touched my chest!" Ross said. "She can't keep her hands off me."

Carl smiled uncomfortably.

"I don't know what's going on," she said, and suddenly, she was more than hurt, she was annoyed, "but—"

"Form it up!" a drill sergeant called.

Octavia hurried into the ranks, hating that the conversation had ended so abruptly—yet not so much as she hated the look on Carl's face: pure relief.

8

THEY JOGGED IN FORMATION ACROSS THE BASE, through the gates, and onto the jungle road, singing cadence. Mere paces out of camp, the jungle ate them. Trees arched from both sides of the road, blocking out the morning sun almost entirely. The air was cooler in this living tunnel, damp and heavy with the bad smell of decaying vegetable matter. In the gloom to either side of the road, dark and twisted trees with shaggy bark rose between deep green stands of fern.

Carl had never been good at hiding his feelings. When he was little, a counselor told him learning how to mask feelings was part of growing up, but his mother always said, "Nobody likes a two-face, Carl. Your openness is a blessing."

Right now, it felt like a curse. He didn't want to talk to Octavia until he'd wrapped his head around the newspaper article he'd discovered. He wished he had never seen the stupid thing.

He liked her very, very much—her eyes, her smile, her brains, her laugh, even her white hair, which was so different—but then he thought of the article and felt sick.

Well, what did you think she did to get here, he asked himself, *shoplift?*

But murder . . . burning someone alive . . .

He slapped at the first of the stinging flies that plagued them whenever they entered the forest. Then, all at once, the air thickened and buzzed with the things, and the drill sergeants cranked the run to a sprint. When they all broke from the woods into the sunlit clearing where the obstacle course began, the flies ebbed away back into the darkness to await the platoon's return trip.

The drill sergeants led them to the starting line and stood with clipboards and timers. "You know the drill. Two by two!"

Anxious to avoid Octavia, Carl pushed to the front and ended up side by side with Mitchell, a tall Alaskan with an enormous Adam's apple. Mitchell could run fast, and he climbed like a monkey. He, Campbell, and a wiry guy named Sanchez were the only ones who'd come close to Carl's time.

Mitchell nodded at Carl.

Carl nodded back.

Drill Sergeant Rivera said their names, and his assistant, a tough-looking girl not much older than eighteen, wrote on the clipboard. "Well, Mitchell, you going to beat him this time?"

"Yes, Drill Sergeant!"

"Motivated! What do you think, Freeman?"

Carl grinned. "I could win this running backward, Drill Sergeant."

"Talk's cheap, boys. Timer ready? All right, then. On your marks, get set, go."

Carl ran down the path, letting Mitchell keep beside him. He'd pace himself for the first half, then pour it on midway, once they swung over the stream. He could sprint it from there. The pencil wound in his thigh wasn't really bothering him.

They crossed ditches on balance beams, vaulted over log hurdles, swung across the monkey bars, and hit the dirt to crawl under ten yards of low-strung barbed wire. Here and there, drill sergeants yelled at them to push it. They ran down a long curve that took them for a time through the forest, with its gloom and dampness and the sounds of birds, then broke from the woods and ran uphill to the cargo net ascent.

Carl leapt into the net and scrambled up. Throwing one leg over the top, he turned to razz Mitchell—and saw the spiderweb. Strung through much of the netting on Mitchell's side, it was a foggy mass straight out of a Halloween nightmare. At its center, an entangled bird struggled and cheeped, eyes bright with terror.

Carl broke out in goose bumps. "Watch your head."

"Whoa," Mitchell said. "Thanks." He climbed up beside it and whistled. "That's a bird trapped in there. A little bird."

"Yeah," Carl said. "Creepy, huh?"

"I got it," Mitchell said. "You're all right, little buddy," he told the bird, trying to free it. "This web's crazy. Really strong."

A spider the size of a plum crossed the web so fast Carl barely had time to yell a warning.

"Whoa," Mitchell said, and ripped the bird free just in time. He leaned away, laughing and cursing, and tossed the bird into the air.

Then the spider jumped.

It landed on Mitchell's neck, just under his chin. He screamed, whipped his head back, and batted at it . . . with both hands.

He fell ten feet and hit the ground with a horrible crunch.

"Mitchell!" Carl started down the netting.

Mitchell screamed in pain, then came off the ground with his left arm jutting at impossible angles and the huge spider clinging to his face. He ripped the spider away and threw it into the trees, cursing. "It bit me! That thing bit me!" Then he lifted his broken arm into view, saw the right angle in the middle of his forearm, the white bone there, the blood, and passed out.

Carl crouched beside him. On his forearm, Mitchell had a homemade Bart Simpson tattoo so poorly drawn that no one had even known what it was until the kid had grinned with his bad teeth and told them. Splintered bone had pushed completely through the skin there, splitting Bart in half.

Worse still were the bites, a pair of them, one on his neck, the other just below his eye. In mere seconds they had swelled to the size of tennis balls, bright red fang marks distinct as logos at the center of each lump.

Carl shouted for help.

Mitchell groaned and twitched. Spit foamed from his mouth.

A drill sergeant pushed Carl out of the way, looked at the bites, and lifted Mitchell's shoulders. "We have to take him back. Get his feet."

Carl grabbed them and lifted.

"You!" the drill sergeant called to kids coming up the hill. "Run back to Drill Sergeant Rivera and have him radio a jeep. Go."

They carried Mitchell back up the trail. He continued to foam and twitch, and the bites continued to grow, swelling one eye shut and obscuring his prominent Adam's apple.

Carl felt sick.

Back at the clearing, they loaded him into the jeep.

"Get him to the Chop Shop," the drill sergeant said, and the jeep sped off, turning left.

Toward the medical center, Carl thought. The Chop Shop. One more macho joke. Right now, with the image of Mitchell's break and bites fresh in his head, nothing could seem less funny. What kind of twisted people would call a children's hospital the Chop Shop?

CARL SPENT THE REST OF HIS DAY going through the motions of training, avoiding Octavia, and trying to forget the image of the spider and the awful breaking sound Mitchell had made hitting the ground. The whole thing made him feel cold and nauseated.

On their way back to the barracks that night, Ross said Mitchell would be lucky to survive.

"Survive?" Carl and Campbell said simultaneously.

Ross raised his palms. "Don't shoot the messenger. I'm just saying, a spider that size, a wound in the neck, another in the head, the swelling. I mean, the guy looked like he was fighting for his life. My diagnosis: anaphylactic shock."

"Ana-what?" Carl asked.

"Anaphylactic shock. Like kids get from beestings when they're allergic. Back in Massachusetts, my next-door-neighbor went into shock from a wasp sting. He looked just like that."

"Did he live?"

"Well, yeah. They jabbed him with an EpiPen, and he was all right. But I didn't see anybody doing that for Mitchell, and besides, we're not talking a little wasp here, right? We're talking about a spider the size of—"

"I'd rather not talk about it," Carl said.

In the barracks, when everyone started polishing boots, Carl locked himself in the book man closet.

While preparing the whiteboard, he remembered the diary atop the ductwork and pulled it down. He needed a distraction.

Dear Diary,
    Um . . . hi. I've never written a diary before, but this is the craziest thing that's ever happened to me, so I figured I might as well start. Well, here goes.
    My name is Eric Flemmington. I'm seventeen. Up until a little while ago, I lived in Tucson, Arizona. Then I got into some trouble and had to come here.

Carl skimmed along. This kid Eric had moved from orphanage to orphanage, group home to group home, with stays in juvie here and there. Then he'd been arrested for stealing cars, and they'd sent him to Phoenix Island, where he'd become book man.

The kid had a pretty good sense of humor.

Carl flipped ahead and knew instantly by the handwriting that something had happened. The opening pages were neat and tidy. A few pages in, the writing went sloppy and dark. The page itself was all wrinkled up, like it had been crumpled and then flattened back out again. In the margin, Carl saw what looked like rusty fingerprints. Was that dried blood?

Ralston died today. They put him in the sweatbox again and just left him there till he died. We could hear him screaming all night. Then this morning they formed us up and made us watch while they dragged him out. They were laughing, of course. Some of the kids were, too. I hate them. Someday, I'm going to let the whole world know about these murdering psychopaths.

Carl stared at the diary. They'd killed some kid on purpose?

For a second, he tried not to believe it—but certainty settled over him like a shadow. Hadn't he known something was off here? Way, way off?

With a shiver, he remembered Parker's whispered threat, the day he'd stabbed Carl with the pencil: *I'm going to fix your wagon once and for all.*

Once and for all. . . .

His mouth suddenly went dry.

Skipping ahead to the last page, there was only one entry:

If you're reading this, I guess I'm dead. If you're stuck here like I was, you know what you have to do. Do it. We have to beat these monsters before it's too late. That's it, then. I got one chance, and I'm going to take it. I'm so afraid.

That was it.

Carl was shocked. What had happened? Was Eric really dead? What did he mean, *you know what you have to do*?

Was Parker planning to kill him? Was that what he had meant?

But Rivera would never let that happen. Right?

He turned back to the first page and read the thing straight through as fast as he could.

Then he read it again.

Then he just stared at the wall.

PERHAPS AN HOUR LATER, someone knocked. Carl had been waiting for it, knowing Ross came on duty at midnight. He opened the door.

Ross looked tired. He made a crude joke about what Carl was doing alone in the closet, then Carl pulled him inside and closed the door. "We have to talk."

Ross nodded at the door. "I'm on duty, in case you forgot. If Rivera comes up here, and I'm not walking the hall—"

"Ross, they *kill kids here*."

"Well, I don't think he'd kill me, precisely, but—"

"I'm serious," Carl said. "That's why they only take orphans. Some kid steps out of line, they kill him."

"Riiiight. I think somebody needs a glass of warm milk and a good night's sleep." Ross reached for the door.

Carl blocked him. "Listen, Ross. I found something. A journal. You can't tell anybody about this."

"Okay."

"The kid who wrote it was book man a few years ago. He talks all about it. Torture, murder, everything. Something else, too, something about the doctor down at the Chop Shop. I don't know what was going on there. He wasn't sure. Something—the doctor doing stuff to kids, to their brains. It made me think about that kid we saw, the first day, driving in—the zombie kid—and it makes me worry about Mitchell."

"Hold on," Ross's hand dropped from the doorknob. "You're serious? *Murder?*"

Carl nodded. "His early entries, everything sounds like it's been for us so far. Rough, but . . . you know, like it's been. But then, thirty-some days in, they shifted to Blue Phase, and this guy they keep talking about, the Old Man? He shows up, and everything changes. People start dying. Lots of people. You ever see the pictures in the drill sergeants' office, the ones with the faces blacked out?" Carl stopped himself. He didn't like the panic he was feeling, and he didn't want to overwhelm Ross.

Carl and his friend looked at each other for a few tense moments, then, to his surprise, the other boy smiled. "You found it in here, right?"

"Yeah. So?"

Ross spread his hands. "It's obviously a joke. The guy made it up, hoping somebody would find it. He's probably sitting somewhere right now, back in the world, laughing about it with his buddies."

"No. It wasn't in a place where people would find it."

"*You* found it."

"It's real, okay? If you read it, you'll see."

Ross rolled his eyes and held out his hand. "Let's see it."

Carl handed Ross the journal.

Ross grinned at the beginning. "This guy seems way cooler than our book man."

"This is just the normal stuff," Carl said. He flipped the top page.

"Hey," Ross said, "he was talking about how fat his dog was."

"Look," Carl said, pointing partway down the second page. "Here's where the Old Man shows up."

"This kid sounds pretty impressed."

"Yeah. Apparently, the Old Man is way different than the other drill sergeants. Like the ultimate poet-warrior or something. Way smarter, and way more dangerous. Turn the page. Look."

"Yadda, yadda, yadda . . . somebody mouthed off to a drill sergeant, pushed him." Ross read on for a second and frowned. "No way. This has to be joke."

Carl didn't say anything, just let him keep reading.

"Public execution?" Ross said.

"Right in the quad. Everybody was made to watch. And look who did the killing."

"Parker?"

Carl nodded. "At first. Then some kid tried to sneak ammo off the firing range. They shot him on the spot. Another kid got caught trying to sneak into the girls' barracks. He died in the sweatbox after being left there for *eight days*. Another one, this kid who started crying in formation, they threw him to the sharks."

"That's ludicrous."

"When people started dying, it changed everybody." Carl grabbed up the pages and started reading from them. "'Some of the kids went with the program, got mean. Others ran.'"

"And?"

Carl looked up at Ross, who had gone white. "'They hunted them.'"

"That's sick."

"It gets worse. It wasn't just the soldiers hunting runaways—the kids helped."

"No way," Ross said, shaking his head.

"That's what they're doing here. They're turning us into killers."

Ross looked at him. "Why?"

Carl said, "According to Eric—that's the guy who wrote all this—the Old Man turns Phoenix Island grads into mercenaries."

Ross gave him a look.

"You don't believe me?"

"Oh, I believe *you*," Ross said. He shook the papers. "I just don't be-lieve this guy. Look, if I had Parker on my back and Davis giving me trouble, maybe I'd buy into this stuff, too, but believe me: this is some kind of joke. There's no way. They'd get in so much trouble."

"How?"

"Well, they can't just kill kids."

"Why not?" Carl leaned forward. "If somebody kills me, who's going to know?"

"I'd know."

"And what would you do about it?"

"Tell somebody."

Carl crossed his arms. "Who? One of the drill sergeants?"

Ross made a face. "Somebody on the outside, obviously."

"How?"

Ross opened his mouth but said nothing.

Carl said, "If somebody kills me tomorrow, who's going to come ask-ing? No one. How about you?"

Ross threw the papers on the desk. "This is stupid."

"Who would check on you?"

"Somebody would. I have an aunt in Vermont."

"Okay, let's just say she did wonder about you. Who would she ask? Nobody knows where we are."

"Somebody does. The judge does."

"You sure about that?"

"Well, someone does," Ross said, scowling. "The system does."

"Maybe. And what would the system do? Your aunt calls, are they going to come all the way out here, check up on us? No way. At best, they'd call or email, and the drill sergeants could say, 'Ross, oh, he's doing fine. Sorry, no, he can't talk. Strict policy. Wouldn't want to ruin all the hard work he's done. We're so proud of him.'"

Ross looked uncomfortable.

Carl said, "Or they could even admit you were dead. 'Oh, we're so sorry, ma'am. We didn't have your contact information. Such a tragedy. He drowned while swimming.'"

"But if enough people checked . . ."

"How many people would? Not many. And they'd all be trying different judges in different towns, different states. Who's going to connect the dots? And this is just me, thinking off the top of my head, but if the Old Man can set up an *entire island* with guns and a military and stuff, I'm pretty sure he has a whole plan set up. He could forge letters, let people talk to graduates who work for him—a huge smoke screen that hides us forever." Carl shook his head, truly frightened. "We're stuck, man. We're all alone."

"I still don't believe it," Ross said, but he didn't sound so sure of himself anymore.

Carl climbed onto the chair and returned the journal to its hiding spot. "I guess we'll see soon enough. Blue Phase is right around the corner.

"So what are we supposed to do?"

"Do?" Carl put a hand on the smaller boy's shoulder. "We have to escape Phoenix Island."

"Escape?" Ross said. "In case you hadn't noticed, we can't exactly call a cab."

Carl patted the journal. "According to this, every week or two, a plane brings supplies."

"So what do we do, ask for a ride?"

"We sneak onboard. That's what Eric was going to do."

"Pardon my skepticism," Ross said, smirking, "but it didn't seem to work out so well for him."

Carl nodded. "I thought about that. Maybe he got caught."

"If even half of what he said is true, I do *not* want to get caught."

Carl tapped his knuckle on the journal. "Maybe we'll think of something he missed. You're smart."

Ross gave him a *yeah, right* look. "Whole lot of good my brains have done me. I'm here, aren't I?"

"There might be another way." Carl turned to Eric's crude map of the island. "We're here," he said and pointed to an *X* labeled HOME SWEET HOME. Then he ran his finger over the long, dark line that crossed the island. "This is the road we came in on. Here's the obstacle course. The Chop Shop. The reception area."

"Some reception."

"Tell me about it." He pointed to other X's. "Firing range. Urban training center. Battleground. This, I don't know." He moved his finger to the other side of the island, where a weird phrase spread across a large shaded area. "Hic sunt dracones?"

Ross chuckled. "It's Latin. 'Here are dragons.' Roman cartographers—sorry . . . mapmakers—used to write that on sections of uncharted territories, basically saying, 'Look out. We don't know this area. It's probably dangerous.'"

"How do you know all this stuff?"

Ross shrugged.

"You're a weird guy, Ross."

"Thanks. Your predecessor was making a joke. He only knew this half of the island. Everything he'd seen—and everything we've seen, for that matter—is on the west side of the island. Look." He pointed at a jagged line that split the island roughly in half, top to bottom, just east of the road and the mountains. "It's a fence . . . an electric fence, I'd guess. These squiggles are lightning bolts probably."

Carl nodded. "You're right. We've only seen stuff on this side."

"Yup. And woe to he who ventures here," Ross said, poking the uncharted spaces beyond the fence, "for here be dragons. Get it? A joke . . ."

"Yeah, I get it," Carl said, then pointed to an X not far from the landing strip, "but this is no joke. Camp Phoenix Force."

"Where the mercenaries train?"

"I think so. I'll bet the Old Man has been there this whole time, training survivors of last cycle."

"Today's class," Ross said, "twenty ways to kill a man without breaking a sweat."

Neither of them laughed.

Carl tapped Camp Phoenix Force again. "Eric said there were boats here."

"So . . . what? You're suggesting we break into a compound of trained killers, steal one of their boats, and head for Mexico? I respect your bravado and everything, but I don't consider that a sane course of action."

"What else can we do?"

"If we knew this bad stuff was really going to happen, I'd swim with the sharks to get out of here. But right now, nothing's certain enough to risk everything by breaking in there. Don't get me wrong. It would make a great movie. I'm just not ready to live it."

Carl exhaled slowly and ran his hands over his stubble.

Ross snapped his fingers. "I've got it. Campbell's leaving soon, right?"

"Too soon."

"What if he gives the journal to someone back in Texas?"

"Who?"

"The news. It's a story, right? Innocent orphans getting tortured and murdered south of the border? Somebody would pick it up. They could do some research, get our location, and send in fact finders."

Carl allowed a tentative smile. "It might work."

"Of course it will work," Ross said. "Campbell will help us."

9

YOU GUYS ARE CRAZY," Campbell said between bites of chili mac. "You honestly think they kill kids here?"

"Yes," Carl and Ross said practically in unison. The platoon was eating MREs in the field rather than heading back to the chow hall. The three of them sat in the shade some distance from the others.

Campbell laughed as if Carl had just told the greatest joke he'd ever heard. Parker, who was eating down by the jeep, looked up angrily. Campbell didn't notice. "And Mitchell's a zombie now?"

Carl hesitated. The night before, someone had blacked out Mitchell's face with a Magic Marker. The black mark reminded Carl of the spider. "I don't know. Maybe."

Ross said, "Officially, he's been recycled, meaning he'll start over with the next cycle of orphans, but we know that's not true now."

"Look," Campbell said, shoving trash into his empty MRE sack, "I don't have time for your conspiracy theories."

A little spike of panic stabbed Carl. "Wait—we really need your help."

Campbell frowned. "My help?"

"Just listen, okay?"

Campbell nodded toward Carl's lunch. "Give me your ranger pudding."

"Sure," Carl said and handed him the hot chocolate mix.

"Go ahead then," Campbell said, tearing open the pouch, "but just for the record, you guys sound pretty crazy. You know that, right?"

"If we're so crazy," Ross said, "where are all the recycles from last cycle?"

Campbell shrugged as he tipped water from his canteen into the pouch. "Haven't seen any."

"Exactly," Ross said, and gestured across the sprawling platoon. "Nobody's a repeat. Not one kid."

"So?"

Ross leaned in. "Are you trying to tell me no one fell out last cycle? Not one broken leg? Not one heat casualty? Not one psych case? If they really recycled kids, we'd have repeats with us right now."

"That doesn't prove anything," Campbell said, stirring the powder and water into a thick soup. "Look—if all this nonsense is true, how come they haven't killed anybody yet? In fact, from what you're saying, Carl shouldn't be here right now. They should've killed you on day one, my man, made an example of your 'individuality.' So why not?"

Why, indeed, Carl thought. He'd wondered the same thing. "Well—"

"We haven't worked that out yet," Ross said. "Maybe it's part of their cover."

"Their cover?" Campbell shook his head, chuckling. "Paranoid."

"Maybe," Carl said, "but take a look at this." He glanced around, saw no one watching, and handed Campbell the journal.

"What's this supposed to be?" Campbell said. "Dear diary . . . aw, come on." He shoved it back in Carl's direction.

"Don't wave that thing around," Ross said, and glanced nervously downhill. "Just read it, okay? I'll give you my hot chocolate, too."

At that, Campbell shrugged and they struck the deal. He flattened the journal on his lap, weighed it down with Ross's powder, and grinned as he read and spooned makeshift pudding into his mouth.

Carl and Ross exchanged looks. Ross crossed his fingers.

Campbell turned the page. "So far the guy likes Rivera and hates Parker. No big surprise."

"Keep reading," Carl said. It was crazy, showing Campbell now, out in the open, but at least here they could see someone coming. In the barracks, you were never alone.

As seconds passed, Campbell's smile faded, and his eyes narrowed.

His spoon paused halfway to his mouth, dripping dark syrup on his uniform. "What the . . . ? No way."

"Keep reading," Carl said again.

Campbell's eyes flicked back and forth more and more quickly. When he turned the page, he looked up, frowning, and glanced downhill toward the cadre. It was the first time Carl had ever seen Campbell look nervous about anything.

Five minutes later, when he had finished reading and looked up again, he looked more than nervous. He looked scared.

"It's real," Carl said.

Campbell launched into a series of questions—mostly the ones Ross had asked—and Carl and Ross both answered him. Right from the start, Carl could see that Campbell knew, just as they knew, that the journal was real. He put his hand absently to his chin, where his goatee had been. "This is insane."

"We have to stop them," Ross said.

Campbell looked at him like he had suggested wrestling a grizzly bear. "Stop them? How? You said it yourself. We're stuck."

"We are," Carl said, nodding toward Ross, "but *you're* not."

Campbell turned to him. "What do you mean?"

"We're stuck here for a long time, but your birthday is right around the corner. You'll be out of here soon. See, they don't know you know. How could you? They won't start the bad stuff until you're gone."

"Why?"

"So you can be like an ambassador for them," Ross said. "In the unlikely situation that anyone ever did start asking questions, whoever runs this place—the Old Man or whatever—could point to you and a bunch of guys like you all over the country. 'Phoenix Island?' you'd tell them. 'Oh, that place sucked. Shaved our heads, made us run all the time. What? Kill people?' And then you'd laugh your head off, and that would be that. Investigation closed."

Campbell nodded slowly.

Carl said, "We need you to take the journal home with you and show it to news people."

Campbell's eyes went wide, and he shoved the journal off his lap as if it were a poisonous snake. "No way. They shake me down, find that thing, who knows what they'll do? Make me stay, send me to prison . . . if you guys are right, they might even execute *me*, man, mount my head in the quad."

Ross smiled nervously. "Well, when you put it like that . . ."

Carl nodded. No matter how badly they needed help, he couldn't ask Campbell to take that kind of risk.

"That's sixteen hundred," Rivera called uphill at them. "Time to pack it in, orphans."

Sporadic hooahs rippled across the platoon, which came to life, people standing, gathering trash.

"I see one wrapper on the ground," Parker shouted, "I smoke the whole platoon!"

The three of them gathered their trash in silence, Campbell obviously deep in thought, Ross looking like he'd been punched in the stomach, and Carl worrying about the journal, which he'd just tucked back into his boot.

"Tell you what," Campbell said, as they walked together toward the trash can. "I get home, I'll put on a tie, go see a senator or a state rep."

Ross's features brightened, understanding dawning on his face. "That's brilliant." He laughed and slapped Carl in the arm. "Why didn't you think of that?"

Carl turned to Campbell. "It could work, man."

Campbell nodded, his face solemn and his eyes far away. "I just hope my birthday gets here before we switch to Blue Phase."

THE NEXT MORNING, Drill Sergeant Rivera formed everyone up outside the gear sheds, and Carl could just tell that something bad was coming.

"All right, orphans," the soldier began, "here's the deal. It's the end of the trail for Drill Sergeant Rivera." He patted the air until the groans quieted. Rivera wasn't only Carl's favorite; he was everyone's favorite. "That's right. My tour's finished for this cycle. Some of us drill sergeants, our specialty is getting you started. Then we hand you off to the Blue Phase cadre, some of whom you already know. Now it's time for me to head home to my family, just like someday, it'll be time for you to head back to the world. Hooah?"

"Hooah."

Hearing their weak response, Rivera crossed his arms. "You're gonna do me like that after all we've been through together? Not my orphans. My orphans are motivated—hooah?"

"Hooah!"

Rivera smiled. "That's a troop, right there. Just remember: be the person you want to be. That's all we are: the decisions we make, the things we say, and most of all, the things we do. You keep doing the things you should be doing, and you *will* become fine men and women, people who can hold their heads high. Hooah?"

"Hooah!"

"During Red Phase, you've learned to march and drill and take care of your gear, and you've learned Phoenix Island's rules and etiquette. With Blue Phase, you'll move on to advanced training: land nav, field communication, survival skills. You'll learn to work as a team. Hooah?"

"Hooah!"

"Don't slip up, orphans. You can lose that blue flag a lot easier than you can gain the green one you'll be aiming for."

We'll lose the blue flag right after the Old Man shows up, Carl thought, remembering Eric's journal. Everyone would complain about the demotion and the loss of privileges, completely unaware that everything that happened here was scripted, start to finish. If Eric was right about losing the blue flag, way worse things than extra chores were coming their way.

Rivera said, "Now, it's not just the end of the trail for me today. You're losing another leader."

Carl's breath caught. *Let it be Parker. . . .*

"Campbell, come on up here, son."

"Yes, Drill Sergeant." Campbell left the ranks to join Rivera on the gear-shed loading dock.

"Oh no," Ross moaned.

"Campbell has been one squared-away platoon guide, hooah?"

"Hooah!" the platoon responded. Carl noticed Davis smirking at his buddies.

"Campbell," Rivera said, "you're just days away from turning eighteen, and you have decided to leave us, correct?"

"Yes, Drill Sergeant," Campbell said, looking relieved.

"Well, son, I'm sorry to hear that. You'd make one heck of a soldier." He placed a hand on Campbell's shoulder. "I could see you in a marine's uniform. The few and the proud. Semper Fi."

"Thank you, Drill Sergeant."

"Well, here's the deal, Campbell. The next plane out of here leaves at thirteen hundred. After that, the next flight is two weeks out . . . six days *after* your birthday. Now, I talked to the Old Man, and he said, in light of your performance and everything you've done for the rest of these sorry orphans, we could out-process you today, hooah?"

Campbell smiled wide. "Hooah!"

"All right, soldier." Rivera clapped him on the back and pointed toward the gate. "We'll get you over to processing, then. The flight leaves in two hours, and believe me, those hombres wait for no man."

"Yes, Drill Sergeant."

"Your last duty as platoon guide, then, will be to be to surrender the red flag. When I replace it with this blue flag, you orphans are officially in Blue Phase, hooah?"

"Hooah!"

Carl felt sick to his stomach.

Campbell returned to the ranks, casting a cautious smile toward Carl, and retrieved the platoon standard. The flag fluttered as he carried it back up the steps, the crimson phoenix at its center barely visible against the bloodred banner.

"Sanchez," Rivera said, withdrawing a scroll of blue fabric from a nearby box. "Prepare the platoon for the exchange of flags."

"Yes, Drill Sergeant!" Sanchez said, stepping from the ranks. Stepping into Campbell's spot, forward and left of the formation, he faced the platoon. "Atten-shun!"

The group responded as one, coming crisply to attention. Carl could feel anticipation thrumming through everyone.

It doesn't mean what they think it means, he thought. *It's one more piece of the game. They're just giving it to us so they can take it away.*

Campbell held the flagpole as Rivera, moving slowly and deliberately, detached the red flag and fastened the new one in its place. Against the blue banner, the red phoenix now burned brightly.

Turning to the platoon, Rivera said, "Welcome to Blue Phase, orphans. Now, I don't know if you're interested, but the Old Man cleared me to give you liberty for the rest of the day. Hooah?"

Their cheer was an explosion.

Rivera told them to fall out, and most of the kids sprinted off toward the barracks, hooting with joy. A full day of free time? It didn't seem possible.

Carl and Ross approached Campbell, who stood talking to Rivera.

Rivera shook Carl's hand. "Freeman, you stick with this, you'll make a fine soldier."

"Thank you, Drill Sergeant, and thanks for treating us like human beings."

Rivera smiled. "No problem, Freeman. You're *almost* human. Now drop and give me ten for suggesting I went easy on you."

"Yes, Drill Sergeant." He dropped and racked out ten.

"Ross," Rivera said, offering his hand, "you, on the other hand, would make a terrible soldier."

Ross beamed. "Yes, Drill Sergeant."

"But I suppose society will find something for you. Stay out of trouble."

"Yes, Drill Sergeant."

"You got about thirty seconds to say good-bye, Campbell. Meet me at the gate, and I'll drive you over to processing."

As Rivera strode off, Campbell said, "Looks like I hit the lottery, huh?"

Even though Carl hated to see him go, he was happy for him.

"Don't forget," Ross said.

"Don't worry," Campbell said. "I'll get in touch with people. And you," he said, turning toward Carl, "watch out for Davis and Parker."

He gave them both a quick embrace and jogged off toward the gate.

"Good for him," Carl said.

"Yeah," Ross said, "but bad for us. I have a feeling—"

"Hey, Carl."

Carl turned. It was Octavia.

"Hey," he said.

"Can I talk to you for a second?"

"Sure," Carl said.

"I'll see you inside," Ross said, and headed for the barracks.

Carl and Octavia stood several feet apart. She looked at him with those beautiful gray eyes and said, "Campbell's really gone then, huh?"

"Going," Carl said.

They looked at each other for a second. Even here, even now, with everything going on, his heart gave a little jump as they stood face-to-face, close enough for either one of them to reach out and touch the other.

"Carl, I'm no good at this stuff," she said.

"What—"

"Carl, don't. You know what I'm talking about. Don't pretend, okay?"

"All right," he said. "Octavia, there's something you need to know."

"Are you finally going to tell me why you've been acting so weird?"

"What?" Then he realized she meant the way he'd been avoiding her. So much had changed since he'd found the journal, all that other stuff seemed trivial now. "Oh—no . . . it's something *big*, about this place. I found this journal—"

She shook her head. "Wait. I'm not listening to anything until you explain yourself. What's been up with you?"

"Nothing," he said, and it even sounded lame to him. But he couldn't deal with all that now—he had to tell her the truth about this place.

"Just say it, Carl. I'm sick of this game, whatever it is. You've been acting weird for days, avoiding me."

"Really, it's nothing. I just have a lot going on."

"Yeah, right. And you didn't before? I didn't think you'd be like this—that's what I liked about you. You seemed like you were above all this stupid stuff and all the games. You seemed different. Shows what I know."

"Wait," he said. "Don't leave. I'll tell you. But then you have to listen to this other thing, okay?"

Octavia just looked at him.

He said, "Look, I'm the book man, right? And I was filing stuff, and I saw this thing in your file, something about—" And suddenly, he found he couldn't say it.

"What? What did you see?" Her eyes flashed with anger.

"A newspaper story," he said, staring at his feet. "Forget it."

"No, Carl. I won't *forget it*. What did it say? Man up and tell me what you think you saw."

Carl looked her in the eyes and hated the fury he saw there. "It said you set a fire and killed somebody."

She spread her hands wide. "It's true. Happy?"

"No. I . . ."

She crossed her arms, her gray eyes dark as storm clouds. "Did you read the whole thing, Carl? Did you bother to get the whole story before going all high and mighty on me? Did you ever think of asking me about it before passing judgment and getting all weird?"

"Octavia, look . . . I didn't want to cause some big problem. That's why I didn't say anything about it. I thought maybe over time—"

"Over time what, Carl? You'd find it in your heart to forgive me?" She laughed dismissively. "That's very big of you. You're a really amazing person to consider hanging out with scum like me."

"That's not what I meant." He reached out.

She batted his hand away. "Oh, shut up. I thought you were a nice guy, Carl, but it turns out you're just as bad as the rest of them. You snoop through my files, see one thing, assume the worst, and then you don't even have the nerve to ask me about it. You play this stupid game, make me chase you. I really didn't think you were like this."

"I'm not."

"Whatever. Do me a favor, and leave me alone, okay? Just stay away from me. I wouldn't want to contaminate the perfection that is Carl Freeman." She started to walk off, her hands balled into fists.

"Octavia."

She turned, and for a mistaken moment Carl was relieved. "And next time you snoop around somebody's personal stuff, get the whole story, genius. That guy who died in the fire? Yeah, well he killed my mom, okay? And he molested me for years. But of course you didn't bother to figure any of that out, did you, Hollywood?"

With that, she stalked away. This time, she didn't turn back.

10

THE BARRACKS RANG WITH SHOUTING AND LAUGHTER, everybody going nuts over free time.

Carl trudged upstairs, feeling like his head might explode. Campbell was gone. Rivera was gone. Now Octavia was good as gone, too. He still had to warn her about this place, but it didn't seem like she would ever talk to him again. He wanted to be angry at her for being mad at him, but all he felt was empty. It was horrible, the whole thing, and he felt awful about what she'd gone through with her mother and stepfather. . . .

Ross stopped him as he reached the bay. "Wait," Ross said. "Don't overreact."

"What?" He walked around him into the bay.

His locker was open. His stuff lay all over.

"Great. Another tornado." While the platoon was out, the drill sergeants would come in and mess up their gear, their beds, everything. One time they'd piled everyone's boots in the middle of the hall. That had taken forever to sort out. "It doesn't look so bad this time."

"Yeah," Ross said. "Um . . . look down."

Scraps of glossy paper lay sprinkled like confetti on the floor. Carl glanced up and saw the bare surface where his photographs had hung. "No . . ."

He crouched in the destruction and with shaking hands picked up a thin strip that held half of his mother's smile. He stared at the teeth, the eye above them. Who would do something so cruel?

Parker.

He let the torn photo fall to the floor. His throat started to tighten, but he tightened his fists instead. Better to shed blood than tears.

Ross said, "Carl—wait! Don't do anything stupid."

Carl strode down the hall. Taking his medal was one thing, but destroying his pictures? They were all he'd had left of his parents. And now they were *gone*. Forever . . .

He pounded on the closed door of the drill sergeants' office.

Nothing.

He tried the handle. It was locked.

"They already scribbled out his face," Ross said, pointing at the platoon photo hanging on the door. Ink masked Campbell's face. "That's going to be your face, too, if you don't settle down. Can't you see that you're playing right into Parker's plans?"

"Leave me alone," Carl said, and started back down the hall. Maybe Parker was in the bays.

Ross followed, trying to talk.

"Not now," Carl said.

Kids crowded the entrance to the second bay. Carl saw their bright eyes and nervous smiles, and his anger burned higher. Parker . . .

Laughter roared like a monster from the bay.

Laughter and cruelty, always laughter and cruelty . . . no matter where he went, there they were, waiting for him.

His fists ached with the old pain.

"Wait," Ross said. "I'm begging you."

Carl ignored the smaller, weaker boy. Since coming to Phoenix Island, he'd avoided situations he would have confronted in the past, fearing trouble, yearning for a clean record and a normal future—and every time he'd turned away he'd hated himself for doing it.

"Stop it!" a high-pitched voice cried in the bay.

One of the kids standing in the doorway laughed nervously.

Carl pushed past him and saw Medicaid on the floor, sobbing.

Parker wasn't in there. It was Decker, the redneck with weird eyes, and his toadies who stood over the redhead, laughing.

Carl started for them.

"Stay out of it," Ross said. "This is just what Parker wants."

Carl hesitated, gritting his teeth. Some part of his mind—a faint whisper toward the back—said Ross was right. He couldn't fight. Not now, with the threats implied by the journal. Everything was on the line: his freedom, his whole life, that magical word, *expunged* . . .

Decker pushed Medicaid with his boot. "Now do a car."

"Vroom," Medicaid said through his tears.

Decker reached down and yanked Medicaid's underwear in a hard wedgie. "Brake pedal!"

Medicaid squealed and fell flat.

The bullies roared with laughter, and Carl understood: they were pushing Medicaid to the breaking point. They didn't care how he felt. They only wanted pain. Pain and power.

Some power, Carl thought, *breaking a kid who was already broken when he came here.* He hated them.

Medicaid struggled weakly. "Stop! Please stop!"

More laughter.

"Do a dog," Decker said.

Medicaid let out a strangled bark.

"Louder," Decker said.

"You get free time, this is how you spend it?" Carl shouted.

Decker looked up, his icy blue eyes twinkling.

Carl said, "Leave him alone."

Decker smiled. "What's wrong, Hollywood?" He was short and thick, maybe ten pounds heavier than Carl, fifteen at the most, with muscles that suggested he'd spent most of his childhood lifting engine blocks. He just stared, amusement and fury burning in his eyes, waiting for Carl to make a move.

Carl glanced at the others, gauging them. The other three would jump in, but it would boil down to Carl and Decker. If this was going to happen, Carl knew he had to show them all. This had to be decisive. Otherwise Decker would become a slow bleed in his life. This was it.

"We're trying to motivate him," one of the kids said.

Somebody laughed. Decker just kept staring, a terrible amusement playing across his face. It was a cold humor Carl had seen in other bullies. The toughest ones. The ones with real confidence. Counselors and teachers told you bullies were insecure and cowardly, and, sure, some were. But guys like Decker, guys who got that look in their eyes, were neither insecure nor cowardly, and they weren't just acting out for attention. Guys like Decker were confident and tough and mean to the core, and they hurt people because they liked causing pain. He'd been pushing Carl for weeks, trying to get something out of him, but Carl hadn't fallen for it. Now this. Decker's eyes shone with interest.

Meanwhile, Medicaid looked at Carl with pleading eyes. His mouth twisted into weird shapes, and his face was red and wet with tears. A natural target. Carl didn't like the kid, had no reason to like him, but he couldn't just let these guys ruin him like this.

Decker grinned. "What do you care, anyway? You don't like him, either. I can see it in your eyes."

Decker wasn't stupid. He was just mean. "Look," Carl said. "We're all in this together. They're trying to break us. We don't need to work on each other."

Decker straightened. "I've been wondering when you were going to step up." He gestured toward Medicaid. "Come on over and have some fun. Medicaid's gonna imitate a monkey." He took a step in Carl's direction.

Carl stepped back. Decker was a wrestler—Carl had seen him pin guys in the back bay—so Carl wanted to keep his back to the open space, wanted plenty of room to move. He didn't want Decker to get ahold of him.

Decker smiled. "Easy there, Hollywood. Little jumpy, aren't you?"

Kids laughed, gathering around. Davis and his buddies came into the room, hooting with their eyes sharp. Ross stood nearer, shaking his head.

Decker turned to his friends. "Ever see somebody so jumpy?"

One of Decker's toadies, Stroud, started walking toward Carl.

Carl put out a hand. "Hold up, Stroud."

"Here, let's shake on it," Decker said. He took a step closer and stretched out a thick arm, the hand looking boxy and strong.

"No thanks," Carl said. If he shook Decker's hand, he'd be on the floor in about half a second. He'd seen this routine with wrestlers before, and it didn't play to his strengths. "Just leave the kid alone. And leave me out of it."

"Ooooo," someone said.

"*And leave me out of it,*" Stroud mocked, making his voice go all high.

Carl ignored him, keeping his eyes on Decker. "Look, you know I'm right. If we fight, the sergeants will flip. They wait for something like this, then crucify everybody." Carl gave the rest of the barracks a quick glance. Then, to Decker, he said, "You and me, we'll get it bad. They'll turn us into examples. But everybody else will get it, too. Parker will smoke us all, take away our privileges, keep us in Red Phase. You know I'm right. If you want to do this, let's do it later, just the two of us, some-place where everybody else won't get in trouble. I don't—"

"You talk too much," Decker said. "I think you're all talk." He nodded, and a hand grabbed Carl's arm, and Carl reacted instinctively. He dipped low, stepping back, and snapped his arm free.

Stroud lunged.

Carl sidestepped and flicked out a jab, caught the kid on the point of the chin, and spun his head around. Then, instead of drilling Stroud with a right hand, he stiff-armed him in the chest and tossed him into Decker, who was coming for him at last.

Low to the ground and moving fast, Decker blasted through Stroud like a nose guard gunning for a quarterback. He flashed his eyes up to Carl and clapped his hands high, a kind of feint, and shot low, reaching for his legs, meaning to take him to the floor.

Carl jumped.

Decker whooshed underneath him.

Carl turned, and the side of his head exploded. Instinctively he got his hands up, drove his shoulder in, and buried a right hook into the gut of his attacker. Stroud oofed and folded.

Another fight had broken out a few feet away. Ross was down on the ground, wrestling with one of them; another bully hovered, looking to kick him.

Carl started for them, but then someone had him by the legs. A high-pitched voice squealed, "I got him! I got Hollywood for you!"

It was Medicaid. *Medicaid* of all people. . . .

Ross yelled, "Look out!" and Carl was lifted off his feet.

It was a hard tackle. He jarred to the floor, most of the wind leaving him, and before he could roll away, Decker wrapped one arm around Carl's legs, controlling them, and then proceeded to climb up him, clamping his strong arms around Carl as he went, like a boa constrictor wrapping its prey.

The crowd howled with delight.

Decker said something Carl couldn't make out. Carl propped onto one elbow, and Decker lurched into the air over him, his big fist drawn back. Carl didn't even try to block the punch, and he didn't bother throwing one of his own.

Instead, as Decker's fist came crashing down, Carl tightened his stomach muscles, yanked his upper body upward, and snapped his head forward as hard as he could.

The punch grazed his ear.

The top of his head slammed square into Decker's face, nailing him like a ball-peen hammer right between the eyes.

The head butt stunned Decker and opened a cut on the bridge of his nose. Carl lurched the rest of the way up and twisted the bully to the floor, reversing the position. He longed to drill punches into Decker's stupid face, but he didn't want to cut or break his knuckles, so instead he grabbed him by the ears and slammed his head into the tile floor, hard, once, twice, three times. It was too late to stay out of trouble. All he could do now was to teach them, make them understand. It was all he had.

The crowd yelled on, cheering for blood.

"I told you to let it go," Carl said, and he picked up Decker's head again. This time, instead of slamming it back down, he held it by the ears and blasted it with another head butt. Decker's eyes rolled back in his head. His nose was a fan of blood.

Rage consumed Carl. He got to his feet and lifted Decker off the floor. Decker reeled, barely conscious.

Carl shook him. "Still think I'm all talk, you stupid redneck?"

Decker raised a fist.

"Ha!" Carl shouted. "You're going to punch me?" He turned his whole body with an uppercut that snapped Decker's head back and launched him over the nearby cot. Decker fell on the other side, his feet up on the bed, and lay still.

The crowd stopped yelling.

Carl turned to face them, vaguely aware of Stroud running off, shouting.

Carl had to work fast, then, had to leave his mark, had to show everyone. It was too late for anything else. The remaining two toadies—Funk and Chilson—backed away, hands high. Carl saw Davis watching with keen interest, smiling. The rest of the crowd watched with wide eyes, backing away themselves.

Squaring himself with the toadies, Carl yelled at them, "Why do you always have to push?" He brought his left arm around with blistering speed and blasted through Funk's pitiful guard. This time, Carl left his hand open, and his palm cracked loudly off the kid's face. Funk cried out and stumbled. "How do you like it?" Carl threw three rapid-fire, hooking slaps with his left, *wap-wap-wap*, then slapped so hard with the right that Funk dropped.

Carl's palms burned. He grinned at the pain.

Chilson ran. Ross threw himself low underneath him, and the bully tripped, sprawling onto the ground. Carl jumped over Ross, lifted Chilson by the back of his shirt and his pants and rammed his head into a footlocker with a loud crash. He drove a kick into his gut, and Chilson gave a high-pitched squeal.

Carl faced the rest of the platoon. "Any of you want to bully somebody," he said, and he was breathing hard now, not from fatigue but from rage, "you bully me. Got it? If I catch you bullying anybody, I'm going to beat you worse than this."

He searched out Davis and stared him in the eyes. "We have anything to settle, you and me?"

Davis shook his head and displayed a wry grin. "We're cool, baby."

Carl turned and pointed at Medicaid, who was crying again. "And you. You're a pitiful piece of crap, that's what you are. Grabbing hold of me when I was trying to help you? I ought to shove all your teeth down your throat. But you're not worth it. No heart. Just a punk, punking out for the bullies."

Then a deep voice thundered, "What's going on in my barracks!" Drill Sergeant Parker stepped into the bay, carrying something that looked like a woman's curling iron. He glanced at the kids on the floor, then at Carl. Stroud was behind him, talking rapidly.

And then Parker pointed at Carl with the short rod. "Now you're going to pay, Hollywood. Get ready to ride the lightning." He flicked the rod he held, and an arc of blue electricity crackled at its end. "This is my bug zapper. Five hundred thousand volts. I carry it for hotshot punks like you, smart meat brig rats who think they can come in here and do things their way."

Screw that, Carl thought, looking at the cattle prod. "They started it, Drill Sergeant."

"I didn't ask you a question, Hollywood!" He walked toward him. "Parade rest!"

Carl obeyed the command, spreading his feet and folding his hands one on top of the other at the small of his back, but spoke out of turn, too, saying, "You ripped up my pictures, didn't you?"

"Shut up, Hollywood," Parker said. He advanced slowly. The stun gun sparked and crackled.

"Drill Sergeant," Carl said, snapping into protocol, "Private Freeman requesting permission to speak, Drill Sergeant."

"Permission denied," Parker said—and Carl had never seen a more wolfish grin. This guy was the ultimate bully, a man who'd made a full-time job out of hurting people. Carl knew teen boot camps filled their ranks with bottom-rung drill sergeants, guys who'd washed out of the army or the marines. Whether they'd washed out for being too cruel or just washed out, they were so pissed off about it, they wanted to spend ten or twenty years hurting kids. Whatever the case, Carl knew then and there that Parker was the rock star of these bottom-rung monsters, these professional bullies, and he was about to have himself a good time. And something else, too—Carl could see it in his eyes—Parker didn't just want to hurt Carl; he wanted to kill him.

"Now we'll see how tough you really are, Hollywood. If you can stay at parade rest while you ride the lightning, I'll zap you once, and we'll call it a night."

Carl's muscles tensed.

"You cry out, though, or break parade rest? Well, then you ride the lightning all over again."

"Drill Sergeant—" Carl began.

"Denied!" Parker said. He was right in front of Carl now, glaring into his eyes.

Carl forced himself not to eyeball the man, forced himself not to break parade rest. Picturing the torn photographs, he wanted to nail Parker with a hook hard enough that he'd hit the wall before that Smokey Bear hat of his even had time to drop. He didn't, though. This was a crucial moment. If he messed up here, Parker would kill him— literally end his life.

Parker raised the cattle prod between their faces. It snickered, flashing blue.

Carl stared straight ahead.

"You afraid, Hollywood?"

"No, Drill Sergeant."

"Bull. Why are you shaking, then?"

"I'm angry, Drill Sergeant. This whole situation is unfair, and I don't deserve to be punished, Drill Sergeant. You destroyed my—"

"I don't want your life story, Hollywood!" Parker shouted. "I just want everyone here to understand what happens to hotshots who don't follow rules. Remember: you break parade rest or cry out, you get it again. And again. And again. Until you die or I get bored. And don't go pissing in your pants, either. That's what most of them do."

"This is stupid!" a voice behind Parker called. "Freeman didn't do anything wrong, Drill Sergeant. Decker started it."

Ross. Carl saw his small friend standing there, his nose bloody, his hands spread, looking nothing like a soldier. The little guy had guts, but Carl wished he'd just shut up before he got himself hurt, too. A guy like Parker, all he wanted was pain, and once he'd flipped the switch, the only place to go was up. More pain and more pain and more pain.

"Drop and give me thirty, Ross!" Parker said.

"This is absurd. We're not really in the army. And—"

"Make that fifty push-ups, Ross! You will *not* speak again unless spoken to." Turning to Stroud, he said, "You, Tattletale, make sure he does all fifty, and if he cheats, kick him in the ribs."

"Yes, Drill Sergeant!" Stroud said, and he turned toward Ross, who was getting into front leaning rest position.

Turning back to Carl, Parker said, "And away we go."

Carl steeled himself. *Don't cry out,* Carl thought. *Don't break parade rest. And don't hit him. Whatever you do, don't hit him.*

11

"You know what, Hollywood?" Parker said . . .

11

CARL BRACED HIMSELF.

Parker held the baton close to Carl's face. "Let's see how tough you really are, Hollywood."

Carl tensed as the stun gun crackled and an arc of blue energy snickered between two blunt points at the end of the baton.

"It's not fair!" Ross shouted from the floor.

Carl heard the dull thud of a kick and heard his friend grunt with the blow.

"Gather around, orphans," Parker said. "I want you to see what happens to *individuals* on Phoenix Island." The others pressed closer. Decker pushed to the front, his face smashed and bloody.

"You think you're a star, Hollywood," Parker said, "so let's light you up." The baton crackled, and two needles of energy plunged into Carl's forearm. Electricity coursed through him and locked his muscles rigid, filling him with sparking, yellow pain. His teeth clacked shut, but he didn't cry out.

It was kind of like getting punched hard—when somebody with fast hands cranks you a good one, when you don't see it coming. White lights flash in your head, and you feel like a surprised cartoon character, all these little spikes shooting out of your head. That's what this was, only the explosion was in his arm, not his head, and all those shock lines, instead of shooting out of him, stayed inside of him and shot up his arm and into him, spreading and multiplying the pain.

Withdrawing the stun gun, Parker looked angrier than ever.

Somehow, Carl had passed the test, had managed to maintain parade rest position and avoid crying out. For that he was thankful.

He let out a shuddering breath. He'd done it. He'd taken a blast of 500,000 volts and hadn't given Parker an inch.

Parker grinned through his anger. "Not bad for the first one."

The first one . . . And then the horror of it dawned on him; Parker had no intention of stopping no matter what Carl did. He was going to keep shocking Carl until Carl couldn't take it anymore. He was going to keep pushing and pushing and pushing until Carl finally broke, and then he'd push a little more. *Well,* Carl thought, *he's going to have to work at it. I'm not going to just lie down for him.*

"You know what, Hollywood?" Parker said. "I'm feeling kind today. You want to stop, we can stop." He pushed his boot forward. "All you have to do is be humble. Kiss my boots, and I'll let you go."

"Just do what he wants," Ross said.

Screw that. I won't give him the satisfaction.

"No? So be it. . . . In nonlethal combat school, they taught us the three best places to stick somebody with a stun gun: the hip, shoulder, and neck. What do you say we go in that order?"

Parker reached out again. Carl heard the snicker and saw the blue flash, and needles of pain tore into his hip. His muscles went tight as a fist, his jaw locked, and he strangled a scream in his throat. His body jerked more this time, but he stood his ground. The pain was bright white. The initial shock felt like the explosion of a hard punch, but the pain was nothing like the pain of a fight. Fighting generated suck-it-up-and-take-it pain. This stun gun pain was something else altogether. Not worse exactly, but abrupt. It seized him, taking control of his body, and this lack of control filled him with wild desperation. Fighting it was more like fighting panic than pain. It was more like drowning than getting punched.

The electricity cut off. Somehow, he'd managed to hold position and keep from yelling.

Parker roared with laughter. "How'd that feel, Hollywood? Huh? Let's see what you do when I touch this thing to your shoulder. Right where you got your shots today . . . that ought to tickle. Unless you're ready to quit playing games. You know what you have to do: just give Daddy's boots a smooch."

Carl said, "You're nothing like my dad."

"You're right," Parker said. "I'm still alive."

Carl opened his mouth to tell Parker what he really thought of him, but then a yellow jolt whacked across his shoulder and through his chest, and it felt like there was a bird in his heart, flapping its wings. The shock flashed up through his head, and Carl's skull felt like a shining lantern. With the pain came the panic, but still he did not cry out, and though his upper body jerked involuntarily, he managed to keep his hands behind his back and his legs spread. He had to. . . .

"Woo-hoo! That was a good one!" Parker yelled. "Well, Hollywood, you took it to the arm, the hip, and the shoulder. You don't really want it in the neck, do you? Be a smart little individual. Kiss the boots, and I'll make all of this stop."

Carl shook his head. He'd rather die than play Parker's stupid game.

Parker turned to the others. "See? Hollywood thinks he's better than you. Always showing off. Now he's the superhero. He gives you guard duty, and while you're up in the night, he sleeps like a baby."

Carl saw people nodding, angry, eager . . . crazy. Like animals smelling blood. How could they buy into this? But he knew the answer, didn't he? This was the whole point of Phoenix Island. Parker was setting him up for the kill. Had been since day one. Eric's journal was right. Parker, this place, they didn't just want to kill kids; they wanted to turn kids into killers. He was trying to transform the kids in their united hatred of him. And by the looks of the faces he saw around him, it was working.

With one noteworthy, unexpected exception.

Davis.

Carl saw Davis looking at him, his face slack, unhappy. Davis, who had seemed to want to kill Carl mere days ago, now looked like the only sane face in the crowd. Davis, of all people, looked restrained, thoughtful. Seeing Carl look at him, he nodded.

Parker said, "Last chance, Hollywood. You want to get humble or keep showing off and take it to the neck?" He grinned. "Well, what do you say? You want me to stop?"

Want him to stop? It hurt so much, he wanted him to stop more than just about anything. . . . But punk out for Parker, after all he'd done?

Carl looked straight ahead, waiting.

"Well," Parker said. "Aren't you just the show-off?" He turned to the others. "I gave him a chance. You all heard me. I tried to show mercy, but Hollywood insists on being an individual. It's all right. We've got all night."

The drill sergeant triggered the stun gun, and blue light snapped from prod to prod, flashing. *Crack, crack, crack.* He held it close to Carl's face for several seconds, and once again, Carl had to force himself not to close his eyes. Suddenly, strangely, it came into his mind that he had nothing in the world. No possessions, no family, no future. All he had was himself. His self-respect. He would rather die than let Parker take that.

"Go ahead," Carl said, and he had just enough time to hear people shout with laughter before the prods plunged like fangs into his throat, and his whole head filled with white light, and his body jerked, and this time his mouth *did* make noise, a quiet animal sound that was not crying. Parker pressed the points deeper. Everything in Carl wanted to scream. Everything in him wanted to jump away. But using every last ounce of willpower, he remained in place as lightning coursed through his neck and made his head feel like it was cooking. Parker bore on, and the light turned from white to blue, and everything in the world flashed and crackled as if Carl's head were nothing more than the end of the stun gun itself. *Crack, crack, crack!* And it felt like his eyes would pop from his head like bottle rockets riding tails of flame.

Parker pulled away the prod.

"Woo-ee! I thought his head was going to blow up."

Carl shuddered. His muscles shook from fatigue and shock and anger. He forced them to stay in place as best as he could, his legs spread, his hands folded at the small of his back. He kept his chin out and his eyes forward as Parker walked around him in a wide circle, as if inspecting him.

Parker said, "You jerked around like a little girl that time. I think you're ready to quit. You ready to quit, Hollywood?"

"Yes, Drill Sergeant."

Parker smiled. "You know what to do, then. Get down there and pucker up."

"No, Drill Sergeant."

Parker shook his head. "In nonlethal combat training, they also taught us to target the red zone during emergencies." He tapped Carl's chest three times with the baton but didn't trigger it. "The red zone can kill. See, a stun gun works through the muscles. That's why you look so stupid every time I touch you, like you're having a fit or something. Well, the heart's a muscle, too. What do you think will happen if I put half a million volts through it?"

Carl said nothing.

Parker shook his head. "See, this is what I call an emergency situation. The emergency here is that you need an attitude adjustment. You are tore up from the floor up, and I don't mean that in a good way. FUBAR. The most FUBAR soldier I have ever seen." He turned to the group again. "Hollywood's too good for us, too cool. Thinks he's better than us. What do you think? Is he better than us?"

Angry shouting filled the room.

Carl saw what Parker was doing, knew he was feeding the platoon's bloodlust. He wanted them to howl for Carl's death.

"Last chance to make it stop, Hollywood. We go to the red zone, you'll be crying for your mommy." He stared into Carl's eyes. "Though you might as well save your breath, seeing as how your mommy's dead."

Rage leapt up in Carl, and it was all he could do not to bring his fists around from behind his back. But he knew that was just what Parker wanted. He was waiting for Carl to strike, hoping he would swing. Then he could justify anything . . . *anything*. Even public execution.

Parker raised the stun gun again. "Get smooching, Hollywood, or we're going to the red zone."

Before Carl could even think about what he was doing, his mouth opened and words came out. "Go to hell, Drill Sergeant."

The platoon cried out with delight.

Parker looked like he'd been slapped. "What did you say to me? You worthless piece of crap, you're going to wish I fed you to the hammerheads." The cattle prod crackled to life. "So be it. Say hi to your parents for me."

"Stop!" Ross shouted. "You're a monster!"

Carl's heart surged with gratitude and concern for his small friend.

Ross broke free of Stroud and grabbed Parker's arm. "What are you trying to do, kill him?"

Parker drove a crushing right into Ross's mouth. Ross flew backward into the others and dropped to the floor. His limp body hopped with convulsions.

That's when Carl started punching.

12

CARL DIDN'T HOLD BACK. He didn't worry about hurting his hands. He just unloaded his punches with the full force of all that pent-up hatred. Parker had pushed and pushed and pushed, and if he'd been smart enough to just keep pushing, he could have melted Carl into the floor with that stupid stun gun of his, but then he'd punched Ross, and now he was going to pay, even if it meant Carl's death.

Carl's punches landed at full extension with full power, and they caught Parker off guard—*smack, smack, smack, smack*—but they did not knock him unconscious. This was no boy. This was a man who had led a life of pain and who'd spent most of that life lifting weights, shooting steroids, training his body, and preparing for situations just like this. He had a thick neck, a square jaw, and broad shoulders so heavy with muscle that he looked like an ape. He wouldn't go easily.

But that didn't bother Carl. He had nothing left in the world, nothing but this. And he didn't care if somebody shot him. He didn't care if they hung him or nailed him to a cross. . . . He was going to finish this now. He had tried his best not to get into trouble, to just get along, but they pushed here just like they pushed everywhere else, and Parker was the worst bully of them all, and Ross was down and hurt very badly, and now Carl was going to hurt Parker just as badly, no matter what the cost.

The other kids roared like savages.

Before the drill sergeant could recover from the first barrage of punches, Carl moved in and drilled him with half a dozen sharp blows: hooks and uppercuts and a right cross every bit as crisp as that stun gun.

Parker's hat flew off his head. He put up his hands. His face was already lumped and streaming blood. He cursed and rushed at Carl.

Carl danced away and caught Parker with another jab on the way out.

Parker crashed into a bunk, spun, and roared, "I'm going to kill you!" He raced toward Carl again, going low like Decker had, and Carl lashed out with his foot and landed a kick square to Parker's face. There was a shock of two powerful forces slamming together, and Carl hitched backward, his foot exploding with pain. On the other end of the collision, Parker's head snapped back on his thick neck. His arms went wide, and he sat down hard with a grunt, then fell over onto his back.

There was a lot of shouting. Carl was aware of people running off, hollering for other drill sergeants. He knew he should run, but he had to finish this first. Besides, where would he run? This was the end of the road. *A terminal facility*, the judge had called it. *Terminal*. The same word the doctor had used for Carl's mom's cancer.

Carl suddenly knew that he was never going to see the world again.

Parker grunted as he grabbed the corner post of a bunk and pulled himself up. Carl could see the tattoo again, the skull and crossbones, *Death Before Dishonor*, and he remembered the first day, Parker digging through Carl's stuff and taking his medal. Today, the drill sergeant's nose lay flat against his face, the tip jutting off to one side, and beneath it he wore a mustache of bright red blood. He huffed with exhaustion and frustration, and his eyes burned with hatred.

And Carl saw something else there, too: fear.

At long last, Parker was starting to realize what he was up against. It didn't matter that he'd been hurting kids year after year. It didn't matter if he could bench-press four hundred pounds. It didn't matter that he was thirty and Carl was sixteen. None of that mattered now. All that mattered was what was happening and what was going to happen, and Carl was in control of that. For a brief moment, Carl could read the internal struggle behind Parker's eyes, the tug-of-war battle between rage and fear as Parker decided whether to back down or march forward.

Hatred won. Carl saw it in the man's eyes, saw the fear and rage uncouple, saw the eyes narrow and set with purpose. Parker came at him more slowly this time, hands up, moving his head side to side like a novice boxer imitating a slugger.

He's a southpaw, Carl reminded himself, seeing Parker advance with his right foot forward, *and he's had just enough training to do everything a southpaw is supposed to do.* He would fight with his right foot forward and try to nail Carl with a straight left hand, maybe a right hook. *All I have to do is keep my lead foot outside his lead foot, and I'll eat him alive.* If Parker came at him like that, looking to land the big left, Carl could just quarter-pivot, and Parker would turn and chase him and run into Carl's straight right.

As Parker shuffled toward him, Carl saw another advantage. Parker's right hand was loose and pawing, and his left arm was tense, the knuckles of that hand white around the handle of the stun gun. He was thinking too much about his weapon, relying too much on it. It was like being able to see inside Parker's head. The drill sergeant had latched on to the idea of shocking Carl again. . . .

Carl made a small adjustment, stepping to his left, repositioning his lead foot—his left—outside Parker's lead right.

Parker didn't seem to notice. He just shuffled forward, ticking his head back and forth but forgetting to keep his hands close to his face whenever he bobbed or weaved. He had just enough training to work against him. An untrained fighter is dangerously unpredictable. But Parker knew how to fight, had been taught, and this made him susceptible to Carl, who'd fought thousands of rounds and hundreds of street fights.

Carl laughed. He rocked forward and back and side to side, moving his shoulders. Then he licked out with a quick jab just to see what Parker would do.

Parker swung at him with the snickering cattle prod, bringing it in an overhand arc like a nightstick, and Carl slid out, going to the left. He quarter-pivoted and rocked back on his right leg like it was a coiled spring. This motion cocked his right shoulder. Then, just as Carl had assumed, Parker turned to face him and stepped in, drawing back with the stun gun, and Carl drilled him with a straight right that cracked loudly, snapped Parker's head back, and sent spears of pain up Carl's wrist. *That's all right*, Carl thought. *I have to keep punching now, no matter what.*

Parker shambled toward him until Carl doubled him over with a hard hook to the liver.

Bent at the waist, Parker covered his liver with his hand. He smiled through his pain, blood from his shattered nose making his lips look big and red like those of some demented clown. "You know what we're going to do to you, Hollywood?" he said, and Carl could hear the pain in his voice. His eyes seemed to burn with sudden inspiration . . . or perhaps insanity. "We're going to lock you in the sweatbox. Cook you for an eternity. Then I'll form everybody up and show them what we do to show-offs like you." His laughter was an ugly sound full of pain and madness.

Carl stopped it with a hook to the jaw.

Parker dropped to all fours but recovered faster than Carl expected and lunged at his legs, trying to tackle him. It almost worked. He had Carl's leg, but Carl was able to spin to the side and break loose, and Parker sprawled onto the floor. The stun gun skittered away. Parker fell facedown and was slow to rise. If he'd been a weaker opponent, Carl would've jumped in then, locked up Parker's legs with his own, slid one forearm under his chin, wrapped his other forearm behind the big neck, and cranked until the King of All Bullies went to sleep. But Parker was too dangerous for that, too strong, and it was better for now to keep him out in the open and cut him to ribbons with his fists.

As Parker made it onto all fours, Carl noticed Decker picking up a metal shoeshine box and motioning to his toadies. They were about to hit him with everything they had, all of them, and Carl knew he couldn't withstand that. Instead of attacking Parker, he backed up and scooped the stun gun off the ground. Decker and the others looked at him warily. Parker rose, moaning. Carl felt around the handle of the stun gun until he found the button, pushed it, and the blue light crackled to life.

"You guys come any closer," Carl said, "and it's your turn to ride the lightning."

The others paused, looking toward Decker.

"He can't take us all," Decker said. "That thing hurts, but it won't kill us. He can't take us all." Then, raising his voice, he said, "Everybody, Freeman's way out of line. We gotta stop him. We gotta help the drill sergeant."

"Bull," a familiar voice said. "Let them finish. It's their fight. You feel me?" And Davis stepped to Decker. The gang guys massed around him, united, and Carl suddenly found himself laughing. He couldn't help it. This was all so crazy.

People murmured and shifted their weight. A few moved forward and picked stuff up. Blankets, boots, shine boxes like Decker had grabbed. Somebody came from the back, double time, carrying a mop.

"Y'all are punks," Davis said.

Decker was right, Carl knew. There was no way he could take them all, even with Davis's help.

"On three," Decker said.

Carl tensed.

"One," Decker said.

Parker spit blood onto the floor.

"Two."

Parker glared at Carl, drooling blood, and raised one fist into the air. "Stand down," he said. "I'm going to finish this myself. Right now." He reached into the cargo pocket of his camouflage pants, spat more blood, and pulled his hand out of his pocket. Sneering, he flicked his arm sideways. There was a sharp snapping sound, and six inches of steel flashed from his fist.

"Now," he said, advancing on Carl, "I'm going to gut you like a fish."

He meant it. Carl could see it in his eyes. All the hate and the fear and now the embarrassment at having been beaten in front of the kids, it had all boiled together in Parker to create a true psychotic rage. He shuffled forward in a low, knife fighter's crouch, and Carl knew this was real trouble. Guys like Parker trained in knife fighting, spent their whole lives dreaming of do-or-die situations like this. The stun gun would do very little good, as far as the shock went. Parker could definitely push through the shock and pain long enough to sink the blade into Carl.

Forget the trigger, then, Carl thought. *Just use the thing like a bat and try to knock the knife away.* He glanced around the room near him, looking for anything he could use to protect himself.

There was nothing.

Parker kept coming.

Ross shouted from the crowd, restrained by the others.

Good, Carl thought. *Hold him.* Otherwise, Ross would get himself stabbed. The kid had guts enough for somebody three times his size.

If they'd been at the other end of the barracks, Carl might have run out the door and into the night, but he had his back to the rear wall, and the door might as well have been a mile away. Between him and it were a knife-wielding psychopath and at least a dozen kids who would happily join the attack.

Parker flashed out with the knife. It didn't come close, just flicked out and back in. *He's judging my reaction,* Carl thought. *Trying to see what I'll do, trying to set me up.* Carl sidestepped, not wanting to back into the tighter space between the final pair of bunks, and Parker rushed him.

Carl jarred into a bed and slid away, panic at the unexpected speed of the attack popping up inside him. He spun past, but a line of fire lit across his elbow. He'd been cut. He felt the warmth of the blood and the burn of the cut, and when he shook his arm, an arc of blood splattered onto the tiles.

"Like it?" Parker said. "Even better than the pencil, huh?" His voice sounded thick and stuffy, and Carl knew Parker's nose was broken. Good. He hoped Parker choked on the blood.

Carl's eyes panned the surroundings again. Nothing. Then . . . wait . . . He reached out and pulled a pillow from the nearby bunk.

Parker laughed, edging toward him again. "Think this is a pillow fight?"

Carl held the pillow out in front and gripped the baton in his right hand. He found his rhythm again, rocking side to side, ready to spring one way or the other. This had to work. He had to time it just right, or he was going to die.

Parker surged forward, and Carl jagged left. The blade went past.

Carl started to bring his arm around, seeing the opening—and then something cracked hard into his head.

It was such a surprise and such a sharp blow that he lost his balance. The blade drove in again, and Carl had just enough time to suck in his gut. The edge of the knife sliced across his side, opening his shirt and burning across his ribs. He felt the steel rub across the bone and slip away. Pain raced along the wound—another line of fire—and he spun away again, tripping over the thing on the floor. A shoeshine case lay at his feet, its lid cracked open, its contents spread across the tiles like spilled intestines.

Decker. Decker had thrown it at his head, had almost gotten Carl killed.

Then the whole room seemed to explode. Carl saw Davis catch Decker with a looping hook, saw Davis's friends tearing into Decker's toadies.

Carl could figure that out later . . . if he lived that long. For now, he had to survive this attack. His ribs burned, badly cut, and his arm burned, and his whole body ached with fatigue.

Parker seemed to sense this. He was grinning again, the fear gone from his eyes. They still burned with rage, and now they shone with excitement, too, anticipation, bloodlust. He bobbed and weaved toward Carl and flashed out with the knife again.

This time, Carl didn't hit a bed, and nothing hit him in the head. He timed the blade, read its arc, and bent away from it, letting it miss by inches rather than feet. His left arm brought the pillow around hard, slamming it into the exposed side of Parker's head hard enough to make the big man stumble. Then Carl smacked down, sharp and fast, with the baton. It cracked across Parker's thumb and wrist. The knife fell away, and the drill sergeant stumbled clumsily into a footlocker, grabbing at his wrist. Carl jabbed the stun gun into the thick neck and pushed the button. He heard the quick *crack-crack* and saw the blue flash, and then Parker was shrieking. He shook away and batted at the air, terrified.

Carl kicked the knife under a bunk and thumbed the button again. The thread of blue lightning snickered. "How you like it?"

Parker backed into the small area between the final bunks. He flashed a desperate look toward the bunk under which Carl had kicked the knife.

"Don't bother," Carl said. "You'd never make it."

Terror flashed in the drill sergeant's eyes. He dove for the floor.

Carl kicked him hard in the ribs.

Parker grunted but plunged his hand under the bed, reaching for the knife.

"Give it up," Carl said, and let him have another blast from the stun gun.

Parker shrieked and flailed, but he was determined. He kept after the knife. He had his head and shoulders under the bed now.

I can't let him get that thing again, Carl thought. He was losing a lot of blood from his cuts, enough that he felt oddly chilled. Soon, he would feel weak. If Parker got the knife again, he'd kill Carl.

"Ha!" the drill sergeant yelled, and Carl knew he'd found his weapon. The big man lurched backward, his wide, muscular shoulders coming into view, and he reached back with one hand to pull himself free.

This was it. Carl's last chance. He drew his knee up, all the way to his chest, and stomped down as hard as he could on the exposed collarbone. There was a loud snap, and Parker screamed. Carl stomped down again and again and again, targeting the broken bone. Then, when Parker slid screaming from under the bed, meaning to kill Carl, Carl stomped down hard on the bully's face. Once, twice, three times. Parker waved the knife uselessly in the air, and Carl stomped again. He had to end this. Had to finish it. Now. He saw the jaw give. Stomped again, saw the knife hand drop, saw the knife go free onto the ground again, and was just thinking about picking it up and ending this monster once and for all, when something smashed into the back of his head, and darkness ate him.

13

CARL AWOKE IN HELL.

The air itself seemed to be made of flame, and in his great pain and confusion, his body felt indistinct, as if it had melted into the heat around him.

Slowly, he came to his senses, only to wish he hadn't. He knew where he was.

The sweatbox.

The cage smelled of filth and decay, sweat and blood. It was perhaps five feet long and half as wide, small enough that he couldn't straighten out, and so short he would have to stoop if he tried to stand. Not that he felt like standing; he didn't feel like moving it all. He was awash in a hazy semiconsciousness steeped in pain and ripe with fever. Through blurry eyes swollen nearly shut with bruising, he registered the tightly spaced bamboo bars, the corrugated metal ceiling, and, beneath him, the filthy matting of straw. His vision was so unsteady that the straw itself seemed to shiver with a subtle vibration.

He was in a lot of pain.

Some of his injuries came from the fight. His knuckles, massive with swelling and crisscrossed in deep splits, throbbed, as did the bones in his swollen hands. His right hand wouldn't work correctly and was almost certainly broken. Both wrists ached deeply. The knife cuts, one a strip of fire on his arm, the other an urgent burning across his ribs, hurt so much even in his semidaze that it felt like the wounds themselves were moving. General bruising had inflated his entire body, making him stiff and achy, head to toe.

Much of the damage had obviously occurred after the fight, after they'd hit him from behind. This part of the story he pieced together from evidence: the sore knot at the base of his skull, the extreme bruising and tenderness and swelling all over his face, the lips split and especially tender, the ears ringing and sore to the touch. His entire head roared with the worst headache he'd ever felt . . . doubtlessly a concussion. In the back of his mouth, he was missing a tooth. He wondered vaguely if he'd swallowed it. Worst of all were his ribs, which pulsed with pain from top to bottom on both sides and felt like they were splintering whenever he took a deep breath. They hurt so much that they seemed to quiver gently. They were bruised, maybe cracked or broken. He'd had bruised ribs before and knew the pain and how long it took to recover. Only forever or so and then maybe another week or two.

Pain and this methodical inventory of injuries brought Carl further out of his unconsciousness. His throbbing nose drew no air, feeling as if it had been packed with dirt as he slept. Blood and mucus, he thought. Probably broken, too. He wondered, in the conditioned response of all boxers, what his nose would look like this time, and then considered just how bad the smells in the sweatbox must really be, if they were this pungent through a broken nose. Awful. His mouth tasted coppery with blood and was sandpaper dry from dehydration and breathing through it for however long he'd been unconscious. His throat was raw, and his tongue felt shriveled, somehow reptilian. It kept sticking to the roof of his mouth. He knew he was in the grips of a fairly serious fever, but he couldn't be certain how much of the heat was coming from within and how much of it was the cage itself, which was certainly over 110 degrees. He needed water desperately.

A bowl sat in the corner near a hole in the floor. Staring at this, readying himself for the pain he knew would accompany movement, Carl began to piece together something troubling. That strange, incessant movement he felt in his cuts and over his ribs slowly fell into step with his unsteadiness of vision. Then the subtle vibration of the straw covering the floor coordinated with a soft whisper barely audible behind the ringing in his ears. Finally, in a moment of dawning horror, his tactile senses sharpened, and through the deep foghorn of pain that had been deafening his perception of the world, Carl detected one final sensation.

A light tickling covered his flesh.

Movement. On his skin, under his clothes, in his hair. Everywhere.

Bugs.

He was covered in bugs.

He surged off the floor, slammed his head into the low ceiling, bumped into the bamboo bars, and screamed, his voice low and raspy—the scream of a ghost long dead—and shook his broken body and swatted at himself and raked, twitching, clutching things from his body and clothing. For several seconds he was lost to madness, slamming back and forth in the small cage, making animal sounds of rage and terror, clawing and plucking and smashing, while within him erupted an absolute volcano of pain. Some of the bugs fought him, biting and gripping into his clothing and flesh with legs like briar thorns. He screamed again to find his cuts bubbling with feeding insects and tore at them with his dirty nails only to utter another hoarse cry upon discovering a hard-shelled black centipede the size of his index finger buried in the open wound over his ribs. He struggled with stiff and swollen fingers to grip the nightmarish thing, which broke in half as he pulled, then broke again and again so that it took an eternity for him to believe that he'd removed it completely.

Later, convinced that all the bugs were off him, he collapsed into a crouch, the whole world pulsing in and out of focus around him. He was out of breath, weak with fever, and nearly blind with pain. Crouching there, he focused on his breathing and willed the pain into its proper place as best he could, channeling the faint ghost of the wisest man he'd ever known—his boxing trainer, Arthur James—until he could almost hear Arthur's soft voice cooing in his ear, as it had between rounds, telling him, *That's all right, son. Catch your breath. That's it. First the breath, then the mind.* Once able, he crawled across the straw to the bowl. Without water, he would die.

Large black bugs with yellow stripes swam in the murky water. He scooped them from the bowl, crushed them with his hands, and flicked them through the bars of his cage. He raised the bowl to his lips and gagged. It smelled like rotten eggs. This stench married with bad smells coming from the nearby hole in the floor, and Carl crawled to the other side of the cage, careful not to spill the water.

Ignore the smell, he told himself. *This is life or death.*

He drained half of it at a gulp. It was warm and tasted awful, but it was water, and instantly, he wanted more. *Slow down,* he told himself. *Be smart.*

He sipped more water, but this time he didn't swallow it straight away. He let it sit in his mouth. *Like I'm sitting in the corner between rounds,* he thought. Arthur would dig out Carl's mouthpiece and give him only a short squirt of water in order to avoid stomach cramps. He swished it around, letting it soak into his tongue and wash away the blood, then tilted his head and gargled, soothing his throat, and finally swallowed. Only another mouthful or two remained in the bowl. He debated what to do with these. What if no one brought him more? Should he use the last bit to clean his wounds?

No. He needed the water now. If they didn't bring more soon, he would die before infection had time to really set in.

He inspected the wide, ugly gash on his ribs and pulled from it dirt, pieces of straw, and bits of broken insects. The edges of the wound were swollen and very red, like the lips of a leering mouth smeared in lipstick . . . or blood. Carl thought again of infection, which would probably develop quickly in this climate and filth, and he wondered if his apparent fever was an early sign. He wondered, too, if bugs might've burrowed in and laid eggs in his flesh. He'd heard things like that, stories where bugs or ants planted eggs inside people, awful stories, the eggs hatching, the babies eating the person from the inside out.

Just thinking about it made his cuts itch and his whole body crawl with invisible insects, but he put a lid on that nonsense straightaway. No use worrying about it when there was nothing he could do. Not yet. He had to deal with what was real, not what he was afraid would happen. At a time like this, worry was as dangerous as hope. Another lesson he'd learned from boxing: if you wanted to win, you couldn't let either fear or hope blind you. You had to see things for what they were and make the right choices and adjustments.

He had to do what he could to keep bugs and dirt out of his wounds. Tearing away the bottom of the shirt, he soon discovered his right hand was so damaged and so swollen that he had no grip, so he used his teeth and his left hand to rip the shirt. He did a clumsy job of it, tearing away more of the fabric than he had wanted. Tying it off was very difficult. It took him several tries, and in the end, he used his right arm to press the fabric up against his ribs and the left to do all the tying. The resulting bandage wasn't nearly as tight as he had hoped, but it would have to do.

Repeating the process and covering the cut on his arm, he finally turned to eyeing the world outside his small prison.

Through the bars, he could see the barracks and the parking lot, the cattle trucks parked beside the flagpole, atop which fluttered the flag with its burning phoenix. *Well,* Carl thought, the unbelievable heat pressing down on him, *at least they got the fire part right.* He saw the fence, the gate, and, at a distance of perhaps two hundred yards, the guard towers, where a pair of soldiers stood close to each other with rifles slung over their shoulders.

He saw none of the trainees. Thinking of Ross, he felt a fierce rush of affection for his small friend. Ross had known the dangers—he'd read the journal, too—but he'd stood up for Carl anyway, first against Decker and then against Parker himself. The kid had heart. Real heart. He'd taken a beating for defending him, and who knew what he was going through now? Carl hoped he'd be okay. Octavia, too. He cursed himself for his stupidity toward her. Shutting her out over the newspaper article, never bothering to get the whole story straight from her, failing to warn her about the journal . . . he'd really messed up.

He could do nothing to help them right now. He had to keep fear and hope in check and focus on reality.

He knew he might die here. Maybe in the cage. Maybe on display, as an example, in front of Ross and Octavia and everyone else. Maybe they would release him into the jungle and hunt him like an animal.

He drank the rest of the water and dwelled on the possibility of his death for a moment. Somehow, it lacked the sting he would have ex-

pected. He did not want to die, but the thought of death neither saddened nor panicked him. It was merely fact, something to recognize, to
know. It could happen.

Everything drew down tight. He thought of the journal tucked
away in the book man's closet, the stories of death and how they had
started, one boy dragged out of the sweatbox and executed in front of
the platoon.

By Parker, of course . . .

Well, there was nothing to do about that now. They'd had their fight,
and now Carl was here, in the sweatbox, and he'd just have to wait and
do what little he could to prolong his life. At least he had won. At least
he had shown them.

Locked here in this sweatbox, he was completely at the mercy of the
soldiers. He pictured Parker aiming a pistol at him through the bars of
the sweatbox, pictured himself smiling at the muzzle in one final act of
defiance. That would drive Parker crazy, denying him what he craved—
the fear of others—even at the end. With this image, Carl laughed aloud,
hurting his ribs, and this pain, highlighting the absurdity of laughing at a
time like this, only made him laugh harder.

*They can hit me from behind and beat me while I'm down and lock
me in this cage, but they cannot determine who I am. They can deny me
food and water, but they cannot change me. They can shoot me through
the bars of this sweatbox or hang me from the flagpole or throw me to
the sharks, but they cannot make me cry or beg. I will not allow them. I
will determine my own self. I will not look to them for mercy. I will not
show them weakness. I will stay strong. If they kill me, they will remember my strength; I will force them to live with the memory of my strength
forever.*

*And if I live, I will escape from Phoenix Island, and I will tell the
world. I will bring these people down.*

HE AWOKE when a bug crawled into his ear. He roared at the feel of it,
tried to pick it out with his damaged right hand, failed, and used his left
to pull it free and crush it to paste between his fingers.

At some point, without even knowing it, he'd passed out and slid onto the floor, and now there were bugs on him again. Forcing himself to remain calm, he swatted, brushed, and plucked them away, then smiled grimly to find his homemade bandages had protected the cuts.

It was late in the day. The corrugated metal overhead clicked and pinged as the air outside cooled, yet it still felt like a microwave inside the sweatbox.

Where one leg had lain against the bars, the ankle was red as rare steak and bubbled with blisters. He pushed down his pant leg and forced this new complication from his mind.

The quad remained quiet. He wondered where everyone was. Probably off training. Or maybe in the mess hall. Or getting smoked because of him. He hoped Ross was okay. He hoped Octavia was okay. He hoped Campbell was well on his way back to Texas.

His mind drifted briefly into possibilities: Campbell reaching home, getting in touch with the right people, raising the alarm . . . helicopters landing, journalists and police and soldiers—good soldiers—filling the island, freeing the kids, freeing him . . .

But he shut down this line of thought. It could happen. Could. But *could* was dangerous right now. *Could* led down the dark path of hoping for things he didn't have enough reason to hope for. He had to stick to the facts, had to remember his plan.

Which was . . . ? He wasn't quite sure. Wait. Keep his wounds as clean as possible. Look to escape. And above all else, show no fear.

He was very thirsty.

His stomach growled, too, but with the great heat and his fever, the pain and the damage they'd done to his mouth and jaw and ribs, he had no desire for food. Only water.

As daylight died, a great whining rose from the jungle. Carl gripped the bars of his tiny cage and knew . . .

He was trapped in the sweatbox, and the mosquitoes and biting flies, rising with the coolness of dusk, would eat him alive.

A mosquito landed on his arm. He slapped it, wincing at the pain. He felt another on his neck. Another on his face. More on his lower back where he'd torn away part of the shirt. Heard a buzzing in his ear . . .

And then he was slapping as fast as he could with his left and using his demolished right hand to brush at his skin.

It was no good. Insects swarmed to his cage, covered his flesh, and attacked every bit of exposed skin, no matter how small, biting and stinging and sucking his blood. They packed his ears and his nostrils, whining and biting. They flew into his mouth, and he spit and screamed and breathed through clenched teeth. He swatted his arms, his neck, his face, crushing them by the hundreds, but no sooner had he cleared a patch of skin than they would descend upon him again, covering it, biting, sucking, taking. Finally, he rolled into a tight ball on the floor and covered his head with his arms, and they ate him alive for what seemed like an eternity.

He rolled in the straw trying to crush them and slammed up against the bars of his cell, making his ribs feel like they were breaking all over again. The pain in his head grew worse and worse so that after a while he just fell to the floor and brushed himself in a mindless repetitive motion. The mosquitoes became a living blanket, and Carl rolled onto his front and howled with rage and frustration in the filth and straw at the base of his cage. How long this went on he didn't know—after a time, the unrelenting mosquitoes pitched him into a kind of madness—but then it was full dark, and all at once, the mosquitoes and flies disappeared. He returned to his mind, rolled over, and sat up. His skin burned with their bites, his head burned with fever, and his throat burned with thirst.

With the hard darkness of night, the jungle became a madhouse of sounds: cries and squawks, squeals and snorts, hoots and gibbers—something large bellowing deeper in the woods. And under it all, the constant, deafening chorus of insects pulsed with noise, and this peeping, bleating rhythm was to him the heartbeat of night in the jungle, wild with hunger and menace.

RAIN WOKE HIM.

It fell gently, pattering overhead, a soft sound like mice running across marble. He sat up, awake at once, ignored the several bugs he felt crawling over him, and instead patted the darkness until he found the bowl, which he pushed out between bars.

The rain was cold and good on his throat, and as he washed his cuts and bites and wiped away at least some of the grime covering him, he said a silent prayer of thanks.

He believed in God and feared him, and tried to believe in heaven, hoping one day to see his parents again. But, despite his faith, he could not bring himself to wholly believe what others said about God, and he certainly didn't think he could know the mind of God. He often said prayers of gratitude, but long ago, he had stopped praying with any real conviction for favors or protection. Life had not prepared Carl to believe in the power of those sorts of prayers. Nonetheless, he offered a sincere prayer of thanks, and the rain continued to fall, and Carl drank his fill and cleaned himself and then poured handful after handful over his head to battle the fever.

After a time, the rain slackened, and in the soft rhythm of its fall, Carl slipped once more to sleep, like sand before the tides.

HE DREAMED OF THE PAST.

His father, before the tragedy. Walking together, dirty snow flecked in cinders flanking the sidewalk. The old neighborhood in winter. The cold, the wisp of their winter jackets, his father's height. Happiness.

Older boys, gathered around a shape on the ground. Mean laughter.

His father's voice, loud and strong. The boys scattering, gone.

The lump, a man—old Cobbie, the drunk—his father helping him up, walking him down the street to Rose's Diner. Seating Cobbie at the counter, handing Rose money. Telling her, "Coffee and a sandwich."

Back out on the street, Carl asking what had happened. His father crouching down, placing his big hands on Carl's shoulders. His father's eyes, staring into his. His father telling him, "This is what I do, Carl. And someday when you grow up, it will be up to you to protect them, all the people who can't fend for themselves. A good man won't give in to fear when there's work to be done and someone needs him. Will you do it?"

His own voice: "Yes. I promise . . ."

* * *

CARL WOKE IN THE HEART OF THE NIGHT, still crouching. The dream had been lucid, like a window on the past. He brushed at his wounds and listened to the sounds beyond his cage. Dripping leaves. Jungle sounds, quieter now, birds calling back and forth, sounding somehow lost and mournful. A light breeze rustled the palm fronds and shed a patter of raindrops. The flag clasp dinged rhythmically against the metal pole, like a distant bell tolling a funeral.

He sat back against the cage bars and stretched out his stiff legs.

A deep voice said, "Carl Freeman." It was not a question.

14

DEEP IN THE NIGHT, Octavia scratched the toothbrush across the bathroom tiles, pressing not the bristles but the plastic handle as hard as she could into the floor.

Periodically, her nerves got the best of her, and she stopped and rushed to the toilet. And each time she vomited, she hated herself for her weakness. She had to be strong.

Strong like Carl.

They said he'd fought Decker and three others all at the same time. Beaten them. Then beaten Parker.

She thought of his hands. The big knuckles, the scars. Thought of his square jaw and slightly crooked nose and the light scars around his hazel eyes. Remembered the way those eyes had pleaded with her the last time they'd talked.

And she'd turned on him.

Now she wished she could take it all back.

So what if he'd flipped when he'd seen the article? Of course he had—anybody would have, not knowing the story, just seeing the headline.

She remembered the night she'd set her house afire. Remembered the things her stepfather had done—again—and remembered how he'd looked, passed-out drunk, remembered the strength it had taken to spread the gasoline and strike the match. Counselors and psychiatrists and even the judge had urged her toward remorse, and she'd lied and told them she was sorry, but she was glad she had stopped him, glad she had killed him. After all, hadn't he done his share of killing? He had driven her mother to suicide, and he had so completely killed the innocent girl Octavia had once been that it was difficult now even to believe she'd ever existed as a happy child; it was as if, in destroying her innocence, he'd killed some sweet sister she once had. He was a monster, just as Parker was a monster, and it was not with remorse that she remembered his screams in the fire but with pride.

She just prayed she'd have the strength to slay another monster tomorrow.

It was too late to do anything else. Too late to explain herself to Carl or apologize for flipping out. Too late to really get to know each other.

Back and forth she scraped the brush, back and forth.

They said Carl's fight started because he wouldn't let Decker bully Medicaid. Then Parker came in and tried to break Carl with a stun gun, but Carl wouldn't give in. He didn't let Parker have it until Parker hit Ross.

Oh, Carl . . . they're going to kill you for being decent.

She couldn't stop them all, but maybe she could stop Parker. Maybe then Carl would see who she was. Maybe he would see what she really thought of him. And maybe they both could spend their final moments in the comfort of knowing what could have been between them. In a place like this, where there could be no hope or mercy or justice, what more could one really want?

She paused at her work, not because of the cramping in her hand— she could grit her teeth through that—but to check her progress.

Good.

The end of the toothbrush handle now formed a crude point, still too blunt for her purposes but recognizably dangerous. She brushed away the fluffy shavings of scraped plastic, then got to work again.

Back and forth, back and forth.

By morning, she would finish, even if she needed to stay up all night. By morning, she would have a killing point and, God willing, the strength to use it.

15

FOR ONCE, CARL'S PAIN AND FATIGUE WERE A HELP, as he managed not to jump at the unexpected voice. He would show them no fear. He would give them nothing. He would die with honor.

"That's me."

A pair of eyes shone in the darkness. "And how are you, Mr. Freeman?"

Carl shrugged. It hurt. "You're looking at it."

"Indeed."

Carl studied the darkness around the eyes. The shape of a man, crouching near the cage. Clothed in black. Face painted the color of night. A large man. Very large, Carl realized.

Not that that mattered. Locked in a cage, he was helpless. A six-year-old with a sharp stick and a mean streak could do him in. All Carl could do was wait and see . . . and show no fear.

The deep voice spoke again. "'To tell the secrets of my prison-house, I could a tale unfold whose lightest word would harrow up thy soul, freeze thy young blood, make thy two eyes, like stars, start from their spheres, thy knotted and combined locks to part and each particular hair to stand on end, like quills upon the fretful porpentine: but this eternal blazon must not be to ears of flesh and blood.' Do you know Shakespeare?"

"Nope."

"World War Two? The presidents? Dwight D. Eisenhower once said, 'A soldier's pack is not so heavy a burden as a prisoner's chains.'"

"Well, good for him."

"Perhaps you're more attuned to the wisdom of another president and military man, John F. Kennedy. 'Conformity is the jailer of freedom and the enemy of growth.'"

Carl said nothing.

"They were both right, of course," the man said.

Carl slapped a bug. "Look, let's get down to it, huh? Are you here to kill me?"

A pause. The man leaned his head back and looked up at the stars, and Carl saw his teeth, very white and straight in the darkness. "I'm here to *see* you."

Carl waited.

The man looked at him again, his eyes bright liquid, the eyes of a black panther in the darkest jungle. "I wonder . . . what would you do if I were here to kill you?"

"I'd try to kill you first."

A chuckle. "Excellent. And how would you attempt this?"

"Pretend I was weak. Hope you'd open the box, let me out."

"And then?"

"You could always open the door and find out."

More chuckling, low and burbling, like a subterranean river. "I don't think that would do either of us any good. Some doors are better left unopened. Impatience is a great magnifier of suffering."

"I'm patient enough."

"I believe you are. These are rather unusual circumstances, yes?"

"Who are you?"

"I have many names." Rolling his head back to look at the sky again, he said, "You can call me Captain Midnight."

Carl tried to spit but came up dry. "Sounds like a jerky comic book name."

"It's an old name, the army name for commandos specializing in nighttime maneuvers."

"Is that what you are?"

"Is what what I am?"

"What you said, a nighttime commando."

"It's something I do." The man closed his eyes, and the whole of him became less distinct in the darkness. Carl heard him take a deep breath through his nose. "Do you love the night?"

Carl thought for a second before answering. The man was strange. Carl sensed confidence and power but no meanness. There was a darkness in his manner—something lethal, Carl thought, as if the man himself were a weapon, the personification of violence without the intent—yet for now, the man seemed simply curious, conversational. *I came to see you,* he had said.

All right, then, Carl thought. *No sense holding back.* "I guess I like it all right. I like to walk at night, when nobody else is around, you know, back in Philly. Especially in summer. Like the back streets, the way everything is so still and the way the street seems so wide and you can hear the quiet sounds, like wind in the trees or maybe somebody practicing the piano or people talking on a porch. You see a lot of stuff at night, too. Cats. Skunks, junkies, guys walking their girls. Yeah, I like the night."

He realized he'd been rambling and realized further that his mind was adrift in a sea of fever. None of this seemed real. The man's presence, his immensity, his deep voice, his calm, the spill of words that had flown from Carl's own lips . . . it was all the stuff of dreams, fever dreams, yet from his pain, Carl knew the moment as waking truth.

"I love it, too," the man said, and Carl heard him take another deep breath. "The stillness, the mystery, the sharpening of auxiliary senses. Sounds carry in the darkness, and our fingertips can all but see in the blindness of night. Even taste is enhanced. Have you ever eaten an orange in complete darkness?"

Carl said he had not.

"Here, then," the man said, and after a bit of rustling, an orange appeared in the darkness, as spherical and whole and bright as a miniature sun, and moved forward to the bars of the cage. "It's not an experience to be missed."

"Thank you," Carl said. The orange was cool and damp, and he had to work to get it through the bars. He peeled it slowly with his left hand.

The man waited in silence, watching.

Carl pulled away a section. The first bite was an explosion of taste. It turned to juice on his tongue and filled his mouth, and the man was right; the taste was better in darkness, *more* in the darkness. "Amazing."

"Indeed," the man said. "You're not afraid of me."

Carl shook his head. "I'm from Philly. I don't scare easy."

The man's laughter was deep and dark, a night sound. "You've conducted some primitive first aid on yourself."

Carl looked down to where he'd wrapped his ribs. "I couldn't do much. I washed with rainwater, tore off part of my shirt, and wrapped it around my ribs. The knife got me pretty bad. Mainly, I was just trying to keep the bugs out."

"Before you woke, I was admiring your handiwork." He pointed to the dead bugs littering the ground just outside the cage. "The samurai respected insects. To them, insects represented efficiency and victory."

"I'm not a samurai."

"No? And how do you know that?"

Carl shrugged.

"Miyamoto Musashi—the greatest samurai of all time—encouraged his young warriors to wander the countryside, fighting. He told them to carry no money and to sleep outside and to get thrown into prison on purpose. Do you know why?"

Carl ate his orange and said nothing.

"So they could extricate themselves through their own power and wisdom. Why are you in this cage?"

"They hit me from behind. I didn't see them coming. It was my mistake."

"Ah, yes . . . fair enough, but what I'm asking is why they wanted to put you in this cage in the first place. I've heard one report. Now I'd like to hear yours."

Carl told him. He started with Decker and Medicaid and told it straight through Parker to when they hit him from behind and how he'd awakened here. The man didn't interrupt. "Parker said he's going to execute me."

"Did he?" the man said, but his voice lilted, making his words sound less like a question than an expression of amusement. "From what I understand, Drill Sergeant Parker already did his best to kill you in the barracks."

"He came at me with a knife."

"And how do you explain your survival? Drill Sergeant Parker is older than you, well trained, and combat experienced. He's killed before. Many times."

"Well," Carl said, and paused. Normally, bad-mouthing a drill sergeant was a one-way ticket to trouble, but he was already in trouble, and something told him that this Captain Midnight guy had more respect for truth than he did for Parker. "He was stupid. He forced me into it. He wanted to hurt me since day one, and he kept pushing, and finally, when he hurt my friend, I let him have it."

"I would say you did."

"Honestly," Carl said, "he can't fight. He puts too much faith into muscle. He's always flexing and everything. He lets anger get in the way, too. And he pretends things are what he wants them to be, not what they really are."

"Interesting. Please elaborate."

"When you fight, you have to know the situation. Like I understood he was really strong, so I wasn't going to wrestle him. And I knew he was left-handed, so I moved mostly to my left, away from his power. I just worked speed and angles and broke him down, and that made him mad, so he kept getting sloppier and sloppier, and that made it so I could start landing heavier shots."

"What about his weapons?"

"He tried the stun gun, but I knocked that out of his hand. That messed with his head."

"The knife?"

"I wasn't happy to see it. Blades are scary. But part of me . . ." He shrugged. "Maybe part of me *was* happy to see it. I mean I was scared, but I also knew I had his heart in my back pocket then. If he was confident, he wouldn't have brought it out. But he must have thought he needed it."

"What should he have done instead?"

"Readjusted. He should have let go of what he wanted to happen and taken a good look at what was really happening and done something about it."

"Could he have beaten you if he had?"

Carl was silent for a second. Then he said, "No. Probably not."

"And what about your current situation? What's really happening? And what are you going to do about it?"

"Right now, I'm finishing this orange and having a conversation. Then I guess I'll just wait and see. I figure they'll probably kill me."

"This doesn't frighten you?"

Carl shrugged. "Not really. I mean, I don't want to die, but if I'm going to die, I'm going to die. You know what I mean? Parker's hoping I'll beg for mercy or kiss his boots or whatever, but I'll tell you right now that's not going to happen."

"Musashi said, 'The way of the warrior is resolute acceptance of death.'"

Carl nodded. "Maybe I should have been a samurai, then."

The man showed his teeth again. "Perhaps. And perhaps it is not too late. But speaking of lateness . . . 'the glow-worm shows the matin to be near, and 'gins to pale his uneffectual fire: Adieu, adieu!' Carl Freeman, remember me."

He turned and, silent as nightfall, disappeared into the darkness.

16

THEY WERE OUT ON THE PAVEMENT. It had rained in the night, and now, beneath the rising sun, fog spun and lifted from the blacktop in pale, little rags, like so many ghosts drifting away. Normally, the smell of rain was comforting to Octavia—a reminder of home, Washington State, where it always rained—but this morning, the heavy smell of decay drifted out of the jungle, and the smell of wet earth filled her nostrils, and she breathed the smell of worms until it seemed they filled her, wriggling in her stomach, as if she were already dead and buried. . . .

She was very tired.

"Form it up!"

Octavia pushed close to the front and all the way to the left. She needed to be close.

"Attention!"

She came to attention, wobbling only slightly. Not bad, considering how, after weeks of sleep deprivation, she'd stayed up all night.

The shank was in her pocket. She prayed she wouldn't have to use it. She also prayed that if she did have to use it, it would be good enough to finish the job. And that she would be good enough, too. Strong enough.

"Good morning, orphans," First Sergeant Oteka said.

"Hooah!"

"Motivated," Oteka said. "Today, orphans, is a special day. A very special day. Today, at seventeen hundred hours, you are meeting a great man, the man who created Phoenix Island, Commander Stark."

Everyone hooah-ed again.

Octavia swayed with fatigue. She took a deep breath and forced her eyes wide open. *Wake up,* she told herself. *You have to be on point . . . for Carl.*

"We will spend this day in preparation," Oteka said. "Training Base One will be completely squared away. Spit and polish, orphans, spit and polish. Everything dress-right-dress: the barracks, your footlockers, your gear, yourselves. Everything must shine. But first, we must see to cleaning of a different kind. As you know, I will soon be leaving Phoenix Island for my next assignment. It has been my pleasure to oversee your initial training, and it is with complete confidence that I pass you to Drill Sergeant Parker, who will oversee Blue Phase and prepare those lucky individuals who will one day train full-time under Commander Stark."

Oteka nodded toward Parker, then stepped aside, flanking the formation.

"Thank you, First Sergeant," Parker said, and swaggered to the front, whooping like a motivational speaker entering a school auditorium. A sling cradled one arm, and bruises covered his face. "Woo-ee, orphans! You're in for a treat today. Yup, you're finally going to see how things really work around here." A long machete hung in a sheath at his side. From what everyone had been whispering, he was going to use it to kill Carl.

From the machete, her eyes went to Parker's thick neck, made cartoonishly thick now by the foam brace he'd been wearing since the fight.

She pictured the shank passing through that foam, pushing through the thick muscle, and sinking into the veins. Severing them. Pictured it pulling free, plunging in again. Pictured an indistinct spray of blood and a struggle that ended badly for her. How many holes would she be able to put in him before they took her down? Would she even have the strength to do it? Fatigue and anxiety played tag in her empty stomach, making her feel like she might hurl again.

Her hand gripped the shank.

"Bring him out," Parker said to the trio of muscular soldiers beside the sweatbox. "Careful. He's scrappy as a Chihuahua."

Her muscles tensed. Parker was just ahead of her, with his back turned. *Not yet,* she told herself, staying in the ranks, keeping the weapon concealed. She had to be certain Parker was going to go through with it, had to be sure it wasn't another bluff.

But then, seeing Carl for the first time, she forgot all about Parker.

Oh, Carl . . .

Her heart broke at the sight of his limp body as the soldiers lifted him from the sweatbox. His head lolled loosely in semiconsciousness, and his face, always so handsome and intense, was a purple balloon of bruised swelling.

Carl, Carl, Carl . . .

She squeezed her eyes shut, fighting back tears, and breathed through her nose. *Hold it together,* she told herself. *You have to hold it together.*

She heard thumping and laughter and opened her eyes only to wish she hadn't. They had spilled Carl onto the ground. Parker laughed as they kicked him, hard, over and over.

Nausea filled her shaking body. Why didn't Carl cry out? Was he unconscious? How else could he keep from crying out?

No . . . he wasn't unconscious. As they bent to lift him, he punched one soldier hard enough that the muscle-head wobbled and fell on his butt. So they started kicking Carl again.

She hated the intensity of the other kids, the excitement shining in their eyes. Many smiled. She saw them nudge, saw them crane their necks for a clearer view. They sickened her.

"Leave some for me," Parker said. "Jenson, stand up. I told you he was scrappy."

Just do it, she told herself. *Just do it now, while he's distracted. Walk calmly out of the ranks. Be quiet and act natural and then run the last couple of steps and bury the point in his neck again and again and again until it's over for both of you.*

She took a deep breath and smoothed her hands on her pants, drying the palms. She would need a good grip.

They dragged Carl across the pavement. Seeing his battered face broke her heart all over again. He sagged between them, his head bobbing as if he were fighting unconsciousness. They dumped him on the pavement at Parker's feet.

Parker smiled. His hand went to the handle of the machete, but he didn't unsheathe it.

Octavia's hand went to her own weapon.

"Well, well, well," Parker said, "what do we have here?" He turned to the platoon, smiling so hard the scabs on his lips split open, sending blood running down his teeth. "Our old friend Hollywood, the individual." To Carl, he said, "I told you what would happen, didn't I? Scripture and verse. And lo and behold . . . so it has come to pass. Like a miracle, Hollywood . . . our own little miracle."

Carl stirred and pushed himself off the pavement with shaking arms.

Parker took a step back. The other soldiers hovered, ready to start kicking again.

But Carl simply fought his way onto all fours, then rocked back, kneeling before Parker.

Parker laughed. "That's it. Just as I said. It's a pity you spent all that time in the box. Probably don't even have the voice to beg."

Carl lifted his head and stared through swollen eyes at the drill sergeant.

"Leave him alone!"

Everyone shifted.

Ross broke the ranks, his bruised face twisted with indignation. "Leave him alone, you animal!"

"Ross—*again*? What are you, brain damaged?" Parker snapped his fingers. Decker and his friends tackled Ross and dragged him off toward the barracks.

Parker chuckled. "We'll deal with him later. But right now the spotlight's on this individual. You know what time it is, Hollywood. You know what you have to do. You remember." He shoved one muddy combat boot toward Carl. "You don't have to say a word. Just bend down there and kiss my boots. Lick 'em clean in front of your audience, and I'll let you rejoin the ranks."

Just do it, Carl, she thought. *Just give in this once.*

Carl shook his head.

"Last chance, Hollywood! Either kiss my boots, or I'm going to cut off your stupid head!"

Carl rocked back and extended both of his middle fingers.

Parker roared curses.

Tears burned Octavia's eyes. *Oh, Carl . . . you just got us both killed.* This was it.

Gripping her weapon, she prayed, *Please, God, grant me strength.* She broke ranks, starting for Parker.

Parker unsheathed the machete.

Octavia pulled the shank from her pocket, keeping it low and hidden at her side.

"Now," Parker said, raising the machete overhead. "Now, you miserable son-of-a—"

"Stop!"

Everything froze. The command was so loud and deep, so full of power, even the wind seemed to cease.

Parker looked toward where the voice had come from and lowered the machete to his side.

Octavia put her own weapon back in her pocket. A hand closed on her shoulder, and Oteka's voice whispered, "Back into the ranks, Gregoric," then, louder she yelled, "Attention!"

Octavia returned to her spot and snapped to attention. From behind the ranks strode a man who looked like he had stepped straight from the pages of a comic book. Easily six and a half feet tall, with broad shoulders, a narrow waist, and bulging muscles, he moved smoothly, embodying all the fluid grace and power of a panther. He was dressed in all black—black combat boots, black cargo pants, a black tank top, and a black beret—and his dark eyes stared with withering intensity out of his ruggedly handsome, deeply tanned face.

"Drill Sergeant Parker," the giant in the black beret said.

"Yes, Commander Stark!" Parker said, standing at rigid attention.

Commander Stark, Octavia thought. Oteka's special guest had shown up early.

"Sheath your weapon, Drill Sergeant," Stark said.

Relief flooded through Octavia.

But Parker did not sheathe the machete. "Commander, he attacked me—"

Stark took a step forward and dropped his voice. "Are you questioning my authority?"

Parker took a step back. "No, Commander. It's just—"

"I have given my order."

Parker's muscles twitched. His knuckles were white on the handle of the machete. "Yes, Commander."

"Unless, of course, you wish to challenge Mr. Freeman to an official duel."

Parker's face underwent an amazing transformation, in a split second going from a mask of frustration to one of wide-smiling excitement. "Yes, Commander!"

No, she thought, *not a duel . . .* Carl couldn't even stand up; how could he fight?

"Of course . . ." Stark said, a sly smile coming onto his face now, "I would give your opponent time to recover." With this comment, she saw an understanding pass between the men. The drill sergeant's smile fell away, and she had to fight to keep one from appearing on her face. "And, observing the rules of dueling, if Mr. Freeman were to accept your challenge, as I assume he would, the terms of said duel would be of his choosing. He could, for example, choose weaponless combat." He paused, his smile growing.

Parker said nothing.

"Well, Drill Sergeant? Do you issue an official challenge?"

Parker said something she couldn't hear.

Stark's smile disappeared. "Sound off, Parker. I want everyone to hear your answer. Do you or do you not challenge Carl Freeman to single combat to commence upon his full recuperation and under provisions selected by him?"

"No, Commander," Parker said.

"I see. One more of Caesar's many deaths."

Half a dozen soldiers appeared behind Commander Stark, four men and two women, all looking around twenty years old, incredibly fit, and intensely dangerous. Each dressed like the commander, with one exception: instead of a tank top, each wore a black T-shirt emblazoned with a red phoenix.

"Help that soldier to his feet," Stark said. "Pay him the respect he deserves."

The soldiers who'd kicked Carl moved away, and these new soldiers lifted Carl to his feet. Carl managed an exhausted smile, and Octavia's heart cheered. Maybe everything was going to be all right after all. Maybe this was the end of something. A new beginning. Her legs felt rubbery as her adrenaline faded away.

Stark unclipped a canteen from his belt. "You must all remember this day forever. Remember the manner in which this soldier faced his own death. Resolute acceptance, orphans . . . resolute acceptance of his own demise." He raised the canteen overhead and gestured with the other hand toward Carl. "Behold Carl Freeman! A true warrior! I call him brother and ask that he drink from my own water." He extended his canteen in Carl's direction.

Carl shook himself free of the hands holding him, staggered to accept the canteen, and drank greedily.

"Hooah!" Stark bellowed.

The platoon's thunderous response puzzled Octavia—only minutes ago, they'd clamored for Carl's blood—but she didn't care. She wanted very badly to join their cheer but could not. Tears overcame her. It was over. The nightmare was finally over. . . .

17

CARL OPENED HIS EYES to see fan blades whirling overhead. He lay in a comfortable bed with low metal rails on each side. Next to the bed stood a metal pole, from which hung a bag of clear liquid. The liquid dripped slowly into a skinny tube that snaked from the bottom of the bag into an IV inserted in his arm.

A hospital room.

Smelling swampy decay, he tensed.

The Chop Shop . . . .

He pictured the kid he'd seen while sitting on the cattle truck, the kid raising his hand, his mouth hanging open, and remembered Eric's journal: *We saw them standing at the fence, guys we knew, guys who went to the Chop Shop and never came back. They just stared, moaning like zombies. . . .*

Carl shuddered.

But he felt fine. Better than fine. He felt good. It didn't seem possible.

He remembered Parker raising the machete in the air, sunlight flashing off the blade, and then the voice, deep and familiar, telling Parker to stop. . . .

The voice belonged to his shadow visitor, Captain Midnight.

Commander Stark.

He'd stopped Parker and saved Carl's life.

After the nightmarish ordeal in the sweatbox, his survival felt like nothing short of a miracle. He said a prayer of thanks and studied the room around him.

It was small and neat, with pale blue walls the color of a robin's egg and a single window, through which Carl could see bright daylight.

Despite the bars on the window. . . .

That's it, Carl thought. *I'm out of here.* He'd had enough of cell bars. He needed to get out of here and find a way off this horrible island.

He tried to sit up, but broad canvas straps bound him to the bed. Restraints clutched his chest, arms, hips, legs, and ankles. He strained against them, but it was pointless. There was no escape.

A door opened.

"Already awake?"

Carl turned his head and saw the bearded man he'd seen from the cattle truck the first day, the doctor, the man with eyes of fire.

Without light flashing upon the glasses, the thick lenses made the doctor's eyes look big and round and eager. A smile parted the beard, the teeth very white against the glossy black whiskers. "You supposed to sleep thirty minutes more . . . so soon." His accent was heavy. Maybe Mexican, maybe South American. Carl didn't know.

He crossed the room and leaned over Carl.

Carl pressed back into his pillow as the doctor held his index finger in front of Carl's face. "How many fingers you see?"

"One."

"Now?"

"Three."

"Is good. *Tres. Sí.* Is strong boy. Many boys come to me, never I see one so strong as this boy. As you. What I think I like most . . ." The doctor extended his index finger again and lowered it toward Carl's face.

"Hey," Carl said, "What are you doing?" He tried to make his voice strong, but it was raspy, the voice of an old man. "Don't touch me."

The nut was going to poke him in the eye.

Carl closed his eye just as the fingertip pressed softly into its inside corner. He could hear the doctor breathing through his nose, could smell garlic on the man's breath. Then the doctor said, "What I think I like most is to see how you do with the *cheep.*"

"Get off," Carl said and turned his head side to side. He was trapped. The more he fought, the more the restraints seem to tighten, crushing him in his own fear.

The doctor chuckled and withdrew his finger. "So much fire this boy has. So, so much. So machismo. Could he be the one?"

"You let me go, or I'll break your nose."

The doctor laughed. "I like this very much. You American boys . . . sometimes, I think it is only you who are like this. You all tied up, but still you say these things to me."

Carl gave him his hardest stare. "I'll do it. I swear. You don't let me up, I'll break your nose. I don't know when, but I will."

The doctor stroked his beard. "A boy from my country, he tied up like you, is gentle like a little baby. He look around, say to himself, this is bad. And he is right." He tapped his head. "He believe in his mind the bad thing, it can happen to him."

"You don't let me up, you know what's going to happen to you."

The doctor's smile fell away, and Carl didn't like the way bearded face changed, the man looking angry, thoughtful, and amused, all at once, like Carl was a fly and he was thinking about plucking his wings.

The doctor said, "Perhaps maybe you will be the one. Perhaps maybe you will not. We will see. But he makes me wait." He crossed the room with his hands folded behind his back. He paused beneath the window, face upturned, and once again his lenses gleamed, looking this time not so much likes circles of flame but more like the headlights of an oncoming car. "I feel the pain to wait. I see a boy such as you, the good muscles, the good reactions to medicines, and I ask myself: Is this the boy? And I want to know. But he makes me wait." He sighed.

"Let me up, and we'll see about things right now."

The headlights aimed directly at him. "Ah—no is problem, the waiting. What else do I have but to wait? There is no opera, no café, no jai alai. They even take the greyhounds from me. So I wait. But I think perhaps maybe when he say it is time, I bring my tools and make you sing first. I miss the music."

Carl was trying to think of something to say when the door swung open again, and a loud voice Carl recognized said, "Awake already? Carl Freeman, you amaze me."

"Commander Stark," the doctor said, and bowed slightly.

Carl filled with relief.

Stark approached the bed, smiling widely, all six foot six of him reminding Carl of a gymnast, all speed and power and no extra bulk, every movement fluid. He stood with his combat boots spread wide, hands on hips, his broad shoulders squared with Carl. Above a neck corded with muscle, his square chin gave way to a warm smile, a crooked fighter's nose, and piercing, dark eyes that flashed with intelligence and vigor. A black beret sat atop his close-shaven skull. "Dr. Vispera, has anyone else ever woken early from one of your timed comas?"

"No, Commander. He is first."

"Indeed," Stark said, and smiled. "Well, Carl, let's get you unbuckled. Ready to get out of this place?"

18

THEY WALKED SIDE BY SIDE DOWN THE ROAD, talking easily, Stark refusing formalities and treating Carl like an old friend. It was surreal. Strangest of all was how natural it felt, the two of them matching strides and chatting like father and son.

For one reason or another, Stark liked him. Carl wanted to keep it that way. If he could stay close to Stark, he'd be safe from Parker until Campbell blew the whistle on Phoenix Island.

Carl asked how long he'd been unconscious.

"Two weeks, minus half an hour or so. Dr. Vispera induced the coma to maximize healing, then got busy fixing you. Rehydrated you, stitched your wounds, drove out infection."

"Two weeks? Really?" Fear goosed him—a lot could happen in two weeks. "Are my friends okay?"

"Friends?"

"Neil Ross and Octavia Gregoric," Carl said. "Are they all right?"

Stark patted his back. "Don't worry, Carl. After everything you've been through, it's understandable that you might assume the worst, but trust me: everyone is fine."

"You're sure?"

Stark laughed. "Positive."

Carl relaxed . . . a little. He was afraid to ask what he really wanted to ask.

Stark picked up on it. "You must have a million questions. Fire away. Anything you like."

"Do you, um," Carl said, deciding to go for it but feeling his face go hot. "Do kids . . . get executed here?"

Stark stared at him for a long second—then burst into laughter. This was no chuckle. It was an explosion of deep, rich laughter that stopped Stark in the middle of the road and bent him in half, the sound of it so full and cathartic that by the time Stark straightened again, wiping tears from his eyes, Carl realized he was sputtering laughter himself.

"Sorry to laugh like that," Stark said, and put his hand once more on Carl's shoulder. "Really, I shouldn't. Boot camps breed the wildest rumors and speculation. If I'd gone through everything you've been through, I'd believe something like that, too. Here's the simple truth: things got out of hand. *Drill Sergeant Parker* got out of hand. None of that was your fault. You're safe now, and I've talked to Parker. I'll check on your friends, too. What were their names, Ross and Pandora?"

"Ross and Octavia," Carl said, feeling enormously relieved. "Thank you."

"No problem," Stark said. "I'm sorry you went through all that, but now I'd like you to move past it and dwell on the positive. Your healing, for example. Amazing isn't it?"

"It still doesn't make sense," Carl admitted and shook his head. "I feel better than ever. My cuts are almost healed. My bones feel good as new. The pain's gone."

"Welcome to the post-human age. Dr. Vispera used titanium oxide nanotubes, stem cells, and electrical stimulation to mend your bones. You've been receiving human growth hormone since your arrival on the island, along with daily doses of the best vitamins, herbs, protein, and creatine. It's all coming together. But of course your new body will take some getting used to."

New body? Carl thought. He held out his hands and looked at them. They were fixed up—that seemed miraculous enough—but new? Looked like the same old hands, scarred knuckles and all. . . .

Stark chuckled. "And more: Dr. Vispera gave you certain enhancements during your coma. He implanted numerous small chips into your organs and glands and injected hundreds more into your ventricle, and now they've spread throughout your body, attaching to smooth muscle along your circulatory system."

Suddenly, Carl felt like he was crawling with ticks. "What for?"

"For now, they're mapping you, electrically and chemically. Don't look so startled, Carl, and don't worry. Even now, chips at various points monitor your organs and record your movement, your muscle contractions, the transportation of oxygen, the firing of nerves. They're learning your processes. Later, they'll help to improve those processes."

Imagining the things burrowing into him, Carl had the wild urge to start scratching.

Stark said, "They are like musical instruments. The master chip will be the conductor."

Vispera had talked about music. The memory sent goose bumps over Carl's flesh. "I don't want another chip."

Stark patted his shoulder. "Well, that will be entirely up to you when the time arrives. Presently, certain risks remain. We're moving to an improved version, and Dr. Vispera still needs to fine-tune implantation. Soon enough, however, the procedure will be completely safe, and you'll be allowed to choose. Personally, I can't wait for the opportunity. The chip will change our lives forever."

"You're getting one?"

"Wouldn't miss it for the world. I myself have also received the blood treatment he gave you while you were out."

"Blood treatment?" This kept sounding worse and worse.

"You'd lost a lot of blood. Dr. Vispera replaced it with special blood, blood to which he's added his blood virus."

"Wait—he put a *virus* in my *blood*?"

Stark chuckled. "Relax, Carl. It's not really a virus. It just acts like one. When a real virus invades our system, it hides for a while and then starts pumping out copies of itself. It reproduces inside us. Much like the Special Forces, it enters the back country of its host with a relatively small contingent, then raises an army behind enemy lines."

Carl imagined little silver triangles tumbling along through his blood, breaking into smaller triangles, these swelling to full size, breaking apart, filling his veins. A shudder of revulsion went through him.

Stark laughed and patted his shoulder again. "This is great news, Carl. The virus is strengthening your white blood cells and making your red blood cells capable of carrying more oxygen. That will make you stronger, help you build muscle, and greatly improve your endurance."

"Like blood doping?" He remembered a top amateur boxer in Philly getting stripped of his medal for that.

"No—this is much more effective . . . and permanent. For the rest of your life, you'll heal more quickly, and you'll be more resistant to everything from infection to malaria. Look—a pig." Stark pointed into the forest, and Carl saw a dark shape disappear into heavy vegetation. "Vicious animals, these island pigs. See that peak?" He motioned toward the tallest of the stony ridges that ran across the center of the island. "The forest on the opposite slope is thick with pigs. Avoid it. End up among them, and you'll be lucky to keep your fancy new blood."

Carl nodded. Nothing seemed quite real.

"Dr. Vispera is no stranger to blood," Stark said. "Before political unrest brought him to Phoenix Island, he was the 'inquisitor' for a particularly brutal South American dictator. Give him a sewing needle and thirty minutes, and he can reveal the deepest secrets of any prisoner."

"He was a torturer?"

Stark nodded. "You've heard the saying 'The eyes are the window to the soul'? Dr. Vispera has his own saying: 'The nerves are the keys to the truth.' Clever fellow, his 'keys' have a double meaning: they unlock truth, but he's also referring to the keys of a piano."

A chill went through Carl as he remembered the doctor saying he'd make him sing, that he missed the music.

"He considers himself a musician of pain. A maestro. Pain is his piano, and the victim's nerves are his piano strings."

Great, Carl thought. *I threatened to break his nose.*

Stark said, "Despite his monstrousness, he is not so different from you."

"Not so different from me? The guy's a psycho."

"You are both individuals of pronounced talent . . . but born in the wrong place at the wrong time."

"I don't get it."

They passed under a thicker canopy, the roadside trees arching overhead, meeting imperfectly, dappling the road in sunlight and shadow. Stark said in an airy voice, "If Dr. Vispera had been born in London or Detroit, he would no doubt have risen through the ranks of respected physicians and scientists and established himself in more *conventional* ways. Unfortunately for him—and even less fortunately for his symphony of victims—he was born in place that valued power over science. Sometimes, the only difference between a Nobel Prize winner and a war criminal is geography. Do you understand?"

"Not really," Carl said.

"Consider your strengths: fighting ability, physical endurance, battle courage. You have a gift for remaining composed during moments of extreme emotional duress, moments that would tear most boys and men to shreds. Like Dr. Vispera, you suffer from the importability of assets. It's a paradox. In today's society, where the American child is rewarded for sitting still in a grid of chairs day after day, your natural strengths have become liabilities. Because you are a young man of action who believes in his view of the world, because you fight when you deem it necessary, you've ended up here."

Carl nodded. "The stuff I'm good at gets me in trouble."

"Yes—because of the time and place of your birth. When you stand up to bullies, American society deems you an animal. They keep putting you in cages and finally send you here. To me."

"It's so stupid," Carl said. "At school they have these anti-bullying programs, but they never do anything. Nothing real. Then you do something, and they punish you for it."

"Institutionalized hypocrisy works only in corrupt and convoluted systems. If you were born in a cave during prehistoric times, Carl, you would be a respected leader. Strong enough to protect your people, smart enough to make the right decisions, consistent enough to make them believe in you. You were simply born in the wrong place at the wrong time. Even a slight adjustment—say one hundred years and one hundred miles—and you would've made a very successful farmer or stonemason."

Carl thought for a few strides. "But if I'd been born someplace else or at a different time or whatever, I wouldn't be me, right? I mean, I'd be somebody else, with different strengths."

"Perhaps. The good news is you're here now." Stark spread his arms. "This is a world outside of time, a world that recognizes your strengths. And here you will have guidance. I'll give you skills that will empower you to make your own destiny."

Initially, Carl had assumed Phoenix Island was just another teen boot camp, a bunch of gung ho ex-soldiers forcing kids to play army in an olive-drab hybrid of punishment and rehabilitation. Now, after everything he'd read in the journal and all the brutality he'd experienced, he wasn't sure of anything. Still, after his stupid question about the executions, Carl wasn't about to ask Stark about mercenaries and the mysterious Old Man.

Instead, he kept it simple. "Army stuff?"

"That's part of it, but I'll teach you to be far more than a grunt, and in the end, it will be your choice whether you want to become a soldier."

A soldier? It was a job he'd considered while growing up, one that had always seemed real to him, and he knew a lot of cops—his own father included—had gone into the military before joining the police force. But now, after everything he'd experienced here? Not likely. . . .

Stark gestured toward a side road. "Turn here."

They left the main road and walked uphill.

Stark said, "Many places in the world still value men like us. We can get rich in these places. I have. But what is money? In the United States, it's everything. Money is status, power. In that world, the kings of the caves drive Jaguars with Harvard stickers in the back window. Nonsense." He spat into the weeds alongside the road. "I wouldn't last one week in American suburbia. The first person who tried to involve me in small talk about mulch would soon find my thumbs jammed into his eye sockets."

Carl laughed. "People do talk about stupid stuff. I've seen kids sit around and talk about nothing. Somebody will bring up a TV show or a singer or something, and then they'll just sit there and agree about how they all like the same thing and then talk about it for *hours*. It's weird—it actually makes them happy."

"Indeed. How could you ever succeed in a world like that? They're asleep, and everyone—their teachers and parents and future bosses—wants them to stay asleep. A boy like you might wake them up."

It made sense. School and pretty much everything else—except boxing and hanging out with friends—had often seemed entirely pointless to Carl. He'd always assumed it was a problem with him, not the other way around.

Stark said, "Here, your strengths will make you a great man. Just as Dr. Vispera's strengths have made *him* a great man."

That made Carl stop for a moment. "A great man? He's a torturer."

"The world outside America is full of people who would eat our livers raw for the simple pleasure of filling their bellies. If I capture one of these murderers and he has information that could mean life or death to my men, I will use any means necessary to extract that information. The comfort of one bad man is not worth the lives of ten good ones."

"I guess it sort of makes sense when you put it that way."

The continued walking, and, winding uphill out of the dark forest, the road opened onto a plateau, where at the center of a bright green clearing sat a massive camouflage hangar easily a football field in length and probably three or four stories high. It looked like the sort of thing the military would use for aircraft, but Carl saw no landing strip or planes. Behind it rose the tall mountain peak, its gray raw rock towering overhead like an enormous, unfinished statue, a half-sculpted bust, humanoid yet not necessarily human, God's rendition of man or monster. . . .

Stark spread his arms, an epic gesture from a man of his great size, and said, "Welcome to my home."

THE STEAKS WERE RARE, served with crisp salad, wedges of bright red tomato on top, alongside mashed potatoes on heavy white plates beside tall glasses of ice water beaded with condensation. Carl sawed off another chunk of steak and forked it into his mouth.

Nothing had ever tasted so good.

Stark watched Carl like an amused parent. "Slow down, Carl. Chew your food. Taste it. This isn't the mess hall."

Carl smiled without showing his teeth, the piece of steak a lump in one cheek. With conscious effort, he slowed his chewing. It was all so good, and he was so hungry, he felt like tilting the plate and taking it all in a swallow.

Stark gestured with his steak knife. "Do you find it strange that I eat my meals here, in this . . . garage?"

Carl shook his head. They sat in folding metal chairs at a folding plastic table, at the center of the large, open space partitioned from the rest of the hangar by a long curtain. An old white refrigerator hummed against the wall between an oven and a sink. Two-by-fours and wallboard partitioned off a few small rooms on either side of the hangar. Everything was clean and simple.

"Since you're polite enough to lie, I'll be polite enough to pretend I believe you."

Carl laughed. "No, I mean it. It's nice."

Stark was quiet for a moment, seeming to think, then said, "I lead a very simple life, Carl, what you might call a Spartan existence. You know the Spartans?"

Carl said he'd seen 300.

"Ah, yes, the brave Three Hundred at Thermopylae. A timeless story and an important bit of history. It's long been a favorite of US special ops: the SEALs, Berets, Rangers, Recon, Delta. It's a story we can all relate to: a small force of well-trained warriors, vastly outnumbered, waiting for reinforcements that never arrived." A fierce smile came onto his face. "But kicking a lot of butt while they waited."

Carl nodded, shoveling another spoonful of mashed potatoes into his mouth.

Stark said, "To Spartans, only warfare mattered. Everything else— money, jewelry, decoration of any kind—meant nothing. Their simple lifestyle suits me. I have no desire for fine things: flashy cars, expensive homes, big-screen TVs. None of it. You get a few things like that, you know what happens?"

Carl shook his head. "I've never owned much."

Stark put down his silverware and tented his fingers. "I'll tell you, then. You get a few things, you want more. And more. And more. For the common person, owning nice things provides the only sense of power they'll ever know. Ownership is poisonous, Carl. Never accumulate things for the sake of having them, and never confuse possessions with power."

Carl nodded. It made sense.

Stark asked, "Are you familiar with Greek mythology?"

Carl shrugged.

"Zeus?"

Carl swallowed a particularly delicious bite of steak. "He was king of the gods, right?"

This earned a smile. "Correct. He lived atop Mount Olympus, where he could look down on the world of his worshippers, the humans. Do you know the story of Prometheus?"

Carl shook his head.

"When the world was young," Stark said, "mankind dwelled in caves and lived simple, happy lives, existing only to worship the gods."

"Like Adam and Eve?"

Stark smiled again. "Yes, and ancient Greece was these worshippers' Garden of Eden until someone—not a serpent but a titan named Prometheus—destroyed paradise . . . with a gift."

Carl thought for a second. "An apple?"

Stark shook his head. "Fire. Prometheus stole fire from the gods, carried it down Mount Olympus, and shared it with mankind. At first they feared the flames, but when Prometheus showed people how they could cook their meat, brighten darkness, and make themselves warm and dry on even the coldest, wettest nights, fire seemed a great blessing."

"But it was really a curse?"

"It was both." Stark leaned back in his chair. "Before this, Zeus had paid little attention to his primitive worshippers. To him, their lives were as brief and predictable as the lives of houseflies are to us. But he woke one morning, looked down from Olympus, and saw a changed world. Mankind had abandoned their caves and moved into houses, towns, cities—some with castles at the center. Women wore fine clothes and jewelry and played harps of exquisite design. Men brandished swords and spears and wore shining armor and helmets. A few even wore *crowns*."

"Zeus was pissed?"

Stark nodded. "He unleashed three punishments. One for Prometheus, which we won't discuss while you're eating. Here, have some more." He pushed more steak onto Carl's plate.

Carl grinned. "Thanks." Everything was so great. The food was awesome, and there was plenty of it. No rush, no one glaring at him while he ate. It was so nice to just relax and talk, and not about how everything sucked or about bad stuff that might happen. Stark was interesting. Out of nowhere, Carl realized he'd like to look into this stuff, maybe even read a book about the Greek myths.

"The second punishment," Stark said, "came in the form of a beautiful woman and a golden box. We'll save this one for later, too."

Carl shrugged, chewing.

Stark said, "The final punishment was mercy."

Carl slowed his chewing, tilting his head and narrowing one eye. He swallowed. "How can mercy be a punishment?"

"Zeus knew that, left on its own, mankind would punish itself—would eventually destroy itself—with the offending gift. Fire had given them not only light and heat but also ambition, imagination, and invention. You see, fire begat technology, which remains both a blessing and a curse—and with which we still play gods . . . and punish ourselves. Do you understand?"

Carl nodded. "I think so."

"I feel for the children of today," Stark said. "Pampered like little godlings, they are weak and unhappy, with nothing to hold on to, nothing to worship but their own desires. Nothing is honored. Nothing is sacred. In a world where nothing matters, they are overfed and put to pasture. Is this how we're meant to live? No, it's how sheep are meant to live. That's what most children are today—fat little sheep, content in their electronic pasture fields. They spend their lives staring at television screens and blabbing on cell phones, escaping into video games, and talking for hours on end about nothing on the internet."

It was a lot to take in. What Stark was saying seemed true enough, but before Carl could really think it through, Stark spoke again.

"But," Stark said, and raised a finger, "what happens when one child isn't a sheep? What happens when he disrupts the flock? They punish him. If that doesn't work, they medicate him. If that doesn't work, they cage him. And if that doesn't work, they send him to me."

"What if that doesn't work?" Carl asked.

"It always works."

They were silent for a time. Stark ladled more potatoes onto Carl's plate. Carl thanked him and went to work on the potatoes, wondering exactly what Stark had meant by *it always works*. Certainly Phoenix Island didn't work for some kids. Sure, he had probably seen only the worst of it, and a lot of them would adapt, but what about a kid like Medicaid? What happened to someone like him?

"I was thinking of ancient Greece and the Spartans when I designed this place," Stark said. "At the age of seven, Spartan boys left their families and entered military training they called the *agoge*. Training was intense, even brutal. Boys learned to fight and steal to survive. Childhoods were destroyed, but survivors emerged as respected men and fearsome warriors."

Carl remembered the movie *300*, the part with the little kids fighting, the main character kneeling on top of some other kid, beating him. Then he pictured Medicaid again. Never in a thousand years would Medicaid be the kid on top. . . .

Stark said, "Phoenix Island is the *agoge* for the twenty-first century. I take orphans discarded by society and offer them meaningful lives. The ancient Greek historian Herodotus wrote about the Spartans, including your Three Hundred. He also wrote about the phoenix, a bird like an eagle that had the ability to burst into flames, die, and come to life again, reborn from the ashes. During your time in the sweatbox, it must have felt like you were about to burst into flames, eh? But look at you now: reborn."

Carl nodded, but Stark's mention of the sweatbox stunned Carl's appetite. Yes, this experience was like being reborn, but Ross and Octavia were still back there, suffering under Parker. If only he could get them here, with Stark, where everything was so different. They wouldn't just be safe. They would be happy. Then he thought of Campbell, who was headed home with a promise to expose Phoenix Island.

And what if he did? What if the authorities showed up, asking for Carl?

Watching Stark finish his meal, Carl sagged with guilt. Stark had been kind. Stark believed in him. In a flash, Carl saw all of the adults who had looked down on him, punished him, misunderstood him. Then Stark. And Stark was so much more impressive than the others. Smarter, stronger, more experienced. Was it all true, what he'd said on the walk? Had Carl's strengths caused all the problems that brought him here? Was Parker the only real problem here, a mean dog Stark had since muzzled? Could it be possible that Phoenix Island really was the best place for Carl, the only place that would recognize his strengths and help him make the most of them? And if so, how would Stark react when the authorities showed up, shutting down the place and blaming it all on Carl?

Watching Stark chew his last piece of steak, Carl felt like the biggest punk in the world. In this moment, rescue seemed a horrible idea. He would never be able to face Stark again. The betrayal . . .

And as Carl tried to imagine the consequences, Stark rose from the modest table and went to the sink, where he stood, a giant of man with rippling muscles in his back and neck and arms, and washed blood from his plate and knife.

19

CARL FREEMAN," STARK SAID, leading Carl through the curtain into the main hangar later that evening, "meet the dojo."

Carl beamed. The dojo was huge. An elevated boxing ring sat at the far end. Along the walls Carl saw speed bags, heavy bags, double-end bags, and all kinds of training equipment: jump ropes, headgear, and laced gloves hanging from hooks; stacks of medicine balls, kicking shields, and punch mitts; and racks of what looked like wooden swords.

"This is the first time I've seen you really smile," Stark said.

"What? Oh . . ." Carl walked a few steps deeper into the room, taking it in.

Stark said, "The ring must seem like an old friend."

"It sure does," Carl said. Even with everything that had happened, it was a rush being in a gym again, and nothing brought it home more than the sight of the elevated ring and its red, white, and blue ropes.

"Go ahead. Climb up and check it out."

Carl thanked him, crossed the room, and ascended the short steps to the ring apron. He slipped through the ropes and into the ring, and his whole body thrilled to feel it surround him—the turnbuckles, the taut ropes, the subtle give of the flooring—as if the ring had scooped him into an embrace.

He shook out his arms, did a couple of deep knee bends, and then started circling. The padding was good, soft beneath his feet but not too soft, and the floorboards greeted him with familiar creaking and thumping as he glided over them. He tested the ropes on all four sides. They were a bit tighter than he preferred. You put a guy on tight ropes like these, a good counterpuncher could use that extra bounce, really crack you if you weren't careful.

"You like?" Stark stood on the floor beside the ring, looking like a professional wrestler ready to come through the ropes.

"It's perfect," Carl said, and he shuffled toward the center of the ring, where he picked up his traditional rocking motion—forward and back, forward and back, side to side—flicked out a light six-punch combination, and quarter-pivoted. Out of the pivot, he bobbed into a squat, launched a stronger combination, and pivoted again.

It was amazing. There was no pain. Stark was right about Vispera. Psycho or not, the guy was a miracle worker.

After a minute of shadowboxing, he could feel his new muscles cooperating and knew with a little practice he'd have all his speed back and a lot more power. He shoe-shined a flurry of light, fast uppercuts, shook out his arms, and came to the ropes near Stark. "Thanks for this. I mean, it feels awesome to be back in the ring again."

"It's my pleasure. I respect skill, and I have a deep interest in combat. It seems like you've recovered pretty well from your injuries."

Carl laughed. It felt great, being well again, moving in the ring, no one making fun of him, egging him on. He wondered when he would have to go back to camp and face Parker. Then he pushed that thought away. Parker had already done enough to make his life miserable; he wasn't going to allow him to ruin this perfect moment, too. "My punches are rusty, and my footwork's off, but I feel like I could spar ten rounds."

"And perhaps you could. But we won't start with sparring. We'll stretch and do some circuit training, work off that rust and try out your new muscles."

"What . . . now?"

"The great samurai Musashi said that if we are to learn the way, we must train morning and night. It's night."

While they stretched, Stark asked Carl about his boxing experiences. Carl started with the end—winning the national championships—then worked his way back, telling how it was, going from gym to gym in Philly and sparring against pros, grown men who outweighed him by five, ten, even fifteen pounds. Stark asked if it was true, what everyone said about Philadelphia gym wars, and Carl smiled, telling him it was. In Philly, fighters go at it harder than anywhere else. There was even an old saying used all over the world: "Sure, the kid is good, but how long would he last in a Philly gym?"

"Did your father teach you?" Stark asked.

"No," Carl said. "I got into trouble, and the judge made me try boxing."

Stark laughed. "Smart judge."

"Yeah, right?" Carl said. "That's where I met my trainer, Arthur James. He was awesome."

"Tell me about it," Stark said, and made a broad sweep with his arm. "All of it. Everything."

So Carl told him about how he'd loved boxing right from the start and about Arthur James and how Arthur barely looked at him, let alone talked to him, other than to point out what he was doing wrong. Carl hit the gym every night and worked hard. Three months into training, he earned the chance to spar.

Arthur threw him in with Cliff, a slick boxer with several amateur bouts who was a couple of years older and outweighed him by twenty pounds. As Arthur laced and taped the big sixteen-ounce gloves and tightened the headgear strap uncomfortably across Carl's throat, he quietly reviewed things they'd trained, cooing reminders softly as a pigeon. Hands up. Chin down. Step when you punch. Use lateral movement and mind the angles. Work the body. Start with the jab; finish with the jab. Punches in bunches. Then, as he held open the ropes for Carl to slip through, Arthur offered a rare smile and said, "Well, son, here you go. This is what you've been wanting."

Cliff was already in the ring. He smiled, all mouthpiece, but Carl knew the smile didn't mean Cliff would take it easy on him. In sparring, you went hard, only backing off if your trainer told you to. Carl respected that. He didn't want anybody's pity or B-game.

The bell rang. Twenty seconds later, Carl dipped a right cross, threw a left hook, and dropped Cliff to the canvas. Carl went to the neutral corner like he'd seen other fighters do. Cliff got up, still all business, and Arthur said, "All right, son," and called them back together. Cliff brushed his gloves off on his tank top and proceeded more cautiously, tending a wider gap and using more movement, more jabs, keeping his hands high and tight whenever Carl got close.

The rest of the sparring session went Cliff's way, but Carl had a few good moments and did what Arthur told him, keeping his guard and his cool and throwing lots of punches. By the end of the third, he had a bloody lip, and a pleasant, buzzing emptiness filled his head. At the final bell, Cliff spit out his mouthpiece, grinned, and whacked Carl on the back with one big, puffy glove. "Woo-ee, Carl. You punch like a middleweight!"

Arthur told them to quit jabbering and do twenty minutes of stairs and six rounds of jump rope. He allowed each of them a quick drink at the water fountain, a rare treat, and said to Carl, quietly as always, "Good job in there, son. You'll be all right." Carl thanked him, went to the steps, and fell in behind Cliff. He'd never felt better about anything anybody had ever said to him in his whole life. "Good job. . . . You'll be all right" from Arthur Marcellus James was like a gold medal from anybody else.

Carl stayed on Cliff's heels, up and down the stairs, up and down, wishing he could tell his dad what Arthur had said. One of the older boxers joined them on the steps, and together they sang "I want to be an airborne ranger" until one of the trainers, a loud guy named Benson, came to the top of the stairs and told them they were horrible and laughed and threw a bag glove at Cliff. Cliff ducked it and ran downstairs, cackling like a madman, and Carl followed after him, laughing just as hard.

Carl chuckled now, remembering it all as he told Stark, but then the chuckle died away.

"What?" Stark said.

Carl shook his head. "Nothing. That's it."

Stark narrowed his eyes slightly. "We need to trust each other," Stark said. "Tell me."

Carl sat in silence for a second then said, "It was that night, that same night, when I went home, that an ambulance was parked in front of the house." He paused, rocked by the memory. And then it all came back to him: the panic he'd felt, standing there, the whole block flip-flopping with the flashing ambulance lights, and the cold dread that filled him when the paramedics closed the back doors and his mother's wail cut through the night, through him, through everything he'd ever known.

Stark put a hand on his shoulder. "You okay?"

Carl nodded and let out a shuddering breath. "That was the night my dad died."

"Oh, Carl," Stark said, frowning. "I am so sorry." He gave Carl's shoulder a light squeeze. "I shouldn't have pushed you to tell me."

Carl shook his head and forced a weak smile. "It's okay. Really. Just . . . took me back, you know?"

Stark nodded. "Life is hard—and sometimes, hard to understand. Victory and defeat. Pleasure and pain. Blessings and curses." He stood, a smile coming onto his face. "The trick is to keep moving, my young friend, keep living." He dropped into a full split without so much as a groan, then came out of it, gave Carl a good-natured slap on the arm, and said, "Let's do some warm-ups."

"Sounds good," Carl said, meaning it. He hated being sad and tried not to dwell on sad stuff.

They ran through jumping jacks, push-ups, sit-ups, and deep knee bends. "Grab a jump rope," Stark said. He went to the wall and flicked a switch, and the big timer mounted there rang out *ding, ding, ding,* and its green light flashed to life.

"Time!" Stark said.

It felt good to jump rope. Carl loved the simple rhythm of it, the familiar rattle of the ball bearings inside the wooden handles, the whirl of the leather rope and its ticking slap against the floor. After mere seconds, he found his comfortable old rhythm, and his feet started doing their traditional dance with the spinning rope. He added double jumps and crossovers, and when the thirty-second buzzer sounded and the yellow light came on, he spun the rope so quickly he had to sprint to keep up with it.

He felt great. No pain or stiffness, no cramping, no burn in his muscles. He wasn't even breathing hard.

They jumped for three rounds, then climbed into the ring together and moved in their own circles, shadowboxing for another three. Stark was impressive. He didn't fight like a boxer—he stood a little straight, and his stance was a bit wide—but his punches were loose and fast, and Carl could tell the big man had real power in his fists.

"Wrap your hands," Stark said, pointing to the wall, where sets of hand wraps hung from hooks. "We'll do a little bag work."

Carl hesitated. Shadowboxing was one thing, but pounding the bag was another.

Stark laughed and shook his head. "Still worried about your bones? Carl, you must learn to trust me."

Carl grabbed a pair of wraps and wound them over his hands, loving the solid, tight feel they gave his fists. Stark helped him pull on a pair of training gloves and pointed to the heavy bag. "Let's see what you've got. On the bell."

Carl got into his stance. Stark slipped behind the bag, holding it with his hands and leaning into it with his shoulder. "Start with jabs."

The bell rang. Carl flicked out jabs, nice and easy at first, relieved to feel no pain whatsoever. It was a good bag—very heavy but not too hard and made of well-worn brown leather—and he loved the way his jabs felt popping the bag, loved the sound of his work, the thump of his fists, and the jangling of the chains overhead. He shuffled side to side, jabbed, cut back, jabbed, dipped, jabbed, circled the bag. He started to time his jabs with his footwork. When he added a little twist to his shoulder and lead knee, the chains sang.

"Great, Carl," Stark said, grinning around the bag. "Work in some right hands."

Carl started to protest—his right hand had been way more messed up than his left—but then remembered Stark saying, *You must learn to trust me*, and nailed the bag with a right hand.

There was no pain.

He worked the bag up and down. Jab, jab, straight right, jab out. He started working his angles, and this made his combinations sharper.

It felt awesome. All the rust and clumsiness disappeared. Gradually, he let his punches go a little more and a little more, and by the end of the round, he shocked himself with the new power he found in both hands.

His punches sounded like rifle shots. When the thirty-second warning buzzed, Carl launched a fierce barrage that battered the bag with such speed his rifle shots sounded like machine-gun fire, the bag chains jangling like spent brass casings.

The bell rang, and Stark yelled, "Hooah!" and banged fists with Carl, who wasn't even short of breath.

"It's amazing," Carl said. "I feel like I could keep going forever."

"When you came to Phoenix Island, you were already a top-notch athlete with superior genetics and years of solid training. Here, the food, supplements, and inoculations are helping you to maximize your potential. Those things and your new blood, of course. Give it a few more weeks. You'll be amazed."

"Sounds good," Carl said, thinking, *A few more weeks*? Was training like this going to be a regular thing? Then he thought of something. "Are the chips making me stronger, too?" He'd been pretty freaked out by that stuff, but suddenly it didn't seem so bad.

"Not yet—but I can see you're warming to the idea. Good. That's one reason I wanted to train together today. I wanted you to glimpse the future opening before you. For now, the chips are merely studying you from the inside. Once you receive the master chip, you'll be able to call upon them as you please, and you'll have such power, speed, and endurance that you'll look back on today and remember yourself as slow and weak."

The bell rang.

Carl went back to work. Stark called specific punches and combinations, and Carl delivered. When the thirty-second warning buzzed, Stark told him to let his punches go, and Carl finished the round just as he had the first, in one long, rocking combination.

They trained for an hour, fifteen rounds split between jump rope, shadowboxing, bag work, and Carl's favorite, mitt work, where Stark called out combos and caught Carl's punches with hand pads. On the mitts, Carl's punches were even crisper and louder than they had been on the bag. They echoed off the high ceiling. Carl never tired.

"I'm impressed," Stark said. "I knew you were a good fighter, but that was amazing."

Carl grinned. "Thanks again. I mean, you saved my life. And now all this."

"Carl, you're not like the other orphans. Mentally and physically, you're ahead of them. Well ahead. Morally and philosophically, as well. Your courage, your history, your fighting ability, your sense of honor, the way you bore up under hardship, the way you faced your own death—resolute acceptance—all these things tell me you're on your way to becoming not only a great man but also a great leader of men."

Carl barked out a laugh. "Me—a *leader*? I'm nobody. I *just* started Blue Phase."

"Blue Phase?" Stark said. "What would a man like Parker teach someone like you? All of that is behind you now."

"Really?"

Stark looked him in the eyes. "Really."

"Wow," Carl said, and he could feel the stunned smile coming onto his own face. He'd been wondering when Stark would send him back to camp, back to Parker. "Thanks."

"Ever since I built Phoenix Island," Stark said, "I've been waiting for a worthy candidate, whom I could train intensively and raise like a son. And now my wait is finally over. You, Carl, it's you I've been waiting for all these years."

Carl's face was suddenly hot with emotion: surprise, gratitude, pride, and almost overwhelming happiness. For so long, he'd been shuffled from place to place, unwanted—a nice kid, sure, but that temper!—and no matter where he went, trouble always followed. Adults had gone from looking at him with hope and pity to regarding him like some kind of dangerous beast, and even he had started to view his future as a succession of cages. But now this man, this amazing man—and Carl's throat tightened as he tried to make the moment real—this man, who was smarter and stronger than anyone Carl had ever met, was telling him . . . "Me?"

"Yes, Carl, you." Stark put his hands on Carl's shoulders and smiled. "Say you'll be my apprentice."

But Carl couldn't say anything—he was afraid if he tried to speak, he'd start crying—so he just smiled and nodded instead, kept smiling and nodding until Stark pulled him into a crushing hug.

20

TWO WEEKS LATER, Octavia ran.

As usual, the platoon started their morning before first light with PT, a trip to the obstacle course, and a long run, which looped back to the chow hall. What was unusual was Octavia's hunger. During the month since Carl's departure, she'd barely eaten. She'd always been thin, but now you could count her ribs through her shirt, and her hip bones poked out like fins. Worry for Carl had stolen her appetite.

But this morning, inexplicably, she was so hungry she could have eaten her combat boots.

Dreaming of food, she ran even faster than usual and pulled away from the pack. When she reached the chow hall, the only person who'd beaten her, Sanchez, was kicking the dirt outside the doors.

"What is it?" Octavia said.

"It's locked."

She tried the handle, hoping he'd made a mistake. He hadn't. "At least we'll be first in line," she said.

Other runners started showing up.

Tamika plopped down beside Octavia and launched into a colorful rant about the locked door. Octavia laughed. Tamika was a poet of profanity.

As others arrived, complaints got louder. People pounded on the door and checked the back, but nothing worked. When stragglers started to show, Sanchez, who'd been named platoon guide after Campbell, tried to get everybody to stretch. Octavia went along with it.

At least stretching gave her something to think about other than how hungry she was.

"Here comes Carl's friend," Tamika said. "He don't look so good."

"Oh," Octavia said.

Ross's face looked like a Halloween mask from some fresh beating he'd taken, the whole thing black-and-blue and so swollen it seemed like he was having a hard time opening his eyes and closing his mouth. Octavia felt horrible for him. She remembered how brave he'd been, standing up for Carl.

Medicaid stumbled into view, crying again. He had a bloody nose. She noticed with a wave of involuntary disgust that he had also wet his pants.

Decker and his thugs surrounded the miserable kid, laughing and prodding him with clubs.

Clubs? Octavia narrowed her eyes. *What was up with these guys carrying weapons?*

Then she noticed that each of them also wore a shiny black armband with a bright red phoenix at the center.

"They look like the damn Hitler Youth," Tamika said.

"Yeah . . . or the Parker Youth."

The kid next to them, a timid type named Soares, said, "I wouldn't joke around if I were you. Things have changed around here, so watch out." The kid had a fat lip, a little split there, some dried blood. Wide-eyed, he watched Decker's crew prod Medicaid into the group.

"What do you mean, *changed*?"

"Just be careful," Soares said, and then he sidled away, like he was afraid they would get him in trouble or something.

Tamika said, "One of them tries to use a nightstick on me, I'm turning him into a Popsicle."

Octavia laughed, but she had to force it. This was no joke. She didn't know just what the weapons and armbands meant, but it was bad—really, really bad. In her dread, she could all but hear the voice of her dead stepfather. *You didn't really think it would all be okay, did you? Has your life taught you to believe in happy endings?*

No, it hadn't. Not at all. And here it was at last, she thought, the next wave of bad luck . . . in the form of cloth and sticks.

Decker's club smacked loudly on Medicaid's butt, and Medicaid fell, squealing like a little kid.

"Get up, Porky Pig," Decker said, jabbing Medicaid's belly with his baton.

Octavia jumped to her feet. "Leave him alone."

Decker looked up at her, smiling.

Oh no, she thought, seeing the terrible, amused cruelty in his eyes. *What have I done?*

The chow hall doors sprang open. Parker's voice boomed, "Form it up, orphans!"

Octavia turned away from Decker and got into the ranks.

"Smooth move," Tamika whispered, "picking a fight with an armed psychopath."

Octavia rolled her eyes. Why did they have weapons? And Parker obviously didn't care that they'd used them on Medicaid.

When that Stark guy had saved Carl, she had hoped—had almost believed—the nightmare had ended. She'd been wrong. It was all starting again, only this time, this time, it wouldn't just be Parker and the drill sergeants. . . .

The soldier in question circled the formation, eyeballing everybody. Parker looked so stupid, standing there with his stupid neck brace and his stupid sling and the same old stupid scowl on his face. She hated him like she had hated no one except her stepfather, hated him like she'd thought she'd never hate anybody again.

He grinned at them. "Guess you orphans are hungry, hooah?"

"Hooah!"

Octavia hated all this hooah crap. After she got off this island, the first person who hooah-ed her, she was going to hooah in the nose.

Parker said, "Today you move on to land navigation. You'll work in teams. Instructors will drop each team at a different location. You'll use a compass, a topo map, and coordinates to find a series of checkpoints. Hooah?"

They sounded off.

Not bad. At least she'd get away from Parker for a while. Decker, too. Then a dark thought clouded her mind. What if Parker put her in the redneck's group? She thought of the club, the cruel laughter in his icy eyes. She did *not* want to be stuck out in the jungle with him.

Parker said, "You get no breakfast today."

Everyone groaned.

"Lock it up," Parker said. "We want you motivated. Always, always, always. First group to reach the finish line gets extra chow at dinner. The last group goes without again. Hooah?"

"Hooah!"

"Now that's motivation. And here's some more: first group back pulls no guard duty this week. Last group back covers their shifts. Hooah?"

Everybody sounded off, Octavia included. For extra food and sleep, she would *run* the stupid course. Besides, they'd studied map reading and compass use. That stuff was easy.

"One more thing, orphans. Commander Stark is looking for motivated orphans who can listen to orders and get tough when they need to. Someday, some of you might be invited to join Phoenix Force. That's the varsity team, hooah?"

They sounded off louder than ever. She didn't give a crap about Phoenix Force—the day she turned eighteen, she was out of here—but she yelled just as loud as everybody else, dreaming of food and sleep.

"Great balls of fire, orphans, what have you been eating, whiskey and gunpowder?"

"Straight meat, Drill Sergeant!" they yelled—just one more stupid response Parker had hammered into them.

"Hooah! That's what I like to hear. Now lock it up, because most of you have about as much chance of making Phoenix Force as I have of becoming the Queen of England."

There's an uncomfortable image, Octavia thought.

"These are your groups for land nav. Group One . . ."

Here we go, she thought. Her stomach clenched.

"Decker . . ."

No, no, no, no—

"Funk, Chilson, and Stroud."

Decker and his toadies cheered.

She relaxed. She wasn't with them.

"Group Two," Parker said, "Gregoric, Ross, and Medicaid."

Group One roared with laughter, and Parker paused to find Octavia and give her a big smile. She looked away. So be it. He'd paired her with Ross, who currently looked like he should be in the emergency room, and Medicaid, who *always* looked like he should be in an emergency room—or a mental hospital. So friggin' be it. . . .

When it was time to group up, Ross found her. "Sorry about the face," he said. "I left my real one in the barracks. . . . Uh . . . it hurts to smile."

She looked around. "Where's Medicaid?"

Ross shrugged. "We're screwed. Having Medicaid on your land-nav team is like having an acrophobe on your rock-climbing team."

"Where is he?"

"See, that was a joke. An acrophobe is somebody who is afraid of heights—"

"I know. I get it. Look, Ross," she said, putting a forceful hand on his shoulder. "I don't care if we have to take turns carrying Medicaid, we're going to win this thing."

"Win it?" He looked at her like she was crazy. "It'll be a miracle if we don't come in last."

"Win it. I want that extra food and rest."

"You're serious, aren't you?"

"Serious as a ten-car pileup. Let's go find the third musketeer."

21

CARL PUSHED OUT ANOTHER REP and set the barbell on the rack.

"Good form," Stark said. "Rest for thirty seconds. Then you'll do one more set. That's all, though. You have a big day in front of you."

Carl nodded. It was amazing. Even after two weeks of training, working out several times a day—mostly boxing, cardio, and what Stark called combatives, which was basically mixed martial arts and gymnastics—he felt zero fatigue.

"Three, two, one, *go*," Stark said.

Carl racked out a dozen reps, focusing on form and breathing, just as Stark had told him. With each rep, his muscles swelled. By the time he finished the set, his chest muscles were massive and rounded, twitching for more work.

"Great work, Carl." Stark slapped his hands together. "My turn. Give me a hand."

Carl's mind conjured an image of Ross making one of his lame jokes: Stark asking for a hand, Ross shrugging and applauding with a little golf clap. . . .

He missed the little weirdo. Stupid jokes and all.

Octavia, too. He wondered if she knew he was all right. He wondered if she cared. The last time he'd seen her, she was pretty mad at him. That had been a long time ago—jeez, probably a month.

Other than missing and worrying about his friends, life was perfect. The weeks he'd spent here as Stark's apprentice had been truly awesome. The man was amazing—smart and strong, cool and interesting, upbeat and encouraging—and life had been a blissful collage of top-notch training, reading and discussing books, and endless conversation, all of it fascinating. He encouraged Carl to embrace "self-efficacy," which he said was the key to long-term success. Self-efficacy meant having absolute faith in your mission and yourself, so much that it freed you from worry or overthinking, allowing you to live in the moment and concentrate on whatever action you were supposed to be doing at that very second. In Carl's situation, it meant unwavering faith in his abilities, their work together, and his destiny. Forget the past, don't question the future, and focus on the moment at hand.

Carl loved his new freedom. Stark allowed him to choose his own books, and Carl's questions drove their reading discussions. He had a voice in which training to do when, and Stark allowed him to come and go as he pleased on solo runs, so long as he promised to avoid other trainees. He even had his own bedroom in the hangar, complete with a small bookshelf and a minifridge stocked with good food he could eat—without asking permission. Life was great.

Or was, anyway, until he pictured Octavia's eyes or imagined Ross impersonating Rivera. Then all the happiness whooshed out of him. But what was he supposed to do? Quit his apprenticeship and head back to Blue Phase? That wouldn't do anybody any good. As soon as he could help them, he would. Until then, it was best to embrace Stark's self-efficacy and focus on the moment at hand.

Distracted by these thoughts, Carl moved as mechanically as a robot, helping Stark load heavy plates onto the bar. Only as they slid the final plate into place did the reality hit him. "That's a lot of weight."

"Seven hundred pounds," Stark said, lying down on the bench and squaring himself beneath the bar.

"Really?" It made no sense. Seven hundred pounds . . .

"Really. On three. My count. One, two, three—" The bar flexed as Stark lowered it smoothly to his massive chest and pushed it up again with seeming ease.

"Awesome!" Carl almost yelled.

Stark pumped out seven more reps before racking the weight. He didn't need a spot.

"That was amazing!"

"Thank you," Stark said. There was no show, no roaring, no flexing, nothing. He acted as calm as someone who'd just done eight push-ups. "Last month, I maxed out at nine hundred and eighty pounds. I'm only ninety-five pounds under the world record."

"That's crazy."

Stark smiled. "Yeah, it's pretty cool. In a couple of months, I should be able to beat it, too. Not that I care about the record books. I want strength in case I need it. If a mission goes hand-to-hand, I want to be able to punch a hole through the enemy's chest."

"Or rip his arm off and beat him with it." Carl couldn't imagine fighting Stark. It wasn't just the power. The guy was sharp and fast and threw smart punches. He could kick or grapple, and probably knew how to use every weapon in the world.

"You'll be just as strong," Stark said.

Carl laughed.

"I'm serious. I wasn't born at this level. You're eating what I eat, taking the same supplements I take, training like I train. You'll be squatting Humvees in no time." Stark crossed the room to a set of scales. "Let's check your height and weight, get a baseline."

Carl stepped onto the scale. Stark checked his height first. "Five eleven. Congratulations, you've grown two inches since coming to Phoenix Island."

Carl couldn't believe it. He was nearly six feet tall. . . .

Stark adjusted the balances atop the scale. "One hundred and eighty-seven pounds," Stark said. "And I'd guess you're at about six percent body fat, if that. Six percent is good. Go much lower, and you'll cut into your energy reserves."

"Unreal . . ." Carl wondered aloud. He stepped off the scale and flexed. "It doesn't seem possible."

"You're not finished growing yet. You'll get taller, heavier, and stronger. I'd rather not pack a lot of excess muscle on you, but your genetics might have something to say about that." Stark uncovered a freestanding mirror beside the scale. "See for yourself."

Carl turned toward the mirror. He'd been so preoccupied he hadn't really looked at himself in weeks. His reflection didn't seem real. He looked like a smaller version of Stark. He raised his arms and flexed. "Those shots we were getting back in camp, those were that stuff? HG-whatever?"

"HGH, human growth hormone. And yes—you and a few others received it. Not everyone. HGH is expensive, after all, and let's face it: it would be a waste on many of them."

"But I did. . . ."

Stark laughed. "Carl, I've had my eye on you for a long time. I have employees throughout the juvenile justice system. Think of them as talent scouts. Counselors, probation officers, judges. For cash under the table they identify at-risk youths who display considerable potential. The names come to me, and I conduct research. Your name came to me shortly after you'd won your boxing titles."

Carl started to laugh—this had to be a joke—but stopped as he remembered his file, the handwritten note, *National Boxing Champion*, beneath his sixth-grade photo. "But that was . . . years ago."

"Indeed," Stark said. "Several years. I kept track of you, and when the time was right, I made the proper arrangements."

A feeling was building in Carl, something like getting punched, like getting nailed with a shocker of a right hand you hadn't seen coming, but in very slow motion. "Wait." He pictured the summary sheet he'd found in his folder, the strange note about Idaho and North Carolina, the date that he'd assumed was an error. "You're serious?"

Stark smiled. "Completely."

For a stunned moment, Carl could only stare. It felt like his brain had turned to stone. "So you're saying . . . that you—"

Stark waved dismissively. "I can't take all the credit—your choices and actions led to each move, after all—but I made sure that your path led here." He laughed again. "Didn't you think it bizarre, getting moved all over the country? Idaho? North Carolina?"

"Yeah," Carl said, his own voice sounding strange to him, distant, the rock in his skull crumbling now, falling into dust, "I guess I did."

Stark half turned and started sliding the cover over the mirror again. "Well, I had to get you away from home, break old ties, and eventually wrap you around to one of my judges. I have a couple dozen friendlies spread from Alaska to Florida, and they keep me in business, without ever really knowing what they're doing."

The debris of Carl's crumbled brain now whirled around his skull in a tornado of confusion. All these years, Stark had been watching him, waiting, pulling strings to bring him here? It called a lot of things into question. That gray-haired judge back in North Carolina, sitting there joking with the cop . . . he'd just been following Stark's orders? Implications shuddered through him. "Did you put me places where you knew I'd slip up?"

Stark laughed. "You make me sound like the villain from some crazy conspiracy theory."

"Am I right?" Carl asked, his knuckles starting to ache. "Did you set me up?"

"Set you up?" Stark asked, almost like he was hurt by the question. All at once, his smile died, and his eyes went dark. "I *saved* you."

In that moment, everything changed, Stark's anger clicking into place with the simple efficiency of a cocked hammer. Like it was always there, at the ready when he needed it. Carl tensed, certain he'd just crossed a very dangerous line. He had to deescalate this before it was too late.

"Tell me," Stark said, taking a step closer. "If I hadn't *set you up*, as you put it, where would you be now? More to the point, *what* would you be?"

I'd be living my own life, Carl thought, but with caution lights flashing in his mind, he kept that thought to himself and simply shrugged as if he was unsure and open to Stark's opinion.

"I'll tell you what you'd be," Stark said. "Without me, you'd be the neutered pup of some suburban foster family that would pump you full of happy drugs twenty-four/seven. Would you like that?"

"No," Carl said, telling himself, *Fix . . . this . . . now. . . .* "I wouldn't like that at all." He shook his head for effect.

"I didn't think so," Stark said, and leaned back a little. "I only want what's best for you, Carl. That's all I've ever wanted."

Carl forced a smile onto his face. "I know. Thanks."

Stark smiled and clapped him on the shoulder. "My decision to facilitate your direction might seem bold, but that shouldn't bother a person like you. Life is a series of choices. People pretend these choices are simple—right versus wrong, good versus evil, heads or tails, take your pick—but in the real world, we face dilemmas. No simple answers. Nothing black or white, everything gray. You and I both know it."

Carl nodded, thinking, *Keep nodding. Keep him happy.*

"Boxing success brought your name to my attention," Stark said, "but it was your handling of dilemmas that won me over. A single charge, repeated ad infinitum."

Carl stiffened. The exact phrase he'd seen in his folder . . .

Stark started pacing again. "When you saw bullies picking on someone, you acted decisively, intervening even though you knew it would bring you trouble. Even as boy, you were a man of action." He grinned.

Carl looked at the ground. "They made me mad."

"Understandable," Stark said, "Anger is a natural response to a world gone mad, where schools fearing public opinion claim 'zero tolerance' for bullies, then punish a boy for showing that exact lack of tolerance, the same world where a government fearing global opinion declares a 'war against terror,' then betrays an elite soldier who actually tries to wage that war."

"Is that what happened to you?"

But Carl could see that Stark was lost in his speech and didn't seem to hear the question. "The world needs us, Carl, needs us to set things right. We don't hesitate during dilemmas, we act—decisively—because we understand and accept that the price of progress runs high at times. That's what we do: we affect progress, making the world a better place, even if that means breaking rules, even if the price runs high at times."

Carl nodded again, feeling like a puppet on a string.

"No matter how you got here," Stark said, "you've come to the right place. Phoenix Island is the heart of a much larger organization committed to making the world a better place. We have additional operations, albeit cruder ones, all over the world."

"Wait," Carl said, rattled out of the nodding routine. "There are more places like this?"

"Many," Stark said. "We have facilities in Africa, Asia, Central and South America, the Middle East, and the former Soviet Union. The best children end up here, though, where I train them as Phoenix Force troopers."

Carl tensed, remembering Eric's journal. Phoenix Force, the Old Man's killers-for-hire. But he just said, "You train Phoenix Force?"

"Abso-hooah-lutely," Stark said, beaming with obvious pride. "I'm company commander, the father of this organization. That's why they call me the Old Man."

22

THE JEEP DROPPED THEM a couple of miles from camp. Thick forest hugged both sides of the road. A little way back, they had driven over the big swamp. Octavia opened the map.

Ross, pretending to call after the jeep, said, "On second thought, I've changed my mind. Drop me off in Massachusetts instead."

The guy never quit with the jokes. Here he was, with a face like a train wreck, stuck out in the woods, still joking around. In a way, it was pretty cool. In another way, not so much—and Octavia hoped she could control her temper.

You will, she told herself. *You will do everything you have to do because you're going to win this thing.* She had to get these guys on board.

"All right," she said, "Medicaid— Uh, what's your real name?"

Medicaid looked at her and laughed. A light breeze passed, and Octavia smelled urine.

Lord, give me strength, she thought. "All right, then. We'll just continue with Medicaid. Go on over to that checkpoint. They said there should be some paper in the box."

To her surprise, Medicaid went straight to the post, pulled out the paper, and brought it to her.

"Look," Octavia said. "We can do this, guys. I mean it. We might not be the most athletic group, but we're smart. Map reading was easy. I liked it."

"Stockholm syndrome," Ross said. "You're going native. Next thing you know, you'll develop a love for camouflage, plan a wedding dress in green and black."

"Ross, for as much as I admire your spirit, if you don't stop screwing around, I'll strangle you."

"Whoa—" Ross said, putting up his hands. "I'm all for trying to win, but don't ask me to stop making jokes, like, ever."

"Whatever. Just take a look at this map, okay?"

They flattened the map on the ground, took out the compass and a pencil, and got started. Medicaid scuffed around on the road, talking to himself, while she and Ross plotted the course.

"That's where he got it," Ross said, pointing to the right side of the map, which showed the outline of the island but no detail, just dark cross-hatching, save for a single, short phrase she couldn't understand.

"That's where who got what?"

Ross glanced over his shoulder toward Medicaid. "Nothing. I saw another map, and it used this phrase, *hic sunt dracones*—here are dragons. It's a figure of speech—an old one—meaning an uncharted area, maybe dangerous, maybe not. Besides, whatever's on the other side of the island, there's a fence between it and us."

She didn't like the way he smiled at her then, like it was forced, like he was worried or afraid or something. Like he was lying. She started to say something but stopped. There wasn't time. "All right. Let's shoot this azimuth."

"The girl speaks Mapese!" Ross said, and this time his smile was genuine. "Shooting the azimuth, ma'am."

She knew Ross was smart. It showed as they worked out the best path together.

"Sometimes," Ross said, "the shortest distance between two points is not a straight line." He traced his finger across the map between their location and the first checkpoint. "See how all those lines and circles get tight here? See how the numbers get lower and lower?"

"The swamp?" Octavia said.

"Bingo," Ross said. "Let's walk back up the road past it, *then* head into the woods. Then we won't have to cross the swamp on foot. We can use the bridge."

At a glance, the route he'd charted looked silly, a long curving line that went way off before looping back to a point that lay straight ahead of them, but she knew he was right. If they traveled in a straight line, they would get stuck in the marsh with all those snakes and spiders and who knew what else.

"Good idea," Octavia said. Then, to Medicaid, she said, "All right, let's go."

She and Ross started walking. Medicaid followed. *Note to self,* she thought. *Look over your shoulder every now and then. Make sure the kid hasn't wandered off and gotten lost.*

They walked up the road and crossed the bridge.

"Let's step it up," she said. "I want to win this thing."

Medicaid laughed, perhaps a little cruelly.

"I hate to say it, but the kid has a point," Ross said. "I just want to avoid coming in last. If ever anybody needed a beauty rest, it's me. I mean, really"—he pretended to fluff nonexistent hair—"I don't think these bruises do a thing for me, do you?"

She wanted to punch him. This place, the constant pressure—they were driving her nuts. She fought to keep her voice level. "I'm serious, okay? We have to win. I don't care about the food—well, I do, but that's not the point—we have to show them they can't control us. Did you see Parker's face when he read off the group? Did you hear Decker laughing? They obviously expect us to take last. I'm not giving them the satisfaction."

Ross started jamming on an air guitar. "I can't get no . . . satisfaction!"

She grabbed his throat and glared into his eyes. "Ross! Enough . . . with . . . the . . . jokes! Now get serious, or I swear I'll beat the crap out of you."

Ross wriggled free and backed away, rubbing his neck. "Honestly, I'm not sure I *can* stop. It's a thing with me. I mean, I can't control it, really. Last night, those guys were beating the crap out of me with their clubs, I made a crack, and they gave it to me all over again. I mean, what I said wasn't even a *good* joke."

"Wait a minute. You said 'those guys'—you mean Decker, those guys?"

"Well, yeah . . . you see anybody else walking around with clubs?"

"I assumed Parker did it. He let *them* hit you?"

"Let them? He *told* them to do it. Not that he had to tell them twice."

"That's crazy. I don't know why I'm surprised, but—"

"There's a lot about this place that would surprise you." Ross stared at her for a second, and she'd never seen him look so serious. Those eyes weren't within a mile of joke.

"Don't make me play guessing games, Ross—talk."

But Ross turned his bruised eyes to glance at Medicaid, who bumbled after them vaguely. "I'll tell you later."

"Hey," she said to Medicaid, who was laughing and mumbling to a bright blue butterfly fluttering around his head, "you want to step it up? Stop fooling with the butterfly and let's go."

"Pretty butterfly!" Medicaid said, and then giggled like the thing was tickling him.

Turning to Ross, she said, "He's not listening."

"Don't be so sure. The kid's gone completely insane over the last couple of weeks, but he hears a lot more than he seems to. Isn't that right, Medicaid?"

Medicaid laughed.

Ross raised his brows.

Octavia sighed. "Whatever. Let's just step it up, okay? Wait—does this have to do with Carl?"

Ross shrugged. "Yeah. I mean, it has to do with all of us, but yeah . . . I'm worried about him. But seriously, not now, okay? It's not worth the risk, with our partner."

"Tell me now. I don't care about—"

Abruptly, she walked back to Medicaid—not one but two blue butterflies fluttered around him now—grabbed him by the shirt, and shook him. He shrieked.

"We're having a private conversation," she told him. "Keep your nose out of it, or I'll kill every butterfly I see. Got it? I'll rip their wings off and crush their little heads." She demonstrated, rubbing her thumb and forefinger together, crushing an imaginary one. "Got it?"

The kid's eyes went wide and scared. "You don't hurt the little butterflies!"

"I won't—unless you get nosy."

Medicaid shook his head.

Octavia went back to Ross.

"Remind me not to get on your bad side, all right?" he said. "That was—um—kind of twisted."

Octavia ran a hand over the stubble atop her head. "I know. This place is getting to me. What were you saying?"

They glanced back. Medicaid followed at a distance, hands pressed to his ears. The poor kid was crazier than a soup sandwich. Maybe she'd been mean, but there wasn't time to be nice. This place punished you for being nice.

"Well, it's just . . . I'm afraid they're going to . . ." Ross said, halting his stride. "I'm afraid they might have already—"

And then Ross really surprised her. The eternal comedian started sobbing.

"What is it? Are you all right?" She put an arm around him. It was awkward. She'd never been a touchy-feely person. His shoulders felt really, really small under her arm. In that second, it came clear to her all over again just how warped Decker and his buddies were. Ross was the size of a twelve-year-old.

Ross wiped at his tears, cursing. "I hate crying. I mean, I really, really hate it."

"Don't worry about it. Just tell me." The cold feeling in her stomach intensified. A part of her was worried that it knew what he was going to say and didn't want to hear it.

"They blacked out his f-f-face."

"What?"

Ross rolled his head back and blinked away tears. "The platoon photo. Parker blacked out Carl's face."

"So?"

"I'm afraid they killed Carl."

As a reflex, she looked over to make sure Medicaid had stopped at a distance from them. "That's stupid. Nobody killed Carl."

Ross just looked at her. Then he started walking again and she followed, but she felt like shouting. "Stark *saved* him. What are you talking about?"

"We found this journal. Well, Carl found it, and it told all about Phoenix Island."

"What—wait—why did you say that about Carl?" Panic rose in her, melting the cold spot in her stomach and bringing it to a boil. Any second, she'd start shrieking like a teapot. . . .

"I'm trying to tell you, okay?" He glanced at Medicaid, then leaned toward her, whispering, "We found somebody's diary. This guy Eric. He used to be book man. During a previous cycle, I mean. He talked about everything that happened then. And it's all been happening to us the same way."

"So?"

"When Eric's platoon reached Blue Phase, the drill sergeants started killing people."

"Wait." She shook her head. "What?"

"Don't look at me like that. I'm serious."

She took a deep breath. He certainly looked serious . . . but no . . . this couldn't be real. "Killing people? *Actually killing?*"

"Parker started it. Then . . . others joined in."

"Well, Parker wanted to kill Carl, but Stark stopped him."

"True, but then he sent Carl to the Chop Shop."

"Don't call it that," she said, grimacing. "I hate when they call it that."

Ross gave a slight bow. "I hate it, too, but whatever its name, that's where Stark sent him."

She spread her hands. "Duh—where else would they send him? He was hurt."

"They do stuff there. That's what the journal said. This guy Eric, he didn't know just what they did, but he was suspicious. He said people went there and never came back. Then he went past and saw people walking around like zombies. Carl and I saw some kid like that on the first day."

She held out her hand like a traffic cop stopping a car going the wrong way. "Slow down. You're not making any sense."

"I think they do stuff to people's brains there. Operate on them or whatever. Lobotomize them."

"Loboto . . ."

"Lobotomize. It means they take something sharp and poke it into somebody's brain."

"And kill them?"

"No. They used to do this back in the old days. I mean doctors. Psychiatrists. They saw it as treatment. They poked it in there and jabbed around the frontal lobe, and—"

"Enough," she said. She felt sick. Just the thought of someone doing something like that to anyone, let alone Carl . . .

"Anyway, the operation pretty much wiped them out, made them like zombies."

Octavia shook her head. This was crazy. "Stop, all right? I don't want to hear anymore. You're wrong, okay? Carl's fine—he's fine!" Unbidden laughter tumbled out of her—and she wasn't entirely comfortable with the slippery hilarity even she heard in it. "Tell butterfly boy to quit his hear-no-evil monkey routine, and let's find that checkpoint."

"Wait. Don't shut me down. This is important."

"No." She pulled away from him. "This is over. I never should have listened to this crap."

His hand grabbed her arm. "Octavia, please."

She spun and pushed him with both hands. He fell hard onto his butt. "Mistake, Ross! Do *not* touch me." Her hands shook, and she breathed hard, as if she'd been sprinting. Suddenly, she felt like she might cry, too. She marched deeper into the woods.

For the rest of the hike, Ross stayed ten feet behind her. Medicaid stayed even farther back. He still had his hands on his ears, but he was smiling now and singing some kind of gibberish song.

They dipped into a wooded ravine. Thick vines and heavy undergrowth forced them slightly off course, but then things opened up, and they entered into a section of the forest straight out of a children's book. The kind of children's book with witches. And palm trees. That kind.

Five minutes later, she kicked a tree.

"We're lost, aren't we?" Ross said.

She rolled her eyes skyward. "Yes. I was so upset, I—crap. No breakfast, no lunch. I don't want to go without dinner."

Ross approached slowly and tugged at the map. "May I?"

"Go ahead." Map reading had been so easy in class. Then again, her brain hadn't been under this kind of stress.

Ross worked loudly, trying to flatten the map on uneven ground and fumbling with the compass. "Um . . ."

She closed her eyes and pinched the bridge of her nose. On top of everything else, a killer headache was carving a tunnel through her skull.

"All right," Ross said, trying too hard to sound cool, calm, and collected. "We just have to walk back to the road and start over again."

She growled. "That will take too long. There has to be a landmark, something."

Ross shook his head. "I'm lost. Completely lost."

"Crap!" she shouted.

A flight of birds lifted, squawking into the canopy.

The trees, bigger here, taller, rose limblessly up like so many columns, branching out far overhead to block most of the light. Down on the ground, everything was dim and cool and damp. Here and there, light fell in heavy shafts, standing out in sharp contrast with the gloom.

"We," Ross said, shaking his head, "are officially screwed."

A mosquito buzzed in her ear. She swatted it.

Medicaid waddled up, leaned over Ross for perhaps two seconds, and kept walking.

"Hey," she said. "Don't wander off."

"This way," Medicaid said, and kept going.

"Wait!" Octavia called after him, but he disappeared into the darkness beyond a thicker copse of trees. "Grand," she said. "If he gets lost and we waste time searching for him, we'll come in dead last."

Ross took forever folding the map.

"Come on," she said, and they trotted off in the direction Medicaid had traveled.

But he was gone. They saw only trees and vines, shadows and mosquitoes.

"Medicaid?" she called. "Where are you?"

Off to the left, something big moved through the forest, snapping branches. She heard a grunt.

"Uh-oh. Not good," she said. "Hey, Medicaid? Medicaid!"

"Hey! Wait for us," Ross said.

She scanned the forest. Nothing.

Ross shook his fists in the air. "Why does everything suck?"

"Wait," she said. Something—she heard something. . . . "Be quiet." There.

"I hear it," Ross said.

"His nonsense song," she said. Relief swept over her. "Come on. Let's find him before he stops singing."

They hurried, pausing several times to try to locate his singing, turning back twice. The jungle did weird things to sound. It was easy to see how people got lost, with so little light, the grinding sameness of the forest, and no long views whatsoever.

At last they found him in a small clearing, leaning on a post with a box nailed to it.

Ross pumped a fist overhead. "Yes! The checkpoint!"

"Medicaid, you found it!" Octavia said. She ran forward to where Medicaid stood squinting at a butterfly that had inexplicably landed on his finger. She was so relieved, she nearly gave him a hug . . . but then saw the blood and snot on his face and smelled urine again and gave him a soft pat on the back instead.

Medicaid cringed. "Don't hurt the butterflies."

Octavia stepped back. "I won't. Really. You did great. I'm not going to hurt the butterflies."

Visibly relieved, Medicaid started walking again.

"Wait," she said. "We have to write our names in here and get the coordinates."

"This way," he said, and kept walking. The butterflies followed, flitting in circles around his head.

Ross scribbled furiously in the book and put it back in the box.

"Go after him," Octavia said. "I'm going to check the map. Just call out every minute or something, and I'll catch up."

Ross nodded and jogged off.

All right, she told herself. *Focus. You can do this.*

She looked at the map, noted the coordinates, and circled the next checkpoint. Using the compass and protractor, she marked the azimuth.

In the distance, Ross called out to her.

All right, she told herself. *See it.* She glanced at the topographic lines. There was the depression from the map, the rise, so that meant . . . they had to go *that* way. . . .

Exactly where Medicaid had gone.

Could it be? No—it had to be luck, coincidence . . .

Didn't it?

Ross called again. This time it was faint.

Octavia ran after them.

23

NO SOONER HAD STARK CALLED TIME than Carl's first opponent was across the "ring"—they sparred outdoors, in a cinder-packed square at the center of Camp Phoenix Force—and Carl was tasting blood.

Stark had only just introduced him to the members of Phoenix Force that were on the island when he announced an impromptu boxing exercise, a round-robin sparring session with Carl facing a fresh opponent at each turn.

Carl covered, slipped to the side, and retreated to the center of the ring—then dipped away as the Phoenix Forcer blurred past, swinging wildly.

The guy was sloppy but fast. *Crazy* fast. And not just his hands. His whole body.

So was the next guy. And the girl who followed. All of them were fast and strong and aggressive, gunning for Carl as soon as Stark called time.

Their speed messed up his rhythm and ruined his sense of the gap, that space between an opponent and yourself, which Carl had learned to control by watching Philadelphia legend Bernard Hopkins. Somebody wanted to fight at a distance, you stuck on his chest. He wanted to in-fight, you stayed an inch outside his range and played gatekeeper.

Those first three rounds, Carl couldn't even gauge the gap, let alone control it. He ducked a lot and kept his hands high.

Then he adjusted. The others were fast, but once his mind and body synced, he realized he was, too. He found his old rhythm, only everything had sped up a beat. His body had been ready. He just hadn't recognized it.

After that, he had let them know, dropping them, one after the other, some with headshots but mostly digging to the body.

And they'd loved him for it.

Now he sat in the front row of a Phoenix Force classroom, the sweaty platoon gathered around him, talking over one another, vying for his attention.

The light swelling under his eye, combined with the swelling in his upper lip, made him feel like he had a goofy grin pasted to his face. He took another drink of water from the canteen, loving that buzzy, empty-headed feeling he always got after sparring hard. Back home, boxing had helped him put his troubles in perspective, and here it was, helping again. So what if Stark was the Old Man? That didn't necessarily mean the journal was true. After all, these troopers weren't exactly blood-thirsty savages. They were treating him like a celebrity, the undisputed, undefeated, pound-for-pound champ of the world.

"I caught you with that hook," Cheng said, leaning in from behind him. She'd been his fifth opponent. She looked Asian and sounded English. "Lucky for you I didn't land the right cross as well."

"Yeah," Henshaw said, "too bad Killer Carl knocked you the eff out before you could even throw it. Agbeko, did you see Cheng jerking on the ground? I thought she was break-dancing!"

Agbeko laughed but said nothing. No one had complained when Agbeko had taken the seat next to Carl. He was the leader of this Phoenix Force squad, a recruit from somewhere in Africa, Carl thought, by his accent. He was the biggest of the group—nearly Stark's size—and the best fighter in the bunch. He'd managed to clip Carl a couple of times hard enough that Carl was happy the punches hadn't been flush. Carl had dropped him twice, but Agbeko wouldn't stay down. When the round was over, he spat out his mouthpiece and gave Carl a hug, saying, "You are a killer, Carl."

Henshaw had crowed "Killer Carl!" and it had stuck.

Now Agbeko spoke, and at the sound of his deep voice, the other troopers quieted. "In my country, the generals who make soldiers out of children, they teach you nothing. Only what to do. They give you a gun; they tell you where to point it, who to shoot. 'There, shoot him,' they say. 'But that is my father,' you tell them. 'Then shoot him in the head so he won't suffer,' they tell you. So you do. Or they shoot you." He gestured at the room. "We are all so blessed. The Old Man, this place, they are great blessings. There is a plan, you see?"

Everyone hooah-ed.

And before Carl could really ponder what Agbeko had said, Cheng said, "Here he comes," the door at the front of the room opened, and Phoenix Force shot to its collective feet.

"Atten-shun!" Agbeko said.

Everyone, Carl included, snapped to attention.

"At ease," Stark said, and walked to the front of the room. "After-action report on this morning's sparring session: Carl kicked your butts." He grinned, and the troopers busted up with laughter. Someone patted Carl's back again.

Stark went to the computer at the front of the room, and the image of its desktop appeared on the large projection screen covering much of the front wall. "Carl, each week, I deliver the 'sitrep,' a situation report outlining Phoenix Force activities around the world. Henshaw, get the lights."

"Yes, Commander." A second later, the room went dark.

"Here we go," Stark said. A map of Russia and a bunch of smaller countries filled the screen. Stark pointed to perhaps the smallest of these, saying, "Zurkistan. Former member of the Soviet Republic. Bordered to the north by Russia, to the west by Georgia—that's the country, not the state, Henshaw."

The troopers laughed, none harder than Henshaw.

Stark continued, pointing to various locations on the map as he spoke. "Zurkistan is bordered to the east by the Caspian Sea, and to the south by Azerbaijan. Area: roughly forty thousand square kilometers, most of it mountainous. Population: a little over two million. Per capita income: around two thousand dollars a year. Topography: hills and mountains. Primary assets: mining, agriculture, and wine making. Significant income from taxes on an oil pipeline running through their country from the Middle East en route to Russia. But that's not the only pipeline running between these regions."

He dragged the tip of his pointer along a black line that stretched from the south of Zurkistan up and across the country into Georgia. "This is the Taakvili Trail. Thousands of years old; a former caravan trade route. Now it's a pipeline for all things terrorist. We're talking weapons, drugs, money, and the terrorists themselves. Ground zero for any extremist looking to stick it to Russia, from Al Qaeda all the way down to 'Al Smith' or any other recent 'revert' who wants to join the fight. You read me, troopers?"

"Lima Charlie, Commander!"

"Hooah!" Stark said. "The Zurkistani government hates these terrorists. More than anything else, Zurkistan wants a seat on the UN, but until it can stop the flow of bad guys into neighboring countries, that's not happening. Speaking of the bad guys, who are we talking about?"

Hands went up all around Carl.

Stark pointed. "Boudazin."

The pretty girl who had outshot everyone at the range spoke with a French accent, saying, "The Tigers, Commander Stark."

"Correct," Stark said, and pointed to a mountainous region in the southwestern corner of Zurkistan. "There are two main ethnic groups in Zurkistan. You have your indigenous farmer types—poor as dirt and dumb as turnips—and a hodgepodge of Muslims to the south. Lots of ethnic Chechens and a bunch of mujahedeen who relocated after the Soviets pulled out of Afghanistan. Against all odds, they actually seem to get along with each other most of the time, at least well enough that the terrorists among them have formed an organization called the Taakvili Tigers.

"Meanwhile, back in the capital," Stark said, tapping a star on the other side of the country, "what's the Zurkistani government to do? The Tigers don't live in barracks; they mix with the locals, so the Zurkistani government can't root them out without killing thousands of noncombatants. The international community would cry genocide. Why not ask Russia for help?"

Hands shot up. It was twisted, seeing these hardened troopers, most of them older than Carl, act like anxious schoolkids.

"Nachef?"

"The locals remember life under the Soviets," Nachef said, "and fear Russian occupation."

"Great explanation," Stark said.

"Nerd!" Henshaw squawked, and everybody busted up.

"All right, all right," Stark said. "So they can't handle the Tigers themselves, and they won't ask Russia for help, but they want that UN seat. So whom do they call? Phillips?"

"The United States."

"Bingo," Stark said. "Truthfully, the US would love to wipe out the Tigers and all the anti-American terrorists they're training and harboring, but no can do. Why? Cheng?"

"Multiple reasons, Commander," Cheng said. "Russia wouldn't like it, for starters, and even if that weren't the case, American troops would face the same problem as Zurkistani troops. The Tigers are hidden in the mountains, spread out among noncombatants."

"Excellent." Stark smiled. "You get an extra belt of ammo next time we're on the range."

Someone fake-coughed, "Brownnoser!" and that got everyone laughing again.

Stark waved them into silence and said, "Killing noncombatants remains a big no-no, despite the fact that the women and children in question are terrorists and future terrorists, too. So once again, the greatest army on earth, who could flatten this entire region with a tactical nuke, bows to the all-holy rules of engagement and does nothing." He smiled. "Well, at least *officially* they do nothing. Unofficially, a few of the more forward-thinking individuals in certain government agencies quietly call us and make arrangements. Because Phoenix Force has only one rule of engagement. Carl, do you know what our one rule of engagement is?"

Carl shook his head. The pleasant post-sparring buzz was gone now, and the weird unreality of the people he was around—people who spoke in these military terms that were sort of plain but still sort of unsettling—was rapidly darkening into dread. "I don't know what you mean by *rule of engagement*."

Some of the troopers laughed.

"That's all right, son," Stark said. "And you jokers out there, pipe down. Carl just got here. That might be tough for some of you to remember, considering the way he kicked your butts sparring today, but he's new."

Someone hooah-ed and a hand patted Carl on the back.

"The rules of engagement," Stark said, "are rules of warfare. Vote-grubbing politicians use them to please foreigners and bleeding-heart liberals who know nothing about combat. So they tell the army, 'Play nice, tie one hand behind your back, don't fire until fired upon,' that sort of thing. Luckily for the world, however, Phoenix Force has only one rule of engagement, which brings me back to my original question. Troopers, what is our one . . . rule . . . of . . . engagement?" He drew it out, like a teacher prompting a conditioned response.

"Win!"

Stark leaned toward them, cupping a hand to his ear dramatically. "What? I can't hear you."

"Win!" they roared.

Stark looked very pleased. "Hooah!"

"Hooah!"

"Outstanding," Stark said. "And as your reward, here is fresh footage from Zurkistan, taken about two hours ago, just after midnight, local time." He tapped some keys, and the map disappeared, replaced by nighttime video: the outskirts of a mountain village, everything otherworldly in that weird, green night-vision glow.

The Phoenix Forcers leaned forward. Carl stayed still; he didn't like the eager look on everyone's faces.

The video erupted in gunfire and shouting. Carl saw muzzle flashes, then made out vague shapes firing from behind boulders, parked vehicles, and a stone well casing. Bearded men in robes emerged from houses, shouting and firing rifles, and died quickly. A string of bright green explosions obscured everything, and the houses were gone and the rocky ground itself burned.

"Thermite," Stark said, and the troopers hooah-ed.

On-screen, some of the soldiers were up and moving, while others remained crouching, laying down cover fire. One of the upright soldiers, a sharp-featured man with a hawklike nose and a goatee, drew near to the camera and barked orders to the other soldiers. Then he glared into the camera with the most intense, predatory eyes Carl had ever seen.

"Baca!" some the troopers shouted, and the room rang with the name and a wave of hooahs.

Then the man with intense eyes—*Baca*, Carl told himself, *a name worth remembering*—ran off at a sprint, firing his weapon.

Stark paused the playback. "Baca is the personification of an optimized OODA loop: observe, orient, decide, act. Watch him. He's executes the OODA loop as quickly as any SEAL or Delta commando."

He restarted playback, and the camera followed the prized soldier, who turned down a side street and sprinted between two rows of buildings, lighting up the night with machine-gun fire with one hand and tossing grenades with the other. Other soldiers followed behind him, working in teams, kicking in doors—and killing anyone in sight.

Carl watched numbly as a woman ran into the street carrying a child, then watched in horror as Baca ended her with bullets and charged on without a thought, as if he she barely registered. The scene became a blur of atrocities. More gunfire and explosions; homes burning; men, women, and children falling dead. An animal—a dog, Carl thought, and truly didn't want to know—ran, completely engulfed in flames, from one of the homes, to be shot dead by one of the soldiers.

Carl looked away.

Awful sounds filled the room—worst of all the cheering of Phoenix Force.

Five minutes later, an eternity, it was over.

A massacre.

The troopers whooped with appreciation.

Carl felt sick. He couldn't believe what he'd seen, didn't want to believe it. . . .

"We'll break down the after-action report once I've had time to review it, but overall, this was a home run," Stark said. "Phoenix Force suffered only a single casualty, and she's in stable condition."

"Hooah!"

"It gets better," Stark said. "Bad-guy body count: 184."

"And one dog!" someone shouted, and the others roared with laughter.

Carl forced himself to join in, hating every second of it. This was madness.

"Best of all," Stark said, "we positively ID'd the guy we were after. Known terrorist dead, mission accomplished."

As Phoenix Force hooah-ed, Carl thought, *They massacred an entire village just to kill one man?*

Then, turning to him with a glow in his eyes, Stark said, "I'm glad you were able to see this, Carl. I didn't want you to get the impression you'd joined some cut-rate mercenary force, Merc Depot or something."

"'For all your mercenary needs,'" Henshaw said, and everybody laughed some more.

"Indeed," Stark said. "But you'll see for yourself one day, Carl. Once you finish initial training, I'll drop you into Baca's team and let you get your feet wet."

Carl's dread and revulsion shifted to terror. *Baca's team? Get my feet wet?*

"Helots!" someone yelled.

The others laughed, many of them repeating the strange word.

"An inside joke," Stark said, "You remember the Spartans and their *agoge*? Helots lived within Sparta but weren't really citizens. They were dime-a-dozen peasant types, trapped somewhere between serfdom and slavery. But they served a higher purpose, too. In order to graduate from the *agoge*, a young Spartan had to kill a Helot."

"Zip!" someone shouted.

"Zap!"

"Ka-boom!"

More laughter.

Stark chuckled along, and when the noise died down, he said,

"You'll love your final exam, Carl." He grinned, staring at Carl with shining eyes. "It's way, way better than knocking someone out."

"Killer Carl!" Henshaw squawked, and the room exploded in hooahs and laughter.

Carl forced one more smile onto his face, but inside he was reeling. Eric's journal was true—all of it. Parker's executions, the Old Man, killer kids, everything. Were Ross and Octavia okay?

24

WHEN MEDICAID LED THEM straight to the second checkpoint, they were impressed. Maybe a little freaked out. Cautiously optimistic, even. But impressed.

On their way to the third checkpoint, Medicaid cut left when the map clearly suggested they should go right, then fell into a screaming tantrum when they tried to redirect him. "This way!" he shouted over and over, until they finally gave his way a shot.

Fifteen minutes later, they had written their names in the logs of both the third and fourth checkpoints and were hurrying across swampy ground to catch up with the kid. It was as if he had memorized the map at a glance. Stranger still, he now had more than a dozen bright blue butterflies fluttering around his head.

Octavia and Ross ran after him, laughing. Amazing . . . absolutely amazing.

Medicaid bobbled along, crowned in living blue, babbling his nonsense song.

"Do you understand what this means?" Ross asked her.

"Medicaid is some kind of human GPS?"

"Yeah, that, a miracle and whatnot, but more important: we don't have to starve tonight."

She laughed. "Thank God."

Fifteen minutes and two more checkpoints later, Octavia looked up at the sky and said, "It's not even noon yet. I don't want to jinx us, but at this rate, we might beat everybody."

"I know. I think we're actually going to win." A huge grin spread across his face, closing his swollen eye. "We're saving a ton of time not having to consult the map. I never thought I'd say this, but Medicaid is a genius."

"One more checkpoint, then on to the finish line."

"And extra food."

"And sleep. I can't wait to see the look on Parker's face."

They slapped a high five and hurried on.

Medicaid led them up a steep hillside, moving with uncanny speed for such a roly-poly, normally clumsy guy.

They scaled the ridge and started down a slight counterslope, weaving through trees that grew farther and farther apart, until they stumbled laughing to the brink of another clearing. Perhaps a hundred yards away, down through the trees, Medicaid stood at the center of the open space.

Ross threw out his arm, stopping Octavia before she left the trees. "Oh no," he said. "Look who it is."

Decker leaned against the next checkpoint. He hadn't seen them yet, but he was staring directly at Medicaid, who stood only a short distance from the redneck.

Her guts tightened, her mouth went dry, and her stepfather laughed in her imagination. *So stupid! How could you ever believe things would work out for someone like you?*

The memory amplified her fear, weakened her.

You're not exactly Lady Luck, his voice reminded her, and she felt she could crumble into herself.

But no—she had to be strong.

She pictured the strongest person she knew—Carl—and used his image like a silver cross before a vampire to drive the voice of her stepfather from her mind.

Then real laughter floated up to her, and Decker's thugs entered the clearing.

Medicaid stopped singing. The butterflies puffed out and away in all directions like living confetti scattered into the air.

She balled her fists. "Okay, let's go."

Ross looked at her, wide-eyed. "Are you crazy? Do you know what's going to happen if we go down there?"

"No—but we both know what's going to happen if we don't."

He reached for her arm, but she stopped him with a glare.

"You don't know these guys," he said. "We should just wait."

"No. Carl wouldn't abandon him, and I won't, either." Half-mad with fear, she marched out of the trees, forced a smile onto her face, and said nonchalantly, "Hey, guys. You beat us here."

"Not yet we haven't," one of them said. Stroud chuckled. It was a mean, dirty sound.

She pretended not to hear. She tried to make her voice sound natural and upbeat. "So, are you guys, like, almost finished? I mean, is this your last checkpoint?"

For some reason, all of them started laughing . . . except Decker. He came off the post, staring at Medicaid, who started to whimper. Decker's face held little expression—no fake grin or tough-guy scowl—but somehow, he'd never looked scarier. It was his eyes. The rest of his face, its bruises faded green and yellow, was relaxed, almost sleepy, but his eyes stared at Medicaid with frightening intensity. They burned a liquid blue, like a gas flame without warmth, and always looked oddly out of place in his square, brutal face with its black stubble: the eyes of a movie star set in the head of a caveman. They stared from either side of his broken nose. *More of Carl,* she thought. *Like Parker's brace and bruises.* More of Carl's work, lingering like an echo, reminding her of his absence. And with that thought, a kind of fatigue weighed down her chest.

Even though she felt like running back into the trees, she forced herself to keep going downhill. "Did you guys sign the book yet? If not, go ahead. You obviously got here first." She made her face smile again.

Decker moved quickly. She saw his face change, saw his body shift, and had just enough time to understand what was happening before she heard the thump and Medicaid's yelp. Medicaid fell to the ground and curled up, clutching his stomach.

"Hey!" She pointed at Decker. "You can't do that."

Now he looked at her, and there was his smile again. She wondered if he ever smiled over anything other than pain. "Haven't you heard? I'm the sheriff. I can do anything I want."

He swung his shiny black baton overhead and brought it down hard on Medicaid's butt. There was a loud crack, and Medicaid screamed.

"No!" Octavia said. "Leave him alone!"

Stroud, the tall, skinny bully, laughed. Bruises encircled his eyes, too. More of Carl.

Oh Carl, she thought, *I wish you were here now.* But he wasn't. She had to handle this on her own. She wished she had her shank.

Medicaid tried to crawl away, but Decker stomped on his lower back and pinned him to the forest floor with his combat boot.

"Let's take his pants," one of the bullies said.

She pointed at Decker, trying not to show her fear. "If you don't knock it off, you'll be in big trouble. I'll tell on you." And then she thought, *I'll tell on you? What is this, third grade?*

Decker laughed and turned away from her. "Go ahead, Funk, take his pants."

"You can't be serious," she said. "That's just sick."

"You got no idea how sick I am." Decker stared into her eyes. "Want to find out?"

"No." *Okay—crap—*that was it. No more pretending to be brave. This guy was crazy. And out here in the woods—*oh God—*he could do anything.

"She's Hollywood's girlfriend," Stroud said. His hand reached for her.

She slapped it away. "Don't touch me."

"I'm thinking about making her *my* girlfriend," Decker said. "But she's flatter than roadkill."

Stroud reached for her again, grinning. "Yeah, but she's still *Hollywood's* girlfriend."

She swatted his hand away again and took a step back. That single step backward filled her with the urge to run.

Decker held up his baton. "She keeps looking at my club." He waggled the thing in her direction. "You like it, baby? You want to touch it?"

Stroud said something and laughed.

She pretended not to hear.

Medicaid jumped up and ran for the trees. Funk and the other one chased after him.

Decker didn't seem to care. He stepped toward her instead. "How come you got white hair?"

"Maybe she's an old lady."

Decker grabbed her arm. "She doesn't feel like an old lady." His grip was very strong, and she could feel his rough calluses.

"Ouch," she said, and instantly regretted it. Guys like Decker, you couldn't let them know they hurt you. It just wound them up. She couldn't break his grip. She felt the heat of him, and his smell—sharp and sour—filled her nose, making her want to turn away, to scream out.

He laughed. "Where are you going? The long arms of the law have got you now."

She felt Stroud's hands on her hips. Without thinking, she kicked backward. Her boot heel drove into something soft, and Stroud let go with a loud *oof!*

She swung her free hand at Decker's face, but he blocked it easily and yanked her toward him.

She screamed.

He twisted as he pulled, wrapping an arm around her and lifting her off the ground. For a second she was in the air, then she slammed into the ground so hard that light flashed in her head and all the air whooshed from her lungs.

Then he was on her. His body was hard and strong, and he pushed her into the forest floor and turned her onto her back and pressed her shoulders into the ground, hurting her. His blue eyes, coldly sane, stared from a face otherwise consumed by rage as he spoke. "You like to hit?" Then he slapped her hard in the face.

The world exploded with white-hot pain.

Suddenly, it was like her stepfather was alive again, like he was on her again, holding her down, hurting her, and she only wanted to kill or die. She cursed.

"Sounds good to me, honey. We got all day out here. All night, too, if I want. Because the sheriff can do anything he wants." He stared at her with something like curiosity and pinched her arm, hard.

She cried out and tried to bite his hand. He moved his hand a little, and her teeth clicked down on air.

Stroud appeared behind him, looking murderous.

Decker laughed. "Oh, you want to bite, hmmm? That's a bad little doggie. I have to teach you some manners. Like my daddy used to say, 'A dog, a woman, and a walnut tree—the more you beat 'em, the better they be.'" He raised his hand in the air, and she closed her eyes, waiting for it.

Then there was a thudding noise, and his weight tilted, lifting a little.

She pushed hard. He rolled off, and she scooted backward, expecting Stroud to jump on her, but he was looking up at the trees.

Atop the rise, Ross bent over, picking up another rock.

Decker cursed loudly, holding his face. Blood trickled from between his fingers.

She jumped up and ran. Running where, she didn't know, didn't care. Just running. Away from them. Away from Decker and Stroud and the voice of her stepfather. Off in the distance, she thought she heard Medicaid scream. Behind her, Decker yelled, "Get her! Ross is mine!"

Fear consumed her like fire. She ran, burning with terror, into the trees, making the most out of the lead she had on Stroud. She was a good runner, and as she wove through the trees, she fought her fear until her mind started working again. Her eyes scanned the forest. There: a steep uphill grade.

She sprinted for the slope. She heard him behind her, snapping branches and huffing for breath, but she didn't look back. No. She was going to run and run and run.

She scrambled higher, grabbing vines and saplings, yanking herself uphill like a monkey climbing a tree. The sounds of Stroud fell back, but she didn't slow. She rocketed up the slope, cleared the top edge, and entered a thicker forest, everything lost to shadow. Diving behind a huge plant with wide fronds, she crouched and drew air, giving her lungs a break and watching the ridge for Stroud.

Seconds later, as her breathing came back into her control, she heard him gasping for breath. She smiled grimly. Decker and his buddies always poked along at the back of the runs, too cool to try hard. Now

Stroud suffered for it. He stumbled over the rise and fell onto all fours at the crest. He didn't see her. He lifted his head, sucking air, with his eyes squeezed shut.

His weakness twisted her fear into rage. Had he really thought he could take her so easily? She charged from behind the bush.

He opened his eyes, saw her coming at the last second. "What the—?"

She swung her leg as hard as she could, and her combat boot smashed into his face. His head snapped backward, his arms lifted off the ground, and the top of him arched back and disappeared over the hill. His legs kicked up and then whipped away, too, and he was gone, screaming as he tumbled down the steep slope, bouncing and pitching into the air, smashing down again and bouncing, all the way to the jungle floor below, where he slammed into a tree and lay still.

Good, she thought, shaking with rage. *I hope he broke his back.*

Off in the distance, someone screamed.

Ross?

She had to go and help him, like he had helped her.

But she was so afraid. She looked down the hill. Stroud still lay on the ground, not moving.

She took a deep breath. She had to help Ross. But she pictured Decker, pictured his face over her, his cool blue eyes, and for a second she couldn't move.

Oh God, she thought. *Please. I need to be strong. I need to help Ross.*

That's when she spotted the club lying at her feet. Stroud's club. He must've dropped it when she kicked him.

Down below, he stirred. There wasn't much movement, but he was alive.

She picked up the club. It was lighter than she expected, made of wood. Its surface was smooth, but the handle had ridges for a better grip and a little leather loop attached to the butt end. She slipped her hand through the loop and started downhill.

She descended sideways, careful not to fall, and when she reached the bottom, Stroud cried out and tried to scramble away. She chased him down, knowing she had to beat him badly enough that he wouldn't follow her. He would've shown her no mercy. She would show him none.

She nailed his face with the nightstick. His body went loose, slumped forward, and lay still. She considered hitting him again and again, just finishing him. Forever. But there was just enough of her rational mind left to know that that was a bad idea, a horrible idea, that there would be no turning back.

Looking down, she saw one of his hands lying atop an exposed tree root. "You shouldn't touch people who don't want to be touched," she said, and she swung the club hard. She heard the bones in his hand break, and she stepped back, startled by her own ferocity. Her stomach squeezed and churned, and her gorge rose, but she didn't vomit. *Forget it,* she told herself, and ran toward Ross.

She paused at the edge of the clearing, which sat empty. A trap? She didn't have time to worry about that now.

She stepped into the open and waited. Nothing.

Across the clearing she sprinted, fear rising in her as she imagined Decker's rage.

Be tough, she commanded herself. *Be like Carl.* Reaching the other side of the clearing, she hammered up the hill but slowed when she passed the point from where Ross had thrown the rock. She wanted to have her full breath if she needed it. Besides, she'd be able to hear better if she walked and breathed quietly.

Scanning side to side and listening hard, she crept ahead. She hoped this was the right direction. Where was Medicaid when you needed him?

This thought saddened her. She pictured Medicaid, happy for the first time in this horrible place, bumbling along with his entourage of blue butterflies, leading them almost magically from checkpoint to checkpoint. Then she remembered his cries in the forest and went cold. What had they done to him?

A branch snapped.

She crouched behind a tree.

A large brown pig with long, curling tusks emerged from the undergrowth. The thing trotted across her view and disappeared into the gloom. She hoped it found Decker.

She stood, then dropped again into a crouch.

A loud shuffling . . .

And there he was: Decker.

Stalking through the jungle, blood on his shirt, a club in his hand, his eyes scanning side to side, he looked like some primitive subhuman out of the primordial depths of prehistory, a bloodthirsty savage that hunted its meat and ate it raw and steaming in the forest. Octavia crouched low and clutched her weapon, taking shallow breaths and praying he wouldn't see her.

Then, like the pig, Decker disappeared into the gloom.

Moving as quietly as she could, she hurried out his back trail. Fear filled her afresh. What if she found Ross sprawled in a pool of blood? She knew only basic first aid and had no supplies.

But these were bad thoughts, panic thoughts, dangerous to her now, and she pushed them from her mind and hurried on.

She was just starting to wonder if she'd gone in the wrong direction when a voice called softly from the undergrowth, "Octavia."

"Ross?"

A thick bush shook, and Ross emerged. She saw no new damage, but his eyes were wide. "Where's Decker?"

"He went that way." She nodded and then started moving in the other direction. She grabbed his hand and pulled him with her.

"Where did you get the club?"

"I'll tell you all about it later. We have to find Medicaid."

Ross shrugged. "Honestly? I don't want to sound like a coward, but I don't think there's much we can do for him. Not here. We have to tell Stark what happened."

She didn't say anything. Her face still ached where Decker had slapped her, and with her adrenaline receding, she felt pain creep into her shoulders and the back of her head, where the psycho had slammed her into the ground. The day's events didn't seem real, but here she was, hurting and holding a club in her hand.

It was real. It was all real.

"We can't leave Medicaid," she said. Ross started to protest, but she stopped him. "Hear me out. Earlier, when you started to talk about Carl and how they might've done something to him, I didn't want to listen. I didn't want to believe it. But now, after all this? Everything's different. I believe you. The journal, all of it."

"A step in the right direction," Ross said, "but I still don't see what that has to do with us putting our necks on the line for Medicaid."

"He needs us. Decker's 'the sheriff' now, right? He can do anything he wants."

Ross made a face like he'd bitten into a rotten lemon.

And in that wavering moment, she saw it, saw all at once, what her plan would be.

Ross sighed. "Fine. We'll take a quick look, but then we find Stark."

She held up one finger. "Not quite. I have to do one more thing first."

Ross waited, looking sick.

"I have to find Carl."

"What . . . at the Chop Shop?"

She nodded. "He might need us, Ross. And if he does, I'd rather die right here and have the pigs eat me than let him down. I mean it."

"I know you do." He was quiet for a time after that. His mouth moved like it was working a seed back and forth. "All right. Let's go. But I'm not spending all day looking for Medicaid. We'll try to find him, then we'll go looking for Carl." He rolled his eyes. "We are so screwed."

"Basically," she replied. "Do you have the compass?"

He shook his head. "The map is gone, too."

"Crap."

They moved along through the woods, checking the sun when they could, continuing in what they hoped was the right direction. After a while, she said, "If you hadn't thrown that rock—thanks so much, Ross. I mean, you saved me—"

He put on a cheesy smile. "That's me, always ready to save a damsel in distress."

She laughed. "For the first time ever, I actually appreciate you joking."

"It grows on you."

Seconds later, Ross hissed, and they both crouched. She heard movement but saw nothing. Looking at her with wide eyes, he pointed downhill and raised four fingers.

She saw Decker in the distance, passing through the trees. Then came Funk and the one whose name she couldn't remember, and finally Stroud, who limped along, holding his broken hand. The four of them headed off toward where she thought the road was. Good. Now she and Ross could hurry in the opposite direction and hopefully find Medicaid. She hoped he was okay.

She motioned to Ross, and they started moving again. Avoiding the clearing altogether, they entered the part of the woods into which Medicaid had run.

They followed a pig trail into a dim, muggy forest where so many mosquitoes brushed against them, it was like walking through a dark room filled with cobwebs. She risked a few quiet calls out to the kid. Nothing.

They moved slowly, looking behind bushes and under trees, anyplace Medicaid might hide. He was probably so freaked out that he wouldn't trust even them.

"Look," Ross said.

His tone filled her with dread.

Medicaid's pants lay on the ground. One boot lay nearby. Both were bloody.

Ross cursed. "Beating him up is one thing, but why humiliate him? All jokes aside, the jungle's no place to be going around without your pants."

They called a few more times. Nothing.

A little further on, she spotted a drop of bright red blood lying atop the muddy pig trail, round as a screaming mouth. Seconds later, they found another drop. In this way they tracked him, like hunters following a wounded deer.

That's how he must feel, she thought, *terrified, like some wounded animal.*

Blood led them to another clearing, at the center of which pulsed something large and blue . . . something blue that made no sense. At first she thought it was alive, some type of shimmering alien—something—a blue lump the size of a bathtub, wavering like a pile of blue eyes, all of them blinking. Then, drawing closer, she saw what it really was: a mound of bright blue butterflies, all of them fluttering and jostling.

"Weird," Ross said. "There must be thousands."

"Come on," she told him. "We have to find him."

Suddenly butterflies lifted into the air like an eruption of blue lava.

"Oh—oh no . . ." she said.

A few of the insects remained, their wings opening and closing rhythmically, like so many beating hearts. One sat atop his white kneecap. Another wobbled on his red hair. Still another—and this was the one she noticed just before she started screaming—perched on his open, unblinking eye.

Medicaid was dead.

25

SHAKING WITH EXHAUSTION AND WILD WITH FEAR, Octavia fought through the dense vegetation. Mud swallowed her feet. Roots tripped her. Vines clutched her. Thorns tore her flesh. Broad leaves covered her face, making her blind, trying to smother her, as if the forest itself wanted her dead.

She growled, struggling forward.

The hooting drew closer.

Just behind her, Ross sobbed. He couldn't keep up. Whenever they hit open patches, she longed to sprint away, but she couldn't abandon him.

Not now. Not when she knew the truth.

Decker's gang had killed Medicaid.

And now they want to kill us.

She and Ross had stayed staring too long at the body in disbelief, and the killers had returned to find them.

She crawled under a fallen tree, remembering things in flashes: Medicaid, the bright blue butterfly sitting atop his open eye, its wings winking at her, as if the whole thing, his death, Phoenix Island, the world . . . everything . . . was one big cosmic joke.

That's right, her stepfather's voice said. *The world's one big joke, and you're the punch line. . . .*

As she remembered the awful discovery—the screams that had ripped out of her, and the murderers shouting, coming for them—a touch of madness shivered through her again.

No. She couldn't afford madness. Panic had already cost them enough time.

She had fled blindly into the forest and only after she-didn't-know-how-long had finally calmed enough to head for the road. Or where she hoped the road would be.

They had to find a road and get to an adult before Decker could catch them. If he caught them . . .

"Rossy-poo!" someone yelled in the forest behind them. He sounded close. So did the laughter that followed.

Octavia jolted ahead and slammed into a thick screen of wide leaves that slapped against her face, blocking out the light of day. Their sap burned her skin, setting fire to what seemed like a thousand scratches and cuts that covered her body. She pushed at them with her hand, swiped at them with the club, and powered forward, sure that any second now, the air behind her would fill with the screams of Ross and the laughter of the killers.

"*Greg-oh-ric!*" Decker called in a mocking voice. "We're gonna get you, baby!" It sounded like he was maybe ten feet behind her now. . . .

Driving through the blinding vegetation, she could all but feel Decker's hand close on her shoulder.

Then she stumbled out of the green mouth of the jungle and into the light and fell hard on the packed dirt of the road. The club clattered away, and she scrambled after it, her palms burning. As her hand closed on the club, her heart surged.

The road stretched away in both directions, hedged by dark forest.

A loud thrashing sounded behind her. The vegetation shook, and Ross struggled free with one hand over his eye, wincing with pain.

Something must have jabbed him. So be it. They had to run.

Octavia grabbed his hand. "Come on, man. They're right behind us."

They ran as fast as they could up the road.

The hunters spilled out of the woods behind them, hooting like cannibals, their jeering loud as gunfire out on the open road.

A scream ripped involuntarily from her lungs. She pulled away from Ross without realizing what she was doing, then slowed going into a bend in the road, waving blindly with one arm for him to hurry. She turned halfway as she ran and saw Ross struggling after her, his face a bruised mask of terror. Perhaps a football field behind him and closing fast was Decker. With the ancient terror of stalked prey, she watched Decker eat the distance.

She shouted for Ross, fear an erupting volcano in her now, unable to tear her eyes away from the terrible sight of Decker drawing closer and closer. One hundred yards . . . eighty . . . fifty . . .

And fleeing with her face turned, she nearly ran into the jeep parked in the middle of the road.

She stopped herself at the last second, throwing out a hand and catching herself on the hood. *They were safe!*

"What's going on here?" A familiar voice boomed.

Drill Sergeant Parker stood beside the jeep, glaring at her.

For the first time in her life, she was happy to see him. "They . . ." she said, fighting to catch her breath, "they killed him."

Parker stepped toward her. "What did you say?"

One of his soldiers stepped from the forest to her left.

Ross slammed into her, gasping for breath.

"Him," Octavia said, pointing at Decker, who stopped running and walked toward them now with a big smile on his face. Farther back, the others pumped their fists in the air and shouted. "Them. They killed Medicaid."

"Bull," Parker said.

His word stopped her like a punch to the gut.

Parker's soldier gestured for her to hand him the club.

She ignored him. "What did you say?"

"Bull," Parker said. He pointed to the club. "Where'd you get that?"

"What?" she asked. None of this made sense. She'd just reported a murder, but he—

"She took it off Stroud," Decker said, walking up to them.

She turned and drew back the club. "Stay away from us, you murderer!"

Ross stepped between them, facing Decker. "You're in big trouble."

Still smiling, Decker said, "I think you're the one who's in trouble, buddy."

A hand closed on Octavia's wrist. She screamed and tried to pull away but couldn't break the grip. Parker tore the club from her hand. "Cuff her."

"What are you doing?" she said.

The soldier she hadn't noticed before grabbed her from behind and slammed her up against the jeep. He pressed her hips against the grill and flattened her chest and face against the hood. "Arms back. Wrists together."

She struggled briefly—vaguely aware of the sounds of fighting behind her, Ross's crying out—but the soldier was too strong, and as the cold steel cuffs closed around her wrists, Parker's face leaned in close, smiling.

"You're just like your boyfriend, huh? An individual." He reached out and pinched her nose like he was some playful uncle. "Well, you messed up this time, sugar britches. You and Ross killed that poor carrottop sack of crap, and now you're going to pay."

Then she understood. "You planned this, didn't you? You told Decker to . . . do *that* so you could blame us. You're crazy!"

He crossed his eyes, stuck out his tongue, and burst into laughter. Then, standing straight, he said, "Throw Ross and Mrs. Hollywood in the back of the jeep. It's hunting season!"

26

THE RUCKSACK SQUEAKED with every stride. Carl tugged at the chest straps, and then it stopped, leaving only the pounding of combat boots on the hard-packed forest trail, the sounds of the birds, and the easy rhythm of breathing—Stark's and his own, synchronized as neatly as their strides. For now, he had to pretend to be completely in step with Stark's plans and vision . . . when everything in him wanted to run in the opposite direction.

They chugged up a steep hill without slowing. For the hour or so since they'd left all that madness back at Camp Phoenix Force, they'd been sprinting up and down the twisting network of jungle trails, dressed in full-length fatigues and combat boots, a good sixty pounds on each of their backs. Despite the sparring session and heavy pack, Carl's "new body" was well up to the challenge.

His mind wasn't doing as well.

Stark was none other than the Old Man from Eric's journal, a six-foot-six, combat-experienced soldier who could bench-press half a ton and who planned to cart Carl off to some war-torn corner of the world to kill people. That would mean the death of everything Carl stood for, the death of the person he'd always been, the death of his father's son . . . and the birth of a new person, a cold-blooded killer, the son of Stark.

He *had* to escape.

The pack started squeaking again.

He tugged the straps.

Ahead of him, Stark laughed. "Welcome to the soldiering life. Since the days of the Spartans, soldiers have struggled with equipment. We'll doctor your pack back at the hangar. Sound good?"

"Sounds great," Carl said. He'd never been good at hiding his feelings, but he deserved an Oscar for his recent performance.

They sprinted up another steep incline.

How could he escape?

Armed guards watched over the boats at Camp Phoenix Force, and stowing away on the supply plane seemed impossible. He didn't know its exact schedule, and even if he did, how would he sneak on board? Stark let him go out alone for runs and sometimes left him alone to study, but Carl couldn't exactly time these moments with the plane's arrival. Even if he did get on board, where would he hide?

Insanity . . .

Come on Campbell, he thought. *Get somebody over here before it's too late.*

Breaking his thoughts, Stark whooped, and Carl watched a small herd of pigs move off into the deeper darkness of the forest.

"Vicious animals, those pigs," Stark said. "Run into a big boar, you better be prepared." He slapped the large knife that rode always in a sheath at his belt. The man loved knives, a fascination likely stemming from the samurai and their Bushido code—just one more piece of his well-educated madness.

They broke from the trees onto the wide stone ridge that ran like a spine across the island. Despite Carl's anxieties, the view here above the tree line staggered him, the whole of the island sprawling greenly beneath them, the surrounding Pacific misty in its vastness. To his right, beyond the slope they'd just ascended, Carl could see sections of road, a broken brown ribbon barely visible through the canopy. Beyond the road, a straighter, unbroken line split the jungle, dividing this half of the island from the eastern "here are dragons" side. From this height, Carl could see that the fence ran from one end of the island to the other, the trees just on either side of it cleared away. Considering this half of the island had vicious pigs and psychopaths with automatic weapons, what "dragons" were so dangerous to necessitate an electric fence like that? He didn't even want to know. . . .

Turning to the other side, he took an instinctive step backward, his gut clenching like a fist. The ridge plummeted away in a sheer cliff of raw stone, a hundred-foot drop to the lower forest. Straight ahead, like a stone skull rising from the rocky spine, towered the tallest peak of the mountain. Beyond, the ocean stretched darkly into infinity.

"To the summit," Stark said, waving Carl forward. "No better place to watch the sunset."

Carl followed, sticking to the center of the ridge. He'd never really been afraid of heights, but the sharp cutaway to his left—all that open space!—felt like it could just suck him out into the void. He locked his eyes on the trail and kept putting one foot in front of the other.

At the summit, Stark dropped his pack and hooah-ed.

Maintaining his Oscar performance, Carl did the same.

Around them stretched the blunt peak of raw stone, flat as an observation deck, and roughly the size of a boxing ring. Stark went to the edge and stood, facing the void, with his hands on hips.

"Alexander the Great conquered the known world before his thirtieth birthday. Marched an army all the way from Greece to India. Destroyed the Persians, everyone. In Afghanistan, they thought he was a god. As legend has it, he scaled a mountain not unlike this, and reaching its peak, looked out upon the vast lands beneath him, and wept." He turned to Carl. "Do you know why he wept?"

"He'd lost a lot of soldiers?"

Stark shook his head. "He wept because there was nothing left for him to conquer."

"Wow," Carl said, doing his best to sound impressed.

Turning to face the ocean, Stark said, "Whenever I come here, I imagine Zeus looking down from Mount Olympus and laughing at a world still punishing itself with the gift of fire."

One push, Carl thought, staring at Stark's back, *would send him over the edge.*

"Prometheus's fire has given the leaders of the free world everything they need to annihilate our enemies," Stark said. "Satellite surveillance, drone planes, tactical nukes, genetically tailored super-flus . . . everything. But while our citizens and soldiers die, they play Hamlet and hesitate. Why?"

He would never see it coming, Carl thought, taking a step forward. *One push, and I could end this thing.*

"Because Prometheus's fire also created the information age," Stark said, "and with several billion idiots watching CNN and whining on the internet, the most powerful men on the planet are afraid to act."

Carl stopped. He couldn't do it. He was no murderer.

Stark turned with a smile. "But you and I, son, we're different. We understand that progress comes at a price. It's not ready yet, but soon, when Prometheus's fire gives us the master chip, we'll act very decisively. Then, when it's our turn to look down on the conquered world, we won't weep like Alexander. We'll laugh like Zeus."

"Awesome," Carl said, and even managed a smile. What did Stark mean, *conquered world*? What was he planning to do with the master chip?

Stark checked his watch, unzipped his rucksack, and came away with two pairs of binoculars. Handing one set to Carl, he said, "Come on. I want to show you something."

They went to the edge, where the mountainside sloped steeply away in a storm-damaged swath of forest. From a dense tangle of low vegetation jutted the splintered ends of snapped trees . . . compound fractures of the jungle that had been. Carl thought of Mitchell's broken bone.

Stark pointed downhill. "Look familiar?"

Carl raised the binoculars to his eyes and saw an all-too-familiar scene: the ocean, the low block buildings, the ramp, the pier, the landing strip, the parking lot where Parker had stolen his medal.

"Oh, yeah," he said, "that's where we landed the first day."

Stark said, "From what I understand, you got to know the pavement pretty well that afternoon."

Carl forced a laugh. Stark knew everything.

"Keep watching. Something genuinely interesting is about to occur."

But instead of looking where Stark seemed to be indicating, Carl's eyes stared at what he'd just spotted.

A boat.

A lone vessel bobbing up and down on the tide, moored to a dark pier that jutted out like a finger pointing to the mainland, to Mexico, to the United States beyond. . . .

"Here they come," Stark said. "I hear them."

Carl heard an engine down there somewhere but didn't look away from the ship. Hope rose within him and popped, bright as a flare, in his chest. *A boat!* He'd thought all of them were at Camp Phoenix Force, but no—on the far side of the low buildings flanking the landing strip, the boat bobbed as rhythmically as a beckoning hand.

"Right on time," Stark said, and glancing away from the boat, Carl saw a jeep back to the end of the pier.

Two soldiers wrestled a large drum out of the back, tilted it, and dumped a wet mash off the pier. The water went cloudy, and Carl saw things floating on the surface.

"Garbage from the chow hall," Stark said. "Keep watching."

All at once, the water boiled. Dark shapes thrashed beneath the surface, swirling and splashing. One of the soldiers took a step backward.

Stark laughed. "Hammerhead sharks. Some of nature's finest killing machines scavenging our scraps."

"Jeez," Carl said. Even from this distance, he could see their dark, muscular bodies thrashing.

"Now for the main course," Stark said.

Down below, the soldiers took something else out of the vehicle.

At first, Carl didn't believe what he was seeing. It was a body. A *person's* body.

"The price of progress runs high at times," Stark said. "Never forget that, Carl."

As if it were but a sack of potatoes, the soldiers swung the mass and launched it off the pier, out into the feeding frenzy.

"No," Carl groaned, and watched in horror as the body jerked under the surface, watched as the legs wobbled back and forth, then dipped under, watched as the water turned red . . . as red as the hair of the boy being consumed.

Carl turned and puked his guts out.

27

PARKER SMILED AT HER through the bars of the sweatbox. "How'd you sleep, Mrs. Hollywood?"

There it was again—Mrs. Hollywood—further convincing her that this was all about Carl, Parker's way of getting back at the only person who'd been good enough and strong enough to defy him.

His smile disappeared. "I asked you a question, orphan. How did you sleep?"

"Like the dead, Drill Sergeant."

The smile came back, wider this time. "Like the dead. Good. I like that."

In reality, she'd barely slept, her whole body throbbing like an open nerve. Her arms and neck and face bubbled with what looked like the world's worst case of poison ivy, an oozing red rash that burned and itched until she thought she'd lose her mind. She'd passed in and out of sleep ragged with nightmares, and spent her waking hours killing bugs, slapping her burning rash, crying, praying, and trying not to picture Medicaid dead in the meadow. Now the sun boiled overhead, cooking the sweatbox, baking the air until it seemed her flesh would crack open on her bones, steaming like meat on the grill.

"What's that stuck in your nose?" he asked.

"Pieces of my shirt, Drill Sergeant. It stinks in here."

Parker shook his head in mock disappointment. "That's not *your* shirt. All uniforms are property of Phoenix Island."

"Sue me, Drill Sergeant."

Parker laughed. "I should've locked you up a long time ago. You're funny in a cage."

She said nothing. It didn't matter. What you did, what you said, it didn't make any difference here. If Parker had it in for you, you were screwed. That's all there was to it.

"Well," he said, "you look pretty dumb with your nose plugged up. Maybe if you didn't keep it so high in the air, the stink wouldn't bother you so much."

"How long do I have to stay in here?"

"That's 'How long do I have to stay in here, *Drill Sergeant?*' And here's your answer: until I let you out."

She rolled her eyes. "And when are you going to do that . . . Drill Sergeant?" She stretched out his title, making it sickly sweet with sarcasm. Maybe it was dumb, sassing him, but she couldn't play the good little girl anymore. He was evil—pure evil, that's all there was to it—so why hold back?

He shook his head, laughing again. "You're just like your boyfriend."

"I don't have a boyfriend."

"I can see why," Parker said. "You got white hair like an old woman, and you act like you're the Queen of France. Who would want you?"

"Where's Ross?" She hadn't seen him since the previous night, when they'd dumped her in the sweatbox and dragged Ross into the barracks. Throughout the long night, his screams cut the darkness, like echoes of her nightmares.

"Decker and the boys are getting him ready."

She was afraid to ask him what he meant, afraid she already knew.

He unsnapped his canteen from his belt pouch, took a long drink, and smacked his lips. "Mmm . . . cool, cool water, know what I mean?"

"What do you want from me?"

"Everything."

"Stop playing around. You know I didn't do anything to Medicaid. Ross didn't, either. It was Decker. You know—"

"Medicaid's shark food. Just quit your whining, sweetie pie. I'm the boss around here. Judge, jury, and executioner."

"Oh yeah? Tell that to Stark."

Parker's face went deep red, and his eyes bored into hers. "When they hunt you down, I'm going to throw you in a hole and tamp your mouth full of dirt. The last thing you'll see on this earth is my boot heel."

She pressed against the back of the cage.

"Well, I'd love to stay and chat, princess," Parker said, standing up, "but it's hunting time."

Down by the barracks, people started shouting.

"Here we go," Parker said, and whooped in the direction of the shouting.

When he swaggered downhill, she saw them, coming onto the quad: boys and girls waving sticks in the air.

No . . . not sticks . . .

Spears.

At the front of the pack, Decker shoved Ross onto the ground.

Ross, barefoot and bloody, dressed only in shorts, staggered to his feet, looking small and fragile as a third-grader.

Parker yelled at him, pointing toward the gate, which stood wide open.

The kids roared and pumped their spears as Ross ran through the gate, out of the compound, and into the jungle.

"Start the timer!" Parker said, and she saw Funk poking at one of the stopwatches they used on the obstacle course. "Ten minutes!"

"Hooah!" a voice shouted from the guard tower, and gunfire tore into the open sky, making her jump.

"That boy is a thief and a murderer!" Parker yelled to everyone. "He killed one of your own! And now we're gonna hunt him down like the rabid dog he is!"

"Hooah!" the mob yelled, real excitement clear on their faces even from this distance.

Monsters . . .

"When you see the flare," Parker said, "the hunt's over. Come back to base. We'll have us a gay old time. A bonfire and everything. We'll put Ross's head on a stake and dance around it like a bunch of wild in-juns! And then, in a couple of days"—he turned and pointed uphill—"we hunt *her*."

28

ALL THROUGH THE SLEEPLESS NIGHT, Carl's mind replayed with merciless lucidity the nightmare scene he'd witnessed from the mountaintop. He endured, focusing on one thought: he *had* to get off Phoenix Island.

At dawn, he rose to face another day with Stark. They launched straight into training, no mention of the previous day, as if nothing at all had changed in the world. For Carl, it was harder than ever to smile and pretend everything was all right, but he did it. He had to keep Stark happy. . . .

They started with a grappling session that devolved into a discussion of this samurai book *The Book of Five Rings*, which led to a full-armor kendo session, which took them back to grappling when Stark knocked Carl's wooden sword to the mat.

During a lunch of frothy protein shakes, Stark said he had to step out for a while.

"Okay," Carl said, careful to keep his voice nonchalant. "I'll probably take a run, then finish *The Book of Five Rings*."

Stark just stared for a second, looking thoughtful, then he gulped down the rest of his shake and set it down hard on the table. "That works—but stick to the north end of the island, okay? Parker has the orphans out in the woods today."

"Will do," Carl said, and meant it.

The north end, after all, was exactly where he needed to go.

* * *

HE SPRINTED ALL THE WAY FROM THE HANGAR, bursting with excitement, and literally laughed aloud when he reached the water, looped around the building, and saw the boat, still floating there, unguarded.

"Yes," he said, and threw a quick combo.

Then he looked closer, and it was like getting hit below the belt.

Thick chains secured the boat to a stout post.

He stared at the chain and lock and tried to think around them. A key. Or something to break the chain. One or the other. That's what he needed.

Hefting the chain—each link larger than his hand—he thought he'd better hunt for the key. His eyes flashed to the nearby building.

He smelled garage smells: oil, grease.

He tried the door. Locked, of course. Like so many things on Phoenix Island, this building would surrender no secrets. Just a block building with a single metal door, locked, no windows, no clues. Just another roadblock.

Why wasn't this boat with the others? It made no sense. Unless . . .

He looked from boat to shed, shed to boat, smelling oil.

He returned to the boat and examined its outboard motor. A quick glance inside the tilted case revealed a charred interior gunked with . . . something. The motor was dead. The boat was useless.

Inside Carl, something faded. This boat useless, the other boats guarded . . . he was back to the plane, and after a night of believing he might be able to use this to escape, he realized more clearly than ever how desperate, how suicidal, his supply-plane plan really was. How in the world could he even get on board?

Maybe escape was impossible.

No, he told himself. *Don't give in. Keep fighting.*

Meanwhile, he had to get running again. He couldn't take too long. The last thing he needed was Stark getting suspicious. He needed Stark's trust, needed the freedom to keep doing solo runs if he was going to find a way off this island.

So yeah, time to head back.

Still, he lingered for just a moment to admire the sparkling blue ocean. Amazing . . . even here, even now, amid his frustration and concerns, the ocean pulled him. Its beauty, its tranquility . . . he longed to run off the dock and do a flying cannonball into its warm, blue depths . . . and again he imagined swimming in an ocean and wondered how the salt would taste, how badly it would sting his eyes, and how the currents would feel, pulling as he swam.

But these waters were full of sharks.

Sharks and the dead.

He pictured the horrific scene again, the soldiers flinging the pale, red-haired body out into the roiling chaos of the sharks.

Medicaid.

It had happened right here. He paused. Shouldn't he feel something? Some deeper emotion? Should he say some sort of prayer? But there was nothing to do or say. Location meant little. The whole island was stained in blood and haunted with the dead. Horror stories lay beneath every square foot of this awful place, and at any time, hidden atrocities might surface like sharks rising from the surf to take a bite out of whatever faith he tried to maintain.

Enough, he told himself. *You have to keep moving.*

There was no time to dream of swimming in the ocean, no time to mourn the dead. He needed to head back to the hangar and finish reading Stark's warrior book, needed to stay in the man's good graces, no matter what, and find a way to escape.

Carl started running again, pointing himself toward home and putting one foot in front of the other while his brain worked without success at the problem of escape. His legs carried him uphill, out of the sun and into the dark and humid jungle. He had just rejected a ridiculous idea—maybe he could find a repair manual and fix the boat, a little at a time!—when an all-too-familiar marshy stench filled his nostrils. Looking to the left he saw the foreboding structure called the Chop Shop and felt the same bone-deep dread he experienced every time he saw it.

Like something out of a horror movie, he thought. The stench, the tall fence topped in razor wire, all those low buildings rounded with thatch and dark with shadow, squatting in the gloomy compound like giant mushrooms. Poisonous ones . . .

He jerked with surprise.

Someone stood at the fence, staring out at him.

Someone huge. Someone familiar.

Carl lurched to a stop, a grin coming onto his face. No way . . . it couldn't be.

"Campbell?"

Carl laughed. It *was* Campbell, standing against the fence of the Chop Shop compound, staring at him. Good old Walker Campbell, too cool to show any excitement, even if they hadn't seen each other for a month.

"What are you doing here?" Carl asked, leaving the road and going to the fence. This was insane . . . and awesome. Campbell! "I thought you left a long time ago. Man, it's awesome to—"

But he stopped then. Stopped talking, stopped walking, even breathing for a second, alarm mounting in him now that he could really see his friend.

It was Campbell, all right, but there was something wrong with him. Horribly, horribly wrong.

The big guy's head drooped against the fence, as if his neck muscles could no longer support its weight. His face, always so expressive, was a mask of slack flesh. His strong jaw dangled beneath his open mouth. His eyes, always alert and burning with intelligence, stared emptily at Carl, through him . . .

"What's happened?" Carl asked in a frightened whisper.

Campbell said nothing, showed no sign he'd heard the question, no sign he'd even noticed Carl. His thick arms dangled loose at his sides, and where his ashen forehead leaned into the fence, the chain links seemed to be pressing into his flesh, into his skull.

"What did they *do* to you?"

Campbell didn't answer, but Carl's own mind did, telling him in a cold tone born of a hard life, *You know what they did. You know exactly what they did.*

Fighting down his terror, Carl reached out and touched his friend's forehead through the chain link. It was cool and dry.

Campbell uttered a low sound like a winter draft moaning out of a dry well, and its chill shuddered through Carl.

"Are you all right, Campbell? Say something."

The mountainous kid stared ahead, eyes glazed. The lid over his left eye was swollen and discolored, the eye itself badly bloodshot. A long strand of drool hung from his lower lip.

Maybe he got hurt on his last day, Carl thought. *Hit his head, got a concussion . . .*

No. You know better than that, the cold voice in his head corrected him. *You know exactly what happened to him.*

And he remembered the Chop Shop, remembered Vispera leaning over him, touching his eye . . . his left eye.

Panic shuddered through him. "Oh, man, Campbell. Can you hear me? It's Carl. Carl Freeman. Can you hear me?"

Another moan, another winter draft from the well, only this time, it didn't just chill Carl, it froze him solid.

He stared, unable—or unwilling—to make it real.

It wasn't possible. Not Campbell. Campbell escaped. Campbell was back in Texas, partying it up with his girlfriends, laughing, listening to music, growing back his dreadlocks. Campbell was setting up meetings with his senator, with the news media. Campbell was too big, too strong, too smart, too cool for any of this. . . .

Campbell burped airily.

Carl felt like screaming.

He knew just what had happened here, no matter how much he wanted to deny it. Campbell never left the island. Instead, he got a one-way ticket to the Chop Shop, where Dr. Vispera used him like a guinea pig.

What had Stark said about his beloved master chip?

It wasn't ready yet, wasn't safe yet.

But it was getting close.

How did you think they were testing the thing? he asked himself. *How did they know it wasn't safe yet? How did they know they were getting closer?*

And then it all came clear to him.

Nobody ever goes home. They made Phoenix Force and became professional killers, or they washed out, in which case, they were hunted, murdered, and fed to the sharks, or brought here and used as lab rats. The foul doctor lifted their eyelids, jammed in the newest version of his master chip, and turned their brains into pudding just like that.

Who would miss them? They were just a bunch of throwaway orphans.

He remembered Stark patting him on the back as Carl had puked at the sight of the soldiers throwing Medicaid's body to the sharks. "Be strong, Carl," he'd said, and it had taken all of Carl's strength not to attack him. "Resolute acceptance of one's own death is not enough; one must come to accept the deaths of others, as well. Don't saddle yourself with emotional attachments to your inferiors. The price of progress runs high at times, and you can't afford weakness."

Summoning every ounce of willpower, Carl had wiped his mouth and nodded, to appease the Old Man.

Now, feeling like he might puke again, he once again summoned his will. He had to get control, had to stop himself from tumbling into a complete meltdown.

Forcing himself to breathe, he thought, *You have to be tough. You have to control yourself. If you don't, you'll never leave this place.*

Campbell watched through blank eyes.

The price of progress runs high at times. . . .

To Stark, Campbell was just one more lost pawn.

Campbell, Campbell, Campbell! No matter what he tried to do, horror clanged in Carl like some nightmare clock—like ten clocks, a thousand, a million, all of them tolling and crashing inside his skull.

But no—he fought down his panic. He had to keep his cool. Had to focus on what he could *do,* not what he felt.

"I'm going to help you," he said to his friend. "I'm going to get you out of here, make it better." But even as he said these words, he felt them break in the air, felt their emptiness flutter away.

Get him out of here? Make it better? How? A brain transplant?

His mind drew back like a hand from a hot stove. It couldn't be true.

But it was.

Couldn't be.

Was.

And so his mind clanged, rejecting, acknowledging, rejecting, seeing
. . . and shock gave way to sorrow, which gave way to rage.

Why would they do this? Campbell was so cool, so talented, had so
much potential. . . .

As if in response, Campbell moaned again.

Then the music started.

Carl gritted his teeth and looked past Campbell to the low building
with the thatched roof and porch, out of which spilled what sounded like
opera music. *Just go on in there and kill him*, Carl thought. *Snap the torturer's neck before he can do this to anyone else, before he can do it to
Ross, to Octavia, to you. Then go straight back to the hangar and put a
steak knife in Stark's back. . . .*

But he knew better. A life full of tragedy had given him the strength
to see what was real, and his experiences here were teaching him a reluc-
tant patience. Going after the doctor now would be foolish, and going
after Stark would be suicidal. Neither action would do Campbell any
good at all.

Still, the flash of rage had helped him, had pulled him from shock
and sorrow long enough to cook up bad plans, at least. His whole life,
anger had ruled him. It had canceled everything from fear to common
sense, getting him into trouble again and again.

Well, now it was going to get him out of trouble. He was going
to use it to keep other, paralyzing emotions in check until he got off
this island. That was what he was going to do. Period. He would
rather die trying than end up as a zombie. *That* fate terrified him
more than anything.

The plane was due in mere days. Stark kept mentioning it.

The plane.

Yes, it was a desperate plan, but he needed to risk everything, regardless of the odds, to save Ross and Octavia and stop these madmen
and do whatever he could for Campbell and the others.

"I'm going to help," Carl said, but stopped himself from saying
more, stopped himself from launching into a long good-bye. He couldn't
let sorrow freeze the flames of his anger.

So he turned away from his friend and started running again. Off in the distance, more gunfire sounded. The fourth burst since he'd left the hangar. He hoped everything was okay back at the training base.

He had to help Ross and Octavia before it was too late, had to lock down his emotions, using anger if necessary, but never losing himself to rage. Even though every fiber in his body longed to fight, he had to smile until he found a way onto that flight.

Those tasks seemed utterly impossible. They would demand every ounce of strength, guts, and brains he could muster.

So be it, he told himself, picturing Stark in a prison cell. *The price of progress runs high sometimes.*

And as he turned up the road toward the hangar, a flare from some training exercise or other popped in the distance. Carl thought his anger could be like that: a controlled, useful fire.

29

CARL LOOKED UP from Musashi's *The Book of Five Rings* when he heard a jeep pull in outside the hangar. That was fast. He hadn't expected Stark back so soon.

Here we go, Carl thought. *Back to the act.*

The door handle turned.

Carl forced a smile.

Only to find Parker coming through the door.

A complete surprise—and a weird moment: the last time he'd seen the man was weeks ago, when the drill sergeant had tried to lop off his head.

How things had changed. Now Carl lived here, apprenticed to Parker's boss. Fit and clean, he wore a fresh uniform—a Phoenix Force uniform. Parker, on the other hand, was sweaty and dirty, covered in something . . . blood? That's what it looked like, and knowing Parker, that's probably what it was. Blood. The guy would never get past blood.

So in a way, it was a rush, seeing him step through the door.

But Carl didn't like the look on his face.

He expected anger, maybe shock.

Instead, Parker just grinned.

"He's not here," Carl said.

"I know where he is, Hollywood."

Hearing that name—Hollywood—lit a fire in Carl. "Why don't you go there and see him, then, Parker? I'm studying."

"Ooh la la," Parker said. "Studying. What a brownnoser. I didn't come to see Stark. I came to see you."

Decker, Funk, and Chilson stepped in behind him. They had night-sticks.

"Nice armbands," Carl said. "What are you guys, trick-or-treating as Nazis?"

They said nothing. Funk and Chilson glared. Decker looked like he was trying not to laugh.

Parker took another step inside. "Study break, Hollywood. I got something for you to see."

"Not interested," Carl said. "I follow you out the door, then the four of you jump me, right?"

"Never," Parker said. "Stark wouldn't want his precious baby getting hurt."

"You mean the baby that almost killed you," Carl said.

Parker scowled, then recovered his smirk. "Ross is out there."

"Ross?" He stood. "Where?"

Parker gestured outside. "Right over here in the jeep. Come on out and say hi."

Carl started toward him. "What are you up to, Parker?"

"Just taking your friend for a little swim." He disappeared out the door.

Carl followed, squinting as he stepped into the sunlight.

Decker and his buddies stood at the back of the jeep. Funk and Chilson grinned. Decker just stared, looking amused, interested.

For a second, no one said anything. Carl heard the jeep's radiator clicking.

Then Parker drew his pistol.

"Don't be stupid, Parker," Carl said. "You shoot me, Stark will kill you."

"Pipe down, Hollywood. I'm not going to shoot you. Not unless you make me. You do anything stupid, I'll put a bullet right through your belt line. Spend the rest of your life in a wheelchair, carrying a colostomy bag. How's that sound?"

"Sounds like I'm out of here. You want to talk to me, come back when Stark's around." He turned and started back inside.

"What about your little buddy?" Parker said.

"What about him? You lied. He's not here."

"Sure he is." Parker motioned toward the back of the jeep. "He's taking a nap. Poor kid's all tuckered out from running through the woods."

Funk laughed.

Apprehension sizzled through Carl. "What did you do?" He ran to the back of the jeep.

The others backed away, raising their weapons.

Ross lay there, covered in blood, staring out of sightless eyes grayed with a cloudy film.

"Ross!" Carl plunged forward, prodding his friend, pulling at him, trying to do something . . . anything . . .

Ross!

But the boy's body was stiff and cold and—

"I'll kill you!" Carl roared, and he started around the jeep.

"Stop!" Parker waved the pistol. "I'll drop you in your tracks. Self-defense."

Carl took a step forward. "You think I care if you kill me?"

"You'll care if I kill your girlfriend."

New panic.

"What did you do?"

"Oh, it's not what I did," Parker said. "It's what she did. She killed Carrottop. You know, Mediqueer?"

"Liar," Carl said.

"I speak the gospel truth," Parker said, "as these fine young men are my witnesses."

"Where is she?"

"Sweatbox."

Carl pointed at him and spoke slowly. "You let her out of there, and you leave her alone. You got a problem with me, let's do it. Just the two of us. Leave her out of it."

"Just what I had in mind," Parker said.

"All right, then," Carl said, and cracked his knuckles. "Let's get down to it."

"I'm not going to fight you here. Stark would throw a hissy fit. The man's got a teacup for a temper, he really does. No, you want me? Challenge me to a duel."

There it was. Now Carl understood. "Yeah, right . . . so you can call terms."

Parker grinned. "Pretty much. Dawn tomorrow, in front of everybody, my terms. Agree to that, and I won't do to her what I did to Ross."

"Forget it. Let's just wait for Stark."

Parker got into the jeep. "Nope. Too busy. Gotta feed the sharks and get home in time to start the next hunt. It's open season on white-haired girls."

"You can't do that."

"Oh no? Explain that to your little buddy. Now give him a kiss byebye and get out of my way, Hollywood. I got forty orphans dying to stick their spears in your girl, see how she bleeds."

The engine roared to life. The others got in.

Carl glanced at his dead friend's empty eyes and knew it was true, all of it. . . .

Parker started backing up.

"Wait!" Carl shouted.

Parker stopped and looked at him with one brow cocked.

"Okay—I challenge you to a duel. Me and you, tomorrow at dawn, whatever you want. Just leave her alone. No hunt."

Parker threw his head back and laughed. "You're on, Hollywood. I accept. Tomorrow at dawn, out on the beach beside the lot where we first met. Pistols at ten paces!"

30

DRAW!" STARK SHOUTED.

Carl drew the pistol as fast as he could, stepped to the side, and knelt. He aimed center mass and squeezed the trigger. The gun barked loudly and bucked in his hand. He squeezed the trigger again and again until he'd burned through the clip, and the slide locked to the rear.

"You fight like that, you're dead!" Stark came across the sand, scowling. "Get it together, son. What's wrong with you?"

What's wrong with me? Carl thought. *My best friend's dead, my other friend is a zombie, I'm fighting to the death tomorrow morning, and if I lose, the person I care most about in the whole world is going to die, too.*

They'd been training on the beach for hours. Stark set up a target shaped like a human silhouette and taught Carl the best way to fight, given the circumstances. Parker was an experienced duelist and an expert shot. Few people could hit another person at this range, using a pistol under such stress, but Parker could and had. If Carl rushed it, he'd miss, and Parker would kill him. His only hope lay in simple tactics drilled to perfection: step to the side, forcing Parker to adjust, drop to one knee, aim carefully, and fire center mass. Over and over, Stark cited an old Special Forces adage: *Slow is smooth; smooth is fast; fast is deadly.*

Now Stark looked pretty deadly himself, his face red with frustration. "You stepped in the wrong direction. A fatal mistake. He's left-handed." He did a slow demonstration, drawing with his left hand. "That means he's going to come across the body like this. You have to step right, make him come back the other way. You step left, he's got you."

Carl nodded. The ringing in his ears matched the buzzing of his mind. He couldn't believe all of this was true, couldn't believe Ross was dead and Campbell was lost, couldn't believe Octavia was locked in the box, suffering, her life in his hands.

Stark put a hand on his shoulder. "You have to focus, son."

Carl nodded again. Stark was right. He had to focus, had to kill Parker. For Ross. For Campbell. For Medicaid. For what he'd done since the first day . . . and before that. But most of all, he had to kill Parker in order to save Octavia. Once she was safe, he could worry about sneaking onto the plane.

"These are killing shots," Stark said, pointing to four holes in the paper target. "Aim center mass. That way, if you go high or low, left or right, you'll still have a chance of hitting him."

"I aimed center mass every time."

"You have to do better. Twelve of your rounds missed the target altogether." He pointed to two other holes in the target, one in the arm, one in the shoulder. "A shot like this would cripple him and give you an edge. But sooner or later, you're going to have to put a hole through something important. His heart, his lungs, his guts."

"Okay," Carl said. His hands were ice-cold as Stark stapled a fresh target onto the board.

Carl swapped out clips and started back toward the line.

They would meet in the middle, turn their backs, and walk ten paces apiece, as Stark counted. Then they would turn and face each other—at something like fifty feet apart—and Stark would call for their draw; then everything would blow up, both of them blasting away until one of them went down and couldn't get up again.

Carl found the mark and waited.

"Focus this time," Stark said. "Any questions?"

"Just one," Carl said.

When Stark had learned of the duel, he'd snapped, bellowing as he trashed the hangar, overturning the table and the bookshelf, smashing plates on the floor, and hurling the microwave across the room. When

Carl suggested he cancel the duel and pull Octavia out of the sweatbox, Stark gave him a resounding no. Dueling was an ancient tradition and a sacred piece of the global Phoenix Force warrior culture. Stark could not, would not, make an exception. Once a challenge was accepted, the duel was set in stone.

"I know you can't stop this thing from happening, but what about postponing it? Could we put it off for a couple of weeks, just to give me training time?"

In reality, he just wanted time. The supply plane was coming in five days. If he could delay the duel, talk Stark into springing Octavia from the cage, and then sneak her onto the flight . . .

"No delays," Stark said, ending it. "Dueling is an institution, Carl. If I bent the rules for you, I would dishonor the tradition, and our soldiers all over the world would lose faith."

Carl wanted to argue but nodded instead. He had to stay on Stark's good side.

"We are so close . . ." Stark said, and Carl sensed he was in that melancholy mood that meant more talking in grand philosophical terms. But the Old Man went on to say only, "Once the master chips are ready, no one will be able to stop us. No one will be out of reach. Not the heads of corporations, not even the president of the United States."

Apparently, Carl let his mask slip a little, because Stark said, "Oh, don't look so surprised, son. You didn't think my life's ambition was running a mercenary unit, did you? Killing terrorists is no different than beating up bullies. Both actions treat symptoms, not the underlying illness. Bullies are a symptom of a sick school system, just as terrorists are a symptom of a sick world. You could spend your whole life treating symptoms, but until you cure the illness causing them, there will always be more symptoms, more bullies and terrorists, more people using Prometheus's fire to punish all of us."

Carl struggled to control himself. He couldn't slip, couldn't show his disgust.

"The world is sick," Stark said. His eyes burned like twin furnaces, and in their fiery depths, Carl saw many things: rage and madness, but also self-righteousness and, more than anything else, a horrible purpose . . . everything part of everything else, a molten, hissing lava of destruction. "Someday soon, a great fire will burn it all to the ground. We're going to see to that. Then we will sift the devastation and coax a new phoenix from its ashes."

Carl swallowed and forced himself to nod.

"Retrogression," Stark said, smiling now, "moving forward by moving backward, back through time to a younger world, when life was simple and good. Once we've taken from mankind the punishing gift of fire and driven humans back into their caves, they will be content in their rightful place, overjoyed to worship the gods of a new age: us."

Stark put a hand on Carl's shoulder. Carl managed not to flinch away. "That is our destiny, son, to end the suffering of mankind and establish ourselves as the lords of a new Pantheon. But first"—he gave Carl's shoulder a squeeze—"you must survive." Clapping his hands together, he said, suddenly optimistic, "We'll break from training and meditate. Get control of your emotions. Focus on what's real."

"Okay," Carl said.

"Sit. Don't get sand in the barrel. We'll start with deep breathing, okay?"

"Sure," Carl said. "Thanks. But . . . there is one more thing."

Anger flashed across Stark's features again.

"It's not about the duel. I know I was being stupid. I get it."

Stark's features relaxed . . . a little. He waited.

Carl tried to keep his voice relaxed. "It's about Octavia. If I die, could you make her your apprentice? She's really smart and tough and—"

Stark shook his head, and Carl got a crushing feeling in his chest.

"Forget the girl," Stark said. "Like dueling, the hunt is an important tradition here. Hunting, killing, is a rite of passage. The hunt culls the weak and baptizes the strong. Once a child has killed, his childhood dies, and he is reborn as a soldier, one more phoenix arisen."

"But she's strong. And she's already killed someone—her stepfather—so she's passed the test, right? You could use her."

Stark shook his head again. "Let go of her, Carl. She represents your only weakness: an irrational dedication to others. It's what brought you here, all those fights against bullies. And it's what caused you to fight those boys and Parker. This need to defend the weak. In a sense, it's noble—but it's a boy's idea, not a man's. Let it go. Let her go. This is your opportunity to transcend your only limitation and become a great man. This is your chance to rise from the ashes of your past."

"Okay," Carl said, reeling with desperation but trying not to show it. "Let's forget the meditation, then. Teach me. Show me how to kill Parker. I'll put everything else out of my mind, and I'll kill him, and then, when Octavia's free, you'll see how great she is, what a great apprentice she'd make."

"Carl, Carl, Carl," Stark said, shaking his head. "It's too late for her. Whether you win or lose, she's already condemned. The hunt will go on. You can't change that. You can't save her. You can only save yourself."

"But Parker said—"

"Drill Sergeant Parker lied. He set a trap, and you fell into it. He killed your friend to throw you into a rage, then put the girl out there, like a carrot on a stick, knowing that once you issued a challenge, there would be no turning back, just as he knew that once he'd given the girl to the hunt, there would be no saving her.

"All you can do now is make him pay. Nothing else will change. Tomorrow morning at oh-eight-hundred hours, everyone—the orphans, the cadre, and Phoenix Force—will be here, cheering."

He glanced at his watch. "In fewer than fourteen hours, either you or Parker will be dead in the sand."

31

THE ROOM WAS AS DARK as a grave.

Carl lay awake, his thoughts raging like a storm-tossed sea.

There was no way out, no hope . . .

Then, somewhere beneath his panic, the calm voice of his old trainer, Arthur James, cooed softly as a night bird, reminding him, *When the going gets tough, the tough get cool.* Arthur telling him, *Control your breathing, control yourself. See a picture in your mind. Visualize what you have to do. . . .*

Carl pictured the morning to come. He pictured the beach, the crowd, Parker, Stark, pictured the whole thing, felt the weight of the pistol in its holster and heard the chanting of the crowd and Stark's deep voice telling the duelists to approach the center mark, heard him count, heard him reach ten, felt himself moving at "draw!" and then . . .

Nothing.

He couldn't picture the rest of it.

He'd never had trouble with visualization before. Sure, this was different—a fight to the death—but he needed to make a film in his mind.

He couldn't. He tried again and again, the whole scene real to him, but when Stark's imaginary voice gave the command to draw, the picture went blank.

Why?

Maybe, the ghost of Arthur said, *you're trying to picture the wrong fight.*

But he was picturing the only fight possible. Stark had made that clear. There was no way out. No way to help Ross or Campbell or Octavia now. Only the duel. Oh-eight-hundred, on the beach, to the death, period.

In Stark's world, people got hurt along the way. Got killed along the way. To Stark, the duel represented a glorious opportunity, Carl's chance to stop attaching himself to weak people and end what Stark called his pattern of self-destruction.

Carl couldn't deny the pattern: all those fights, from the brawl in the barracks all the way back to Devil's Pocket, to Liam.

But the pattern's roots went even deeper, stretching all the way back to the promise he'd made on a snowy day long ago, after his father had scared off those punks and gotten Cobbie a hot meal at the diner.

This is what I do, Carl. And someday when you grow up, it will be up to you to protect them, all the people who can't fend for themselves. A good man won't give in to fear when there's work to be done and someone needs him. Will you do it?

And Carl's reply: *Yes. I promise . . .*

And all these years, that's what Carl thought he'd been doing: keeping his promise to his father. Standing up for the weak.

But he'd been fooling himself.

Carl's historical pattern of self-destruction did point toward a deep personal weakness—all those fights, all those placements, all the trouble he'd gotten himself into here . . . always a bully, always a victim, always Carl stepping into the middle.

But Carl's weakness wasn't his need to help the victims. His weakness was his need to destroy the bullies.

The difference hit him now square in the forehead like a .40-caliber round . . .

He'd been fighting not out of love but hatred.

He remembered the fight with Decker, just before they went at it, Decker standing over Medicaid and grinning at Carl, saying, *What do you care, anyway? You don't like him, either. I can see it in your eyes.*

And he'd been right.

Carl hadn't liked Medicaid.

When he fought Decker, it wasn't because he wanted to help Medicaid; it was because he hated Decker. Just like the big fight that had gotten him sent here in the first place, his defense of that kid Eli. He didn't know Eli. Never saw him again. Never cared. Never even wondered how the kid was doing afterward. He hadn't thumped the football team because he liked Eli; he had thumped them because they were bullies and he hated their kind.

For him, all bullies were echoes of Liam.

And on some level, Liam was the echo of Wilson W. Wilson, the man who'd shot his father.

Stark saw this moment in time as Carl's opportunity to break this lifelong pattern, to escape his weakness, and Carl was in total agreement. This was it. His chance to break the pattern and become the person he wanted to be. But to Stark, this meant forgetting Octavia, killing Parker, and moving on to a life where Carl would focus only on himself. That's where he was wrong.

This was Carl's big opportunity, all right. But it wasn't time to *stop* fighting for the weak; it was time to *start* fighting for them.

It was time to start keeping his promise to his father.

Even if it cost him his life.

At 0800, he was supposed to go at it cowboy style on the beach. His chance to gun down a bad man . . .

But that was the wrong fight. Killing Parker wouldn't destroy Carl's weakness; it would surrender his life to it. Instead of casting his fatal flaw away, it would allow that flaw to define him. It would burn the Carl he'd wanted to become, and out of those ashes would rise not a phoenix but a monster.

Parker's death would avenge all that had happened to Medicaid, Campbell, and Ross but would save neither them nor Octavia.

If Carl fought the duel, she would die. It didn't matter whether he won or lost. The hunt would go on.

So the only way to save her was by *not* fighting. But that wasn't possible. Duelists couldn't change their minds, couldn't back out. Once the duel was set, it was set.

He pictured everyone gathered on the beach: Parker, Stark, the orphans, the cadre, the Phoenix Forcers chanting, "Killer Carl! Killer Carl!"

He pictured the abandoned hangar, the abandoned roads, the abandoned camps . . .

Everyone out on the beach, ready for the Phoenix Island Super Bowl.

Almost everyone. There would still be an abandoned girl locked in a cage on the other side of the island. . . .

Carl sat up in bed.

What if . . . ?

And he held two images side by side in his mind: Octavia in the cage, Camp Phoenix Force abandoned . . .

The boats bobbing in the water, unguarded . . .

He stood and paced in the darkness. Just before lights-out, Stark had discussed the morning by way of helping Carl visualize the coming duel. Stark would escort Phoenix Force to the beach, leaving Carl alone for an hour to meditate and focus his mind. . . .

What if, instead of meditating, Carl waited for Stark to leave, then left himself? What if he ran not to the beach but straight to Training Base One. To Octavia . . .

How long would it take everyone to realize he wasn't coming to the duel?

He pictured the crowd shouting, pictured Stark going through a range of emotions: realization, shock, disappointment, rage. . . .

They would all think Carl was afraid. Afraid of Parker and afraid to die.

Parker would get away with everything he'd done, with killing Ross . . . and he'd howl with laughter.

Carl's pride screamed. Could he walk away from the biggest fight of his life?

It has always been that he would rather die than back down to a bully. It didn't matter who, how big, or how many. He'd fought again and again, as if doing so could bring his father back to him. It never had. Just as fighting Parker now would do nothing to bring back Ross and nothing to save Octavia.

Ross was gone. Carl's father was gone.

Nothing would bring them back.

Parker and Octavia remained. The choice was simple: risk everything to kill Parker or risk everything to save Octavia.

He knew what he had to do.

He had to break his pattern of weakness.

He had to start keeping his promise to his father.

He had to stop fighting the bullies and start helping the victims.

He had to defend, not destroy.

Love, not hate.

He had to save Octavia.

32

THE MEMBERS OF PHOENIX FORCE mobbed him, shaking his hand and slapping his back, all smiles and bright eyes and encouragement. Then one of them shouted, "Killer Carl!" and they hoisted him off his feet and onto their shoulders, chanting, "Killer Carl! Killer Carl! Killer Carl!"

Stark smiled like a proud parent as they paraded Carl around the hangar. Then he raised one fist in the air.

Both parade and chanting stopped, and hands lowered Carl to the ground. Boudazin gave him a quick kiss on the cheek. "For luck," she said, and smiled—a pretty girl who shot bull's-eyes at three hundred meters.

"Let's save some of that celebration for after the duel," Stark said. "Carl needs time to prepare himself. Agbeko, form everybody up outside. I'll join you momentarily."

"Yes, Commander," Agbeko said. "Phoenix Force, you heard the Old Man. Outside, form it up."

The troopers hooah-ed and started out the door, many turning for one last wave.

Carl waved back, filled with a sudden and unexpected sense of loss. The Phoenix Forcers really liked him, and no matter how crazy it was, no matter how misguided they were, he liked them, too, all these high-speed orphans from around the world. They, too, had been born in the wrong place at the wrong time, and their strengths had likely doomed them to this fate and madman's vision. It wasn't their fault Stark had cultivated them like a deadly virus. Yes, he liked them. Pitied them, even.

But this was the end of all that. If he ever saw them again—and oh, how he hoped he never did—the Phoenix Forcers would try to kill him.

Agbeko gave him a bone-crushing embrace. "You will win your fight, Carl. I know you will. And then you and I, we will be brothers, yes?"

"Yes," Carl said, and his throat closed with a lump of sorrow, gratitude, and warmth for this hulking killer whom he hardly knew. It was completely insane, made absolutely no sense, but then, when did emotions ever give a flying *crap* about logic?

"To glory," Agbeko said, and then he was gone, too.

"Do you see it, son?" Stark said, coming to him. "Do you the effect you have on them? And in such a short time. You're not just a born leader, you're *their* born leader. It's not just charisma. It's destiny."

"Thank you," Carl said, and then added the words he'd practiced in the night. "It's been an honor to learn from you."

"The honor has been mine," Stark said—just as Carl had expected, word for word—and gave a slow bow.

Carl returned the bow, remembering to dip lower than the Old Man, like a samurai before his lord.

When he straightened, Stark was smiling down at him admiringly, as if Carl were graduating high school rather than fighting a duel to the death.

Outside, Phoenix Force took up the chant again. "Killer Carl! Killer Carl! Killer Carl!"

Stark took him by the shoulders. "You know what you have to do, yes?"

"Yes."

"And you're prepared to do it?"

"I am," Carl said, thinking, *And if you had any idea what I'm really prepared to do, you'd snap my neck right now.*

"Hooah," Stark said.

"Hooah," Carl echoed.

Stark checked his watch. "You have just over an hour. Meditate. Prepare your mind. Self-efficacy, yes? The past is a ghost, the future a mirage. Place yourself firmly in this moment, your moment to ascend."

"I will," Carl said.

Stark gave him a light shake. "I won't wish you luck, my son. This has nothing to do with luck—only fate."

Carl nodded.

Stark released him, stepped back, straightened crisply, and snapped one hand to his brow, paying Carl the ultimate compliment, saluting *him*.

Carl returned the salute, held it—listening to the troopers outside filling the reverent moment with "Killer Carl! Killer Carl!"—and then let it drop.

Stark finished his own salute, executed a smooth about-face, and marched out of the hangar, where the chanting stopped in an eruption of hooahs.

Carl let his breath shudder free and stood for a moment, shaking and staring at the door. Then, as Stark and Phoenix Force jogged away, singing cadence, he started gathering everything he needed.

TWENTY-FIVE MINUTES LATER, hearing an engine's rumble, Carl dove into the roadside weeds. Approaching lights cut the predawn gloom, and a pair of cattle trucks filled with kids passed. He flattened himself to the ground and listened to their loud voices, their excitement. They sounded like kids on a field trip to an amusement park.

How many of them were hoping to see him die?

He was glad he didn't know the answer.

Then they were gone, and he was running again. He'd left shortly after Stark, taking time only to dress in black fatigues and slick nighttime camo grease over his hands, face, and neck.

He glanced at his watch and pressed the backlight. Twenty after. In forty minutes, they would wonder where he was. How long after would they begin to hunt him?

Well before reaching the entrance to Training Base One, he angled off through the woods toward the side of the compound nearest the sweatbox.

He low-crawled out of the trees into dawn's dim half-light. Reaching the fence, he lifted his head and scanned the compound.

A low growl escaped him.

Downhill, a guard stood watch at the gate, a machine gun slung over one shoulder. Another stood in the little room atop the gate tower. Not good. He'd hoped the guards would attend the duel. After all, what was left to guard?

Seconds later, he heard a drill sergeant yelling orders. Over by the barracks, several kids raked gravel and swept the sidewalks. He recognized Sanchez, Octavia's friend Tamika, and Lindstrom, the nice kid from Post Falls, Idaho.

He figured he knew why they were cleaning rather than watching the big fight. Sanchez, Tamika, Lindstrom . . . they were all decent. Ross's murder must have been the turning point. Parker weeded out anybody who refused to hunt. Now they were good for only three things: slave labor, getting hunted, and feeding the sharks. Twisted.

Then he saw someone else down there: Davis. Like the others, he was being forced to work. Carl remembered the barracks, the fight with Parker, Davis standing up for him. Something had changed in him . . . for the better.

Carl wished he could take them all with him, but there wasn't time. The faster he got off this island, the better chance he'd have at alerting people to the presence of this place and thus helping all of them. Only one couldn't wait: Octavia. If he left without her, she'd be as dead as Ross.

His eyes found the dark little sweatbox. Even in the relative cool of the morning, the box would be heating up, its metal roof clicking like a radiator. In its shadows, he made out a darker shadow, a lump. No motion.

It made him sick, her suffering like this.

He scaled the fence easily, thanks to his new muscles. Clearing the top, he dropped down the other side and low-crawled to the torturous device.

Octavia lay inside the box, asleep or unconscious, turned away from him. A surge of pity and concern rushed through Carl. He knew what she was feeling in there, knew not only the pain but also the hollowing hopelessness.

He whispered her name.

She stirred and turned, eyes blinking—eyes that he was outraged to note were badly bruised—and spoke with a voice that sounded like an old woman's. "Carl?"

"Yes. I'm getting you out of here."

She closed her eyes, then opened them again. "Are you . . . real?"

Carl went to the latch. "I'm real, all right. We're leaving, Octavia. We're getting off this island."

She mumbled something.

He slid the bolts free, and the door swung open.

"Feel like I'm dying," she said.

"I know you do. But you're going to be okay." He reached in, took her by the hand, and helped her from the sweatbox. She was hot to the touch, and Carl remembered the fever he'd suffered during his time in the box. She trembled as he pulled her into a quick hug. She felt very small in his arms. He glanced downhill. No one had spotted them yet. "We have to hurry."

He led her behind the box, safely out of sight, and handed her his canteen. They had little time, but she needed water.

She drank. Paused. Let her eyes close. Drank some more. When she opened her eyes again, she said, "It's no use, Carl." Her voice was a raspy whisper.

"Come on, Octavia. I know how you feel. I was in there, too. But I also know you're strong. When they see you're gone, they'll hunt us. We have to leave now."

She shook her head. "I don't think I can walk."

"I'll carry you."

She shook her head again. "I'll try."

"We have to get to the other side of the island. There are boats there."

"Carl, there's something I have to tell you," she said, then trailed off. She took another sip of water and leaned against him. "It's about Ross—"

"I know. I know what Parker did, but he can't hurt us anymore."

Octavia's muscles relaxed a bit, as if no longer having to carry the news of Ross had lifted a physical weight off her body. She managed a weak smile. "All right. I'm with you. And, Carl—thanks."

If this were a movie, Carl thought, he would give her a kiss and some snappy line, but he just smiled and helped her along. Then he realized his mistake.

The fence.

She couldn't climb it in her condition, and even with his new muscles, he couldn't get her safely across. Why hadn't he thought to bring rope?

"All right," he said. "We have to go through the gate."

She looked at him like he was crazy, and maybe he was.

"They'll never let us through," she said.

He tried to look confident. "We'll make it. Come on." He draped her arm over his shoulders and wrapped his arm around her waist. As they started downhill toward the gate, tension built in his body. "I'm going to try to talk my way through. If we have to run, break left and get into the trees as quickly as possible."

Henshaw, the unofficial comedian of Phoenix Force, popped the rifle off his shoulder and brought it around with lightning speed.

"Whoa!" Carl said, forcing a chuckle. "Henshaw, take it easy."

Henshaw lowered the barrel and offered a puzzled smile. "Killer Carl?"

"Yeah, it's me," Carl said, trying to keep his voice natural. He recognized Henshaw's rifle from his trips to the range with Stark: a 7.62mm AK-47—a big, no-messing-around machine gun with a fat banana clip full of ammo. He remembered Stark saying how, if the crap ever really hit the fan, he'd prefer an AK over just about anything.

"Carl," a girl with an English accent called from the tower twenty feet overhead. "What in the world are you doing here?"

Carl looked up. Cheng's rifle lay across the rail, not pointed at him, but not slung over her shoulder, either.

He waved, saying, "Stark sent me," and then moved toward Henshaw, out of Cheng's direct line of sight. Nodding toward Octavia, he said, "This girl's a friend of mine. He said I could bring her to the duel."

Henshaw shrugged and slung the rifle onto his shoulder.

Carl tried to look relaxed.

"What's with the face paint?" Henshaw said. "You plan on sneaking up on Parker?"

Carl forced a laugh, hoping it sounded better to Henshaw than it did to him. "Stark thinks it might psych him out a little."

"Hope so. Hey—do me a favor and kill the guy, okay? I came through here, he really gave me a hard time. Broke my arm, threw me in the box. Dude, it sucked." He grinned. "Besides, I got fifty bucks on you."

"My man," Carl said. He put out his fist, and they pounded it like old buddies. Octavia slumped into him, and for a second, he feared she might pass out.

"I'm pissed to be missing it," Henshaw said. "Of all days to have guard duty. Talk about drawing the short straw."

"Oi, Carl," Cheng said. "Need a jeep? She doesn't look capable of walking very far."

"No thanks," Carl said. If Cheng called in a jeep, everything would come crashing down. "Stark specifically told me to walk her back. Who knows? I'm around him all the time and I still can't figure him out."

"Me, neither," Henshaw said. "The man's deep. Like middle-of-the-Pacific-Ocean deep. There is no second-guessing the Old Man."

"You got that right," Carl said.

Henshaw slapped him on the shoulder. "Don't let us hold you up."

"Yeah," Carl said. "I don't want to be late to Parker's funeral."

Henshaw laughed. "Killer Carl! I should have bet a hundred." He reached for the red button that would open the gate but paused when Cheng leaned over the rail and called down.

"Hold on a tick," she said. Her voice sounded different. Edgy. Carl tensed. "Something doesn't quite add up here. How come nobody called this in?"

"Why bother?" Carl said. He slipped his arm from Octavia's waist and spread his hands in a gesture of harmless puzzlement. "Stark knows you guys know me."

Henshaw's eyes narrowed. He tilted his head a little. "Now that I think about it, how did you get in here, Carl? We've been at this gate all night."

Overhead, Cheng quickly said, "Hold the gate, Henshaw. I'm calling this in. I'm not getting burned over it."

Carl drove a hard right into Henshaw's face. Henshaw never saw the punch, and he fell back against the tower and slid to the ground, unconscious before he even realized he'd been hit.

Carl slapped the red button. With a metallic click, the gate began to swing slowly open. "Come on," he said, grabbing Octavia by the arm.

Cheng yelled, "Down on the ground, Carl! Facedown or I'll blow your bloody head off."

Carl pushed Octavia against the guard tower and plastered himself against the wall beside her, out of Cheng's line of fire, but from where they stood to the forest stretched forty yards of flat, open space, an absolute kill zone.

"What are you talking about, Cheng?" Carl called up. "Everything's cool."

Cheng didn't respond. Then he heard her speaking into the walkie-talkie. "All ears! All ears! This is Cheng at Training Base One. We have a break in progress. Freeman and the girl from the sweatbox. I repeat—"

Carl felt frozen. He'd come all this way, put it all on the line, and now everything was falling apart. He looked again at the stretch of open ground, the kill zone. There was just no way. Cheng would cut them in half.

"Carl, can you use that thing?" Octavia pointed to the rifle lying beside Henshaw, who remained unconscious.

Carl nodded and scooped the rifle off the ground. It hadn't even occurred to him to pick it up—he'd never wanted to shoot anyone—but he had to use it now. After pushing the selector to full auto and racking the charge handle, he risked a quick lean, looked up, and saw the dark line of Cheng's barrel jutting out from the tower railing. Carl leaned out just far enough to put the sights on the black line of her barrel and pulled the trigger.

The noise was incredible. The machine gun kicked his shoulder five times, ten, fifteen—it was impossible to tell—and a spike of bright flame jutted from its muzzle. Bullets whined off metal, and sparks exploded overhead.

"Run," he told Octavia.

She staggered to the gate, and Carl, having no idea whether he'd hit the barrel of Cheng's rifle, sent another spray of bullets into the air.

Do not lean out, his mind begged the Phoenix Forcer. *I do not want to kill you.*

As he looked back toward the road, Octavia disappeared into the darkness of the forest. Good. She'd made it. He ran backward out from under the tower and squeezed off several more rounds.

Back toward the barracks, the flat crack of a single gunshot cut the air.

Carl saw a drill sergeant, maybe seventy-five yards away and running straight at him, arm held out straight, pistol in hand.

The drill sergeant fired again, and a bullet thwapped off the tower.

Carl blasted the ground between them, and the drill sergeant hit the dirt.

Backing through the gate, Carl fired over the tower to discourage Cheng from approaching the railing. The air was an explosion of noise and blinding flame and gun smoke and the smell of cordite. He was halfway to the trees when the bolt locked to the rear and he knew the magazine was dry. He dropped the rifle and sprinted into the darkness.

Just as he hit the trees, gunfire exploded behind him, and bullets tore the ground to his left and slapped loudly into the trees, one hitting so close that bark flew off it, making him squint. He charged deeper into the forest. Gunfire chewed the trees behind him, not so close this time, and then stopped. Carl could see Octavia up ahead, weaving through the woods, looking like she might drop at any time.

He caught up to her and took her hand, and they shuffled along side by side. She was making some kind of moaning, gasping noise, but he couldn't tell if she was winded or crying. A terrible thought occurred to him.

"Are you hit?"

"No," she said. "I don't think so."

He squeezed her hand. "You did awesome back there."

She said nothing, just stumbled on.

He pointed into the darkness. "There should be a trail up ahead. They'll expect us to go the other way, toward the road. This'll take us straight uphill. It's pretty steep."

"Steep? Carl, I'm sorry, but I can't do it." All at once, she stopped running. "I'm done." She started to fall, but he caught her.

"I've got you," he said. He dipped low and scooped her into his arms. "I'm sorry if this hurts. But they know now, and we have to go as fast as we can."

And he started running.

She was very light. His arms felt strong, his legs fast. Even his eyes felt sharper, and he found he was able to navigate through the forest with just the dim morning light falling through openings in the trees.

It was time for Plan B.

Plan A—sneak in quietly and steal Octavia away without alerting anyone—never really had a chance. He supposed he had only deluded himself into thinking it might work because without that shred of dubious hope, he never would have had the nerve to attempt her rescue. And feeling her in his arms, he was oh so glad he had. If they were going to die now, at least they would die on their terms, free, fighting, together.

So Plan B it was. He would throw off pursuit by attempting the unexpected and carrying her straight over the ridge and down the other side, where he would help her hide at the shoreline. Then he would go for a boat. And if he got to it in time—*Oh, please don't let this be another delusional plan,* he thought—he would swing around the island for her. It was their only chance.

He ran on.

The ground angled steeply upward. Far behind, he heard gunfire and shouting.

By now, Parker would be ranting and calling him a coward, and Stark would be burning with white-hot rage at Carl's betrayal.

Now they would distribute weapons and pour into the forest.

The hunt was on.

33

CARL LAID OCTAVIA GENTLY ON THE GROUND beside the fallen tree. His muscles throbbed with exertion, and he was soaked with sweat, but he'd done it . . . he'd carried her over the ridge and back down the other side. A mere fifty feet away, jungle gave way to a narrow strip of sandy beach, beyond which the sparkling blue ocean stretched away into beautiful infinity: a cruel joke. Its gentle susurration beckoned Carl, invited him in his exhaustion to lie down beside his friend. *Relax,* the tide told him. *Sleep . . . forget . . .*

Not a chance.

Octavia's face was flushed with fever, but her gray eyes were hard as twin stones. "You have to go. They'll be here any second. Listen."

Hooting voices drew nearer. Were these the same hunters he'd lost going up the slope? Or another group?

"I'll hide you here," Carl said, "under this tree. I'll go to the boat, and when I have it, I'll loop around the island and pick you up." He pointed to a long arm of rocks that stretched like a natural pier into the water. "That's how I'll find you." He forced a smile that he hoped showed more optimism than he felt. At least his time with Stark had given him *that* ability.

"Okay, Carl," Octavia said. "That's good." And there was something in her face and her voice, something calm and content yet sad and reserved that reminded him of the tone his mother would take when he was very small and she was sick with cancer, and the two of them would talk about the future, chatting idly about Christmases they both knew they'd never share. Its recurrence in Octavia's voice saddened him deeply.

More hooting sounded in the woods.

Desperation flooded him. He covered her over with palm fronds, trying not to think of spiders. He gave her his remaining canteen, held her hands, and looked into her beautiful gray eyes, feeling a lump come into his throat. She was all he had left in the world.

"I'll come back for you. Okay? I promise. I'll get you off this island. All right?"

She nodded, looking very sleepy. "I know you will. Now go. They're almost here."

It sounded like they would break through the forest at any time. He heard someone calling his name.

Madness.

He ran a thumb across her cheek. There were no tears. "I'll see you again. I promise."

"I know." Her smile was as forced as his. "Now go."

He ran back into the woods at a sharp angle, flanking the hunters and heading once more toward the mountain. He had to let them know where he was, where he was going, had to draw them away from Octavia's hiding spot.

Their cries were close.

He waited.

Seconds later, he saw the first of them coming through the trees. A shirtless boy—he was too distant to identify—carrying something . . . a walking stick or spear . . .

"Leave us alone!" Carl shouted in the boy's direction. He paused just long enough to be sure the boy had seen him and then started running again.

Their cries multiplied and turned in his direction.

Scrambling once more up the steep grade, he could hear the excitement in their shouting as they chased. Good. Now that he was sure they were on his trail, he would really sprint. He could beat them all on the obstacle course before he'd even received the blood virus. Now he'd leave them behind like they were jogging in place.

And that's just what he needed: space. His only chance—and Octavia's only chance—was misdirection. He'd drawn them away from her; now he had to trick them again.

He would sprint all the way up the mountain to the ridge where he and Stark had trained. It was a risky move—he'd be far more visible out in the open than he would be moving through the forest—but it was the fastest way across the island, and he needed to reach the boats before Stark figured out exactly what he was up to.

Behind him followed a chorus of bloodthirsty howls. It sounded like he was being hunted by a pack of werewolves. And wasn't that what they were, really? Two months ago, they'd been a bunch of hard-luck kids; but this place had turned them into beasts of another sort.

Up the mountainside he scrambled, using the trunks of small trees like ladder rungs to pull himself along. The uphill sprint with Octavia in his arms had taken its toll, but he scaled the mountainside as quickly as he could, burning lungs or no burning lungs, and he took solace in the fact that the others would be dropping ever farther behind.

When he came to a storm-twisted clearing in the trees, he paused, bending over and pretending to be far more tired than he was. He wanted them to see him, wanted them to keep pushing in his direction rather than looping back past Octavia. Sure enough, he'd paused only a few seconds when shouting rose up at him.

Then a rifle shot cracked through the air, and a bullet whined off a nearby rock. He sprawled onto the stony ground just as a spray of lead chewed the trees overhead. Scrambling uphill, he escaped the clearing and passed once more into the relative cover of the forest. More gunfire rattled from below, but Carl knew they had little chance of seeing him, let alone hitting him, now that he was in the trees again.

Gunfire meant Phoenix Forcers. They had been receiving the same treatments he'd been given. Some of them could run as quickly as he could, some probably faster. And they hadn't passed sleepless nights, then sprinted up and down mountainsides carrying someone in their arms.

He couldn't outrun them. Not indefinitely. Not them or their guns.

At last, the trees thinned, and he crested the steep slope and found himself at the lower edge of the long ridge of stone that ran like an exposed spine across the center of island. With the first twinges of exhaustion starting to pop like fireworks in his thigh muscles, he sprinted into the open. From this high vantage point, he heard what sounded like a thousand voices closing in.

The stony ridge was perhaps ten feet wide. To its left, the ground sheered away into open air, a window onto the lower canopy ten stories below. Its empty vastness made him feel wobbly.

He glanced to the right, looking for the trailhead of the steep path he and Stark had used, and—

"There he is!"

They rushed up the hill, looking like hunters out of the Stone Age, six shirtless boys carrying spears. For a second, he recognized none of them, partly because mud was smeared like war paint on their faces but more so because of the faces themselves, which were so twisted with savage bloodlust, they looked more like animals than the boys he'd once known.

"Aaiiaii!" someone—Fay, Carl thought—cried as he threw his spear.

It was so abrupt, their breaking from the woods, that Carl had frozen, and by the time he saw the spear coming at him, it almost skewered his face. Fortunately, his years of boxing saved him. Out of instinct, he jerked his head to the right, like he was dipping away from a fast jab, and the shaft of the weapon tickled past his ear.

It would've killed him.

There was no place to run. There were six of them, five with spears, the sixth—and yes, Carl saw, it was Fay, who'd always seemed kind of timid but now looked like a starving wolf running down its prey—drew a big knife from his belt. They were less than thirty feet away, charging fast. The ridge was an open, rocky path; whether he ran forward or backward, they would cut him off.

"You're dead, Hollywood!" someone yelled.

Carl turned from them, and the world pulsed in and out of focus. The sheer cliff plunged away to the jagged boulders piled at its base. Beyond that was forest.

Something thumped into his shoulder. For a second, even as he registered the spear falling away into the void and the sensations of warmth and wetness and pain springing to the surface of his shoulder, he teetered on the edge of the cliff, filled with terror as he pin-wheeled his arms to keep from tumbling over the edge.

He caught his balance just in time to dodge another spear, which flashed past him, arched out over the cliff, and disappeared into the canopy far below.

"Hold your spears!" one of the kids said—it was Biscoe, Carl saw, and a memory flashed through his mind, Biscoe standing beside his bunk, laughing at Ross's impersonation of Parker, tears running from his eyes—"Use them to stab!"

They were twenty feet away. He could never beat them all, not the way they were armed. . . .

No way out, no escape.

"Spears in front!" Biscoe commanded. "Knives move in from behind. Push him off the cliff."

But Carl beat them to it.

He ran three steps and leapt into the void.

34

THEIR SCREAMS OF SURPRISE ripped away behind him as his body rushed toward the treetops, adrenaline slowing the moment, giving him time to think, absurdly enough, how like a movie all this was. How the desperate hero evaded certain death by throwing himself from some great height—a cliff or bridge or airplane. Only, in the movies, the heroes jumped into *water. . . .*

Not Carl.

He slapped into the leaves of the upper canopy first, slammed into something hard, and screamed when whatever it was, tree trunk or limb—he didn't know up from down in this tumbling green moment—smashed his ribs like a giant fist. Falling again, he spun in the open air, his thoughts reduced to a string of exclamation points as he grabbed wildly at branches, everything around him a green blur veined in cracks of sunshine gleaming through the upper reaches. His hands raked past branch and bark but couldn't find purchase. He felt a fingernail peel away, plummeted in a terrifying free fall, clipped his shin on something hard as steel, and grabbed a smaller branch, which bent with the force of his fall.

The branch burned his hand, but he held tight, even when his body jerked hard, and it felt like his shoulder might rip from its socket. Then the branch snapped away, and he was falling again. He managed to keep his feet under him and bent his knees as he slammed into the forest floor.

His legs took most of the impact. He tried to roll with it but hit his shoulder hard against the ground. He lay for a second, hurting. His ribs were almost certainly broken. One shoulder felt dislocated, while the other bled moderately, sliced by the spear. His hand burned, a red line ripped raw across the palm where he'd seized the branch. His shin throbbed, and his ankle pulsed with pain. Despite all this, a rush of joy filled him with pure elation—he'd nearly died, but he was alive, alive, alive!—and he struggled to his feet.

He'd done it. He'd jumped off a cliff, smashed through trees, and survived the drop to the jungle floor. He lifted his fists skyward and thanked God for this slice of amazing luck.

Above him, all was green shadow. He could hear the boys far up above hooting and laughing, no doubt thinking he'd killed himself.

Good, he thought. *Let them think that.*

He turned his back on the cliff and took a second to get his bearings. Far off to the left, Octavia waited. Straight ahead, through a wide span of heavy, unfamiliar forest, was the ocean. He needed to push in that direction but angle right. Eventually, he would come to the beach, and if his sense of direction were intact, he'd end up just outside Camp Phoenix Force. His only hope was that the Phoenix Forcers had abandoned camp for the duel and then gone off into the forest, looking for him.

He limped into the unfamiliar forest.

The going was slower than he would have liked. He and Stark had never run this corner of the island, and he kept running into unexpected delays: a natural fence of boulders at the base of the central peak, a deadfall of wind-damaged trees, a veritable wall of thorn bushes. And, just below a stream where he paused to drink water and rest his aching body, a murky swamp buzzing with mosquitoes and stinging flies.

At last he found a narrow trail furrowed into the ground. Wherever the rough path split, he headed left toward the camp, and hopefully the boats and freedom.

When he came to the hillside clearing and heard grunting, he remembered why he and Stark had never traveled this section of the jungle.

A groan escaped his lips as uphill, where the clearing ended in a span of gloomy forest, dark shapes moved.

More grunting. A whistle. A squeal.

A big boar charged out of the trees, white tusks flashing.

Carl ran in the opposite direction.

The clearing ended just as he hit his stride, and he found himself flying through the air as the ground broke away, not to a sheer cliff but to a sparsely wooded hillside. He hit the ground running, fell, rolled, and, against all odds, popped up running again. Birds squawked loudly into the air, as if feeling the pain that raged through his battered body. Leaves and branches slapped into him as he hurtled downhill, expecting at any second to feel the boar's tusk slash into his legs.

At last the ground leveled out again, and he realized the trees were thinning, that a wall of bright sunshine burned just ahead.

Some distance behind him, an angry squeal cut the air, and Carl turned to see the big boar waddling back uphill, looking dangerous and proud at having defended its territory.

Carl slowed to jog and then to a limp. Everything hurt.

Uphill, the pigs squealed and huffed but stayed over the rise, out of sight. It seemed they'd given up the chase. Of course they had; that was natural, wasn't it? They were animals. They were vicious, sure, but this wasn't personal. Their aggression was merely territorial. They weren't so savage as *human* animals who went out in packs to hunt and kill their own kind.

He hobbled toward the light, hoping he wasn't too far off course.

Reaching the forest's edge, he felt like shouting. Across the sand directly in front of him ran a chain-link fence surrounding familiar-looking buildings. Overhead fluttered the black-and-red flag of Camp Phoenix Force.

He'd made it. He'd come out exactly where he needed to be.

And taking in the scene, squinting against the sun, he nearly did shout for joy.

The gate was wide open.

At first he couldn't believe it.

He could see no one at all in the vicinity. Just a hundred yards of sand between him and the gate, not far beyond which, he knew, the boats marked on Eric's map waited, bobbing in the water, unguarded.

It seemed impossible, this stroke of good luck . . . and yet the open gate made sense. Everyone had gone off to watch him duel Parker—and now they were spread all over the island, hunting him.

He chuckled, crouching there in his sweat and pain, and swatted mosquitoes while he eyed the gate, making sure. He saw no movement.

Yes. At last things were going his way.

He slipped from the trees and started toward freedom.

He was halfway across the sand when someone with a rifle stepped into view.

35

CARL LURCHED TO A HALT, spraying sand, turned, and sprinted back toward the forest.

The trees were so far away. It was a nightmare: running through the clutching sand, the trees impossibly distant, across a wide-open space. He pumped his arms and legs as hard as he could, a flat-out sprint across the sand. He heard the shouting and waited for the gunfire, knowing it would come, pushing his hardest toward the trees, waiting for the loud bark of the rifle, waiting for fists of lead to slam into his back and open great gaping holes out the front of him. He knew this was it, knew he was finished. . . .

Then gunfire did bark, and a line of bullets tore along the beach beside him, pitching fountains of sand into the air so close he felt the grit on his face. The forest drew nearer and nearer—twenty yards, ten—but the gun was firing again, and he could hear the bullets racing up the sand behind him—five yards now!—and a bullet punched him in the back and threw him off his feet into the tangled vegetation at the forest's edge.

He was shot. They'd hit him.

Pain throbbed in his side, hurting like a hook to the body and a puncture wound all at the same time, and Carl was aware of blood everywhere. His blood. So much of it, on his shirt, on his arms, his hands, even on his face. He tasted blood, smelled it. Glancing down at his shirt, he saw a hole in the front, where the bullet had passed through him, and saw blood leaking down his stomach, down his leg.

More gunfire.

Bullets tore into the forest, thumping against trees, snickering through leaves, and pitching leaf litter into the air. One struck the tree just above his head and rained down splinters. Another ricocheted off a nearby rock with a frightening whine.

He scrambled deeper into the woods. The pain of the gunshot radiated through him, filling him from belt line to throat. It was difficult to breathe. Wild with fear and desperation, he pulled himself up the steep, slippery slope.

The gunfire stopped. Carl risked one look back through the trees and saw them coming for him. Two Phoenix Force soldiers, one of whom, Carl was distressed to see, was their toughest, Agbeko, who was nearly as large as Stark. The other looked like Nachef. They both carried rifles and sprinted his way with what seemed like impossible speed.

He had a lead on them, but they'd also had supersoldier treatments, and they crossed the sand as fast as Olympic sprinters. Coming into the forest, they paused to fix bayonets to the ends of their rifles, which looked like standard-issue M-16s.

He swallowed his pain and rushed farther uphill. Only when he topped the embankment did he realize his mistake.

Lost to pain and terror, he'd run straight back to the dim beach where he'd escaped the pigs. How could he have been so stupid?

He saw the barrel-shaped shadows moving just uphill in the thicker foliage, heard their grunts and something like a whistle.

"I will tell you what is going to happen," Agbeko's deep voice called up to him. "You will come out to us now, Carl, and we will let you live."

Nachef's laughter fluttered up in the wake of Agbeko's words.

They were coming up the embankment.

Maybe I should just wait for them here, Carl thought. *Surprise them as they come over the edge.* But there was no way they'd be stupid enough to come side by side, especially with his blood trail marking the way, not when they'd been trained by Stark. These two weren't like the thugs back at camp; they were combat-experienced mercenaries who'd already survived Phoenix Island and gone off to fight Stark's battles. They'd killed. They'd survived. There would be no outrunning them.

Carl picked up a rock.

A rock versus two machine guns. Long odds.

They were close—coming up the slope, nearing the embankment. Any second now, it would rain lead.

A pig squealed uphill. Soon the whole herd would charge. . . .

Wait, Carl thought. *Wait.*

The big boar strutted out of the trees and snorted at him, its eyes burning with pig rage. Other boars popped from the trees with choppy pig motions, the unlikely speed of their stout bodies and stubby legs making them look like video on fast-forward.

Carl smiled at their tusks, which shone like highly polished knives of bone, and knew what he had to do.

"You're beautiful," he said, and charged straight at them.

He sprinted dead at them for ten feet, then spun. The massive animals launched as one. He gave them perhaps half a second, then sprinted downhill.

With the pigs right behind him, Carl leapt over the embankment and whipped the rock at the nearer soldier—Agbeko—who towered just to the left of him, fewer than ten feet downhill. The stone cracked him in the chest, and Carl saw the hulking soldier tip, his rifle firing lead death up into the canopy.

Carl tucked into a tumble just as Nachef, who stood directly down slope from him, sprayed bullets in his direction, his aim bad because of his surprise. Carl's move took him under the rounds, and he rolled straight at Nachef, launching out of the movement at the last second, just as Stark had taught him during combat gymnastics training, and tackled Nachef at the waistline.

It was a hard tackle.

The soldier folded with a grunt. The force of the impact lifted him off his feet and into the air, and Carl was aware of his rifle spinning away, where it hit and fired once before bouncing downhill, lost to the tangled growth. He slammed Nachef hard into the ground. His own ribs and bullet wound roared in protest, but there wasn't time to worry about pain. He lurched forward and drilled three hard right hands into Nachef's panic-stricken face. The Phoenix Forcer's eyes rolled back in his head as he lost consciousness.

Then the air exploded with screaming, squealing, and gunfire.

Carl scampered instinctively across the ground, waiting for the bullets to strike. He whipped his head around and saw Agbeko firing not at him but into the pack of boars. He saw boars skid away, spouting fountains of blood, heard screams and squeals, saw large slashes open in Agbeko's legs, saw him lose his footing, and saw the battle-scarred boars descend on him, slashing with their razor-sharp tusks.

Carl hauled himself to his feet. It had worked! He turned to run—then hesitated at the sound of Agbeko's shrieks.

Get out of here, he told himself. Run *while you have the chance*!

But the boars were butting the fallen trooper from all sides, ramming their tusks into his body like so many knives.

Agbeko screamed and screamed.

They were killing him.

You are so stupid, Carl told himself, *too stupid to even live!*

Then he was sprinting . . . not downhill, as he should, but uphill, straight into the bloody thick of things. A primitive scream fueled by anger and fear and wild savagery—a caveman's battle cry—exploded unbidden from his lungs as he drove kicks first into one boar, then another, and the pigs, either shocked by his attack or startled by his subhuman cry, scattered as one, fleeing into the forest.

When he turned back to Agbeko, the Phoenix Forcer was on his feet again, swinging the rifle around, not at the pigs but at him.

No, Carl thought, and launched himself desperately at Agbeko just as the gun boomed.

Carl's head jerked, and a line of fire burned across his cheekbone. Then he slammed into Agbeko, hoping for another tackle.

It was like running full-tilt-boogie into a brick wall. Agbeko was six-four or six-five and packed with muscle. Carl fell back on the ground, skidded a few feet, and growled as a fresh eruption of pain filled him.

Agbeko caught his balance and smiled. "That was good, the pigs. You planned it?"

"I kinda hoped it would work," Carl said.

They were both bloody and breathing hard now.

"You're a sturdy guy," Carl said, pointing at the slashes in Agbeko's legs. "You're all cut up, and I still couldn't knock you down."

"My brothers always called me the Rhino." He raised the rifle to his shoulder and pointed it at Carl. "But they are all dead now."

"Wait," Carl said.

"You saved my life," Agbeko said. "Surrender and I will let you live."

Carl thought of Octavia, of his promise to her and what would happen to her if he gave up now. "Let's talk about this." He stood. Agbeko was still several feet uphill . . . too wide of a gap for Carl to try anything.

"Last chance," Agbeko said.

One of the bloodied pigs thrashed on the ground at Agbeko's feet. He swung the rifle around and fired. Blood arched into the air. The pig jerked once and lay still.

Then Carl saw it: the M-16's bolt locked to the rear . . .

The rifle was empty. Agbeko had spent all his rounds on the pigs.

He knew it, too, because the massive Phoenix Forcer smiled and said, "Well, Carl . . . you were good enough with sparring, but we are not boxing now."

Carl moved forward, not straight at Agbeko but to the left. He wanted to get uphill from him, take away some of the big soldier's height advantage.

Agbeko lunged at him, thrusting the rifle like a spear.

He was fast. Really fast.

Carl dodged the bayonet and sidestepped farther uphill.

Agbeko looked him up and down and shook his head. "You are covered in blood, Carl. Give up this game. Save yourself."

Carl started to tell him what he could do, but Agbeko charged him, thrusting the blade at his face.

Carl jerked his head to one side, away from the bayonet . . . and straight into Agbeko's real attack.

The blade had been a feint, and Carl had fallen for it, jerking away just as Agbeko brought the butt of the rifle around in a sharp arc that smashed into his brow. His head snapped backward. He felt the brow split open, felt the cut—a bad one—open over his eye.

Agbeko twisted and brought the butt of the rifle around again, like a puncher throwing the second hook of a double-hook combo, and Carl clamped his arm to his side. The rifle butt slammed into him, but he took it on the arm, not the ribs. He twisted with the blow, just as he would have twisted against a hook to the body, and, out of that twist, he sprang around, countering with a hard left hook.

It caught Agbeko on the point of the chin and dropped him on his butt. Just as he had during sparring, Agbeko started to push straight up again, only this time, Carl stomped his wide face with a kick that stretched the giant onto his back and sent him skidding downhill.

Knowing he had to finish this, Carl ran and jumped on top of Agbeko, riding his skidding body like a sled until it crashed into the base of a tree. Agbeko opened his eyes again and roared at Carl, who rained down lefts and rights on him at full extension, turning his shoulders with every blow and watching his would-be killer's face come apart. He watched the nose squash like a tomato, spraying blood, watched frowning red mouths open over both eyebrows, watched the heavy jaw go askew, watched the eyes roll back, finally losing consciousness. . . .

Then Carl was up again, moving once more uphill. The bullet wound in his side, his broken ribs, and his damaged ankle pulsed pain. The spear wound burned, as did the bullet wound that had creased his cheekbone. He pawed at the blood running into his eye, trying to clear his vision. Now his hands throbbed, too, their split knuckles already swelling, sharp pains shooting up his wrists all the way to the elbow.

None of that mattered now. All that mattered was getting the boat, getting Octavia, and getting off this awful island. Then he had to warn the world about Stark. There'd be time for hurting and healing and dying, if necessary, after that.

For now, he had to push on.

He hoped Agbeko and Nachef were the only guards posted at Camp Phoenix Force, hoped he could make it to the boats. . . .

Nachef.

Carl heard him first, then saw him . . . far below, down at the tree line, shouting out onto the beach. "He's here! Freeman's here!"

Out on the beach, voices shouted in gleeful response.

More hunters. They would come for him now.

Why couldn't they just stop?

He bent and picked up Agbeko's rifle—it was empty, but he could still use it like a club or a spear—and found himself staring straight into the glazed eyes of a dead pig.

He remembered the similar emptiness in Ross's eyes.

That was the only thing that would stop these hunters, these children-turned-monsters: that same glaze in Carl's eyes.

They would keep pushing until they killed him. Or until the pigs killed him. Or he fell off a cliff and smashed his skull on boulders. Or he jumped in with the hammerheads. They wouldn't stop hunting until they were certain he was dead. . . .

At this thought—his mind firing with all the speed that is a survivor's prerogative in the most desperate moments—he looked into the pig's glazed eyes, and the plan dropped wholesale into his mind, like a gift from God. It was yet another long shot, but he was getting used to surviving on slim odds, and he'd learned as a boy fighting in the streets and as a young man battling in the ring to make split-second decisions, to turn his entire game plan in the blink of an eye.

He did so now.

Dropping the rifle, he picked up the heavy carcass of the pig, once again swallowing his pain and fighting through his fatigue, and stumbled uphill, away from the shouting voices entering the forest below. He hurried straight up until he heard another pack of kids hooting nearby, another pack of bloodthirsty hunters closing in from the right. He cut left and headed downhill again, not toward the boats of Camp Phoenix Force but down a lateral hillside toward his original point of arrival: the landing strip, beach, and lot where Parker had stolen his medal and started the whole thing. The spot where he was supposed to have dueled to the death. The spot where they'd dumped Medicaid into the mouths of monsters.

In his haste, he slipped and fell several times, crying out with the pain. Yet each time he fell, he picked up the pig again and kept moving. Pain burned like a fire in him. Fatigue squeezed his lungs flat. Cramps seized his muscles, and blood leaked everywhere, blurring one eye into functional blindness.

When he could no longer run, he shambled. When he could no longer shamble, he walked. When he could no longer walk, he limped. And as he reached the base of the hill and broke the forest's edge, the howls of the converging hunters merged with such urgent nearness it seemed the jungle itself screamed for his blood.

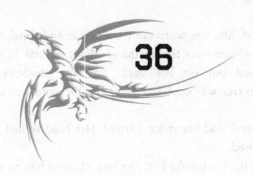

36

OCTAVIA PRESSED THE SHARP SHELL into the flesh between her thumb and forefinger until she came fully awake again. Lying there in the hollow beneath the tree, covered over by palm fronds, she struggled against sleep.

She had to stay awake. Carl was risking his life for her. What if he came around the island with a boat, and she was asleep? She pictured it happening: imagined hearing a puttering sound just audible over the lapping waves, then louder and louder, and pictured herself looking out and seeing the boat. This image blurred with the memory of another boat, one she'd seen long, long ago, when her father—her real father, when he still lived and she was just a happy little girl—took her to the Seattle waterfront, down to the docks. She remembered how warm and nice the sun had been that day, rare weather in coastal Washington, and how small her hand had felt in her father's and the smell of fish and a dog barking on a boat, a little dog and—

She jolted upright.

No! She'd drifted into sleep again. *You have to stay awake.* She pressed the shell into her hand until she had to grit her teeth.

No sooner had she pulled it away than sleepiness settled once more upon her like a heavy fog. She just needed a little rest. That was all. Just a quick nap. She'd been in the sweatbox for days, enduring heat exhaustion and hunger, thirst, and the unbelievable stress of all

that had happened. She was worn out from crying and weighed down
by incalculable sadness over the deaths of Medicaid and Ross. Now
she was stretched out on her back, and the shadowy recess
beneath the fallen tree was cool and dark, and the sand was soft as a
fine bed.

Her lids drooped, and her vision blurred. Her head settled into the
sand. Her eyes closed.

The sound of the boat woke her. The boat shone white as an angel
out there in the water beyond the trees, idling beside the long arm of
stones Carl said he'd use to find her.

He'd found her.

But then the boat was pulling away.

Panic seized her.

She'd fallen asleep, and Carl had come and called for her, but she
hadn't responded, and now he thought she was dead or gone or cap-
tured, and he was pulling away, and—

"Wait!" she cried, struggling upright and scrambling from her hiding
spot. She tripped over the fronds and fell into the open, struggled once
more to her feet and staggered toward the departing boat, waving her
arms. "Carl, wait!"

The boat kept going.

She ran screaming to the water's edge, and just as she was ready to
drop down and cry, the boat turned and came back toward her.

He had seen her.

She clapped her hands and shouted with joy and then did sit down—
fell was more like it—her legs going weak as she plopped onto the sandy
shore and surrendered to the tears, letting them obscure her already
blurred vision.

It was okay to cry now. She was finally safe, finally leaving this horrible island.

The boat pulled in. She heard splashing—Carl coming for her
through the water—and felt guilty for sitting, for making him come all
the way in.

Then she heard more splashing. And hooting. And laughter.

Her heart nearly stopped as she looked up and saw the blurry shapes moving toward her out of the water.

It wasn't Carl at all.

The hunters had found her.

Decker's blue eyes leaned close. "Oh, baby, you are so screwed."

37

CARL LIMPED OUT OF THE JUNGLE, the dead pig heavy in his arms. Its wiry fur pressed like so many bristles into the naked flesh of his arms, which shook with the effort of carrying the dead animal. The cloying, coppery smell of its blood filled his nose and mouth. He struggled across the soft sand, his body roaring with pain and trembling with exhaustion. His eyes burned with fatigue, one of them currently useless with the stream of blood still draining into it, and his ankle screamed with every step, feeling as if the bones there had been replaced with shards of broken glass. Where the first bullet had drilled a hole through his side, the blood flow seemed to be slowing, but the pain hadn't let up at all, making it hard even to breathe.

Coming out of the thick foliage, he squinted against the bright sunlight, his good eye temporarily blinded by the day, and struggled onto the beach. Though he couldn't really see, he trudged on toward the sound of breaking waves, pushing through soft sand that clutched his feet and ankles as if the island itself were in league with Stark.

Through sun-blind eyes, he made out the black mass of the parking lot and, further off, the landing strip. He willed his feet to keep moving as he went around the hot pavement to the right, toward the long pier.

He staggered and fell, sprawling hard across the pig. His ribs screamed with pain, and the cut over his eye spilled fresh blood, further blurring his compromised vision. It would be so easy to stay down. So easy to lie there and rest. So easy to just give up and wait for Stark and his savages to either kill him or drag him off to the Chop Shop. Either way, it would mean an end to the suffering, an end to the struggle, and in his battered condition these endings sounded almost impossibly sweet.

But he couldn't do it. He couldn't quit.

Quitting would also mean the end of Octavia. And quitting would put Stark one step closer to his twisted dream. Quitting here, now, would mean the death of thousands, perhaps millions.

He needed to get back to the compound, back to the boat, but the island between here and there was crawling with soldiers.

His only chance now was the pig.

Growling against the pain, Carl rose from the sand and hoisted the dead pig once more into the air. *Move,* he told himself. *Last round.*

Behind him, in the forest, the hunters' cries drew louder. They would break from the trees any second.

Please, God, Carl thought, and allowed himself a prayer request: *Give me time. Let me make it to the water.*

All his life, he'd wanted to feel the ocean. . . .

And then his feet left the sand and entered the swirling foam of a broken wave. He hurried along the water's edge toward the pier. The salty ocean water rushed in again, almost toppling him, and the spray of the broken wave burned his open wounds. Then he lurched into something hard—the pier—and could have whooped for joy but instead scrambled onto it with his heavy load and hurried out its length, the wooden planks so hot in the tropical sun he could feel the heat coming off them.

Shouting tumbled across the beach. Had they spotted him?

Hurrying, he slipped and nearly fell again, dropped the pig with a heavy thump, bent to retrieve it, and with blurred vision saw the heavy red trail—his blood mixing with the pig's—following him out to the burning planks of the pier. He smiled. *Good. Let them find my track and follow it all the way to the end.*

Grunting with effort, he once again picked up the pig and started moving. Behind him, the shouting grew louder, and someone farther back stitched the air with machine-gun fire.

Reaching the end of the pier, Carl filled with conflicting emotions: joy at having made it this far and fear of what lay ahead. This was it. All or nothing. Finding one last burst of strength, he heaved the pig out into the water.

Then, summoning all his courage, he jumped off the dock.

One dark corner of his mind laughed. In all those years of dreaming about the ocean, he'd never quite imagined his first swim like this. . . .

He swam as fast as he could back under the pier, his wet clothes and boots and the pull of the tide working against him. Salt water stung his eyes but washed the blood from them, and in the shade provided by the dock overhead, his vision returned fully . . . just in time to see the surging wave that lifted him and slammed him hard against one of the concrete supports. He screamed involuntarily at the pain but swam on, and before the withdrawing wave could pull him out, he grabbed hold of a support nearer to the shoreline and clung there beneath the dock, waiting for killers to converge from land and sea.

He didn't have to wait long.

He heard the hunters break free of the jungle, their voices so loud in the open air, they seemed like weapons in and of themselves. Bright and vicious. Full of bloodlust and devoid of mercy.

"Carl," a deep voice called across the expanse. It was Stark. "It's over. Come out now. Face me like a man, and I'll order the others to stand down. We'll settle this ourselves—just the two of us, face-to-face in single combat, two warriors—and I will give you the honorable death you have earned."

Stark meant it. He was offering a duel.

The idea of one last fight tempted Carl, but even if he were whole, he couldn't beat Stark. The man was too strong, too fast, too well trained. Broken and exhausted as he was, Carl would stand no chance at all.

His only chance was the pig. . . .

"Blood trail!" someone yelled.

Teens cheered. Men bellowed.

Stark's voice: "He went toward the water."

Carl heard the sounds of many feet clambering onto the pier and his heart hammered in his chest. *Come on,* he thought, willing the pig to bleed more, bleed faster. *Before the hunters look under here. . . .*

Boots strode directly overhead. Shadows eclipsed the strips of light that had shone between the planks.

"The footprints go all the way to the end," someone said.

"He's under the dock."

No, Carl thought. To have come this far only to be discovered now. He pictured Octavia, her gray eyes staring, waiting forever. . . .

"Fools," Stark's voice said. "Look."

"Sharks!"

In front of the pier, gray fins waggled above the surface, which churned with the great thrashings of the sharks. A rush of joy surged through him—*Yes, pig! Yes!*—but then, suddenly, he was very much aware of his own wounds, of his *own* blood scenting the water. But there was nothing to do about that now. He could only wait and hope that the pig would satisfy them, that he had made it far enough back toward shore, and that hunters would fall for his trick.

"The nutter tried to swim for it," someone said. A girl's voice, British . . . Cheng?

"Hammerheads got him."

"Told you I heard him scream."

"They're eating him."

Someone laughed. "Yes! That's friggin' awesome!"

A loud crack silenced the laugher, and someone fell to the planks overhead.

"You dare to laugh?" Stark said. "Carl Freeman was ten times the warrior you'll ever be. Any of you!"

Silence.

Carl clung to the pier support, waiting.

Something big passed in the water. Something huge. Close. Twisting, it gentled past him with a sliding caress.

A shark had smelled his blood . . . and oh, they were coming for him now.

"He didn't deserve this death," Stark went on.

The shark passed again. This time it bumped lightly, almost lovingly, into Carl. He chilled with its probing, knowing he would soon feel its teeth.

"He deserved an honorable death. In combat." Footsteps marched toward the end of the dock. "He deserved a warrior's death. Not . . . this!"

Gunfire exploded overhead. Bullets tore into the water, and Carl saw sharks thrash with their impact, saw their blood roil to the surface, joining that of the pig.

The shark that had bumped him hurried toward this fresh slaughter.

Carl shuddered with relief.

Overhead, Stark bellowed.

The others were quiet.

"You failed, all of you," Stark said. "Carl determined his own fate and threw himself at the sharks rather than face the disgrace of losing to you. With no chance of victory, he made for himself honor."

Silence.

"Tonight," Stark said, "we will feast in honor of Carl Freeman. We'll have a pig roast, here on the beach, and if any of you speak ill of him, I'll cut off your head and burn it on a stake like a tiki torch. For now, we march back to Training Base One. Phoenix Force, ride tail. Hooah?"

Phoenix Force roared in response.

"On your lead, Boudazin."

"Yes, Commander." And Boudazin, who had, what seemed to Carl a thousand years ago, given him a kiss for luck, started shouting with authority, and Carl heard the kids forming it up on the sand. "All right, orphans! Double-time back to base, hooah?"

"Hooah!"

"Maintain formation. Cadence on me. C-one-thirty rolling down the strip . . ."

"C-one-thirty rolling down the strip!"

"Phoenix Island orphans take a little trip."

"Phoenix Island orphans take a little trip!"

Their singing faded into the forest. So great was Carl's fear of the sharks, he found it nearly impossible to remain under the dock, but he waited until the singing died away before wading to the edge and peeking at the sandy beach. It was empty.

He sighed with relief.

The pig had saved him.

He'd given the hunters what they'd wanted—his death—and now he was free to slip like a ghost the rest of the way to the boats. In fifteen minutes, he'd pull into Octavia's cove, and they would finally escape.

He emerged from beneath the dock, and something yanked him out of the water, into the air. . . .

Laughter boomed like thunder.

Carl crashed down hard on the pier in another explosion of pain.

Stark towered over him. "The prodigal son returned!"

No. It couldn't end like this. He'd fooled them.

Stark took a step forward and held out his hand.

Carl crab-walked backward and struggled to his feet. Half-mad with fear, anger, and dismay, he weighed his options and found them nearly weightless. Behind him fed frenzied sharks; before him loomed a battle-hardened giant.

"Very clever, Carl. Very resourceful. I wondered when I saw pig bristles in the blood trail. Then it occurred to me . . . you have a true will to live, so you most likely had only made it *seem* you'd been eaten. Very impressive. So impressive I decided to spare you from the mob."

"Am I supposed to thank you?"

Stark smiled. "Gratitude is a societal commodity. Men like us deal in realities." He took a step forward.

Carl edged closer to the end of the pier. Behind him, sharks still splashed.

Stark advanced slowly. "Son."

Carl snapped a jab into Stark's chin. "Don't call me that."

Stark laughed, making a show of rubbing his chin. "Nice strike, son. But let's stop this foolishness." He offered his hand. "Come with me. I'm giving you another chance."

Carl stepped back, nearing the edge of the dock. His only chance was to trick Stark into charging him, then slip under his attack, so that Stark went off the dock into the water, into the sharks. "Come on," he said, beckoning.

Stark stepped toward him. "The orphans will be flabbergasted. Carl

Freeman, returned from the dead, resurrected, larger than life, standing at the right hand of his father."

"You're not my father," Carl said. He flicked out another jab. Stark batted it away.

"I could be your father. We are both warriors. We're stronger than these others. Better. Come back with me, and we'll rule over them together."

"And then what? Send suicide bombers to Vegas? Assassinate the president? Set off a nuke at Disney?"

Stark's smile widened. "It would be a start."

"You're crazy."

"Perhaps. But if I am, it's merely one more trait that you and I share."

Carl spat blood. "Yeah, right. I'm not crazy."

"No? What's all this about then? Why fight your destiny, son? What do you owe the world? What do you owe these orphans? Why do you insist on denying your own talent? And why would you sacrifice a brilliant future for some silly girl? It boggles the mind. It truly does. Forget it, and so will I. You're forgiven. Here, take my hand, and we'll put it all behind us." As Stark spoke, he inched closer.

Carl feinted with a jab and drilled his battered right hand into Stark's chest. It was like punching a boulder. Pain shot all the way to his shoulder.

Stark tsk-tsked and shook his head, as if losing patience with a temperamental toddler.

Carl teetered at the edge. Sharks thrashed loudly in the water.

Stark stepped closer.

Keep coming, Carl thought. *Just a few more steps.*

"Come to me in peace," Stark said, "and one day you will inherit my throne."

"No," Carl said.

Stark spread his arms. "If you wish to die in obscurity rather than rise to greatness, the choice is yours. But really . . . what's your next move? Forward, into the sharks? No—suicide isn't your style. What, then? Think maybe you could draw me out, make *me* fall into the sharks? The matador and the charging bull? That trick might work on Parker—the man's a baboon—but I hope I've earned enough respect for you to know it would never work on me. That leaves only one way: straight down the middle."

Stark fell into his loose fighting stance and beckoned him forward.

Disappointment crashed down on Carl like a great stone. Of course Stark had known . . . it was pointless. He was finished. So be it. At least he'd go down fighting. "All right, then." He wiped blood from his cut eye and spat on the planks between them. "I got something for you." He raised his fists and shuffled forward.

"That's the spirit!" Stark said.

Carl feinted with his jab and drove a kick toward Stark's knee.

Stark twisted, Carl's kick missed its target, and then Stark was on him. Carl hammered hooks into the giant's ribs, but Stark wrapped Carl's head and arm into a lock and twisted his upper body.

Carl's feet left the ground, his legs swung high, and his entire body spun like a clock hand racing backward. For a fraction of an instant, he reversed in the air, head nearest the dock, legs pointed skyward. Then his body cracked like a whip, and Stark smashed him into the planking.

He lay shattered on the pier. He couldn't breathe, couldn't move. Stark adjusted his lock slightly, and Carl felt his own arm squeeze against his neck.

Stark said, "I'm sorry it has to end like this, son, I really am. Perhaps your spirit will take the chip further, get us closer to our goal. Onward, progress, onward."

Carl had just enough time to panic—they were going to chip him, turn him into a zombie—then Stark squeezed, cutting off the blood flow, and Carl's vision grew strange. Darkness framed blue sky, then tightened until it was like looking down a long, dark tunnel, the sky a mere blue dot at its end. The tunnel closed, the sky winked out, and darkness claimed him.

38

WHEN OCTAVIA COULD NO LONGER WALK, they lifted her between them—Parker taking her cuffed wrists, Decker holding her lashed ankles—and carried her into the Chop Shop. Over the span of a life that had dealt her no end of misery, she'd never felt such pain, weakness, and hopelessness. She sagged between them, limp as a corpse and wishing only that death would wash her away from all this suffering and injustice into a blissful nothingness. Tragedy had driven her beyond hope and, mercifully, beyond terror, as well . . . or so she believed until, at the end of the hospital corridor, they dropped her just inside a white room.

Misery returned at the sight of him.

Carl, Carl, Carl . . .

He lay still as a corpse on a table at the center of the room. Blood dripped from the table's edge to a puddle on the floor.

All for her. All because he'd tried to save her.

She tried to scream but found only a moan.

A bearded man in spectacles and a white lab coat stood over her friend, speaking to someone she couldn't see.

"Woo-ee!" Parker said. "You don't look so hot, Hollywood!"

"What did you say?" a deep voice said, and Stark came through a door on the opposite side of the room.

Parker tried to smile. It looked like he had a stomachache. "I didn't mean anything."

"You didn't *mean anything*?" Stark said. He gestured toward Carl.

"He was the finest soldier to ever come here, and look what you made me do to him!"

Parker raised his hands, palms out. "Hold on now, Commander. You told me to push him. Told me that before he even got here."

"Push, yes," Stark said, "but you're too stupid to understand the difference between pushing someone and trying to break him."

Parker snorted. "Shoot, if I wanted to, I would've broke him like a promise."

"No, you wouldn't have." Stark's arm flashed out, and across the room, Parker grunted and gurgled. He staggered backward with his hands to his throat, crashed into a wall, and slid to the floor. His hands pushed away from his throat, and something clattered across the floor and came to rest a few feet from Octavia's face: a slender knife, red with blood.

So quickly she hadn't even seen it happen, Stark had drawn a knife, whipped it across the room, and sunk the blade in Parker's throat.

Parker gasped and thrashed. His hands pressed to his throat again, but they couldn't stop the fountain of blood, which just sprayed up from between his fingers. The drill sergeant's mouth worked wordlessly, and his eyes bulged, staring at Carl, as if trying to understand how one boy could have brought all this down on him. The fountain guttered. Parker began to twitch.

Octavia looked away.

There were more sounds, then silence, and when she looked back at Parker, he was obviously dead.

About which she felt nothing.

Bending over the corpse, Stark said, "Some people can't be broken." He reached inside the dead man's collar, yanked hard, and came away holding something shiny dangling from ribbon: a gold medal. "Proceed, Doctor."

Shaking visibly, the doctor glanced at Parker's corpse. "With all due respect, Commander, would it not be wise to use the coma and wait for the new *cheep* to be ready?"

Stark stared at Carl.

The doctor glanced at her and at Decker, who was sidling out of the room, then said, "Would it not be wise to test first on a patient less *importante*?"

"No," Stark said. "I won't keep him like some kind of plant. Fate will decide the matter. Operate."

"Yes," the doctor said. "In time. But with all due respect, Commander, all people have the limit. We should give the boy his chances, especially since he is so close to perfection for this. Use the coma, let him heal. *Then* let fate decide."

Stark stared at Carl. "How long?"

"Is hard to say," the doctor said, tugging at his beard. "Two weeks, maybe three."

For a moment, no one spoke. Then Stark said, "All right. Fix him. I'll want daily updates. Morning and night."

"Yes, Commander."

Stark started pacing. "I won't watch the operation—I've seen him suffer too much already—but you'll keep me informed every step of the way."

"Yes, of course, Commander."

Then Stark stopped pacing, seeing Octavia for the first time. His face twisted with anger. "You," he said, and swept the bloody knife from the floor.

Octavia cringed against the wall. She wanted her suffering to end, but not like this. . . .

His hand slipped under her chin and cupped her jaw, squeezing. The blade descended, and she felt its edge, sticky with Parker's blood, against her cheek.

She forced herself to look him in the eyes. "Just do it, you psycho. Just get it over with and do it."

"Oh, no," he said, and his smile was terrible. "Death would be far too merciful for you."

"Go to hell."

His smile broadened. "Actually, you're headed there now. It's just down the hall. Doctor, once Carl is situated, would you like to make some music with this other little one here?"

"Oh . . . yes, Commander," the doctor moaned. "Yes, very much."

And for as terrible as Stark's smile was, it was nothing compared to the eagerness that shuddered through the doctor.

Octavia had to bite her lip just to keep from screaming.

"Excellent," Stark said, withdrawing the blade. "Make her beg for death every day, but do not give it to her. Don't let the symphony end. She may still prove of use to us."

Biting down even harder, she thought, *Don't scream. Don't beg. No matter what they say or do, don't give them the satisfaction.*

39

OCTAVIA DID BEG—first for mercy, then for death—every day, every hour, every minute, until she could no longer form words in her mouth or mind.

By the time, three weeks later, that Dr. Vispera wheeled her back into the white room, however, she had slipped into a catatonic state. She sat rigidly in the wheelchair, a wasted shell of herself, and saw but did not see Carl spread upon the table beneath bright lights, smelled but did not smell the sharp scent of alcohol, heard but did not hear the slow, steady beat of the heart monitor or the doctor who spoke to his assistant, "Give me the orbitoclast."

The young man in pale green hospital scrubs selected what looked like an ice pick from a tableside cart cluttered with medical instruments and handed it to the doctor.

Dr. Vispera held the tapered wand aloft, as if demonstrating for med students. He leaned over Carl. "I insert the point between the eyelid and the eye. There. It rests against the upper eye socket."

The heart monitor beeped steadily.

"Now the mallet," the doctor said, and the assistant handed him a small hammer.

The doctor lifted a mallet into the air. "I tap the orbitoclast . . ." He leaned over Carl again, and Octavia, mercifully lost within herself, heard but did not hear three sickening taps followed by a cracking sound. ". . . opening the small hole in the skull."

The electronic beep of the heart monitor quickened.

The assistant glanced in the machine's direction.

"Yes, *muchacho*," Dr. Vispera said, returning the tools to his wide-eyed assistant. "Sweat now. Sweat. I think if the beeping stops, you and I are food for sharks." He gave the boy a ghastly smile. "Give me the injection probe."

The assistant handed him something that looked like a clear plastic pistol with a thin barrel that tapered to a point. Dr. Vispera leaned over Carl again. "I enter through the perforation and insert the probe five centimeters into the frontal lobe to plant the *cheep* in the connective fibers between the thalamus and the prefrontal cortex. I squeeze the trigger."

A faint click.

"And insert the *cheep*."

Suddenly, the machine started beeping rapidly.

The assistant gawked. "What's happening?"

"Cardiac arrest," Dr. Vispera said. He stared at the machine, where waves shot across the monitor so quickly the baseline now resembled a jagged row of green teeth.

"Oh, man. How did I get this duty?" the assistant said, and glanced toward the door. "Is he dying?"

"I don't know," Dr. Vispera said, glancing at his watch, "maybe. In ten seconds, the *cheep* will activate. We will see. Five . . . four . . . three . . ."

The beeps came even faster, creating a single note, a shrill whistle of alarm.

"Two . . . one . . . now!"

Carl's body jerked with seizures for several seconds, then lay still.

Octavia heard but did not hear the beep go steady, saw but did not see the monitor's green line go flat as a coffin lid.

"Is over," the doctor pronounced. "The boy is dead."

40

AT THE SECOND OF HIS DEATH, Carl returned with detached lucidity to his childhood and the place in the Pocono Mountains his parents visited to get away from the city: a small cabin beside a wide creek with high banks in the fold between two steep, forested hillsides—where, in springtime, leafless black trees dripped cold rain, and outcroppings of mottled stone emerged from fading caps of ice, and snow that had blanketed the forest floor for months shrank away to reveal pressed black leaf litter and the yawning rib cages and stitched yellow skulls of winter-killed deer. Once, while wandering these thawing spaces, his boots heavy with mud, Carl had lingered over the bleached jawbone of such a deer, imagining its story and thinking about life and death, and his father had placed a hand on his shoulder and warned him of springtime meltwater flash floods. They came all at once, with little warning, his father told him. There would be only a distant booming, then a wall of water would rage past, there and gone, taking things—and sometimes people—with it.

One spring midnight, Carl awoke to one of these floods passing in the darkness outside, thundering and roaring like the end of the world. The following morning, he stood at the edge of the creek and stared at changes wrought by the passing waters: streamside trees snapped to stumps beneath palpable vacancies where once had towered oaks and sycamores of great size and incalculable age; and below these, further change in the creek itself, where disgorged stones, massive and monolithic, canted at strange angles like pagan gods of tribes long vanished, and within the broken creek bank, pendulous roots hung, half-revealed, like the disemboweled secrets of the world.

Within Carl, an approaching flash flood boomed—and the wave of change roared through him. . . .

41

CARL OPENED HIS EYES.

He was on his back in a bright room, pain crashing in his skull, filling it. He decided he didn't want this, and the pain dimmed away.

In its absence, reality gained sharper clarity: the room, the machines, the wires and tubes, the antiseptic smells . . .

He was in the hospital. The Chop Shop.

All of this came to him in an instant, as if sensing the place and identifying it were a single action.

In a flash, he remembered everything—the hunt, the pig, the fight with Stark, Stark talking as he choked him into unconsciousness—and knew they had chipped him.

But he didn't feel like a zombie. Not even close. He felt . . . *incredible.*

"It's beeping again," a voice said. "He's alive!"

Then it was Dr. Vispera leaning over him, clutching paddles in his hands, a look of surprise coming onto his face. *"¡Dios mio!"*

During the brief time it took for those short words to leave the doctor's bearded mouth, Carl's senses and mind fired at lightning speed, dilating the moment. Time, for him, had changed, his senses and consciousness moving so rapidly that they created time within time, time to look and recognize and think, while the rest of the world crawled along in slow motion.

In that second, Carl not only saw the doctor, his look of surprise, and the paddles in his hands, but also identified the paddles as the things doctors used in movies when someone's heart stopped. His eyes and mind worked so quickly that in that same second, he registered the doctor's assistant and the relief on his face, and understood, too, that that relief temporarily nullified the assistant as a threat. Simultaneously, he recognized the feel of his own body, all of it at once, the table beneath him, and the small electrodes—seven of them, he knew—taped to his chest and rib cage.

This was absolutely, far and away, the most incredible experience of his life, all of these things coming to him in the second it took Dr. Vispera to shout *"¡Dios mio!"*

"Amazing," Carl said, and he sat up, tearing the electrodes free with one hand, while his other hand, having balled itself into a fist, smashed into the bearded face.

He felt the crunch of bone and saw the doctor crumbling, saw this and knew he had broken the man's nose but kept moving, body and mind acting as one, thought and action one in the same.

It was unbelievable. His whole life, he had been athletic, and a large part of his boxing success had been due to how quickly he'd been able to convert thought into motion. Someone would take a swing, and Carl would see the punch, dip it, and counter, very little gap between seeing what he had to do and actually doing it. Now that gap had vanished entirely.

So as Carl came off the table, his mind operated at full speed in a world reduced to slow motion, and there was zero delay between seeing what to do and doing it. By the time his right foot hit the ground, he had already oriented himself to his surroundings. All at once, he saw the startled assistant looking toward the instrument cart, noted the guy's muscles tensing, and understood the threat. Before the guy could even reach for a weapon, Carl slammed a hard kick into the cart, toppling it and sending a wave of tools spinning into the air.

As Carl's eyes cataloged the airborne instruments, some of them familiar, others not, eleven tools in all, a tidal wave of adrenaline, joy, and absolute amazement surged in him. This was unbelievably awesome. The assistant winced in slow motion, his arms dragging upward in an awkward attempt to block the rain of instruments, his elbows lifting, exposing his . . .

Carl's hook slammed into the guy's solar plexus.

Amazing!

He'd always been fast, but never *this* fast. It wasn't just his mind working more quickly or the missing gap between thought and action. His body had moved without hesitation, everything synced in perfect co-ordination.

The guy folded, all the air whooshing out of him, and spilled to the floor.

Carl turned.

The doctor stirred, a man who'd tortured hundreds, moaning about a broken nose.

Told you I'd break it, Carl thought, and was about to say the words when he saw Octavia, and his surging tidal wave of elation froze and crashed down on him.

"Octavia!"

Her face was black-and-blue and fixed in a mask of terror. She sat rigid as a mannequin, strapped into a wheelchair. The exposed flesh of her arms was spotted with burns and crosshatched in cuts. What had they done to her?

He ran to her, saying her name, taking her face gently in his hands. She didn't move, didn't react to his touch, just sat there stiff yet alive. Yes, *alive*—he could feel a strong pulse in her neck—alive but frozen, trapped in a moment of paralyzing horror.

"Octavia, it's Carl," he said, and he touched her bruised face. "I'm getting you out of here, okay? Just hang on. Everything's going to be all right."

She just sat there, one eye bright with terror, the other swollen shut, her mouth locked in mid-scream.

No sooner had the radio set crackled to life than Carl's eyes flicked to it.

"Stark to Vispera, come in, over."

Stark.

Carl's fists ached. Stark. He had caused this—all of it—and had to pay. . . .

"Vispera!" the radio barked. "Where's my update, over?"

Carl grabbed the radio from the counter and hurled it across the room, where it smashed into the wall, raining pieces down on Vispera's assistant, who was up on all fours now, crawling away like a frightened animal.

"You!" Carl shouted, his voice an explosion in the small room. "On the ground!"

The guy went flat. "I got no problem with you, man. They just told me to—"

"Shut up," Carl said, "and don't move."

They needed to get out of here, needed a boat to get off this island. Fast. Stark wasn't stupid. He would come for them. Carl knew there were always jeeps parked outside the Chop Shop. Unfortunately, like so many orphans, he didn't know how to drive.

He swept what looked like an ice pick off the floor and grabbed Vispera by the lapels.

The doctor cried out.

Carl held the point an inch from the man's eye. "How many people have you used this thing on?"

"No," Vispera said. "*¡Por Dios!*"

"Look into my eyes," Carl said. "Don't . . . look . . . away. We're going to Camp Phoenix Force. Either you drive us, or I drive this into your brain. Understand?"

"*Sí,*" Vispera said. "Yes, I drive, yes."

Carl hauled him to his feet and pointed to the assistant. "Tie him up. Use those cords. Hurry." He hated taking the time, but he couldn't have the guy calling Stark, and he couldn't bring him along. The jeep would hold only Vispera and three passengers: Carl, Octavia, and the other person Carl couldn't leave without. . . .

"Good," Carl said, and pointed to Octavia, forcing himself again not to really see her, not to think about her. Not yet. He didn't have time for sorrow. "Wheel her out. Hurry."

Outside, in the dim, rank Chop Shop compound, they loaded Octavia into the jeep.

"Is good?" Vispera said. "We go now?"

Yes, Carl thought. *Go now before Stark shows up. Jump in the jeep and pound across the island, hammer it all the way to the boats.* But he said, "Where's Campbell?"

"Who?"

"My friend Walker Campbell," Carl said, and brought the ice pick close again. "You stuck this in his brain."

The doctor shook his head.

"Tell me where he is," Carl said, "or I'll do to you what you did to him."

Vispera pointed a shaking hand toward the back of the compound.

"Where? Which building?"

"No building. The other side."

"Stop stalling," Carl said. "What do you mean, the other side?"

"The other side of the island," Vispera said, and shuddered. "Beyond the electric fence."

And Carl understood. The other side, the secret side, the "here are dragons" side. "Let's go. You're taking me there now."

"No," Vispera said, suddenly looking more frightened than ever. "I will not go there, not that place."

"Yes," Carl said, holding the point closer. "You will."

"No," Vispera said, and actually inched closer to the pick. "I would rather you kill me now."

The guy meant it—Carl could see it in his eyes and hear it in his voice—but why? Vispera would rather die than go to the other side? What horrors was Stark hiding there?

But then, before Carl could even ask, the gate opened, and three truckloads of Phoenix Forcers armed with AK-47s pulled into the compound.

42

"**T**HE CHIP WORKED," **STARK SAID**, stepping down from the lead truck and walking toward him. "Carl Freeman, you are, without a doubt, the most amazing person I have ever met."

No way out, Carl thought. *No escape.* Behind Stark, dozens of automatic rifles zeroed in on him. He had suffered so long, survived so much, fought so hard, gotten so close, only to end like this?

"Stop," he said, and pulled the doctor close, pressing the pick to his throat, "or I kill your pet monster."

Stark stopped, but his smile was unconcerned. "I'd rather not lose him, but he's not exactly irreplaceable, you know. He doesn't make the chips. He just plugs them in."

"Oh yeah?" Carl said. "What about his other talents? You'd need to find a new torturer."

Stark shrugged. "True. He is a maestro of pain, but any kid with a mean streak and a set of vise grips could do the job. Dr. Vispera can be replaced. Only *you* are indispensable."

Carl said nothing. He scanned the scene, studying Stark, the troopers, the compound.

"Dr. Vispera wanted to delay your operation even longer," Stark said. "Weeks, months, whatever it took to perfect the chip, but once your wounds healed, I told him no more waiting. This was bigger than him, bigger than science—this was destiny. And I was right. We didn't need new chips or new procedures. We needed *you.*"

Carl couldn't see a way out. Too much space, too many guns. He imagined all those rifles firing at once, punching holes through not only him but Octavia as well, ending them both.

"Tell me," Stark said. "Is it amazing? I assure you, whatever you're feeling, it's only the beginning. There are many levels to the chip. We'll unlock those together."

Carl's mind raced, but he saw only guns and hard stares, trained killers ready to pull the trigger, the culmination of this brutal place and its bloodthirsty traditions, the end product of Stark's all-holy warrior culture.

His warrior culture . . .

All holy . . .

That was it, his only shot.

"Ah, he smiles at last," Stark said. "You'll join me, then?"

"Not a chance."

"Oh, no?" Stark said, gesturing toward his troopers. "And how do you plan to extricate yourself?"

"Simple," Carl said, and now it was his turn to smile. "I challenge you to a duel."

Stark laughed. "What a flair for the dramatic! You must know that I could, as your commanding officer, sentence you to death for simply making the challenge."

"You won't."

"No? Why not?"

"There would be no honor in it," Carl said.

Stark stared for a moment, the laughter gone from his face. "So you're going to force me to kill you, is that it?"

"No," Carl said. "I issued the challenge, so you set the conditions." He shrugged. "We don't even have to fight to the death."

"A duel to submission?" Stark said. "And why would I agree to that?"

"Because if you win," Carl said, "I'll join Phoenix Force. You'll have exactly what you want: my cooperation and a chance to study the chip in action."

"Intriguing," Stark said. "And if you win? What do you expect in return?"

"Freedom," Carl said. He nodded toward Octavia. "You let us go. Us and anyone else who wants to leave."

Stark shook his head. "Not a chance." He held up one index finger, then the other. "This is a one-on-one duel. It's only you fighting me, not you and some boatload of refugees. One person fights, one person leaves . . . if you win."

Carl hesitated only a second. "Fine."

"Excellent. I hereby accept your challenge, Carl Freeman, under the following conditions. The duel will take place immediately—or as soon as we can gather everyone from the island. We'll skip the prefight meditation." He smiled. "No weapons, no holds barred. Punching, kicking. grappling, everything. When one duelist surrenders or can no longer carry on, it's over. If you win, I provide safe passage back to the mainland."

Carl nodded.

"And if I win," Stark said, cracking his knuckles, "you stop these silly struggles and accept your destiny, and we move forward together into a new age."

43

THEY FACED EACH OTHER ON THE BEACH, under a boiling sun, the sand burning hot beneath Carl's bare feet. A slight breeze, weak as a dying breath, sighed off the ocean, rippling the black flag overhead and stirring the crimson phoenix burning at its center. Twenty feet away, at the far end of the living ring of spectators, Stark lazed through a prefight warm-up, coming out of a stretch and throwing a loose combination.

This was it. All or nothing.

Beyond Stark, beyond the spectators, Octavia sat rigid in the wheelchair, the mask of terror still frozen on her face.

How had it all come to this?

How had a simple promise, made years ago to his father, brought him to this place, this moment?

Stop, Carl told himself, and shook out his arms. *Get your head straight.*

This was it, all there was, all there ever would be. He needed to see this moment for exactly what it was, nothing more, nothing less: a duel to the finish, not a boxing match and not his fight with Parker—who, compared to Stark had been small and weak, slow and inexperienced, a stupid, brutal man lost to rage.

How could he defeat Stark? How could he even hurt him? The man was armored in muscle, and his brain, tucked away in the helmet of his skull, sat high atop his thick neck. To even hit it, Carl would have to get close, dangerously close, right where Stark wanted him.

If they'd been fighting on solid ground, Carl would have tried to kick him in the knee, but kicking here, in the sand, would be too hard, too slow, a fatal mistake.

Stark would stalk him, and unless Carl found a way to stop him, the hulking warrior would eventually walk through Carl's punches as he had on the pier, pull him into a crushing lock, and finish him.

Well, Carl thought, *I just can't let him do that.*

But how could he avoid close combat?

He needed to stick and move, punch and get out.

But the spectators pressed close, tightening the ring, and even now, as Carl rocked back and forth, his feet sank into the soft sand. How could he stick and move with the very ground trying to hold him in place?

No wonder Stark had chosen the beach.

"Duelists," Cheng, who had been named referee, called, coming into the center. "At the ready."

Stark peeled off his shirt, revealing the physique not of a man but a god—the god of pain and suffering, every inch of his torso rippling with muscle and matted with scars, the body of a soldier who had been shot and stabbed, slashed and beaten, blasted and burned, and had come out the other side still moving, still fighting, still waging war on the world. He stretched his thick arms, covering half the ring with their great span.

"Fight!" Cheng said, and the spectators howled with glee.

Carl shuffled forward, heart pounding.

Stark walked toward him, a smile on his face. "Son," he said, "why go through this? Give up this silly game. You've already won the real fight. You've survived. With that chip in your head, I can train you to do amazing things—"

The world slowed as Carl flicked out a jab, ducked Stark's half-hearted swipe, and sidestepped away, toward the center of the ring. His punch had missed—he hadn't dared to go closer—but it was amazing how clear everything was, how much he could see during the brief exchange, and how easy it had been to dip under Stark's attack. Still, he hated the way the sand clutched at his ankles, slowing him, making him clumsy.

"Fast hands," Stark said, still smiling. "But you'll need to come closer if you're going to actually hit me."

No thanks, Carl thought, and threw another jab. He didn't go closer, and he certainly wasn't going to hang in there to throw a combination. Again, Stark reached, and Carl slipped away easily—but then stumbled into the spectators, who roared with laughter and shoved him back into the ring.

That shove almost ended him. But with his mind flashing at light speed and his body moving automatically, he slipped Stark's next punch and scrambled away.

Standing there in this slowed world, Carl saw so much: the doctor, Phoenix Force, his old platoon. Tamika, Sanchez, and Davis stood in front, cuffed and chained together like some kind of road gang. Tamika was crying and Sanchez looked sick. Davis was shouting, urging Carl forward. There was no sign of Lindstrom at all—nor did Carl see Parker or Decker. Most of Phoenix Force cheered, pumping their fists and chanting, "Stark! Stark! Stark!" but Henshaw frowned, Boudazin watched with a pale face, and Agbeko looked on with no expression whatsoever.

All these lives, Carl thought, *all these ruined lives.*

What could he do about it? How could he beat Stark?

So far, he was fighting it like a boxing match, sticking and moving, waiting for his opponent to tire. . . .

Only this wasn't a boxing match, and Stark wouldn't tire. Not now, not ever.

He would continue to plod after Carl, expending little energy as Carl hurried from side to side through the clutching sand. Stark's endurance would not fail him. Neither would his patience. Sooner or later, Carl would slow or stumble, and Stark would pounce.

There was no escape, no way to avoid close combat.

"Come on, Carl," Stark said, his voice light and friendly. "You see it now. Just submit."

Carl shook his head.

Stark said something else—then surged forward, driving a kick straight at Carl's midsection. It was oddly fascinating to see the kick coming in slow motion and even more fascinating to swivel so easily out of its path, the recognition of what he had to do and the actual execution of that thing a single action. Stark blasted past, and Carl moved once more to the center.

And in that moment, watching Stark turn and start another patient approach, Carl finally realized the true advantage of this new speed. His hands were faster, yes, and this new speed would give him more power, but neither of those things would save him now, not on their own.

The real magic of his new speed wasn't in his fists or feet; it was in his eyes and mind.

He had to see everything, had to find a plan before it was too late.

Another jab, another dip under Stark's cautious swipe, and even as Carl slipped away, he felt a glimmer of hope.

That pattern: jab, swipe, slip.

Over and over.

Stark was patient like a hunter and had no reason to change the pattern. He could continue his inexorable stalking, expending little energy, reaching for Carl but never overreaching, exposing only his side to counterattacks, secure in the knowledge that his heavily muscled body could absorb a lot of punishment and that to do any real damage, Carl would have to risk going inside.

"You're bleeding," Stark said, pointing at Carl's side.

Carl didn't look down. Didn't dare to—and didn't need to, either. He could feel the blood, and he realized then he'd been ignoring the pain in his side, suppressing it, but there it was, pulsing away like a distant lighthouse flashing faintly in a foggy night.

"The gunshot wound, no doubt," Stark said. "The blood virus is good, but even you would need more time to heal fully from something like that. Speaking of time, yours is running out, don't you think?"

Carl said nothing, but Stark was right. Time was running out.

Stark put his hands on his hips like an exasperated parent. "Let's just—"

Carl threw another left jab and slipped once more to the left, slipping again under Stark's right arm, which swept overhead. This time, however, Carl focused his speeding eyes and mind on Stark's side, a target he had originally written off, assuming there was no damage he could deliver there that would justify getting that close. But this time, Carl didn't look at Stark's side as a single block. This time, he scanned all of it, every piece, and as he slipped once more to the center of the ring of screaming spectators, he had his target.

It wouldn't work in boxing, with gloves—that's why he hadn't seen it earlier—but this wasn't boxing, and he knew, no matter how much it scared him, exactly what he needed to do.

It would take him straight into Stark's clutches.

So be it.

He had one shot, and he needed to take it before internal bleeding or the sucking sand or a lucky punch from Stark ended him.

"This is all a bit anticlimactic, don't you think?" Stark said, walking calmly toward him again. "Think of it. You've beaten the odds—not once, but twice—first the hunt, then the operation. Amazing! Why ruin your proudest moment with ridiculous cat-and-mouse—"

Carl feinted with a half jab, dipped, and fired his real attack.

No matter how many weights you lifted or how much protein you consumed or what substances you pumped into your body, you could only add muscle to muscle. You couldn't grow muscle where none had ever been. When Stark reached again, Carl drove a left uppercut not into his exposed side but straight into his armpit. He watched in slow motion as the convulsion rippled out of that unprotected bundle of nerves, saw the man's thick arm going instantly limp and useless as a noodle, and drove his right hand into Stark's body. This was a "stop punch," thrown not to inflict serious damage but instead to do just what it did: to interrupt Stark's momentum and jam his turn.

Carl unloaded a blasting one-two-one-two flow of lefts and rights, turning his shoulder with every shot and cranking the combo with all the blinding speed available to him now. This was it, his only chance; he had to finish Stark here, or the man would grab him and crush him and finish him. His fists slammed into Stark's head, *smash-smash-smash*, so fast that even in this slo-mo world, his hands were a blur, *smack-smack-smack*, the punches not just fast but *hard*, explosive with this new speed—and into his mind flashed one of boxing's oldest maxims: *speed is power*—and he was aware of his knuckles breaking, the flesh splitting, *bang-bang-bang*, his wrists fracturing, *smash-smash-smash*, but he didn't hesitate, didn't hold back, didn't stop.

He watched Stark's head jerk, watched the ear twist and tear, saw blood there and then the big head coming around, turning into the blows, toward Carl, the engine of an onrushing train that wanted to flatten him.

Carl had been waiting for this moment. His whole body—every nerve, bone, and muscle—moved in perfect harmony, and as he looped his right fist in a wide overhand arc, he bent his left leg and folded his body forward over it, throwing every ounce of weight and every iota of force into the looping overhand right that orbited Stark's guard and smashed down like a sledgehammer into the opposite side of Stark's head. Carl felt the jaw shatter, and he blew through the punch, clipping its arc slightly inward so that Stark's head twisted with the force of it, then snapped back in the opposite direction.

Dazed, Stark stumbled away with his back turned.

This was it.

Carl surged forward, his whole body moving again in perfect precision. The ball of his foot twisted, his knee turned inward, his hip came around, his upper torso following after, and his right hand shot out, straight as a laser, bringing the shoulder with it, and he nailed Stark harder than he'd ever punched anyone or anything before, blasting him right where the thick muscle of his neck tapered to a thin veneer at the base of his skull. To Carl, it felt like his hand exploded. There was a sharp crack and a hollow *thock* sound, like a baseball bat smacking a watermelon, and the force of the impact jolted up his arm and into him like a jolt of electrical current, as if Stark's strength and willpower and consciousness had raced out of him and into Carl, where, as Stark collapsed to the sand, it exploded, and Carl arched his back, raised his bloody fists, and roared in triumph.

44

CARL FREEMAN IS THE VICTOR!" Cheng announced, standing over Stark's motionless body.

The silence that had followed Carl's knockout punch held a second longer—then broke all at once, the spectators clamoring in disjointed response to this thing they never could have imagined happening. Confused shouting, incredulous laughter, and then someone hooah-ed, and sporadic cheering sounded on all sides.

Something hard pressed into the back of his skull, and Agbeko's voice said, "Do not move."

The crowd fell silent. Some looked shocked, others sad, but most simply adjusted, their eyes as dark and hollow as the gun muzzles they now raised in his direction. A second later, more barrels rose, pointing at him from all sides. Of course, if they actually fired, they wouldn't slaughter just Carl. A circle of machine guns firing simultaneously? They would all die. But what did that matter to them? When someone—Stark or Agbeko or whoever—told them to pull a trigger, they pulled it.

"We don't have to do this," Carl said. "He's down. We can change everything now. Leave this place and head back to the world."

"To us, brother," Agbeko said, "this place *is* the world."

And in that moment, feeling the gun barrel press into his skull, Carl knew Agbeko was right. For many, perhaps even most, of these orphans, the world was gone, burned to ash with their childhoods, leaving only this awful place. You couldn't change that with a pep talk.

"Lower your weapons!" a broken but still-powerful voice said.

Stark staggered to his feet. Cheng tried to help, but he batted her away, reeling as his eyes locked onto Carl. His jaw was crooked, already ballooning, and he wore a beard of blood and sand. He plunged a hand into his pocket.

Carl tensed, watching in slow motion as Stark withdrew his hand, watched and waited and knew this wasn't over, knew what Stark would pull out of his pocket. A knife, of course . . .

"To the victor go the spoils," Stark said, his damaged jaw making his voice strange. His arm flashed out, throwing the knife at Carl—only in that dreamlike moment, Carl saw it wasn't a knife, not a knife at all, but a shining gold disk wobbling through the air, trailing a bit of ribbon.

Carl snatched it from the air and opened his hand to see his only memento of success, the boxing medal Parker had stolen so, so long ago. Even now, battered and bleeding, he couldn't help but smile.

"I am a man of my word," Stark said. "Hempfield, Jackson . . . prepare a boat. Carl, you defeated me. You are free to leave."

Free to leave.

Carl looked past him, past the shocked spectators, past the rigid figure staring blankly from the wheelchair, past the island to the ocean, which stretched away toward . . . what? So much, so much. Mexico first, then north to the States and further north, home to Philly, where he could go back to the gym. No calling ahead—no way—he would show up unannounced, see if he could surprise a smile out of old stone-faced Arthur James. Then they would train together, and with Carl's new speed, power, and endurance, no one could stop him from fulfilling his lifelong dream: winning the professional championship of the world. . . .

"Tempting," Carl said, "but I'm not going anywhere."

45

LATER, THEY STOOD SIDE BY SIDE at the water's edge, Stark's arm draped like a heavy yoke across Carl's shoulders, and watched the departing boat fade into the distance.

"The price of progress," Stark said.

Carl nodded. About that, Stark had been right all along.

The price of progress did run high at times, so high, in fact, that sometimes you had to burn the whole world . . . not to conquer its kingdoms but to keep a promise, not to rise from the ashes but to lift someone else from the flames.

The conditions of the duel had been clear. One-on-one combat with, as Stark had stressed, the freedom of one person up for grabs. One person's freedom, not necessarily Carl's.

It hurt, watching the boat disappear, and he knew that this wound, like the loss of his parents and the death of Ross and the unspeakable thing that had happened to Campbell, would never heal and never stop hurting.

Yet he'd made the right choice.

Octavia would be safe. Stark had guaranteed it—and despite the casual apathy with which he destroyed lives, Stark was a man of his word. Phoenix Forcers would escort her to the mainland and check her into a hospital, where she would receive, no matter the price tag, whatever treatment she required. Nobody would believe her if she tried to speak of Phoenix Island; Stark likely knew this and therefore didn't fear her release. Once she healed, she would start a new life, free and safe . . . so long as Carl lived up to his end of the bargain.

Carl would stay on Phoenix Island, his own freedom exacted as the price of her salvation.

"I hope you can forgive me," Carl said as convincingly as possible. "I was only fighting for her."

"That's behind us now," Stark said, "and you are forgiven. Time, at last, to embrace your destiny."

"True," Carl said, and he was going to fulfill his destiny. For now, that meant this place and training with Stark so he could unlock the chip's powers. But after that . . .

He remembered sitting in the courtroom, what seemed a thousand centuries ago, staring at his scarred knuckles and thinking how they read like a twisted road map of the great lengths he had traveled to arrive there. Now the map had changed again, new lacerations splitting old scars, new fault lines obscuring old roads. With time, these wounds, too, would heal, forming scars upon scars, roads upon roads, delivering Carl . . . where?

There will come a day, son, the judge had told him, *when you will need to determine exactly who it is you intend to be.*

Carl knew now. He was a fighter. Simple as that. Not a throwaway kid, not a cop-in-the-making . . . a fighter.

For the world made its demands of you, whether you set forth to destroy that which you hated or to preserve that which you loved. Life was a constant struggle, an endless fight, and anything else was merely a breather between rounds. Any day now, a great bell would toll, and he'd be drawn once more into combat.

Until then, he would play the part of the willing apprentice, but as soon as he discovered a way . . .

He was going to destroy Stark and his entire organization.

That was his destiny.

Yes, he thought, and the old ache returned to his knuckles. As an experiment, he called out to the chip with his mind and tried to dim away the throbbing. The pain of his new injuries faded at once, but the old ache remained, pulsing away in his fists like a heartbeat . . . the heartbeat of his rage, his purpose, his destiny. *Good,* he thought. *Good . . .*

On the horizon, the boat grew indistinct, faded, vanished.

"Shall we begin?" Stark said.

"Yeah," Carl said, but he lingered for one last look at the empty space where the boat had passed out of sight and out of his life.

Good-bye, Octavia.

Along that far horizon, black spots appeared in the sky, like so many crows flying this way. But no—not crows, he realized, hearing a faint *whup-whup-whup* reverberating across the water like distant gunfire. Helicopters, likely loaded with returning Phoenix Forcers, led perhaps by Baca, the high-speed psychopath from the Zurkistan video. Whoever they were, let them come. He would greet them with simmering contempt befitting the heir to the throne.

A glance at Stark told him the big man hadn't yet noticed the approaching aircrafts.

Interesting.

Had the chip improved Carl's vision and hearing, too? He hoped so, for any advantage the chip gave him, no matter how small or seemingly innocuous, he would carry off into the darkness of his private world, where, with the deadly patience of a prisoner honing a blade in the night, he would sharpen this gift to a killing edge.

"Lead the way," Carl said, turning his back to the vanished boat, the approaching helicopters, and the world. "I'm ready."

CARL FREEMAN'S ADVENTURES CONTINUE IN

DEVIL'S POCKET

ACKNOWLEDGMENTS

LOOKING BACK ON THE UNLIKELY CHAIN OF EVENTS that led to the writing and publication of this book, I am both humbled and awed by the amazing people who made it all possible. I owe thanks to many people—so many, in fact, that I am doomed to acknowledge only a portion of them here. . . .

First of all, thanks to my family and friends, living and deceased, for your love and support. Mom and Dad, I'm sorry I didn't write this book in time for you to have read it.

Thanks to editor extraordinaire Adam Wilson for taking a chance on *Phoenix Island* and for making it a much stronger book, and to everyone at Simon & Schuster/Gallery Books for your hard work. Thanks to Stephanie DeLuca in PR, Liz Psaltis in marketing, John Vairo for creating *Phoenix Island*'s knockout cover, and eagle-eyed copy editor Erica Ferguson, who saved me dozens of times from looking like a complete fool.

Thanks to my excellent agent, Christina Hogrebe; the indefatigable Christina Prestia; and all of the fantastic people at the Jane Rotrosen Agency. You adopted an unknown author and made his dreams come true.

Thanks to my incredible film agent, Joe Veltre, who read this book in a night and then changed everything by shopping it on the West Coast.

Thanks to the coolest guy in the world, Tripp Vinson, whose enthusiasm, vision, and advocacy changed my life and the life of this book, and thanks to everyone who has helped in the insanely complex and collaborative book-to-series creation of *Intelligence*, including the formidable Christine Cuddy, who stepped in when I needed a hand.

Thanks to rock-star publicist Marcy Engelman for helping an unproven writer get his career up and running.

Thanks to my earliest readers, who cheered me on and whose suggestions made this a better book: Adam Browne, Aaron Biscoe, Elaine Prizzi, Chris Von Halle, and the first teen to ever read *Phoenix Island*, the brilliant Makenzie Briglia.

Thanks to the smart, experienced experts who patiently helped me to better understand science, technology, physical trauma, and all things military: Dr. Gary Della Zanna of the National Institutes of Health, Dr. John Dougherty, and combat vets Horace Jonson, Bill Fay, and Don Bentley.

Thanks to the smartest guy I know, Matt Schwartz, without whom this book wouldn't even exist. You guided me every step of the way, and I would have been utterly lost without you. Our next trip to Characters is on me, bud.

Thanks to my writing friends and unofficial mentors, Melissa Marr, Lissa Price, and Doug Clegg, who were never too busy to take my calls, texts, and emails—even when they *were* too busy.

Thanks to all my friends at Seton Hill University, where *Phoenix Island* was to have been my MFA thesis until I ran out of time and money. Thanks to my mentors, Tim Waggoner, David Shifren, and Victoria Thompson; to my critique partners, Swea Nightingale and Don Bentley; the Troublemakers; Chris Shearer; and the amazing community that is SHU's Writing Popular Fiction program.

Thanks to Kimberley Howe and everyone at the ITW, an incredible organization committed to fostering aspiring writers, and all my Thriller-Fest buddies, especially Pete Aragno.

Thanks to the OneFours, the Inkbots, and the Brandywine Valley Writers Group.

Thanks to my brother, Jeff, who taught me to fight *and* encouraged me to write.

Thanks to the world's best mother-in-law, Carole McLean, for all those rides to the train station.

Thanks to all the kids I taught, counseled, or coached over the years, for sharing your lives with me. Many of you, including Tony Delsordo, Reed Shanaman, and Aaron and Michael Faulk, left us way too soon. I'm hoping those who knew you recognize your influence on this story. Another place, another time, you'd have been kings. . . .

Thanks to my third-grade teacher, Mrs. Wolfe. By encouraging me to write, you made me feel like more than a throwaway kid, and by typing up my first story and telling my parents I'd be an author someday, you won my undying gratitude. It took me a long time to deliver on your faith in me, but if there's any justice in the world, you're sitting somewhere comfortable, reading this with a smile on your face.

Thanks to Mrs. Ayers, who also showed me kindness and encouraged me to keep writing.

Finally, thanks to my best friend, first reader, and most honest critic: my beautiful wife, Christina, who has never let me down—not even once—and who has always believed in and encouraged me, even when I lost faith in myself or this book. You're the best, L.O., and I'll love you forever.